C000006024

PETER

DARK HERO

REGINALD Evelyn Peter Southouse Cheyney (1896-1951) was
born in Whitechapel in the East End of London. After serving
as a lieutenant during the First World War, he worked as
a police reporter and freelance investigator until he found
success with his first Lemmy Caution novel. In his lifetime
Cheyney was a prolific and wildly successful author, selling, in
1946 alone, over 1.5 million copies of his books. His work was
also enormously popular in France, and inspired Jean-Luc
Godard's character of the same name in his dystopian sci-fi
film *Alphaville*. The master of British noir, in Lemmy Caution
Peter Cheyney created the blueprint for the tough-talking,
hard-drinking pulp fiction detective.

PETER CHEYNEY

DARK HERO

DEAN STREET PRESS

Published by Dean Street Press 2022

All Rights Reserved

First published in 1946

Cover by DSP

ISBN 978 1 915014 27 6

www.deanstreetpress.co.uk

To

Lieut-Commander (E.)R.B. Bilborough, R.N.

and

Lieut. P.C.G. Eason, R.N.

Once of
HMS *Kimberley*

PROLOGUE
KRAMEN
Germany—April, 1945

BERG lay extended on the ground. He lay quiescent, his chin resting in the dust, the palms of his hands flat against the hot earth. Occasionally he opened his eyes; then closed them as if seeking a relief from the glare of the sun; from the monotonous regularity of his thoughts about the plan.

He was an extraordinary sight. His bare ankles, protruding from the short dark grey and dirty white striped trousers, were so thin that the shape of the bones could be seen as in a skeleton. His face seemed unduly elongated. The two protruding jaw bones and the chin formed a weird and terrible triangle. His eyes, when he opened them, were red-rimmed with dark shadows—entirely lustreless.

He was without actual physical strength. Every effort, no matter how small, to move a finger, a foot, came from the brain—a brain that seemed to have reached the nadir of exhaustion; that desired only oblivion, blackness and peace, from the misery of existence.

When he moved, and he was crawling slowly and almost imperceptibly towards the barbed wire fence, each effort was made after a prolonged mental struggle.

It was afternoon. The sun beat down on the arid compound. Occasionally there was a tiny breath of air which stirred the dry dust. Berg's mouth was open in a fatuous endeavour to absorb into his parched lungs all the air he could get, and when the dust came it settled on his lips and tongue. His bony hands clawed at the ground like the claws of an animal. He progressed very slowly, inch by inch, towards the barbed wire fence.

The process of thought was very difficult in spite of the fact that the sequence of ideas passing through his mind had become a rule of life; had become an organised sequence of thoughts which had been going on for a very long time—hour after hour, day after day, week after week. For what seemed to him an eternity, this same process of thought—this plan—had occupied his starved, shattered and broken mentality.

He stopped in his struggle towards the enclosure; rested his bony chin on a shrivelled forearm, and thought about the plan once again. It was not easy to think, because all the time a kaleido-scope of pictures was tearing at his weak and undisciplined mind. When he opened his eyes the shadows cast by the sun on the compound took on the most extraordinary and grotesque shapes, which seem to him to form themselves into the features of people concerned in the plan.

An hour passed by. Now Berg was within three feet of the barbed wire fence. Looking up he could see the loop of telephone wire which was hanging from a post. He had put the loop there. He had put it there six weeks before when the plan had taken possible and practical shape in his mind. He had been a little stronger then. He remembered leaning against the post and fixing the loop to the top of it, praying as he did so that it would support his weight. He had thought with a cynical flash of humour that it was strange for a man who really did not wish to die to be arran-ging his own execution. He had thought then that the process of death by hanging would not be particularly pleasant, and then that nothing could be more unpleasant than those things which he was still experiencing.

He lay there, his head resting on his arms, his eyes half opened, looking towards the gate of the compound. Things had been lax in the Camp for a month. A peculiar atmosphere had permeated the place. Such people as were able to talk had whispered strange things to each other. There was an atmosphere of *laisser-faire*. The discipline of the place was slowly but surely being undermined by some unseen force that came from some unknown place.

Berg watched. The shadows on the compound grew deeper. He looked towards the sentry. About this time in the late after-noon, when this particular guard was on duty, the same things always happened. The girl came up the hill. Sometimes she was singing—sometimes serious. When the sentry saw her he would wave. As she approached he would go towards her. Nine times out of ten he would lean his rifle against the last post in the barbed wire fence. He would take the girl in his arms and kiss her. They would stand talking. On one or two occasions he had not relinquished his grip on the rifle. He had kept it close by him. But not often. Usually, knowing that there was nothing to be feared from the starved wrecks that were inmates of the Camp, knowing that the non-commissioned officer who inspected the guard was not due for two hours, he would lean his rifle against the post and concern himself with the girl. That was what usually happened.

Both the sentry and the girl had become accustomed to seeing Berg lying there in the dust. Once or twice the sentry had jerked his head in the direction of the prone figure and said something to the girl, and they had both laughed. Once something about the sight of Berg leaning his head wearily against one of the fence posts had brought something amusing to the mind of the girl. She had pointed to him and then she and the guard had indulged in a long and spirited discussion on the subject brought up by the vision of Berg's starving body.

But usually, at this time in the afternoon, when this guard was on duty, the same things happened. The sequence of events was almost standardised.

Twenty yards away across the compound was the window in the Sub-Commandant's office. The window was set at an angle facing obliquely on to the enclosure so that the sentry could not see the window, and any one in the Sub-Commandant's office could not see the sentry. But from the position which he had so carefully worked out, Berg could see the sentry and one end of the office window. At this end of the office window was a high seat and on this seat about this time in the afternoon, with his back to the window, the Sub-Commandant—Kramen—used to sit. Berg had lain there in the dust for many afternoons; had seen the movements of the Commandant's back and shoulders as he gesticulated, talked to the unseen person in the office. Berg knew that the unseen person was usually a woman—one of the privileged prisoners with whom it amused Kramen to dally when he had finished his day's administrative work.

Berg wondered if all these things would happen now as he had planned them to happen; whether the girl would come and the sentry would place his rifle against the post. Whether Kramen would go into his office at his usual time, for his appointment with the unfortunate of the day, and sit in his usual seat. If those things happened, then everything depended on Berg's ability to summon up sufficient strength for a matter of a minute or two to carry out the rest of the plan.

He closed his eyes. He was very tired. He found the greatest difficulty in keeping his mind attuned to any practical events. He wished more than anything else to sleep. He thought that perhaps he would try to count fifty, and when he had counted fifty, and not before, to open his eyes and to look if the girl were coming up the path towards the sentry. But he was unable to do this. The strain of counting even with the mind was too much. When he got to seventeen he opened his eyes.

For a fleeting second strength came to Berg. *The girl was coming up the hill.* Not only was she keeping her usual appointment at the usual time but she was carrying over one arm a wicker basket. Often she brought delicacies to the sentry who was her lover. Now, thought Berg, the sentry would have to put down his rifle. He waited trembling.

It happened. The sentry—a fat soldier in a Landsturm Regiment—waved to the girl, leaned his rifle against the post, went to meet her. Berg closed his eyes. He, who had never spent much time in his life in prayer, found himself praying to somebody—he was not quite certain who—that the rest of the plan would be possible.

He opened his eyes, looked over his shoulder. *Kramen was sitting on his seat by the window,* lighting a cigarette.

Berg began to think about the sentry's rifle. If the safety catch were right off instead of in the half-on position it might require a certain amount of strength to push it to the off position. He hoped the safety catch would not be too stiff. He hoped also that there would be a cartridge in the chamber of the rifle. But there was little doubt about this. For days past the sentries in different parts of the Camp had been amusing themselves by shooting at those unfortunates who had managed to crawl to the central potato store where there were no potatoes but a heap of potato peelings. It was almost certain that there would be a round in the chamber.

The girl was in the sentry's arms. They were embracing ardently. Berg thought he was lucky. Such an embrace might last long enough.

He tried the great experiment. He pushed his hands against the hot earth, pushed his body up with his hands and his knees and with all the remaining strength of his mind until he was kneeling, with his head hanging down like a dog. Then he turned his head. Looking over his shoulder he could see Kramen gesticulating from the window seat. Berg, in one supreme mental effort, concentrated every remaining iota of strength in his wasted body. He got to his feet, lurched wearily forward, fell against the end post, caught the sentry's rifle on its way to the ground.

With another effort, he pushed the barrel of the rifle against the shorter post that maintained one of the supports of the barbed wire fence. He could see the sentry still busy with the girl. The safety catch of the rifle was at half-cock. He pushed it with his thumb. It was well-oiled. It went over.

Now came the great effort. Berg, who had always been good with firearms, found the greatest difficulty in taking a sight. It seemed to him that ages went past—that years elapsed between his putting his eye to the stock of the rifle sighting the foresight through the V on the back sight. He knew that if he took too long a sight his blurred eyes would lose their object. He must act.

He squeezed the trigger, dropping the rifle as he did so, falling against the post which supported it, cuddling it with his arms, his chin on the top, watching with eyes which had now a tiny gleam in their depths.

The window shattered. The noise of the glass as the bullet cut it was a peculiar staccato sound. Berg saw Kramen pitch forward. He drew back his wasted lips in a death's head grin. Kramen would die. The way he had been sitting must have meant that he must have had the bullet through the back into the liver or the stomach, or better still through the spine.

All these things happened instantaneously. Out of the corner of his eye Berg could see the sentry release the girl. He turned towards the fence, staggered uncertainly the few feet between him and the high post on which the loop of telephone wire dangled.

For he realised that he must die very quickly. He realised that it would be a good thing for him to die quickly before they got at him. He reached the loop. He put up his left hand to the top of the post. The idea had always been that he should put one foot on the lowest strand of the barbed wire, pull himself up to the second strand about three feet from the ground, put the loop round his neck and jump.

That had been the idea. But this part of the plan did not work. His strength was gone. He stood there, his left hand feebly clutching the top of the post, his right hand making sawing motions in the air. He knew that he could not carry out the end of the plan.

He turned and leaned against the post. Across the enclosure he could see the guard running towards him—a big Under-officer, his bayonet fixed, in front. The Under-officer was shouting, his mouth opened and shut like a trap as he flung obscenities at the sentry, at the girl, at Berg. Berg heard, rather than saw, the bolt of the Under-officer's rifle pulled back as he pushed a cartridge into the chamber. He hoped, rather ridiculously he thought, that they would kill him quickly. He waited for death.

Suddenly there was a shattering sound—a peculiar staccato sound which seemed to be coming from a very long way away. Vaguely Berg wondered what it was, but not for long. He pitched forward. The dry dust-laden earth of the ground struck his face. Darkness came upon him.

It was evening when he opened his eyes. It was a long time before he remembered. Now he was aware of certain strange things. Now he was aware of a peculiar sense of comfort. He put his right hand down by his side. Against him was something hard—one of the supporting poles of a stretcher. Berg opened his eyes. Above him, a long way away, was a face—not like those faces to which he had become accustomed. It was a brown, serious but good-natured, face. It had a little clipped moustache. It was wearing a green beret and Berg could see that the uniform it wore was khaki.

The face smiled. It said smoothly: "Not too bad. It looks as if you got at Kramen before we did. Don't worry . . . we're here. We're the British."

Berg was unable to speak. He tried to smile.

The voice went on: "I see you'd fixed yourself a nice loop of telephone wire. I suppose the idea was to finish yourself off before they got at you."

The smile became broader. Berg could see the even white teeth under the clipped moustache. He tried to smile once more. This time he nearly succeeded. His face wrinkled in the attempt.

The voice went on. Berg liked it. He could not realise that it was the first time in months that he had heard a voice that was not vilifying, abusing, hectoring.

The voice said: "You're a glutton for punishment—that's what you are. A glutton for punishment!"

CHAPTER ONE
LAUREN
August, 1945

BERG lay in the bath looking at the ceiling watching the steam from the bath condensing on the walls, forming minute rivulets running down the walls—sometimes disappearing, sometimes joining up with other tiny streams, creating blobs of water on the dingy walls of the bathroom. There was no curtain on the small not too clean window at the back of the room. Berg could both see and hear the rain-drops pattering on it. He lay extended and relaxed in the bath—an adequate, tough, specimen of humanity.

His hair was dark, curly, unruly, his cheek-bones were high, his face, though filled out and recovered from the privations of the prison camp, was still long and oval shaped. His chin was firm and the line of the jawbone from ear to the apex of the chin showed clearly. His teeth were even and white. The two lower ones which had been kicked out by Kramen in one of his more playful moments had been replaced by two well-made false teeth. His eyes were wide apart, intelligent and of a peculiar blue. The humour lines about them were developed. His mouth was well-shaped with a short upper lip.

An intelligent, strong and clever face, hardened by experience but owning little softness or philosophy. Berg was a man who saw one thing at a time, who concentrated on that thing. He did not know the phrase, but he believed essentially in seeing any specific thing that interested him through to its logical conclusion. His limbs were well-shaped; his feet were small. On his left calf was a scar where he had been branded with a hot iron in another of Kramen's more playful moments. Berg, allowing his mind to go back for a minute, to remember some of the things which had happened to him in the Camp, realised with a certain gratitude that it was perhaps lucky for him that most of the tortures which had been inflicted on him were mental ones. Berg had a resilient, flexible, mind which had recovered quickly; perhaps more quickly than his body would have recovered from great physical hurt.

He got out of the bath, dried himself, put on a bath-gown, went into the bedroom. It was not an uncomfortable room but Berg realised that the time had come when he must make a move. He liked comfort when he could get it. He had learned in the old days in Chicago that comfort was a good thing, if only for the fact that periods of ease were often followed by times that were difficult and uneasy. When you could lie soft it was a good thing to do it. He began to dress.

His clothes were well-cut and of good cloth, bought with the special coupons which Ransome had managed to get for him. Berg began to think about Ransome. Definitely a man—that one. But where was Ransome?

Berg thought there was little chance of answering that question. Ransome had always been as elusive as a will-o'-the-wisp. He saw you when he wanted to see you. You did not see him unless he wanted that too. Berg wondered vaguely if he would ever see Ransome again. For a moment he thought of Ingrid. He thought of her because he had been thinking of Ransome; because always he associated the woman with the man. But he dismissed the thought of her quickly from his mind. He concluded he had no right to think about her. If you had no right to do a thing you must not do it. He possessed his own peculiar code of morals—mental and physical.

Now he was dressed. He put on a black soft hat, put the wallet stuffed with five pound and one pound notes and a cheque book—also from Ransome—into his pocket. He took a clean handkerchief from a drawer; then slowly, as if a thought had come to him, diffidently, he opened a small drawer and looked into it. Inside the drawer was a .22 Colt automatic—a toy—a plaything—one of those weapons with which you must hit a man in a vital spot to kill him, otherwise the minute bullet is merely an annoyance. Berg grinned wryly at the pistol. He thought that he had no need for it.

He closed the drawer. He stood looking at the closed drawer, thinking about pistols—things which had been to him for a long time tools—the tools of his trade. He wondered where the pair of .45 automatics were—those two lovely weapons with the ivory butts and the ejector sleeves specially made and greased so that there was no chance of a jam. He wondered where they would be.

Berg turned slowly round and began to look at the wall before him. Now his mind was concentrated on the two .45 automatics. Supposing, for the sake of argument, that somebody had found them where he had parked them—supposing somebody had had intelligence enough to look in the parachute jacket which he had left and found the automatics inside them—who would have them? Only one person—Shakkey. Shakkey—whose name he had mentioned to Ransome—who was a Chief Machinist's Mate in a U.S. Destroyer.

Berg grinned again, lifting his upper lip from his teeth, looking a little like a good-natured wolf. The idea of Shakkey being a Chief Machinist's Mate in the United States Navy was funny—definitely funny—*very* funny. He wondered what story Shakkey had told the U.S. Naval Authorities when he joined the Navy. Berg's grin became wider—if they had known what Shakkey's job was in the old days . . .!

Berg concluded that Shakkey in any event would have been equal to the U.S. Naval people. He would have had a story for them all cut and dried—the sort of story that could be checked. Because he was clever and tough they would be glad of him. Now he was a Chief Machinist's Mate—a responsible person—a good citizen of the United States—a sailor deserving well of his country. Berg's grin developed into a smile. He said softly to the wall beside him: "Jesus . . . is that funny! *Is* it funny!"

He turned and looked at himself in the small mirror. He adjusted his hat to a more suitable angle, pulled up the white handkerchief in the breast pocket of his double-breasted jacket. Berg had always been a neat dresser. He liked tidiness.

He looked round the room. There was something of a farewell in his glance. When you were undecided as to what you should do, he thought, you must leave the matter in the hands of fate. It was not very often that you were undecided but of course there must come times, like this time, when you were not quite certain as to which way you should deal with a problem. In those circumstances you left matters in the hands of fate.

He began to think once more about Shakkey and the pair of .45 automatics. Supposing, for the sake of argument, he thought, that somebody had got the guns. It was odds against it. It was extremely improbable that any of the people who worked for Ransome would have found them. But there was a chance someone might have found them. Ransome himself might have come across them. If this were so, Berg was certain that the guns would have found their way to Shakkey, because he had asked that in the event of anything happening to him any effects should be returned to the Chief Machinist's Mate, and if Shakkey had them what would he do with them?

First of all he would not want them. Berg thought that Shakkey might not have a great deal of use for small arms in these days. Then again Shakkey was an extraordinary person. He had always said of Berg: "That guy's always gonna turn up. Nobody's ever gonna knock off that guy. Jesus . . . if you was to stick him in a pit down the bottom of hell and put a ton weight on top of him, the bastard would get out somehow. I'm tellin' you and I *know*."

Berg grinned again. He could hear the strident nasal tones of Shakkey saying the words as he had heard them several times before in his life. If Shakkey believed that; if he had believed that Berg would come back somehow, there would only be one place for the guns. It would be very funny, thought Berg, if the guns were there. It would be *very* funny. It might be considered to be an act of God! If the guns were there, then Berg would know that it was O.K. for him to get on with the business that he had in the back of his mind. It would be a sign!

Vaguely he remembered from out of the past a small hot Sunday School room in the Ozark mountains where he and other children sang hymns on arid Sunday afternoons. He remembered their teacher giving them a talk on one occasion on a sign from Heaven. It had seemed to Berg that in biblical days one's life was peppered with signs from Heaven telling you what you should or should not do. Well, if the guns were there he reckoned that would be a good enough sign for him.

He went out of the house. He began to walk down the Earl's Court Road towards South Kensington. The rain had stopped now; the evening was cool. It was a nice evening, thought Berg. He remembered an English saying that some woman had said to him some time: "The better the day the better the deed." Berg said to himself: That's O.K. by me. You're telling me. By God, you're telling me . . .!

A cab passed him. Berg whistled sibilantly—a decided, penetrative, whistle. The cab stopped. Taxicabs always stopped for Berg.

The man said: "It's a nice evening, sir. I hope you're not going too far. I haven't much petrol."

Berg said: "I'm not going far." He told the man where to go.

He leaned back in the corner of the taxicab, took a flat cigarette case from his pocket, selected a cigarette, lit it. He looked at the case—a neat case of black enamel with his initials in gold in one corner. He thought it was lucky that the shop where he had bought the case also had some odd initials. The "R.B."—his first name was Rene—gave a touch of quality to the case—of exclusiveness. He thought that was very nice.

He put the case back in his pocket. For some reason which he could not identify, the opening of the case and the taking out of the cigarette, reminded him of Carlazzi's in Chicago. No one in his class called Chicago Chicago in those days. It was always

Chi—the home of the leery ones—the smart guys—the mugs who could always beat the rap.

Had Berg possessed a super memory he would have known that the cigarette case reminded him of Carlazzi's because on his first visit there, Travis, talking to him, had taken from his pocket such a cigarette case and helped himself to a cigarette. With a super memory he would have remembered that at that moment there had flashed through his mind the thought that he would like to possess such a cigarette case. As it was his mind played vaguely with the picture of Carlazzi's, with Travis lolling back in the satin-backed window-seat with Lauren in her exquisitely cut tailor-made seated by his side—her lovely eyes moving slowly and wickedly round the small but expensive restaurant then filled with Chicago's smart guys.

The cab stopped with a jerk. The driver put his head round and said through the open front window: "'Ere you are, guv'nor. This is it. You're a Yank, ain't you?"

Berg got out. He paid his fare and gave the man two shillings for himself. He asked: "Why?"

The driver said: "You haven't got much of an accent, but you look like one. There's somethin' about a Yank. You look to me like an airman. Maybe you are an airman?"

Berg said: "Nope. I'm not an airman." He smiled at the taxi-driver. He said: "Maybe one of these days I'll learn to fly all the same."

The driver said: "Yes. It must be nice—flying." He let in his clutch and the cab went away.

Berg turned, walked a few yards, passed the alleyway near Down Street, looked up and saw the flag flying outside the American Club. He thought to himself that a hell of a lot had happened since the last time he had seen that flag. He went into the Club, walked down the passage through the door at the end on the right. In front of him was the cloakroom and the letter delivery service. Berg took off his hat as the trim girl in the blue-grey uniform of the American Red Cross came towards him.

She stood, her small brown hands resting on the counter in front of her. She said: "Can I help you, soldier?"

Berg liked that. The thought that the girl took him for a U.S. soldier in plain clothes for some reason made him happy.

He said: "Maybe a friend of mine left a parcel here for me, but only maybe. It's just as likely he didn't. There's just a chance that he did. My name's Rene Berg."

She said: "If somebody left a parcel for you what would the name be?"

"The name would be Shakkey—Cyram Shakkey—U.S. Navy. If anybody left a parcel for me that would be the guy."

The girl said: "I'll go see." But she stood for a moment looking at Berg—she didn't quite know why. She thought that his face was rather attractive. His eyes, looking squarely at her, were smiling. She went away slowly. She found herself thinking that this Rene Berg who had come for a parcel must be rather a nice man to know in spite of the fact that he was not particularly good-looking—in spite of the fact. . . . She shrugged her shoulders and wondered why she was thinking about Berg. She did not know that a lot of women had wondered why they were thinking about Berg. How could she?

Five minutes passed. Berg leaned against the counter smoking his cigarette slowly, inhaling the tobacco smoke deep into his lungs, keeping it there as long as he could, exuding the remnants. The girl came back. She carried a package wrapped in stout brown paper, tied with thick naval cord. Berg noticed that the package was heavy.

She said: "Well, you're lucky, Mr. Berg. This package was left for you—some time ago. Your friend who left it said he reckoned you'd come in for it some time."

Berg said: "Thanks a lot, lady." He smiled at her.

She held the package towards him and he took it. He knew by the weight what it was. It was the pair of .45 automatics. It was the sign!

Berg said: "So long, lady!"

He put the parcel under his arm, put on his hat, walked down the passage. The girl stood looking at his back for a few seconds; then she went away.

Berg turned out into Piccadilly and began to walk in the direction of the Circus. The weight of the parcel beneath his arm gave him a peculiar feeling of mental comfort. He was relaxed. He considered that now fate had definitely taken charge. So there were other things to be done—things to be planned. He must be constructive.

The idea came to him. If Shakkey had had enough sense to leave the guns, which he had done, maybe he would have had enough sense to tell Berg about one or two of the things which he knew were of interest—about the whereabouts of people they had known, for instance.

Fifty yards past Bond Street, Berg turned off to the left. He remembered the Club. He thought it might be a good thing to drink a little whisky—to do a little quiet thinking, to endeavour to find out how intelligent Shakkey had been. He turned up Sackville Street, turned again, crossed the road. He went up the stairs into the Club. The girl with the hennaed hair was still behind the bar. Berg had always remembered her hennaed hair, her mascaraed eyes, her fully-blown figure and the four-inch heels. She was bow-legged too, so perhaps it was a good thing she worked behind the bar, because the top half of her was by far the most attractive.

She remembered Berg. She said: "Well, if it isn't Mr. Berg! You're quite a stranger. We thought maybe something had happened to you."

Berg raised his eyebrows. He said: "No? Why should anything happen to me?" He smiled at her.

She bridled a little. She said: "Well, believe it or not, things have been happening to people during the last two or three years, you know."

He ordered a large whisky and soda. He nodded when the girl held the piece of ice and looked at him inquiringly. She dropped the ice in. Berg drank the whisky right off, put the glass down, and nodded again. She re-filled it.

He said: "I wonder have you ever met a side-kicker of mine—a guy called Cyram Shakkey? Did he ever come in here? Do you remember the name?"

She shook her head. She said: "No, I don't remember anybody of that name, and I've got a very good memory for names. I know everybody who uses this place! I never forget a thing."

Berg said: "No?" He looked at her mouth—tight-lipped, unrelieved by the artificial smile she put on occasionally. He thought: I bet you never forget a thing. He said: "Don't let anybody steal my drink, will you? I'll be back."

He went out of the bar, up the stairs. On the half-landing was a lavatory. He went in, locked the door, switched on the light. He opened the parcel that Shakkey had left for him.

When Berg removed the paper wrapping, opened the corrugated cardboard, there was a smaller parcel inside. The parcel consisted of something that looked like a pair of polishing cloths tied with white string. Berg undid the string. He threw aside the wrapping, disclosed the two .45 automatics. He stood looking at the automatics as they reposed on the back of the lavatory seat.

The sight of the guns brought many memories back to Berg—a dozen vibrant scenes passed before his eyes—a dozen acute situations. In his mind's eye he could hear the staccato clatter of the guns. He stood there for quite a while looking at the two inanimate pieces of metal, wondering just how much they were to have to do with his forward life—his life from now on.

After a while he shrugged his shoulders as if he had come to a diffident or not quite certain conclusion. Above him was the lavatory cistern. He looked at it; then looked back at the guns. He picked them up. He stood balancing the two guns in his left and right hands. After a moment or two he selected the one he wanted. He slipped it into the pocket cut under the left armpit of his double-breasted jacket—a pocket which had intrigued the English tailor very much when Berg had ordered it. Berg smiled at the recollection. At the time he had not been quite certain that he would ever want that pocket again, but because he had always had one there he thought he might as well have one now. Well, he had been right.

The other gun he wrapped in the brown paper, tied the string round the parcel, stood on the lavatory seat, put the parcel on the back of the cistern. No one could see it there. He had left the cloths in which the automatics had been wrapped on the seat. Vaguely he had thought he might need them for cleaning the gun he had kept. He picked up the two cloths, folded them carefully. He was about to put the folded bundle in the pocket of his jacket when he noticed something stamped on the selvedge of one of the cloths. He held the cloth close under the dim electric light in the lavatory. The words were quite clear "The Double Clover Leaf Club."

Berg sighed. So Shakkey had wrapped the automatics in a couple of polishing cloths filched from the Double Clover Leaf Club. Berg visualised the Chief Machinist's Mate—possibly a little high—the guns secreted somewhere about his person, planning to leave them at the American Club for Berg, wondering what he could use as a wrapper; then stealing the polishing cloths.

Berg stiffened suddenly. Or was there something more to it than that? Was this another tip-off from Shakkey? Was this a message from Shakkey? Berg smiled to himself. Shakkey had always been an odd one—a weird type—inclined to be a little mysterious, vague. Shakkey was not the sort of man who would take a pencil and a piece of paper and write a message and leave it in a parcel. He might prefer to do it this way. The Double Clover Leaf Club! Berg thought that here was the hand of fate, through Shakkey, taking him to that place. Well, why not?

He put the cloths in his pocket, took one last look at the cistern. He hated to leave the single gun there. He had always used the two of them. Now he had only the one. One day, he thought, he would come back here and reclaim the pistol. He switched off the light, went down the stairs, back into the bar. He walked up to the counter.

His drink was still there. He picked it up. There was one other occupant of the bar—a girl who sat on a high stool to his right. A good-figured girl—a brunette—with a clear complexion, nice eyes and a coat and skirt that looked as if they had been pasted on to her. Berg put the glass to his lips.

She said: "Well, sailor, aren't you going to buy me one?"

Berg smiled at her. He said: "Sure, I'll buy you a drink. But I'm not a sailor."

She laughed. She said: "Does it matter? Usually people who come in here are sailors or soldiers or airmen or something. But it doesn't really matter."

Berg said: "No, I suppose it doesn't. What would you like to drink?"

For some reason unknown to himself he felt strangely superior, almost godlike at this moment. He thought he was possibly a messenger of fate carrying out some series of actions, creating a series of events which had been laid down by some higher power. This girl, with her urgent eyes, hoping for something more than the drink, was to him merely a small pawn in this game—a pawn which would perform its service and then pass on:

She said: "I'd like whisky. The whisky here's good. I'm fond of whisky."

Berg ordered a double whisky and soda. The girl behind the bar served it arrogantly, as if she resented the intrusion of her second customer. Berg pushed the glass towards the girl. She picked it up, drank it greedily.

He said: "You needed that drink, didn't you?"

She said: "Yes, I did."

Berg asked: "Why?"

She shrugged her shoulders. She said: "Well, I haven't had a drink for some time. Liquor's dear here, you know. They charge six and sixpence for a double whisky. How do I get six and six?"

Berg said he wouldn't know. He ordered two more large whiskies and sodas. When he noticed the disapproving look in the eyes of the barmaid he ordered three.

He said: "You have one too, sweet."

The barmaid served the drinks. The three of them stood, their glasses in front of them, leaning on the bar, looking at the drinks, looking at each other. It was for the moment as if they were vague floating personalities who had met by chance, who did not know why, who were looking for the answer.

Berg broke the silence. He said: "Well, here it is." He drank his whisky.

Two or three people came into the bar. They came up to the counter, ordered drinks. A man—big, paunchy, bulbous-faced—

began to tell some rather nasty stories. Berg felt the strange sense of discomfiture which always came upon him when men told nasty stories in a bar.

He said to the girl sitting beside him: "Take your drink and sit in the corner. Let's talk."

He ordered another drink for himself. When it was put before him he picked it up, joined the girl who was sitting in the farthest corner at a small table. Now her eyes were bright. She regarded Berg as a potential customer. She thought things might be looking up.

He sat down. He said: "Listen, Cutie, have you ever heard of a Club called the Double Clover Leaf Club?"

She looked at him for a moment. Then she said: "You're a strange person, aren't you?"

Berg smiled at her. He said: "Am I? Why?"

She said: "I don't know. But you're not like other men. You behave differently. You look different. And what the hell do you want with the Double Clover Leaf Club? Is that all you asked me to sit over here for?"

Berg said: "Did you think I had another idea, baby?"

She said: "Yes, I did. Why not?"

He shrugged his shoulders. His smile was easy and pleasant and caressing. He said: "Look, honey, there are other things in the world besides that, you know—but maybe they didn't tell you. Drink your drink and tell me what you know about the Double Clover Leaf Club."

She gave her shoulders a little shrug. It was almost as if she were dismissing some attractive idea which had come into her head as being worthless—some idea connected with Berg.

She said: "Who don't know the place? One time it was called the Pomegranate Club; then somebody else bought it. It was the Tricorn; then the coppers raided it. Now it's O.K. It's run on the straight—the Double Clover Leaf Club. Just off Duke Street, round to the left and through the passageway."

Berg said: "Thanks a lot. I wanted to know where it was."

She said shortly: "Well, now you know, don't you?"

Berg said: "Yeah, I'll be getting along." He put his hand in his pocket, brought out the fat wallet. He extracted five one-pound notes. The girl watched him with hard eyes.

Berg said smoothly: "You don't have to get tough about this. But life can be a hard proposition. Have a little drink and remember me." He grinned. "That is if you want to," he concluded. He folded the notes between his fingers, pushed them across the table to her.

She said: "You're an odd one, I *must* say. But you've got something?"

Berg got up. He was smiling—a whimsical smile that illuminated the oddness of his face.

He said: "Yeah, I know. I heard all about me. I'm terrific, I am. I'll be seein' you! So long."

He went out of the bar. He began to walk down the narrow dark staircase towards the street. Half-way down he thought of something. He put his hand inside his coat, brought out the automatic from under his left armpit. He slipped out the ammunition clip, examined it. He took out the shells one by one. The clip was full—ten .45 cartridges lay in the palm of his hand. Berg worked them back one by one against the spring into the clip. He reloaded the clip into the gun, put it back into his pocket. Then he went quietly up the stairs, more quietly past the bar door, up the further half flight to the lavatory on the landing. He tried the door. It was open.

He went in, stood on the seat, took down the parcel, unwrapped the gun he had left above the cistern. He took out the ammunition clip from that gun, examined it, found it loaded. He slipped the clip into his left-hand jacket pocket, re-parcelled the automatic, put it back. He went quietly down the stairs and out into the street. He thought to himself: What a goddam fool you are, Rene . . . what a fool to think that Shakkey would leave the rods with no shells in them. You oughta know better.

It was beginning to get dark. Berg walked down the street, turned, went back to Piccadilly. He turned westward, then down Duke Street; walked towards the Double Clover Leaf Club. This was a new one on him. He had never been there before. During his time in London—a time when he thought he had known most drinking clubs—the Double Clover Leaf Club had eluded him. Maybe it had been called something else; maybe he had just missed it as one did miss things in life.

He turned into Duke Street, left and right into the passage before him. At the end of the cul-de-sac was a shaded neon sign. The liquid electricity running through the distorted letters said: *"The Double Clover Leaf Club."* Berg thought it was a nice sign. The background was blue, the letters a peculiar cream shot with the same weird blue. He thought it was wonderful. What they could do with electric signs these days!

He turned into the doorway. Before him was a narrow passage with a small room on the right and through the open doorway of the room was a desk. Behind it was a hard-faced man of about fifty—a membership book in front of him. He looked at Berg casually but inquiringly.

He said: "Well!" The word could have been a question or a challenge.

Berg stood looking down at the man, half smiling. He said: "My name's Berg. I'm looking for a Chief Machinist's Mate in the U.S. Navy—a man called Shakkey. Maybe you know him?"

The man said: "I've never heard of him. If you're not a member of the Club you can't come in. And don't try anything funny because this Club is a very well-run Club and we don't have people we don't know."

Berg said: "O.K. O.K. Say, who does the Club belong to? Is the manager or proprietor here?"

The man said: "What the hell's that got to do with you?"

The smile left Berg's face; suddenly his countenance became very tense and very hard. His eyes narrowed to two little slits. He looked at the man behind the desk, who found difficulty in meeting the eyes that looked down at him.

Berg said easily: "Look, fella, I asked you a simple question. There's no law against that, is there? I asked you who the proprietor or the manager was. You can answer a question like that, can't you?" He grinned. "If you don't," he said, "I'll kick your teeth down your throat." The threat was uttered so easily and so casually that it was all the more efficacious.

The man said: "Mrs. Hahn's the proprietress. Mr. Hahn's the manager."

Berg began to smile. The smile illuminated his face.

He said: "For Chrissake . . .! Travis and Lauren Hahn. Is that right?"

The man behind the desk said unwillingly: "Yes, that's right."

Berg asked: "Are either of 'em in?"

The man said: "Mrs. Hahn's in."

Berg leaned back against the wall. His shoulders drooped; he relaxed. He felt strangely, unaccountably happy.

He said: "Listen, punk, you go inside and tell Lauren Hahn that Rene Berg's here. Get crackin', see? Get goin'."

The man said: "All right." He got up and went away.

Berg thought that the place was very quiet. He leaned against the wall, lit a cigarette. There was no doubt in his mind that fate was definitely behind this job. He had found the guns. From the guns he had found the Double Clover Leaf Club. Now he had found Lauren. He waited there, drawing easily on his cigarette, looking blankly at the wall before him, thinking.

After a while the man came back. He said shortly: "This way."

He took Berg down the passage, through a doorway, at the end through another passage, through two thick curtains and across something that purported to be a dance floor, through a doorway on the other side, through another passage to the left. Then he opened a door at the end.

Berg went in. Lauren was sitting behind a small mahogany desk in the corner of the room.

She said: "Jesus . . . Rene . . .!"

She got up. Berg closed the door behind him, leaned against it. He stood smiling easily, looking at her.

He said: "Well, what do you know, Lauren?"

She looked at him. She was still quite beautiful. Berg thought: By now she must be forty-four or forty-five at least. But she was still the junoesque Lauren of the old days—tall and big, deep-breasted and wide-hipped, with a good waist. Her coat and skirt were beautifully tailored. She still had that thing about knowing how to dress. The coat and skirt were black and plain, the pockets and sleeves trimmed with braid. The tailor had had an eye for line and Lauren's figure. At her throat was a pink lace jabot. Above it her neck rose like a column into the clear-cut jaw, the fine chin and full promising mouth, the dark brown eyes. Her hair, dead black, beautifully dressed, made an adequate frame for the face beneath it.

Berg said: "Life's goddam funny, isn't it, Lauren? Hey? Is it goddam funny or is it!"

She said softly: "Yeah, it's funny all right."

She came round the desk. As she came round he could see that her legs and feet were as perfect as ever. She still wore the high-heeled dull glace court shoes which she had affected in the old days. She still put her feet on the ground with the same quiet staccato step. The old swing of the hips was there. Berg thought, with an inward grin, that Lauren had not changed a lot.

She came close to him. She said: "You sweet bastard! I knew you were gonna come back some time." She put her arms round his neck. She pressed her mouth to his.

Berg stood there quiescent. The kiss had affected him not at all. His shoulders were still relaxed, his hands hanging straight by his sides.

She dropped her arms and stood away from him. She said: "Still the same, cold, icy, sonofabitch. Wherever you've been they haven't taught you a hell of a lot."

Berg said: "No. Where I've been they've taught me damn all."

She went back to the desk, pressed a button. After a minute a man in a white jacket came in.

Lauren said: "What are you drinking, Rene?"

He said: "I'll have a big whisky and soda."

She raised her eyebrows. "An English drink, hey? You doing their stuff?"

He said: "Yeah, I like it that way."

She laughed suddenly. She showed her white even teeth. She said: "All right. Me too. Two large whiskies and sodas."

The man went away. Lauren sat down behind the desk. She opened a drawer, took out a box of cigarettes, put two of them in her mouth, lit them with a silver lighter from the table, got up, went to Berg, put one in his mouth. As she did so he could see the remnant of cerise lipstick on the end of the cigarette.

He said: "Thanks, Lauren."

She went back to her seat. There was a silence. Berg stood just a little way away from the doorway looking at her. He thought that the carpet was very soft beneath his feet; that the office was expensively furnished; that Lauren was well-dressed. He thought things were going well with her. The silence went on. After a moment the man in the white jacket came in with the drinks. He gave one to Berg, put the other on the desk in front of Lauren. He went away.

She raised the glass. She said: "Well, here's to you, Rene." She smiled suddenly. "And the old days."

Berg drank. She finished the drink in one gulp. She put the glass on the desk before her.

She said: "Well, what is it, Rene? You don't look quite so good to me. Maybe you been having a bad time. Do you need a little help?" Her face softened. A smile illuminated it. She said: "You know, Rene, you've hit the right spot if you want help."

Berg grinned at her. He said: "Sure . . . sure . . . sure . . .! I reckon if I needed any help I'd come to you, Lauren. Thanks a lot. I don't need any help. Where's Travis?"

She sighed—a little odd sigh which seemed to indicate that the introduction of her husband's name had jarred on her.

She said: "I wouldn't know where Travis is. He's around. He'll be back. Do we have to worry about him?"

Berg said: "No, I don't suppose we do, but I'd like to know where he is."

She said shortly: "I told you he's around. Why don't you relax and talk to me? I'm not poison, am I?"

Berg said: "Aren't you?"

They stood looking at each other. Lauren said after a pause,

"Listen, cutie, what do you mean by that one? Are you being funny?"

He shook his head. He said: "I'm not being funny." He smiled at her. "I've got over that a long time ago. I'm just asking a simple question. I want Travis. Where is he? You know."

She said: "I told you he's around. But this is my place and you're talking to me in my office. Don't you be rude to me. You always were an insolent sonofabitch—you who used to be . . ."

Berg walked slowly across the room. He went round the end of the desk. He stood looking down at her.

He said: "Why don't you keep quiet? Why don't you tell me what I wanta know. Where's Travis? Don't stall. If you do I'll smack it out of you."

She put her hands on the desk in front of her. Berg could see the diamond rings glittering on her fingers. Her shoulders drooped in an attitude of resignation.

She said: "He'll be around. He's due here now. Maybe he's in the other office checking up on yesterday's takings. If you've got to see him I expect you'll find him there—outside through the passage on the right—the room at the end."

Berg said: "Thanks, Lauren."

He turned and walked out of the office. Her eyes followed him—cold, hostile.

Berg walked along the short passage, rapped on the door at the end. There was no reply. He pushed open the door, went in, switched on the light. The room, furnished luxuriously as an office, was smaller than Lauren's room, but had an air of practical use. There were some steel filing cabinets. The telephone, blotter, pen-stand, were all expensive, neatly arranged on the ample walnut desk. Berg, standing just inside the door, looking at the furnishings with an appreciative eye, concluded that Travis was just as smart and neat as he always had been. A smart neat guy—that's what Travis was, with everything in its proper place, except . . . Berg's lips twisted into a wry grin.

Travis had always been one to have everything in its proper place. An organiser, Travis. Definitely an organiser. A person who took a long view; who believed in the right quantity of audacity mixed with a leavening of caution—especially the caution where he himself was concerned. With regard to others he had the ability to plan with audacity. He had been especially audacious where Berg had been concerned. And the probability was that even now he might think that Berg was unaware of the fact. Which made the situation rather funny.

But Travis had brains all right. He looked as if he was sitting pretty now. This club, probably well-organised and well-run, would have been a little gold-mine during the war years. Travis, with his old-time background relegated to the past, would have been very popular with the American Services in England. And Lauren? Well . . . Lauren would have been a good-looking sister or what-have-you-got! A nice combination—a nice set-up, thought Berg.

He stood regarding the inanimate objects about him. He wondered where Travis had got such a fine walnut desk from in war-time. But then Travis always got the things he wanted—or did he? Berg switched off the light, closed the door, went along the passage, back to Lauren's room. He pushed open the door, went inside; stood just inside the doorway looking at her.

She was still sitting in the big chair, her hands with their pretty, white and slightly plump fingers, lying supine on the desk before her. She was looking at her hands. Berg began to grin internally. He remembered Lauren in the old days when she used to sit, her hands folded in her lap, looking at them. You knew she was planning something. She, who could be so secretive, had never possessed the ability to break herself of that little give-away habit.

The silence seemed to go on for a long time; then Berg said: "Travis isn't there. I'll stick around till he comes back."

She nodded. The silence went on. When she spoke her voice was soft but very clear. She seemed to have made up her mind about something.

She said: "Rene, it's a hell of a time since I've seen you. Where have you been? The last I heard about you, you got yourself into a lot of trouble fighting in some revolution in the Grand Chaco. Did you have a good time? And what happened after that? You always were a hell of a fellow for sticking your neck out, weren't you, Rene?" Now her eyes were smiling at him.

Berg thought to himself: "Poor sweet bitch, so you're getting around to it. Getting around to a little cross-examination to find out if I'm wise. To find out if I ever got wise to the big idea in the old days."

He shrugged his shoulders. The movement was so slight that it was hardly noticeable. He said evenly: "Yes, I got around a bit down there but I didn't do myself much good, Lauren."

She said: "No?" She raised one eyebrow—a charming and provocative habit. She said: "Why not? You've got what it takes, Rene. We all thought you'd clean up in a *very* big way."

So they'd taken the trouble to find out about the Grand Chaco. They'd known that Berg had been fighting—if you could call his rather peculiar job fighting—down there. He wondered who they knew in South America. How much they knew. He thought that probably they'd heard something casually and that she was trying to pump him.

He shrugged his shoulders again. He said: "I was never very good at the cleaning-up side of business, Lauren. You oughta know that. Maybe I'm not what they call a business man."

She laughed softly. She said again: "No? All right, Rene. So you're not a good business man. You tell me what you are."

He grinned at her. He said: "You ought to know, Lauren. I reckon you oughta know better than I do, but if I were asked to describe myself I'd say I was more of a near-hero than anything else."

She raised both eyebrows. She said: "And what the hell's a near-hero, Rene?"

He said: "Anything that just misses." He laughed. "You know, a near actor, a near beauty, a near any goddam thing you like."

She picked up a pencil and began to drum with the blunt end of it on the desk in front of her. Berg thought she was nervous, restless, impatient.

She said: "Maybe you're right at that, Rene. You always were a guy for heroics, weren't you, even in the old days? I reckon you always wanted to be a hero in a big way. Well, there's been a war on. I wonder why the hell you didn't get around to it—or maybe you had something better to do."

Berg said: "You're trying to find out if I've been serving." He shrugged his shoulders, obviously this time. "I reckon Uncle Sam hadn't very much use for guys like me. Maybe if I'd been any sort of guy instead of being just a punk I'd have tried to do something about it."

(Inside he was laughing. He was thinking: This is goddam funny. This is real humour. I wonder what she'd think if she knew.)

She put the pencil down. She said: "You're no punk, Rene. You've always had what it takes. You've got guts all right, but you look to me as if you've been kicked around a bit." She smiled. "That is if it's possible for Rene Berg to be kicked around."

He considered for a moment. "You could be right at that, Lauren," he said. "I can get kicked around too, even if it's not by a man or woman. Life can kick you around, you know. I reckon this war sort of up-ended everything."

Lauren leant forward a little. She said: "Listen, pal, what's the matter with you? Don't tell me you're losing your nerve. God, I never knew anybody like you. You were about the toughest, slickest, thing I ever met in my life when . . ."

Berg grinned at her. He said: "Yeah, *when* . . . I know what you were going to say. Maybe I wasn't so tough or so slick before then, was I, before the time when 'when' happened? Remember, Lauren?"

She said: "Look, Rene, you wouldn't be going bitter about anything, would you? What the hell's the matter with you? Have you got something on your mind? Why don't you have a drink?"

Berg said: "Yeah, that's a hell of an idea. Let's have a drink, Lauren—a big one. I feel like it."

She pushed the bell on her desk. The man in the white jacket came back. He did not need any orders this time. He brought a bottle, a syphon, two glasses, and a small bucket of ice with him. He put them on the desk and went away.

Berg noticed his linen jacket was well-cut, spotless, well-pressed. He thought, with a touch of admiration, that Lauren was pretty good at having people neat about her. So was Travis. They were a neat couple.

She poured out two stiff drinks, tinkled some splinters of ice into the glasses. She got up, brought the drink over to Berg. When she was very close to him a wave of subtle perfume came to his nostrils. He remembered it. She was still using the old scent. It seemed to him then that no one, except perhaps one person, had ever exuded such femininity as Lauren. Everything she did was a challenge. She couldn't even move across a room without making you think of the forbidden things—or were they forbidden?

He took the glass. He said: "Well, here it is." He drank some of the whisky.

She went back to the desk, sat down. She picked up her glass and looked at him over the top of it. Her eyes were very kind and half-closed.

She said: "Here's to you, kid. I think you're a bloody scream!" There was a tiny note of anger in her voice.

Berg swished his glass round in a circle, making the ice chips tinkle against the sides. He said: "Well . . . why?"

She said: "Well, you're the same old Rene, but you've got a different top-dressing on. Remember how you used to talk in the old days? Goddam it, feller, when you came down from— where was it, the Ozarks—you could have cut your accent with a knife. I've never heard anything so goddam funny in my life. Now you're talking half English and half American. What have you been doing, Rene?"

Berg spread his hands. He said: "I've been getting around." He began to lie. "After that Grand Chaco business I went back to the States," he said, "and the war started. I wasn't quite certain what to do." He thought to himself that he had better be careful about the lies he told. Lauren had always been pretty good at checking up and if she really were curious she might try to find out.

He said: "Aw . . . what the hell! You can imagine the sort of things that happen to a guy like me—a job here, a job there. One day you have a bank roll as big as your fist and the next day you're on your ear. You know how it is." He smiled. "Maybe," he said, "that's because I wasn't ever really trained for anything, except you know what."

She said: "Yeah, I know what. You were pretty good at it too."

Berg said: "I think I was. Maybe that's the only thing I've ever known how to do."

She finished her drink. She got up, came round the desk, came to Berg, took the glass away from him. She refilled the glasses—mixed two strong drinks.

Berg said: "Hey . . . hey . . . you're giving me a real snifter, ain't you? What's the idea—trying to loosen my tongue?" He laughed at her. He moved across to the desk and took the glass.

She said: "No, Rene. You'll never talk unless you wanta talk. You don't wanta talk I think because . . . well, maybe you haven't very much to talk about. I know how it is. A lot of guys have had a bad time the last two or three years. It's been O.K. for those who've been in the Services and had a job, but if you were sort of on the shelf like maybe you have been, it hasn't been so good."

Berg said: "Well, it looks as if it's been pretty good with you. A nice place you've got here. Who does it belong to—you or Travis? And how do you make out? Do the English like Americans to do this sort of stuff here?"

She winked at him—a delightful wicked flutter of one eyelid. She said: "I'm the proprietress here, and maybe you're forgetting something. Travis is a Canadian. At least, that's the story. He's a Canadian and I'm his wife." The eyelid fluttered again. "We been married for years now. So the position over here is O.K. and I've got an idea we're gonna stay here too."

"Why not?" said Berg. "It's a nice set-up."

She nodded. "Yes." Her voice was very soft. "It's a nice set-up, Rene. There is only one thing wrong with it."

"No," said Berg. "No? Don't tell me." He stood looking down at her, smiling—a little twisted smile.

She said: "Yeah, one thing's wrong . . . that goddam Travis. I never liked the guy."

"You don't say," said Berg. "I wonder why you married him."

She spread her hands. "You can ask a few thousand other married women the same question," she said. "I reckon we've all got to learn a lesson." There was a pause; then she went on: "That's why I was wondering."

Berg said: "Yeah . . . wondering what?"

She lifted one shoulder a little; then she moved her arm and examined the bracelet on the right wrist. It was a platinum curb bracelet with a hundred little ornaments dangling from it. When she moved her wrist they shook. They made a tinkling noise—not unattractive, Berg thought.

She said slowly: "Well, you were always a good guy, Rene—one hundred per cent on the up-and-up. There used to be a lot of talk about you one time, but, by heck, I reckon loyalty was your middle name. You're a wicked bastard, but you got something that's damned good somewhere."

Berg said wearily: "Why don't you have it set to music and make a record of it? So I'm a great guy. I'm on the up-and-up and I'm loyal. Ever heard of a raspberry?"

She said: "All right. If you don't want it that way, don't have it that way. But there's a spot here for you, Rene. Look . . ." She leaned forward. "We want a man in the organisation here like you. This Club's gonna be a big thing. We hope to open others in different parts of the country. You know, there's gonna be a lot of Americans coming here. There's a lot of money to be made, I hope. Why don't you come in? There's dough too, Rene." She paused. Berg could see that she was breathing a little quickly, her breasts rising and falling. He thought: You're making this up as you go along, but it's a lovely story.

He said: "And what about Travis?"

She made a little exclamation; then she shrugged her shoulders, made a moue.

She said: "So what! So what about Travis? Any time he doesn't like it he can get out."

Berg said: "That must be a nice thing for him to know. Does he know it or does he?" He grinned at her.

She said: "If he doesn't know it he must guess it."

Berg picked up his glass. He drank half the whisky. He thought it tasted very good. He said: "I wonder when he's coming in. I wanta see that guy."

"Why?" asked Lauren. "Maybe there's something I can do." She seemed to have forgotten her urgency of a few moments before.

Berg asked casually: "I wonder if you've ever run across Shakkey? I got an idea I'd like to meet up with Shakkey again."

She looked at him, her eyes wide. "For crying out loud!" she said. "Who's ever heard of Shakkey? What's that punk doin'? Why should anybody ever want to meet up again with that heel?"

Berg said: "I wouldn't know. But I don't think he was a bad guy, you know—not too bad. I believe he's done a good job in this war. I heard he was a Chief Machinist's Mate in a U.S. torpedo boat. I thought maybe he'd got as far as London and dropped in and visited with you."

She shook her head. She said: "Nope. We haven't seen the guy. I don't know that we want to." She laughed. "Shakkey a sailor! My God! Is that funny or is it! I'd give half a grand to see him in uniform. Shakkey a sailor . . .! Hear me laugh."

Berg said: "And you don't know where he is?"

She said: "No, Rene." She looked at him. There was another silence. "Maybe I could find out." She got up, came round the desk. She came close to him. The perfume enfolded him. "Maybe I can find out," she said softly. "Stick around, Rene, and if you wanta know bad I'll let you know. I'd do anything for you, you sweet heel. You got me all steamed up. You always could."

Berg said: "Yeah . . . yeah. . . . That's what I thought."

Outside he heard a little noise. He said: "Maybe that's Travis. I'll be back in a moment." He looked at the desk, saw the telephone. His eyes wandered slowly round the room, Then he said: "I'll be seein' you."

He closed the door behind him and went up the little passage to Travis's office. The door was half open and the light on. When Berg went in Travis was sitting at the desk. His eyes popped.

He said: "Jesus . . . Rene! Goddam it, I thought you was dead. I thought you'd had it. Some guy told me somebody had croaked you some place—Grand Chaco or somewhere. Although the idea of you gettin' yourself fogged was one I never fell for. For cryin' out loud . . .!"

Berg smiled. He said: "Yeah, it's me all right, and I'm not a stiff. I'm here." He looked at Travis.

Travis was as usual supremely dressed. The shoulders of his coat were perfect, the cloth superfine. Maybe the tailoring was a little too good. Perhaps there was a spot too much shoulders, a little too much waist. Maybe his shoes were a little too pointed, but his shirt was of good silk and his tie was the sort of tie that used to cost five dollars in the old days. Berg wondered where he got the stuff from in war-time.

Travis said: "Look, this calls for a big drink. Lauren'll be excited to see you. Will that babe be steamed up? Why, it's like old days."

Berg thought there was too much heartiness in his voice.

He said: "Yeah . . . she was steamed up. I've been talking to her. She gave me a couple of drinks but I wanted to have a word with you, Travis—just between you and me sort of."

Travis sat down at the desk. "Sure . . . sure . . ." he said. "Anything I can do for you . . . you know that." His voice sounded a little uncomfortable—a trifle anxious.

Berg said: "Believe it or not, Shakkey got himself some job in the Navy. He's a Chief Machinist's Mate. I reckon something or other he's been over here. I don't think he's out east. I sort of got an idea in my head that he's here now. I want to find him."

Travis spread his hands. He said: "Look, Rene, where the hell do you start looking for a guy like Shakkey? I'm asking *you*! Where the hell do you start?"

Berg said: "I wouldn't know. But I want to find the guy. I want to find him bad."

For one second Travis's eye moved to the telephone. Then he shrugged his shoulders again. He said: "Look, maybe I can get a line on him somehow, that is if he's been here. Maybe if you give me a week or so I'll be able to let you know something. Drop in in a few days, Rene. Perhaps I'll have something for you."

Berg moved over to the side of the desk. He stood looking down at Travis. Travis's eyes came up and met Berg's cold blue eyes that looked down at him so steadfastly.

Berg said: "Look, Travis, I reckon you can make it a quicker job than two-three days, couldn't you? It's sort of urgent with me— this finding Shakkey. I want to meet up with that guy. Couldn't you make it quicker?" There was a note almost of entreaty, of pleading, in Berg's voice.

Travis recovered his equanimity. His voice took on a hearty tone. He said: "Rene, I've told you there's not a dog's chance of getting hold of this boy in less than a week ten days, and then I'll have to work hard to find out where he is. Now be reasonable, Rene. You always used to be a reasonable mug."

Berg said: "Yeah." He leaned forward and put his left hand inside the collar of Travis's silk shirt. He brought up his right hand, brought the fist down on Travis's mouth, using the forearm and fist like a sledge-hammer.

Travis made a spluttering noise. He fell back in the chair, his lips cut and bleeding, one tooth missing from the front of his mouth. Berg spoke softly, but his voice held a horrible menace. Travis could remember when he heard that voice before.

Berg said: "Listen, fella, I'm gonna have a drink with Lauren— maybe two, maybe three drinks. That's gonna take a quarter of an hour. At the end of a quarter of an hour I want to know from you where Shakkey is. If I don't do you know what I'm going to do?"

Berg slipped his hand quickly inside the pocket under his left armpit. He brought out the ivory butted .45 automatic. He said: "Remember this, Travis . . . remember it . . .?" He put the gun back in his pocket. "I'm gonna have a drink with Lauren," he repeated. "You come in inside twenty minutes and let me know where Shakkey is; otherwise I'm going to give it to you, and before I do I'll take you apart."

Berg turned his back and walked to the door. He opened it. When he looked over his shoulder at Travis he was smiling. His face had relaxed.

He said: "Get goin', there's a good guy."

Lauren was standing against the desk looking at the door. There was a half-smoked cigarette between the fingers of her left hand. The right hand also resting on the desk held her empty whisky glass.

She said: "You seen Travis, Rene?"

He nodded. He said: "Yeah. He was glad to see me. We had a little talk."

She pushed herself away from the desk, turned, poured out another whisky. She looked over her shoulder at him.

She asked: "You want a piece of this?"

Berg said: "Thanks, Lauren." His voice was smooth and easy. He said: "I ain't been drinking a lot of whisky. It's a good drink."

She said: "Yeah, I like it. Where's Travis? What's he doing?"

He smiled at her. He said: "It looks like he's finding out where Shakkey is. I thought he could sort of do it in about fifteen minutes. I thought we might have a drink while he was finding out."

She poured out the whisky, slowly handed him the glass, She said: "You're a funny guy, ain't you, Rene? I told you I could find out where Shakkey is."

He said: "Sure you told me, but I wanted to know from Travis."

She shrugged her shoulders. She said: "Well, I'd like to know how the hell he's gonna find out."

Berg said: "I wouldn't know. I reckon he thinks it might be a good idea to get crackin' and find out. I don't think he liked the idea a lot anyway."

Her lips broke into a wicked smile. She said quietly: "So he didn't like it and you talked to him, eh, Rene?" She breathed a little more quickly. She said: "Say, what did you do to him, kid?"

Berg said: "Nothing much. I spoilt the shape of that nice mouth of his." Then as an afterthought: "I reckon I've had enough of Travis. I reckon he's sort of worn out like an old suit so far as I am concerned." He drank some of the whisky.

She said: "Yeah, maybe that goes for me too."

Berg smiled at her. He said: "Maybe it goes for you too." He laughed. "Except that nobody could say that you looked like an old suit. I think you look terrific, Lauren."

She went back to her seat behind the desk. She took two cigarettes from the cigarette box, threw one to him. He caught it expertly, lit it. He took his lighter over, leaned over the desk, lit her cigarette. She blew some smoke into his face, looked at him through the small cloud.

She said: "I wish to God I knew what was ridin' you. What the hell's the matter with you? Anybody would think we didn't look after you in the old days. For Chrissake . . .! You're like a guy who's got a chip on his shoulder."

Berg said slowly: "You sound as if you don't like it because I've come back, Lauren. Maybe you weren't so pleased to see me come in here. Maybe you know something."

She said shortly: "I don't know a goddam thing, and I don't know what you're talking about. All I know is you come around here. You got a beef about something. All right. I give you a sweet welcome and what do I get?" She laughed. "Maybe I'm luckier than Travis all the same." Her eyes sparkled for a moment. "Maybe I'm lucky I didn't get smacked down too."

Berg grinned at her. He said: "Maybe."

The door opened. Travis stood in the doorway. His upper lip was swollen. There was a little blob of dried blood on the lower one. Lauren looked at him and there was an amused concern in her eyes.

She said: "Say, honey, what you been doing? Did you walk into a wall or something?"

Travis said: "Aw . . . shut up!"

He had a piece of paper in his hand. He held it out towards Berg. He said: "Well, there's the address. I was quick, wasn't I?" He stood looking straight in front of him.

Berg put out his hand and took the slip of paper. He read it, put it in his inside jacket pocket. He picked up his unfinished glass of whisky from the desk, drained it.

He said: "Well, you've been nice, you two. It's been nice seein' you. It sort of reminded me of the old days. I guess I'll be getting along."

Lauren said: "Well, if you've got to go, Rene . . . you know. But any time you're around here there'll always be a welcome for you, you know. I always like to see you. And that goes for Travis too." She grinned wickedly at her husband. "Don't it, Travis?"

He said: "Sure . . . sure . . . I'm always glad to see Rene."

Berg picked up his hat. "So long, Lauren," he said. "So long, Travis."

He went out of the office. He closed the door behind him, walked a little way down the passage. His eyes were on the wainscoting. He bent down, took a pocket-knife from his trouser pocket. He flipped out the big blade. He knelt down and worked for a moment against the wainscoting; then he put the knife away, got up, walked down the passage, across the dance floor, past the man in the outer office out into the street. He was whistling softly to himself.

Inside the office, Lauren looked at Travis. She said: "You give him the right address?"

He shrugged his shoulders. "I gave him the only one I knew," he said. "Maybe it's the right one. Maybe it's not. I wouldn't know. But don't worry. You know that bastard Berg—if he's out to find Shakkey, by God . . . he's going to find him, and nothing'll stop him. So what's the good?"

She nodded. She said: "You know what he's going to do, don't you?"

He looked at her. He said slowly: "No?"

She said: "Yeah . . . that's what he's gonna do. Well, *I'm* going to do something about it."

Travis grinned at her. "So you're going to put a spoke in his wheel, are you? You're going to do something about it. What did he do—give you the air? I bet he did. You usta be plenty stuck on Rene."

She hissed at him: "You keep your goddam mouth shut. Maybe I was—maybe I wasn't. Maybe I am or maybe I ain't. So what's it to you? But I'm going to put a spoke in his wheel."

She picked up the telephone receiver. She said: "Give me Trunks."

Travis said: "The big tip-off, hey? Well, I think you're a mug."

She jangled the receiver rest up and down. She said shortly: "What the hell's the matter with this telephone? I can't get through."

Travis got up. He followed the line of the telephone wiring, round the floor. He opened the door, went out into the passage. After a moment he came back. He was smiling. He said: "I wouldn't worry. He's cut the line out there in the passage. A clever bastard, Rene. He always was a smart one."

She said harshly: "That ain't so smart. I can use another telephone, can't I? Why do you think he's smart?"

Travis stood in front of the door. He barred her way. He said: "Relax, Lauren. Don't you think *he* didn't know you could use another telephone? Don't you think *he* didn't know there was more than one telephone line in London? That's not why he cut the wire outside."

She said: "O.K. Then why did he? You tell me."

Travis said: "It's a tip-off to you and me, sweetie pie—just a tip-off to mind our own goddam business and keep our noses out of something he considers his. You got it?"

She said slowly: "Yeah, I got it."

Travis said: "So you don't telephone. You just don't do anything at all. It might be healthier."

She went back to the desk. She sat down. She said wearily: "Maybe you're right, Travis. Maybe you're right at that."

Berg walked down Piccadilly towards the Circus. His mind dwelt bitterly on Travis and Lauren. Smart people, Travis and Lauren. Smart guys—tough guys. They knew how to play life those two. Or they thought they did. They had flexible minds too. If they did not want to think about something that had happened they just let it ride. They were aware only of those things that they wished to remember. Other things they forgot—very easily. Too easily, thought Berg.

And they were not worrying about him. Why should they? They thought they didn't *have* to worry about him. He was all washed up. Actually, in their minds, he was in the same sort of picture in which he had presented himself to them years ago. Lauren, of course, still had a lean on him. He had something she wanted. She was prepared to offer him a job and some dough just in order to have him stringing around; just so that Travis should know where he got off.

Life was goddam funny, thought Berg. You were thrown into life and it kicked you around. Things happened to you. As a result of the things happening to you, you thought things—did things. As a result of the things you thought and did other things happened to you. And so it went on, year after year—things happening because of something you had done—without end.

He wondered vaguely who was responsible for the original thing that started off the sequence of events, but he did not continue the line of thought. It was boring. It was boring and it didn't get you any place.

Now he was crossing the Circus. He went into Shaftesbury Avenue, walked a little way. He came to a side turning that he remembered. He walked up the turning. A hundred yards down was the flight of stairs leading down to the Club.

Another Club, thought Berg. It seemed that one part of one's life was divided into night clubs—the times you had used them, what had happened there; what had happened as a result of the things you had experienced. He remembered this place well— an innocuous place where the drink was not bad, the women unattractive and stupid. He went down the stairs.

Outside the Club entrance a man in the usual little office with the usual book asked him if he were a member. Berg said he was. He went inside. The room was long and narrow. There was a bar—two women behind it. At the end of the bar was a door leading to other rooms where you could eat. Berg ordered a large whisky and soda.

He realised he had been drinking a considerable quantity of whisky, but drinking whisky was a rather nice thing, he thought. It hypnotised him. It made life seem a little easier. It made things seem possible. He stood looking at the drink, at the bubbles that were still rising from the bottom of the glass.

When he moved he found a girl at his elbow. He thought it was rather odd that always in a Club you found a girl. He thought there must be lots of girls waiting in Clubs for people like himself.

He said: "Well, Cutie?"

She looked at him sideways. She was a young, pert, thing, with a retroussé nose and lips painted the wrong colour.

She said: "Well, do I rate a drink?"

Berg said: "Why not? Whisky?"

She nodded. He ordered a large whisky and soda.

She said: "You're an American, ain't you?"

Berg nodded. He said: "You like Americans?"

"Who don't?" said the girl. "We've had a lot of 'em here, you know. You've got to like 'em even if you don't and most of 'em are good guys. Besides they got jack."

He nodded. He said: "Yeah . . . that's the answer, hey, Cutie?"

She said: "It's a good answer. What are you—a soldier, sailor, an airman or a tired business man?"

He grinned at her. He said: "Believe it or not I don't have to be any of those things. I'm not even tired."

She drank her drink.

Outside it was dark. Nobody saw the police wagon arrive. The back opened and a score of policemen ejected themselves on to the pavement. Led by a sub-inspector, they were down the stairs and in the vestibule of the Club more quickly than seemed possible.

The girl nudged Berg. She said: "A raid, hey? What the hell! It's in drinkin' hours. What're they after? This place is run straight. For Chrissake! Why do they have to raid this place?"

Berg said: "I wouldn't know." He was thinking quickly. When a place was raided they wanted your name and address. If you weren't English they wanted to see your papers. He breathed a sigh of relief. Well, that was all right. Ransome had even thought of that one.

He said: "Why worry, kid? Just another slice of life. There's always a to-morrow and the cops here are rather nice I think. They're much tougher where I come from."

She said: "Yes? I'm glad to hear it."

The police came into the bar. Nobody moved. It seemed as if the habitués had experienced raids before.

The sub-inspector said: "There's no need to get excited. Names and addresses please. Take it easy."

Behind him, four stolid, helmeted policemen regarded the occupants of the bar in very much the same way as they would have regarded prize cattle.

The girl slipped off the seat. She moved over to the inspector. She said: "Look, what is this? What are you knocking this dump off for? It's in drinking hours—it ain't even after time. What's the story?"

He was very polite. He said: "I just do what I'm told, miss. If I knew I'd probably be the Chief Commissioner."

The girl went away. She disappeared into the far room. Berg finished his drink. He moved towards the entrance.

The policeman said: "Are you a member?"

Berg said: "I think so. I used to come here a long time ago."

The policeman asked him his name and address.

Berg gave them: "Rene Berg—126 Redwood Avenue, Earl's Court."

The sub-inspector moved over. He said over the policeman's shoulders: "Are you English?"

Berg said: "Nope, I'm an American."

The sub-inspector said: "Have you got some papers?"

Berg said: "Yeah." He put his hand in his pocket. He brought out the leather wallet. He produced the cards from the back pocket—the cards that Ransome had left.

The inspector looked at them. He cocked an eye at Berg. One of the permits said that Rene Berg was attached Special Service, American and British Special Intelligence Liaison.

The inspector handed the papers back. He said to the policeman: "O.K. You got the address?"

The policeman nodded.

The inspector said: "It's all right for you to go if you want to, Mr. Berg. We know who you are."

Berg said: "O.K."

He went up the stairs, out into the street, back into Piccadilly. He began to walk westwards. Police raids, he thought, were funny things. He wondered why it was that the English police raided places and just took names and addresses. There was none of the excitement, police wagons and people being taken away that you got in Chicago, for instance. They played it quietly around here.

But you gave your address. He did not like that.

Outside Duke Street he waited on the pavement. Presently a cab came by. Berg whistled. Surprisingly, the cab stopped. He told the driver to go to Redwood Avenue, got in, sat in the corner, lit a cigarette. He thought it was time he was getting a move on. He did not like this business of addresses being taken. Maybe it did not mean a goddam thing, but you never knew. He settled back *in* the corner of the cab; purled slowly at his cigarette.

It was after midnight when he finished his packing. He had not very much—just one suitcase; another suit, some underclothes, one or two odd things that a man collects.

Mrs. Frane—fifty, deep-bosomed and motherly, stood at the door of his room. Berg gave her a little wad of notes.

He said: "You been swell to me, Mrs. France. Thanks a lot. I've got to be gettin' along."

She said: "I'm sorry you've got to go so suddenly, Mr. Berg. It's been nice having you." She smiled at him. "You've been a nice lodger," she said.

He smiled back. He said: "Yeah. All good things have to come to an end."

She said: "Where are you going to, Mr. Berg?" For some reason which she did not know she was interested in him.

Berg said: "I've got to get a move on. Another thing, I've got to get myself a motor-car."

She said: "Yes?" Lodgers in Redwood Avenue who wanted motor-cars were strange people—beyond her ken.

He said: "You wouldn't know where I could get a car?"

She shook her head. "There are places where you can hire cars," she said. A sudden thought came to her. "I've got a friend just round the corner in Claremont Grove. He's got a car. He's in business. He's got some petrol too. Maybe he'd loan it to you."

Berg took the address. He said: "Thank you, Mrs. Frane. I'll go see him."

She stood aside for him to pass. As he went through the doorway, diffidently she held out her hand. Berg shook it. He smiled at her almost shyly.

He said: "Thanks a lot, Mrs. Frane. You've been swell."

He went down the stairs.

The pinnace cut through the dark waters in Dartmouth harbour. The man in the bows peered ahead towards the spot where the dark grey hulk of the destroyer rose out of the water.

The petty officer in the stern blew two blasts on his whistle. The pinnace slowed down, came alongside.

Ransome went up the companionway, touched his hat to the officer of the day, went down to his cabin. He threw his uniform cap in a corner, lit a cigarette. He sat at his desk. He rang the bell. The night messenger—a matelot of two years' service—stood in the doorway, his cap in his hand.

Ransome said: "Good-evening, Curtin. The officer of the day please."

Curtin said: "Aye, aye, sir." He went away.

The officer of the day came into the cabin. He was a young sub-lieutenant in the R.N.V.R. He had red hair and a wide smile.

Ransome said: "Good-evening, Johns. Any messages?"

Johns said: "Yes, sir . . . they're marked important—one from the Admiralty Intelligence." He held the slip of paper towards Ransome, who read:

"To-night at twenty-one hours an individual calling himself Rene Berg arrived at the American Club, Piccadilly. He asked for a parcel which might have been left for him by Cyram Shakkey Chief Machinist's Mate US. Navy. The parcel was given to him. He took it away."

Ransome put the piece of paper down on the desk. He held out his hand for the second message. He read:

"Special Branch Liaison Department informed to-night at twenty-four hours the Blue Peter Club 124 Stanhope Street Shaftesbury Avenue was raided according to instructions. An individual with a special liaison intelligence pass in the name of Rene Berg was present. He gave an address 126 Redwood Avenue Earl's Court and was allowed to leave according to instructions."

Ransome put the second note on top of the first one.

He said: "All right, Johns. Thank you."

The officer of the day went away.

Ransome picked up the telephone receiver on his desk. He said to the shore exchange: "Captain H.M.S. *Whelp* speaking. This is a Government priority call. Give me Whitehall 1212."

He got the number inside three minutes. He asked for an extension number. A voice came on the line.

Ransome said: "This is Captain Ransome, H.M.S. *Whelp,* Dartmouth. Will you arrange to pick up Rene Berg, 126 Redwood Avenue, Earl's Court. Ask him please to proceed immediately to Dartmouth by car and contact me here. He will understand. Repeat please."

The message was repeated. Ransome replaced the receiver. He lit a cigarette, leaned back in his chair, blowing smoke through pursed lips, thinking.

He wished he had come aboard earlier. If he had received the messages earlier it might have been better. Berg would have had time to act.

Probably the raid would have scared him. Ransome smiled at the word *scared.* It would take more than a police raid to scare Berg. But it might set his mind working. It might make him do something. Ransome hoped that they would pick him up before he had the chance to leave the Earl's Court address. He shrugged his shoulders. He sat at his desk, smoking, wondering. . . .

Berg thought that ten horse-power cars were not so good for speed, but anyhow they got you places. It was one o'clock. There was no traffic on the road. He hoped he had enough petrol in the tank to make it. Of course the guy had not wanted to hire the car, but dough always talked, thought Berg.

He settled down behind the wheel, looked straight in front of him, looking at the road, thinking of Travis, of Lauren, of all sorts of things, but thinking especially of the raid. When coppers came round and took your name and address, it was a good time to get out, thought Berg. Maybe there was nothing to it, but you never knew.

It was good and late, he thought. Maybe it was too late to do anything in Dartmouth. It might be an idea to stay at some place on the road; or to pull off the road and sleep in the car. You had to sleep. That was one of the things you couldn't do without. Especially if you wanted to think straight. He slowed down as he passed through a village; looked for some place to stop.

Maybe, he thought, maybe to-morrow he would find Shakkey.

It was nearly dusk when Berg came down through the little street on to the quay at Dartmouth. He took the slip of paper which Travis had given him out of his pocket and re-read the few words pencilled on it: *"Shakkey, U.S. Torpedo Boat Dayton, Dartmouth, South Devon."* Berg screwed the paper into a pellet, threw it over the quayside into the harbour.

He began to walk past the Castle Hotel towards the narrow street that runs between the water and the Raleigh Hotel. In midstream, and in the distance near the opposite bank, line upon line of landing craft were moored, with here and there two or three British or U.S. torpedo boats at anchor. Berg thought that most of the British ships would probably be paying off their crews. The war was over and a certain sombre and lifeless atmosphere seemed to hang over the quiet waters which had been so busy— had seen so much—in the war years.

Berg stood at the top of the steps leading down to the water almost opposite the entrance of the Raleigh Hotel. He lit a cigarette. He stood there patiently waiting for something or somebody to carry him a little further forward in the quest which fate had awarded him.

Two or three minutes later a man pulled up in a dinghy. The man wore the peaked cap and rough jersey of a fisherman. Berg called to him.

He said: "Hey, fella . . . you wouldn't know a destroyer called *Dayton,* would you—a United States ship?"

The man lay on his oars. He called back to Berg: "Yes, she's across the other side. If you want to go there it'll cost you half a crown."

Berg said: "That's all right." He went down the steps. He thought that it would be very funny to meet Shakkey after all this time; that it might be even funnier to hear what Shakkey had to say about this or that.

The dinghy moved across the quiet waters. Just ahead of them lay the long blue-grey shape of a British Fleet destroyer. Behind them came one short blast on a whistle as the bosun in charge of a naval pinnace signalled to his engine room to reduce speed.

The pinnace passed within four or five feet of the dinghy, and the little boat was rocked in the series of small waves that came from the launch.

Berg turned his head. Seated in the stern of the pinnace, his peaked naval cap at its usual angle, his face as thin, as brown, as ever, was Ransome. Berg made a little noise with his tongue. He said quietly to himself: Jeez . . . what do you know about that one! He watched the pinnace come alongside the destroyer, heard the two blasts on the whistle. Then she stopped. Berg held one hand up so that his face could not be seen; saw Ransome go up the accommodation ladder.

He said to the boatman: "Hey . . . you know the name of that destroyer?"

The man nodded. "That's the *Whelp*," he said—"a nice ship— one of the big ones. That's her captain going aboard—Captain Ransome."

Berg said: "Yeah—and where's *Dawton*? Let's get a move on, shall we?"

The man said: "I'm getting there as fast as I can. She's over on the other side. Who you looking for—an officer? I reckon I know most of 'em by sight."

Berg said: "No, I'm looking for a Chief Machinist's Mate—a guy named Shakkey. Would you know him?"

The man shook his head.

Berg threw his cigarette end into the water, sat relaxed in the stern of the dinghy, looking at the shadows on the other bank. Three or four minutes later the boatman pulled his dinghy round.

He said: "There you are."

They floated up close to the accommodation ladder of the U.S. destroyer. Berg stood up in the dinghy. As a figure came to the top of the ladder he called: "Hey, is that *Dayton*? If it is, is there a guy called Cyram Shakkey aboard."

The voice said: "This is *Dayton* all right, but Shakkey's not aboard. He went on a pass three days ago and nobody's seen him since. Do you want him bad?"

Berg said: "Well, not that bad. I wanted to see him, that's all. He's an old buddy of mine."

The voice said: "Well, I reckon *we* want him bad. He's for it when he comes aboard here. I never knew such a guy for being A.W.O.L. If you come across him ashore tell him he's got a date with me sometime. He'll know who I am."

"Sure," said Berg. "If I see him I'll tell him. So long." He said to the boatman: "This is where I go back."

At the landing steps he gave the man a ten shilling note, walked slowly up the wet slippery stone steps, stood uncertainly at the top. On the other side of the road the door of the Raleigh looked inviting. Berg crossed., went into the back bar, ordered a whisky and soda. He leaned against the bar. The place was filled with a mixture of seafaring men—British and American of all ranks. At one end of the bar four or five young sub-lieutenants in the R.N.V.R. drank copiously of beer. In one corner three tall thin American sailors chewed on their cigarettes and exchanged war reminiscences.

Berg leaned over the bar. He said to the girl behind it: "Say, miss, I wonder if you ever met up with a guy here called Cyram Shakkey—a guy with a thin face. I reckon he'd come here. I reckon this is the nearest place to the ship; he was never a guy for having too big a distance between himself and a drink any time."

The girl thought for a moment, then she said: "I remember the name, sort of. It touches something in my brain but I cant quite place it . . . Shakkey . . . Shakkey . . .?" She repeated it, looking inquiringly around the bar in case the sound might strike a chord in someone's memory. There was a silence. Nobody spoke.

A great sense of disappointment, of unhappiness, came to Berg. He thought to himself: "That's goddam tough luck. Everything breaking like that—finding the guns, getting Shakkey's address, coming all this way, and then no Shakkey." He finished his drink, began to walk towards the bar door. He had almost arrived there when a woman, a glass in her hand, sitting in a big chair by the wall, said:

"Just a minute. Were you looking for Cyram Shakkey?"

Berg stopped. He looked down at her. He smiled. His brain thought: By God, this is the Shakkey type. Shakkey had always gone for women like that—plump, dark, women with well-rounded figures and good ankles—a woman who was a foil to his own blond leanness. His smile widened. He thought: Maybe Shakkey has ditched this broad like he used to ditch 'em all in the old days.

He said softly and very politely: "Yes, ma'am, I'm looking for Cyram Shakkey. I wanta find him pretty bad."

She said: "So do I. And so do half a dozen other women I should think."

He said: "You wouldn't have any idea where he is?"

She said: "Yes, I've got an idea. Perhaps I can tell you where he is. But if you find him you might give him a message from me. Just tell him when you see him—my name's Mrs. Hynes—Carlotta Hynes—you tell him if I ever get within arm's reach of him I'll screw his neck for him—the dirty little Yankee tyke!"

Berg said even more politely, hoping by the softness of his voice to stem the tide of rising anger that Mrs. Hynes was experiencing: "I sure will tell him that if I see him, with pleasure. I reckon I know what you mean. He's a bad type—that Shakkey." Inside he was laughing, thinking to himself that Shakkey was still running true to form.

She said: "Look, maybe you know about twenty miles from Sharpham right on the Dart is a swell sort of hotel place called the Chateau de la Tours—one of those French names. Well, whenever that so-an'-so can get leave he goes over there. He's hanging around looking for something—that's what I've been told, and if you know anything about Shakkey there's only one thing he hangs around and looks for and that's a woman. There's some woman over there. I'd like to get my fingers on her too," added Mrs. Hynes darkly.

Berg said: "Thanks a lot, ma'am. Maybe, I'll get over there sometime. If I do and I see him I'll tell him what you said."

He went out of the Raleigh. Now it was almost dark. It had begun to rain. A few large drops pattered uncertainly on to the pavement. Berg walked quickly along the quay, back to the little square where he had parked his car. He got in, drove round the quay along the road that leads past the naval college. He stopped to ask a policeman the way; then he went on. He was wondering who the woman was that Shakkey was so keen on. Berg thought she must be pretty good. Mrs. Hynes looked all right, and if Shakkey had ditched her it was because he must have found something better. He had probably taken her for some dough too. He always did.

With Dartmouth behind and the deserted winding road in front of him, he put his foot down. The car sped towards Totnes.

It was a quarter to eleven when Berg stopped the car, parked it on a grass verge under the shadow of the hedge, walked to the white wooden gate that led on to the wide lawn behind the Chateau de la Tours. The rain had stopped now. The moon had come from behind the clouds, and it seemed to Berg that the old-fashioned country house, now converted into a luxurious hotel and country club, took on a peculiar air of mystery. The rambling "L" shaped house was painted white. It showed up in its green surroundings like a ghost.

Now Berg experienced a peculiar feeling of anti-climax. He was here, but he could not visualise Shakkey in these surroundings. He could not visualise Shakkey even with the encouragement of his naval uniform calling at the Chateau de la Tours asking for the lady in whom he was so interested. Berg grinned.

He thought it would be much more likely to be the lady's maid. Shakkey had always had a weakness for ladies' maids. He remembered the girl in the old days—the girl who had looked after Mrs. Scansci.

Berg began to walk across the lawn. Even in these days of short labour it was well-kept, smooth and velvety. The rain had made it heavy. His feet brushing over the clipped grass had the sensation of walking on a thick carpet. Berg walked quickly and quietly. He did not know why he considered he should be silent. He moved easily from the hips. There was something catlike in his walk. Now he was fifty yards from the back entrance of the Chateau. He could see a glass-roofed conservatory on one side of the house. The blinds were drawn and inside someone was moving. He was on a gravel path, with the shrubbery at his right. At the end of the path fifteen yards from the back entrance to the house was a magnolia tree—a huge fully-grown tree whose leaves still dripped with the recent rain.

Berg moved under the tree in the shadows that surrounded it. He leaned against the tree, took out his flat enamelled cigarette case, selected a cigarette. He thought some plan of campaign was necessary. Some method of finding Shakkey, of making certain of finding Shakkey, must be discovered. He put the cigarette in his mouth, took out his lighter, snapped it on. He lit the cigarette.

A voice said: "Jeez . . . for Chrissake . . . Rene . . .!"

Berg turned. Leaning against the other side of the tree was Shakkey.

They stood looking at each other, their eyes searching each other's faces in the dim light.

Berg said: "Life's a damn' funny thing . . . hey, Shakkey? I bet you didn't think you were gonna see me. How d'you feel about it?"

Berg heard Shakkey chuckle—the weird metallic half laugh which he had heard so often. He imagined the thin lips twisted in the dark, the long narrow face with the screwed-up humorous eyes made alive for a moment.

Shakkey said: "What the hell! Look, Rene, you wouldn't think that anything was gonna surprise me, would you—especially anything about you? I can't see you good but you ain't altered any. No, sir! Still the same tough bastard, hey? Look, what is this? What are you doin' around here?"

Berg said: "I've been looking for you, Shakkey. Yesterday, I was in London. I went to the American Club. I found the guns you left for me." He went on: "It was pretty clever of you to wrap those guns up in those polishing cloths you pinched from the Double Clover Leaf Club. So I went round there afterwards. You can guess who I found there?"

Shakkey said: "I don't know what the hell you're talkin' about."

Berg seemed not to hear him. He went on: "I met Travis and Lauren. They haven't changed much either. I got your address from Travis. He told me you were aboard the *Dayton* at Dartmouth. I went over there."

Shakkey said: "I was due back on that goddam ship three days ago. I reckon they're gonna give me a right royal welcome when I do get back. I got an idea the captain of that ship's got it in for me."

Berg said: "He's not the only one. I met some dame in the Raleigh Hotel—a Mrs. Hynes. She wants to meet up with you too."

Shakkey said: "Ah . . . the hell with that dame! Look, she's had it. Well, maybe she don't like it." His tone became more nasal. "Aw . . . hell . . . that's what they all say."

Berg said: "She said she reckoned you was over in this part of the world—at this place. She got the idea you was chasing after some baby. I think she was a little jealous or something."

Shakkey said: "Yeah. That's the funny thing."

Berg asked: "What's funny? What's so funny about it?"

Shakkey said: "The funny thing is you turnin' up right now. But, just a minute . . . what's this stuff about the guns I left for you at the American Club? I never left no guns there. And what's this stuff about polishing cloths from the Double Clover Leaf Club? I don't know what the hell you're talkin' about. I ain't been to that place. I don't reckon I've seen Travis or Lauren in years. What is all this? Are you stringing me along, Rene?"

Berg said: "Look, Shakkey . . ." His voice was still casual. "What are you givin' me? Are you tellin' me you never left those guns? Are you tellin' me you weren't givin' me a tip-off to the Double Clover Leaf Club? Are you giving it to me on the up-an'-up that you haven't seen Travis or Lauren in years?"

Shakkey's voice was almost bored: "Jeez . . . what do I haveta tell you lies for?"

Berg said: "Yeah?" So someone else had left the guns. He stood looking across the lawn silvered by the moonlight, at the dark shadows caused by the trees on the other side.

He said: "Well, is that goddam funny, or is it? I sort of thought it was the hand of fate, Shakkey, but maybe it wasn't."

Shakkey said: "Yeah . . . and maybe it was."

Berg drew on his cigarette. He said: "What do you mean by that one?"

Shakkey grinned. He said: "Look, this is funny. About this babe that Carlotta said I was stringin' along after. Look, Rene, I ain't goin' after any broad over here. I'm just goddam curious, see? Two three week ago I got some leave an' came over to this district—just kickin' around, see? I was walkin' across the lawn one evening with some jane I'd picked up in the village. I saw some baby at a window in the hotel here and I couldn't believe my eyesight. I thought it just couldn't be true so I made some enquiry an' it *was* true.

"O.K. When I got my last leave I was in a little bit of a jam. I'm all tuckered up with a bunch of dames—Mrs. Hynes is only one of 'em—some of the others ain't even as nice as she is. They're not so pleased with me."

Berg said dryly: "No, they wouldn't be. Go on, Shakkey."

Shakkey said: "So I got a big idea. I thought I'd come over here and see this baby and maybe work the black a little. I thought maybe she might like to slip me some dough—just for old time's sake."

Berg's heart began to beat very quickly. Almost the fingers holding the stub of his cigarette were trembling.

He said: "Look, Shakkey, you give it to me straight. Who was the dame you were going to touch for the dough—the dame staying in this hotel?"

Shakkey said softly: "Who the hell d'you think . . . Clovis . . .! She's there. She's there now."

Berg drew in his breath. It made a little hissing noise. Almost automatically he slipped his hand inside his jacket towards the left armpit. Shakkey saw the movement.

He said: "For Chrissake . . . what's the idea? What is it, Rene?" There was alarm in his voice.

Berg said: "Listen, Shakkey, I wanta have a little talk with Clovis myself. I've been wantin' to have a little talk with her for a long time."

Shakkey said: "Yeah? Look, you wouldn't do anything funny to that dame, would you, Rene?"

Berg said: "No." His voice was smooth and quiet. "I wouldn't do anything funny to her. You trust me not to do anything like that, Shakkey." He took his hand from out of his coat, put it into his trouser pocket, produced a roll of notes. He peeled off a score of the notes. He said: "Look, you get out of here, Shakkey. There's a stake."

Shakkey's ringers closed over the notes. He could feel three or four five-pound notes amongst them. His eyes gleamed in the darkness.

He said: "O.K., Rene. You're the boss. You know what you're doin'. Listen, you wouldn't have anythin' on her, would you? I thought . . ."

Berg said harshly: "Who in hell asked you to think? Why don't you keep your trap shut and get to hell out of here? Button it up, Shakkey. Scram . . ."

"O.K., O.K.," said Shakkey. "I'm on my way. I'll be seein' you, Rene. Where you stayin'?"

"I'm staying in Dartmouth right now," said Berg. "Maybe I'll be there to-morrow. Maybe I won't. If I am, the Raleigh'll find me. I'll be there in the bar to-morrow night at nine o'clock."

Shakkey said: "Aw, make it some place else. Ain't that Carlotta hangin' around. If I go there I reckon shell tear me wide open."

"All right," said Berg. "Make it the Castle. I'll go there."

"O.K.," said Shakkey. "If I can get ashore I'll see you there to-morrow night at nine o'clock." He put his hand for a moment on Berg's arm. He said: "Don't do anything you sort of wouldn't like to think about sometime else, would you?"

Berg said wearily: "Why the hell don't you get out of here?"

He leaned against the tree. He heard Shakkey's footsteps retreating across the wet lawn.

It seemed to Berg that a long time had passed. Leaning. against the trunk of the magnolia tree, the heavy leaves of the outer branches falling around him like an umbrella, Berg allowed his mind to wander back over the years. A series of pictures presented themselves to him. Very few were soft, happy pictures, but even these were unable to alter the peculiar hardness which lay heavy upon him.

Life, thought Berg, was one of those things—and only one of those things. What happened to you depended on the beginning of things; depended on the time when you first started to think, when you first began to feel things.

All the things that had happened to him since he had been in England—the odd strange things which had led him, by accident it seemed, to Shakkey—were not things which he had created. They were the acts of a peculiar fate which was at this time dominating his whole personality.

Had he been able to analyse his own emotions he would have known that all the things he thought were untrue; that in fact he was carrying out an ordained series of acts—things which had been in his mind for a long time—thoughts which were greater than his own personality.

But at this moment he felt himself dominated to such an extent by some superior power that he was content to lean against the bole of the tree—to allow the ultimate act to arrive at such time as this fate was to decide.

Some more minutes went by. Drawing on the fresh cigarette he had lit, Berg considered many of the similar scenes in his Chicago life—especially one—a scene which had impinged itself on his memory—a scene which like many real pictures in all men's lives stayed with them always for a reason which was never known.

A shadow came across the light curtain of the conservatory on the right of the back entrance to the hotel. It moved towards the door. The door opened. The shadow stepped out on to the gravel path, walked with decided clean-cut steps towards the turning of the path where Berg stood. He closed his eyes, leaning against the tree, his hands flat against the damp trunk. Then he opened his eyes to look again.

It was Clovis.

She came towards him down the path—a trim, neat, figure, lovely feet and ankles—with the same graceful, almost mechanical movement. She was wearing a uniform of some dull colour which accentuated perfectly the lines of her still lovely body. Berg remembered. He thought that when he had first seen her she must have been twenty-one or twenty-two years of age. Now she must be thirty-five or thirty-six. The moonlight fell full upon her, illuminated the glory of her tawny hair, showed him that the clean-cut contours of her face were still real, showed him the scarlet mouth, the lovely deep-set eyes.

She came past the tree.

Berg said: "Hallo, Clovis. Howya making out, kid?"

She spun round. In one quick decided movement she turned and faced him as he came out from the shadows of the tree. For one moment she was dismayed; then as he knew it would, the quick brain worked. Her face broke into that same lovely smile—the smile he knew so well.

She said: "Rene . . . my God . . . you . . .! How marvellous to see you again."

They stood on the gravel path a few feet apart, looking at each other.

He said: "So it's good to see me again, Clovis? You sort of like that. It gives you a kick. You like seeing me, hey?"

There was a pause. When she spoke there was a little break in her voice. She said: "Rene, of course. How can you talk like that, knowing what has been between you and me? Knowing what still is to be between you and me. How can you talk like that?"

He was silent. Berg was utterly astounded at this supreme insolence—an insolence which could only emanate from Clovis—a concealed insolence which was part of that amazing make-up.

He said: "So I reckon you sort of been waitin' for me to turn up. The one thing you wanted was to see me."

There was another pause; then she said softly: "Rene . . . what do *you* think? What do you think I am?" She shrugged her shoulders. "I know there've been misunderstandings and odd things between you and me, but you know we've been everything to each other."

Berg said: "Yeah." He looked away, across the rolling lawn behind the Chateau de la Tours towards the dark avenue of trees. Their shadows invited him. Underneath his left arm he felt the hard weight of the pistol.

He said: "Let's walk, Clovis. I want to talk to you."

They began to walk down the path. They came to the place where it finished and their feet trod on the wet lawn.

She said: "Rene, I knew you'd come one day. I knew that all I had to do was to wait. I knew you'd come back to me."

Berg grinned sourly in the darkness. He said: "So you knew that. D'you know where I've been?" He laughed. Not waiting for an answer he went on: "You wouldn't know where I've been, would you? You wouldn't know about what's happened to me? You wouldn't know the sorta things that have been done to me? You were waiting for me, were you? Like hell you were! Or if you were you were just waiting for me to catch up with you, babe, hey?"

She said: "Rene, I don't know what you mean. You were always strange—a strange weird creature, but one who had some lovely things about him." She pressed her arm against his. Her voice softened. "Do you remember, Rene," she said, "when I first asked you to help me? Do you remember all you did for me?"

He said: "Yeah, I remember. My middle name was always sucker, wasn't it? Maybe I'm still going to be a sucker."

She caught her breath. She had taken it, he thought, the way he wanted her to take it.

She said: "Of course, Rene, you'd always be loyal while there was blood in your heart."

He said: "Yeah? Loyal to what?"

They walked across the wet grass.

He said: "You know, I've learned what loyalty means, Clovis. I've been loyal all right. I've been loyal to something that matters."

They crossed another path, came into the shadow of the trees. Now their way had turned itself into a mere footpath, moss-grown, that passed between the thick trees and the shrubbery that surrounded the outer bounds of the Chateau de la Tours.

Berg said: "You listen to me, Clovis. This is the pay-off. Maybe you never heard of a guy called Kramen. You never heard of a guy called Kramen—a nice guy with a thin face, a half bald head and slitted sorta eyes?"

She said: "No, Rene, I never heard of him."

He said: "No? Well, may be that's the truth. But I reckon this Kramen was sorta pally with a guy you *did* know. A guy you knew in London the last time I met you there. A guy called Maston or somethin'—his real name was Schlengel. You wouldn't have known that guy, would you? Like hell you wouldn't. An' you wouldn't have known Schlengel was a pal of Kramen's. That they were both Germans an' workin' for the Nazis?"

Berg drew his breath. He made a hissing noise. He went on: "The night I met you goin' into Shakkey's place I reckon you was goin' in there to find out about me. He'd told you he'd seen me around in London, and you wanted to know. An' after I told you where you got off I reckon Shakkey told you what I'd told him. That I was workin' for Ransome an' the British Secret Service people, an' likin' it. I reckon he told you I was goin over to Norway to get some girl back. I was a mug to trust him an' he was a mug to trust you. But he told you an' you went off an' told Schlengel. They knew where I'd been in 1940 in Norway, an' they knew where I was gonna drop, an' they was waitin for me. An' you told 'em. Kramen told me so. I reckon he thought I'd never get outa that camp. He told me one mornin' while he was having a rest from kickin' me around."

There was a long pause. She said: "Rene, I don't know what you're talking about. I don't know what you mean. What's the matter with you? I don't understand."

Berg caught his breath quickly. He was thinking that she was a supreme artist—an amazing personality—a person really without fear, without scruple, without morals, without anything. For one fleeting second his heart was filled with admiration for her.

He said: "O.K. So you didn't know. You didn't know, you goddam liar!" His voice was quiet and sibilant. It seemed to echo against the heavy rain-laden leaves of the trees. He went on: "You took me for a ride years ago. Everywhere we been—you and I—you took me for a ride. Well, that was all right. I went with you and maybe I could bear it. So you had to do this last thing. You sold me out. You sold me out plenty and this is where the bill comes in."

She said: "Rene, I know you." Her voice was very soft. "You could be very hard and very tough. I know that your, life and upbringing have made you like that. But you'll never be hard and tough with me because you know that deep in my heart I've always been for you; that you've always been the only man for me."

Berg said: "Yeah? I'll take vanilla!"

They had come to a little clearing. The moon was full. He took her by the shoulders, pressed her against a tree. He put his lips to hers. She kissed him and with the kiss she gave everything that a woman gives in a kiss.

Berg stood away from her. He said: "Look, baby, when I was up in the Ozarks, I usta go to a Sunday School, see? I met you soon after I came down from there. Remember, you bitch? O.K. Well, at the Sunday School they taught me about some mug called Judas Iscariot. They taught me that before he sold Jesus out he kissed him. O.K. Well, I never thought very much of the lesson at the time, but I just had a first-class demonstration from you."

She said nothing. She leaned against the tree. Berg looked into her eyes and for the first time saw fear.

He said: "I'm thinkin' about the night when I knocked off Calsimo. You know why I knocked him off. When I came around to your apartment that night, you'd made up your mind I was goin' to knock him off. You gave me a coupla glasses of hooch, and . . . well, you know what . . . because you knew I was goin' out to finish Calsimo. You had it planned. I was just the sucker."

She in a little voice: "No, Rene . . . no . . . that isn't true. Let me explain . . . I can explain everything. . . ."

He said: "You goddam liar."

The wind stirred the leaves a little. The noise sounded like the waves of the sea coming in. Berg put his hand in the inside pocket of his jacket.

He said, not unkindly: "You remember, Clovis, I always wanted to be a hero. You mugs taught me how to be one an' I listened to you. Well, it hasn't been so good. Now I'm gonna do something I think is O.K. and right. They tell me they're tough over here. They'll hang me for it. They don't let killers get away with it in this country. That's O.K. by me. Like the flyers say I've had it. There isn't anything for me, but . . . by God . . . there isn't going to be anything for you either. You're getting what's coming to you . . . and here it is . . ."

He brought out the gun. She stood, looking at him, her eyes wide, her lips a little apart. Berg began to laugh. He said: "You know the old joke they used to tell in school—a corny joke? The goddam funny thing is it's true. This is gonna hurt me more than it hurts you."

Berg squeezed the trigger of the .45 automatic. The first shot took her through the heart, the second below it, the third above it. She gave a funny cough, slumped, an inert mass, at the bottom of the tree.

The moonlight lay full on her.

Berg put the pistol back into his pocket. He stood looking down at her. Then he said quietly to himself: "Well, that's the way it goes, fella. That's the way it goes."

He walked out of the shadows of the trees along the edge of the lawn back towards the gate where he had parked the car.

CHAPTER TWO
CLOVIS
June, 1932

I

TRAVIS Hahn surveyed the midnight scene in Carlazzi's with a feeling of well-being, tinged with a vague regret that everything was not exactly as it might be. He leaned against the satin-backed corner seat behind his favourite table, set with the snowy napery, gleaming glass and silver; regarded the other inmates of the smart night club with a half smile which might have meant anything.

Not that Chicago wasn't good, thought Travis. Chi was all right. The Windy City was living up to its reputation. It was wide open for a smart guy. Prohibition had opened up a dozen professions, trades, rackets for any one with the brains to work them. And he was in the best of them and still going up. Unless . . .

On the other side of the room, drinking champagne, were Rudy and Willie Trazzi—two well-dressed, black-haired, young men, both of whom were carrying guns for Calsimo, and who returned Travis's smile with an equal acidity. Travis thought to himself that one of these days there was going to be a showdown between Scansci and Calsimo. There had to be a showdown. The

North Side liquor traffic's rich fruits of prohibition had been in Scansci's pocket for the last eighteen months, but Travis was more than a little perturbed at some of the rumours which were being picked up by his people in different parts of the city.

Chicago was wide open, he thought—too wide open. The hooch organisation had progressed to such an extent that before long the liquor barons would be declaring open war on each other. He thought that might not be so good.

Travis was good-looking, perfectly dressed—too well-dressed. He was thirty-four years of age, handsome in a rather showy fashion, and clever—*very* clever. As Scansci's right-hand man he had to be. Scansci considered that Travis had all the virtues necessary for a lieutenant. He could talk to people. He was a good organiser. He played in beautifully with the police. He knew when to graft, when to threaten, and when to arrange for the other thing when grafts and threats were of no avail.

But Travis's greatest virtue was that of keeping his nose clean. No matter who else got into trouble, he kept out of it. He was a big shot—a brain guy.

Lauren came through the heavy velvet portieres into the restaurant. Everybody turned to look at her. She was worth looking at. Just over thirty, her beauty was of that rare type which comes to perfect fruition at that age. She was tall, beautifully figured, giving promise of that supreme ripeness which was to come in a year or two.

She was exquisitely dressed. And if Lauren overdid it she had the figure and the poise to carry it off. She wore a close-fitting parma violet coat and skirt, with a chiffon blouse in a paler shade beneath. A matching tricorn hat with a curled ostrich feather, set off her brunette hair; her lovely feet and legs were encased in bronze leather court shoes with exaggerated heels and gossamer bronze silk stockings. The oversize diamond clip that Travis had given her after his last big "take" glittered at her breast. Lauren was definitely a picture to see and remember.

She made her way through the closely set tables on the edge of the dance floor, across the space that separated the inner ring of tables from those on the outer ring—that select circle where the big shots sat; where they talked confidentially about things which necessitated a space between them and more ordinary people.

When Lauren came near to the table Travis got up. He was always a showman and specialised in what he considered to be good manners even towards his own girl—a rare process in a big-time liquor man. He looked at her. He thought: You are sweet and lovely, you bitch. I wonder where you've been this afternoon. I bet if I checked up, you have ten alibis. They would say you were at the hairdressers; they would say you were fitting new frocks; they would say all sorts of things, but I'd like to know where the hell you really were.

He said: "Hallo, Lauren. It's good to see you. How's every little thing and what about a snifter with your best boy friend?"

Lauren said: "Meaning you?" She arched one eyebrow whimsically.

"Meaning me," said Travis. They both laughed. He went on: "You know, I don't know if anybody has ever told you that you are an eyeful, but that's what you certainly are. Babe, you've got something. You're terrific. Every time I see you you knock me for a row of pins."

Lauren said: "Aw . . . honey . . . not after three years! Don't tell me you still feel like that!"

She sat down opposite him, preened herself.

"I certainly do," said Travis. "It gets worse all the time." He was thinking to himself: I wonder who you're two-timin' me with now. I wonder who it is. He asked casually: "Had a good day, honey? Where you been?"

Lauren yawned. There was a little pause. Travis thought: She's making up a story. It'll be a good one. It always is. He looked at her sideways. The scream is, he thought acidly, she doesn't give a damn whether I believe it or not—not one goddam! She's got guts all right. The hell with her! He admired guts, because, in his own heart, he had a vague feeling that he had not a great deal of that commodity. Once or twice when his business had got him into one or two tight spots, he had always got out good and quick. Travis had medals for getting out from under when things got bad. He liked somebody else to carry the baby. Well, that was the way it should be. Gangsters who worked in the organisation, the gunmen who looked after the liquor deliveries, blackmailed, threatened, bulldozed, held up and high-jacked liquor supplies—the rank and file of the Scansci organisation—they had to have courage of a sort even if it was the lowest form of animal courage. That was necessary. But for people like Travis who considered himself to be on a higher plane, rough houses were things to be avoided.

The waiter came over. Travis said: "I didn't wait, honey; I've eaten."

Lauren said in her soft rich voice: "Yeah . . . what did you have, Travis?"

He said: "I had hors d'oeuvres, some duck, apple pie with American cream cheese, and coffee. I didn't have a drink. I waited for you."

Lauren said to the waiter: "I'll take the same. And bring a bottle of hooch."

Travis said with a smirk: "Yeah . . . and one of those White Rock bottles. And see it's good too."

The waiter winked. He said: "It'd have to be good for you, Mr. Hahn, wouldn't it? But it's O.K. It's your own stuff—the special delivery. We keep it for you and one or two others."

"O.K.," said Travis. "Get goin', fella."

The waiter went away.

Lauren said: "I tried on a new coat and skirt, I had my hair done and I did a little window shopping. I went back to the flat, but you weren't there; you'd gone." She threw him an arch laughing smile. She said: "You been good an' busy to-day, haven't you? You're not two-timin' me with some blonde, are you, Travis?"

A surge of black rage swept through him. He thought: You clever trull! You're pretty good. You knew what was in my mind and this is how you play it.

He said: "I've been stickin' around. I'm a little worried." But he was still smiling. Even if you were worried you didn't show it—not in Carlazzi's. There were too many people watching you.

The place had begun to fill up. Well-dressed men and women came in from the bars downstairs where every sort of liquor was served in spite of the law; sat down, ordered their meal. In the corner, on its gold raised platform, a hot band began to play soft swing tunes.

Lauren said, still smiling: "What's worrying you, honey?"

He took his cigarette case from his pocket—a flat enamelled case with his initial in gold on the corner—selected a cigarette, lit it.

He said: "There's gonna be some trouble in a minute, kid."

"Yeah?" said Lauren. "Where's it comin' from? I thought you'd got everything sewn up. I thought it was all sort of straightened out." She smiled. "You don't mean to tell me somebody's gonna muscle in, do you?"

Travis said: "You listen to me, kid. Nothing stands still. It either goes backwards or forwards. In order to stop yourself goin' backwards you gotta go forwards, see?"

She said: "Nope, I don't. Meaning what?"

Travis said: "Meaning this: You see those two mugs over there—Rudy and Willie Trazzi?"

She looked casually round the room. Her eyes rested for a fleeting second on the black-haired brothers.

She said: "Yeah, I see 'em."

He said: "They're two new guys startin' in for Calsimo. They're from New York. They tell me they're goddam tough. That's one thing. The other thing is I heard some news this afternoon that wasn't quite so good. I think there's gonna be a little trouble on the North Side. I'm goddam certain of it. This guy Calsimo is gettin' too big for his boots. I reckon he thinks he can step in there and take our business, or some of it."

She said casually: "That's not so extraordinary. You've had that sort of thing before, hey, Travis? Scansci's good enough for that. Have you talked to him about it?"

He shook his head. "What d'you think I take my cut for?" he asked. "It's *my* business to look after that."

"O.K.," said Lauren. "It's your business. Well, look after it." She dropped her voice. "Why don't you go for the fountain-head? You've bumped guys as big as Calsimo, haven't you—or had 'em bumped—I beg your pardon," she said with a sarcastic twist of the mouth.

Travis did not like that. The planner of a dozen killings, he had never taken a hand in one of them. He had never carried a gun. Some other mug did that.

He said: "Look, why don't you use your head? Calsimo's been throwing plenty jack around this town. He's been gettin' himself in good with the right boys. Some of the ward heelers are beginning to think they're getting pro-Calsimo. I don't like it. I don't like it one little bit."

She said: "Aw . . . what the hell! What's eating you, Travis? Why don't you get somebody to take him for a ride? And that's the end of the trouble."

Travis said: "I wish I could think that. It'd be the beginning of the big trouble. If somebody bumps Calsimo it's gonna be somebody in our set-up. It must be. We're the only people who could possibly be interested in his tryin' to set up an organisation to supply the North Side with hooch. Another thing is the cops have got to do something around here pretty soon. The last eighteen months we've been getting away with everything we wanted to. You seen the newspapers lately? They're not so pleased, are they? I reckon this thing's got to be played good an' smart or else. . . ."

She said: "Well, if it's clever stuff, Travis, that's up your street, hey? Maybe you can arrange it to look like an accident."

He said: "Aw . . . to hell with that. D'you think Calsimo is gonna get himself in a spot where it's gonna look like an accident? He's got these guys from New York. They're tough and clever." He sighed. "I gotta think something out."

She smiled. "You will, honey . . . you will," said Lauren.

The waiter served her dinner, poured out the whisky from the White Rock bottle. They drank, looking at each other over the rims of the glasses.

After a pause she said: "You got something sproutin' at the back of your mind, big boy. I can see it. You got some idea sproutin'. I know you."

He said: "I ain't got any idea. But I'm plenty worried."

She said: "Sure . . . you told me you're worried about this guy, Calsimo. In a minute maybe you'll tell me you wanta resign and walk out. What do I have to do—make a pass at Calsimo to put the job straight—or what?"

He said sourly: "I wouldn't put that above you sometimes." He laughed suddenly. "I was ribbin' you, babe," he said. "But I'm worried, and I'm not only worried about Calsimo."

She said: "Yeah? What else is on your mind?"

He said: "I'm worried about the Big Boy—Scansci."

She sat back, looked at him in amazement. She said: "What the hell . . . worried about Scansci . . .! Scansci's right on top of it, sitting right on top of the heap. Goddam it, he owns this burg. What are you worried about him for?"

He said: "You know, I'm sorta steamed up a little about this Clovis."

Lauren said: "You mean the new Mrs. Scansci?"

Travis said: "Yeah, the new Mrs. Scansci. I wonder what the hell she's playin' at."

Lauren asked: "What should she be playin' at? She's sittin' pretty. What's she done?"

Travis said: "I wouldn't know. I can't get around to it, babe. But there's something going on—something screwy—and I don't like it."

She poured him another drink. She said: "Look, you know what's the matter with you? First of all you need a coupla drinks. You got this Calsimo guy on your mind. The best thing you can do is to get rid of him. You gotta make it look like somebody else pulled it, that's all. If you think the coppers are gettin' leery around here; if you think they're gonna pin it on our organisation, well, you gotta make it look like somebody else."

He said: "Yeah? And that's gonna be too easy, ain't it? Too goddam easy. What you're tellin' me is I've gotta go to somebody I don't know. I gotta put them wise to the whole set up in order to get rid of Calsimo. In order to get rid of that big baboon, I gotta give my hand away an' put myself in bad. What do you take me for?"

She said: "I wouldn't know. Sometimes I don't take you for anything." She laughed. "Don't worry, Handsome," she said. "You'll find a way out. You always do."

Shakkey pushed his way through the curtains. Travis raised his eyebrows inquiringly. Shakkey, who ran the underground garage where the Scansci speed cars were parked, where all sorts of things happened and no questions were asked; Shakkey, who was in charge of the depot from which the liquor trucks operated; who organised and paid the Italian alcohol cookers. There had to be a good reason before Shakkey put his nose inside Carlazzi's.

He stood just inside the heavy velvet portieres, overdressed, with pointed shoes, a tight-waisted suit of too well-cut English tweeds, a dark blue silk shirt and collar, and a near yellow tie.

Shakkey was thin and angular. His blond hair was swept straight back from his forehead. His cheekbones stuck out. His eyes were humorous and laughed all the time. Shakkey would laugh at you while he was cutting your throat. He looked round the room. Travis saw his eyes rest just for a moment on the two Trazzi boys who were now paying their bill; then he came over to the table.

He said: "Good-evening, Travis. How's it goin', Mrs. Hahn?" He stood on the other side of the table looking down at them.

Travis said: "Take your weight off your feet, Shakkey. What's eatin' you? Anything wrong?"

Shakkey looked at Lauren. Travis said: "Go on, you can talk. I got no secrets from Mrs. Hahn."

She said: "Listen, Travis, if you'd like me to scram I'll get out and come back; if you want to talk to Shakkey; if you think there's something I shouldn't hear."

Travis said: "What does it matter? Get yourself a chair, Shakkey. Have a drink."

Shakkey reached out for a gilt chair from a nearby table. He sat down with his back to the restaurant. Lauren poured him out a glass of whisky. He drank it in one gulp.

He said: "You know, I've never been in here before except maybe once or twice. A hell of a dump! It's terrific. If I was to eat around here I reckon I'd be so set on lookin' at the decorations I'd forget what I was eatin'." His voice was high-pitched, nasal.

Travis said: "Yeah . . . yeah . . . yeah. . . . Cut out the comedy stuff. What's the trouble?"

Shakkey said: "It looks to me like real trouble. You know that consignment that was going down to O'Hagan at Bolt Alley—the big one?"

Travis said: "Yeah—six trucks, wasn't it?"

Shakkey nodded. "Six trucks," he said. "O.K. Well, somebody high-jacks the whole goddam lot. You got that? We found the trucks up-ended on Rose Court at the bottom of the Alley."

Travis said: "What about the drivers and guards?"

Shakkey spread his hands. He said: "They killed Mills and Florian. We don't know where the other four drivers are. One guard's wounded; we got him in the garage now; the doc's tryin' to get the bullet out of him. Where the others are, search me . . . unless . . ."

Travis said: "Unless what?"

There was a pause. Shakkey said: "Maybe I'm dreamin' but there aren't any of our boys would take a run-out powder, are there?" He spread his hands again. "I wouldn't even think a thing like that," he said, "except I been hearing one or two things lately."

Travis said shortly: "Calsimo?"

"Yeah, that's it," said Shakkey. "There's been talk about the boy musclin' in. There's been talk that he's gonna have our business. He's got some sweet boys in from New York, they tell me. Two of 'em are just goin' out now—those two Trazzi bastards. You know, boss, we gotta do something about this."

Travis looked at Lauren. He said: "What did I tell you?"

She said: "So it's that bad?"

Travis said: "Look, Shakkey, I reckon I'll have to have a word with Mr. Scansci. I reckon we gotta move. We gotta do something about this."

Shakkey said: "You're tellin' me. Look, there's only one thing to do, Travis. Somebody's got to fog this bastard Calsimo good an' quick. If you can rub that wart out before the rot starts we'll be all right; otherwise some of us are gonna have a bellyful of lead slugs." His voice became reminiscent. "An', you know, we've been sittin' pretty a long time," he said, "right on top of the heap. You know how it is, Travis. You gotta scheme and fight like hell to get there an' when you get there you gotta go on schemin' an' fightin' to stop there. Maybe," he went on a little diffidently, "some of us have been takin' things a bit too easy."

Travis said nothing. He got the implication. He said: "You look after your job, Shakkey, and leave me to look after mine. O.K. I'm gonna do something about this."

Shakkey said: "That's all I wanta hear. Me—I'm just the guy who brings back the empties with one or two other things, but I go for action in a very big way and right now. Otherwise . . ." He spread his hands.

Travis said: "Aw . . . can it . . ."

Shakkey drank some whisky. He emptied his glass, poured out a fresh one. He said: "Well, Mrs. Hahn, here's to you. I reckon you're beautiful. One of these fine days some guy is gonna get around to tellin' Travis how lucky he is. If I had a dame like you I reckon I'd set up to be the President of the United States. As it is I just go on hopin'."

He drank half the whisky. He put the glass down. He said: "Look, here's a big laugh. Something to relieve the monotony of this conversation we been havin'. You know what happens to-day? I'll tell you. I just got the last trucks away and everything is okey-doke an' all set for the evening. The two boys who are watchmen for the night come on an' I got an idea I'll go out the garage the back way. So I go out by Barrell Street. I'm just closing the small door an' gettin' ready to lock it when I see something. I see a guy. This guy is a scream. He's wearin' a suit of overalls like you've never seen before in your life. He's thin; he's gotta lot of black hair an' eyes that look like a coupla safety lamps. While I'm lookin' at him he falls over."

Lauren said: "He was drunk?"

Shakkey said: "Nope, the mug wasn't drunk. He was starvin'. Would you believe it, he ain't eaten in three days. He's been livin' on water."

Laureen said: "Yeah?" Her tone was almost disinterested. "So what?"

Shakkey said: "So nothing. I lean over this guy an' I flip him under the nostrils until he opens his eyes. Then I say: 'How's it goin, kid?' Well, most guys like that would start a long spiel. You

know, a hard luck story. Well, this mug don't. He says: 'Say, Mister
. . . you couldn't tell me where I could get a job around here?'"

Shakkey grinned. "I think this is funny," he went on. "Here's
a kid so goddam weak he can't stand up an' he wants a job. He
ain't even singin' 'Brother, can you spare a dime?'"

Travis said: "Where is this guy from?"

"That's the other scream," said Shakkey. "Will you believe it,
the guy's hitch-hiked it all the way down from the Ozarks. Yeah .
. . one of them goddam hill-billies. Somebody told him the streets
of Chicago was paved with gold an' I reckon he wanted a coupla
pavin' stones."

Lauren said: "Is this the end of the story? I'm waitin' for the
big laugh."

Shakkey said: "There's nothing else to it. I took him inside the
garage. I gave him a snifter—one out of the apple jack bottle. It
knocked him sideways. Then I was thinkin'. You know, Travis,
all the night guys we got on at that garage are pretty cute sorta
bastards. They been with us a long time. We're payin' them two
hundred and fifty-three hundred a week. But what do we know
about 'em?"

Travis said: "Yeah, I got it. What do we know? They been
with us a long time. They've been paid plenty and they're on the
up-an'-up. Well, it pays 'em to be. What's the idea?"

Shakkey said: "Listen, the idea is somebody told the guys who
high-jacked our delivery to-night when the trucks was leavin'.
You know I never let the drivers or guards know what time the
delivery trucks are goin' out—not till ten minutes before. But they
got 'em in the right place—just at the end of Barrell Street where
there's a double turnin' an' it's easy to make a getaway."

Travis said: "So you think somebody's shootin' their mouth
off? You think some of Calsimo's people have got inta one or two
of our boys?"

Shakkey said: "I wouldn't know. I'm guessin', but what I
thought was this: This mug who turns up to-night from the Ozarks
with the black hair. Look . . . he's sort of virgin. You see, goddam
it, the guy's never been in the city in his life before. I reckon he's
one of these guys if I was to give him two three square meals, put

him on the pay-roll, he'd sorta want to die for me. He's sorta like that. You got it?"

Travis said: "I got it. You might be right at that."

Lauren said: "Sure, he might be right. The trouble with an organisation like ours, Travis, is all the guys in it are a goddam sight too smart. They're always playin' it off the cuff. Some of 'em like it both ways. You give 'em three C's a week they want five. You give 'em five C's they want a grand. Don't I knew 'em." She laughed. "They're almost as bad as dames."

Travis said: "Look, where is this guy? What's his name?"

Shakkey said: "I got him down at the garage. His name's Rene Berg—a damn' funny monicker for a guy twenty years old from the Ozarks. He's been brought up there by foster parents. He don't know who his people are—never seen 'em. You only gotta take one look at this mug to know he's on the up-an'-up."

Travis said: "And the idea is what?"

Shakkey said: "Give the guy some food, put him on the pay-roll, stick him down there at the garage on the night-shift. He goes in the office. He don't meet anybody. We have a glass front put in two sides of the office. From there he can see every truck, every man, in the garage. You got that? All right. He can see if guys are talkin' together. He can hear if the phone goes. All we do is not let him meet anybody who's workin' on the supply organisation or drivin' a truck. You got it?"

Travis said: "I got it." Vaguely at the back of his brain an idea was beginning to take shape. He said: "Look, I tell you what you do. I'd like to look at this mug myself. You get out of here, give him a meal, buy him some clothes. Give him a coupla drinks, a few bucks and put him up for the night somewhere. Get him a bed, see? You bring him round to see me to-morrow afternoon around three o'clock. I'd like to talk to this mug."

Shakkey said: "O.K. It's an idea. Well, I'll be seein' you, Travis. So long."

He finished his drink, went away.

Lauren said: "What's the big idea, honey? D'you mean to tell me you're gettin' interested in Shakkey taking on another guy down at the garage at a few bucks a week? What d'you wanta meet him for?"

Travis smiled at her. He said: "Oh, nothing. But maybe I got an idea."

She thought: I bet you have. You got an idea all right because you're gettin' scared good an' plenty. You're gettin' scared because of this Calsimo. You're lookin' for a way out. An' you'd double-cross your own mother to find it.

She said: "Of course you got an idea. Ain't you the brain guy? Ain't you the little fella who always makes out? Why, without you the Scansci organisation would be in the queer."

Travis said: "Yeah . . . now you're tryin' to flatter me. . . ."

She said: "What *me*! How could I do a thing like that, honey?" She squeezed his hand.

II

It was seven o'clock. O'Finnigan—Lieutenant of Detectives for the Precinct—walked two blocks past Mulberry Street, turned right. He walked slowly, pondered on the annoyances of life generally, and more particularly the annoyances of a lieutenant of detectives in a tough precinct in the Windy City. One of these fine days, thought O'Finnigan, he was going to throw his hand in and get out while the going was good. Maybe when he'd netted a few thousand more dollars. . . .

But it would have to be soon. A cop's life in Chicago was no life. With the liquor racket reaching a nadir; with gang warfare open and insolent, all a wise guy could do was to play it off the cuff and try and make both ends meet with a bit to spare.

O'Finnigan walked another block; turned down the stairs into Florian's speak-easy. The speak-easy was olde-worlde. The panelling of the walls and decorations were supposed to be Stuart. The atmosphere was restful and the drinks were all right—sometimes. You took a chance. Maybe the stuff was good and maybe Florian's boys had made the gin up in the bathroom. You just didn't know. Not unless you were a big shot. If you were a big shot then you were O.K. You got the right sort of stuff—liquor that hadn't even been cut. Stuff that didn't even make you sick in the morning.

There were few people there. The habitues of the afternoon were getting over their hangovers. The evening crowd had not yet arrived. O'Finnigan sat down at a table in the far corner of the room. He lit a cigarette.

The bar-tender came over from behind the bar, put the glass in front of him. He said softly: "You needn't worry about that stuff, lieutenant. It's pretty good. I drink it myself."

O'Finnigan nodded. He drank a little of the whisky, put the glass back on the table, sat looking straight in front of him. Five minutes passed. Travis Hahn came down the stairs, looked at the bar-tender, looked at O'Finnigan, winked, went over to the table and sat down.

He said: "Hallo, Pat."

O'Finnigan said shortly: "Hallo to you."

The bar-tender brought a glass of whisky, a bottle of White Rock, a new bottle of whisky with the cork drawn. He put them down on the table. He went out of the bar. The room was empty now except for Travis and O'Finnigan.

There was a silence. Then O'Finnigan said: "Yeah?"

Travis said: "Look, Pat, I'm a little worried. You get me?"

O'Finnigan said: "Yeah, I can understand that. This guy Calsimo is sort of getting above himself, hey?"

Travis said: "Maybe. Something'll have to be done about that boy."

The lieutenant of detectives finished his whisky. He took the stopper out of the bottle, poured a fresh one, added White Rock.

He said: "Yeah ... but you know, Travis, I think you gotta sort of watch your step. This guy Calsimo is getting around a bit. He's gettin' to know one or two people who matter."

Travis said: "Sure, I know what you mean, Pat, but I thought we'd play this sort of easy ... you know?"

The lieutenant of detectives said: "So you're gonna play it easy. Meanin' just what?"

Travis said: "Look, we understand each other around this burg. You know, Chi's a pretty small village whichever way you look at it, but I reckon everybody is agreed we don't want any outsiders musclin' in around here."

O'Finnigan said: "Yeah, so who's musclin' in? What's going on?"

Travis said: "Calsimo's got a pair of guys—two gunsels—Rudy and Willie Trazzi. He's brought these guys in from New York." Travis shrugged his shoulders. "They tell me they're tough," he said. "I reckon something's got to be done about that, you know."

O'Finnigan said: "Yeah? Such as what?"

Travis poured himself another glass of whisky. He lit a cigarette. He said: "You know, Pat, I bought a block of stock the other day—nice stuff they tell me—Incorporated Steel. It's due for a jump. I reckon there's twenty dollars a share to be made on that stock within the next coupla weeks."

O'Finnigan said shortly: "You oughta know."

Travis went on: "I told you I bought myself a piece of this stock. Well, I bought a little piece for you too, Pat. You'll be hearing about it."

O'Finnigan said: "Thanks a lot. You always were a nice guy, Travis."

Travis said: "I'm always nice to a pal."

There was a silence. The lieutenant of detectives said eventually: "You was talkin' about these Trazzi boys."

Travis said: "Yeah. I don't think I like these guys kickin' around here and I think it's time somebody taught Calsimo a lesson—told him where he gets off, you know. I thought it might be a good idea if we did something about those two boys."

O'Finnigan said: "Well, you know what you're doing, but I think you oughta know there's been a lot of talk lately about your boss Scansci and Calsimo. The Federal Government's taking an interest in what's going on around here. It isn't so much what the State coppers think, but what the Feds think. Whatever you do oughta be played nice and easy."

Travis said: "Sure, I get that. What you mean is there mustn't be any tie-up with our organisation—no sort of tie-up between anything that might happen to those Trazzi boys and the Scansci mob, hey?"

O'Finnigan said: "Yeah, that's what I mean."

Travis said: "Look, I got an idea." He leaned over the table. He went on: "You know, Pat, I've always liked you. I've always talked freer to you than any guy I've ever known."

O'Finnigan said: "And why not? What the hell would you have done without me, hey?"

"I know . . . I know . . ." said Travis. "Well, look, maybe you got the idea in your head that Calsimo is goin' up. Is that right?"

O'Finnigan shrugged his shoulders. He said: "I wouldn't *know,* but that's what I think. He's got something, this guy, and you know they're sayin' around the town that Scansci's slippin' a little—not sort of paying the attention he usta pay to business. Maybe he's got other interests—maybe that new wife of his. How old is she—twenty?" he laughed. "He oughta know better."

Travis said: "Yeah, maybe you're right. Scansci was forty-eight three days ago. He's married this babe and he can't see or hear or think of anything else. It would be sort of funny if Calsimo made the grade, wouldn't it? It would be sort of funny if he got away with it."

O'Finnigan looked at him with hard cold eyes. He said: "Yeah . . . are you thinkin that or wishin' that?"

Travis smiled. He said: "I wouldn't know, Pat, but I reckon if something was to happen to those Trazzi boys, Calsimo's gonna get steamed up. He's gonna do something about it, hey?"

O'Finnigan said: "Yeah, I should think that might happen. You mean he might try an' take Scansci?"

Travis spread his hands. "You never know what's gonna happen," he said.

There was another silence; then the lieutenant of detectives said: "So what?"

Travis poured another drink for each of them. He said: "Look, we took a new guy over the other day. Nobody knows him around here. He's a hick from the Ozarks—a punk. He's got hayseeds in his hair. His name's Berg—Rene Berg. I got him fixed up in a small-town hotel in a room, with a hundred dollars a week and a new suit. He thinks he's gonna work in a garage—one of our supply dumps, see?"

O'Finnigan said: "I see."

Travis went on: "He's a simple sort of mug. He's had no experience of anything at all. He don't know a goddam thing about dames or liquor or the big city or anything—just another of those mugs who think you walk down to Chicago and make your fortune. Maybe you heard about them guys?"

O'Finnigan said: "Yeah. I heard about 'em plenty."

Travis said: "These two Trazzi boys are sort of pushers, see? They go for dames in a very big way. Well, I know a coupla sweet babies who might fall for 'em—or look as if they were falling! So maybe these two babies date up the Trazzi boys out at the Rose Dean Roadhouse. You got that?"

O'Finnigan said: "I heard something like this before about somebody else sometime. I got it. So the two Trazzi boys go out to the Rose Dean Roadhouse to meet up with these two broads; then what?"

Travis said: "Well, one of our cars goes out with a coupla smart boys aboard and this guy Berg's with 'em. So maybe he has a few drinks on the road. Maybe he don't know what he's doing. So the Trazzi boys get it. They get bumped off. You got that?"

O'Finnigan said: "I got that. Then what? If they get bumped off we gotta have somebody. I told you Calsimo was gettin' in with some big boys around there. They're working for him an' somebody fogs 'em, there's gonna be plenty trouble. We gotta *have* somebody."

"Sure . . . sure . . ." said Travis. "You'll get somebody all right. You get Berg, see?"

O'Finnigan said: "I don't see. You tell me."

Travis said: "When our car gets out to Rose Dean, this guy Berg is cut. He's high. So he don't know which way he's pointin'. O.K. So the Trazzi boys get bumped. When the cops come they find Berg in the car with the gun that killed the Trazzi guys in his pocket, so you have *him,* see?"

O'Finnigan said: "I see. Well, that's O.K. You know what you're doin'. So long as we get somebody. But I reckon we aren't having any more killings around here without having somebody taken in for it. The newshounds are getting sort of restive, you know. If we get this Berg mug, O.K. But it's the hot squat."

Travis said: "Sure . . . that's O.K. Is that all right with you?"

The lieutenant of detectives said: "That's O.K. by me."

They had another drink. Then O'Finnigan said: "Well, I'll be seein' you, Travis."

Travis said: "Sure . . . thanks a lot, Pat. You always were a good guy. You'll hear from the brokers to-morrow about that block of shares."

O'Finnigan said: "Thanks. So long, Travis. Remember me to Lauren."

He got up, walked across the carpeted floor of the speak-easy, went up the stairs. Travis watched him until he disappeared round the winding stairway.

At eight o'clock Travis went to Scansci's apartment—a penthouse on the fashionable North Side with everything that opened and shut.

He rang the bell. A Japanese butler opened the door, Travis went in. As he stepped into the hallway, Clovis Scansci came out of a room on the right. She looked at Travis. She gave him a long steady look from her large violet eyes.

She said softly: "Hallo, Travis. You wanta see Paul?"

Travis said: "Yeah, it's important. Howya goin', Clovis?"

She said: "Wonderful . . . I feel everything's wonderful. I think I'm a very lucky girl."

Travis said: "Yeah, if I looked like you look I'd think I was lucky." He thought she was the most perfect thing he'd ever seen in his life. Twenty-one years of age, with a supreme figure, tawny hair that framed a heart-shaped face, a superb mouth, little teeth like pearls . . . everything! He thought to himself. I got an idea back of my head you and I understand each other baby, but I got to find out.

He asked: "Is Paul around?"

Clovis said: "Yes, in his room. Go in; have a drink."

Travis said: "I will. I'll be seein' you, Clovis."

She turned suddenly. She was close to him now. She put out her hand, took his. It might have been a gesture of friendship or something else. You couldn't know.

She said: "Do, Travis. I'm lonely sometimes. Give me a ring. Come and talk to me. I like talking to you."

He smiled at her. He said: "Yeah, I will. So long, honey." He crossed the hall, went down the passage, opened the door at the far end.

Scansci was sitting at his desk. He was big, fat, ponderous. His face was round and smiling, his eyes small like pig's eyes. His silk collar was a little too tight for his neck and a fold of flesh showed above it. He was smoking a cigar. Travis noticed that his eyes were rimmed with tired red circles.

He said: "Well, Travis, how is it going? What's new? Everything okey-doke?"

Travis said shortly: "No, everything's not okey-doke, and we got to do something about it. You got that? Something's *gotta* be done."

Scansci said: "Say, what the hell is this, fella?" He ran his hand over his sleek black hair. His hand was plump. There were two diamond rings on the fat fingers.

Travis sat down. He lit a cigarette. Scansci got up, walked to a wall cupboard, produced a bottle of whisky, a bottle of White Rock and two glasses. He poured out two drinks. He said: "Hey . . . hey . . . Travis, what's this? What goes on around here? You look as if you re worried about something."

Travis said: "I'm worried all right, boss. Look . . . two three nights ago we had some trucks high-jacked. That Was Calsimo. You got that? O.K. The word's going round this burg that he's on the up-an'-up and you're on the down an' out. You know what that means?"

Scansci spread his hands. He said: "That means a leetle fight, that's all. We had thees sort of thing before, Travis. Well, we'll feex this. You look after it."

Travis said: "It's not so easy. Listen, Paul, this boy Calsimo has been sprinklin' some ground-bait around City Hall and one or two other places. You got that? He's gettin' himself in with the big boys. He's not try in' to duck trouble; he's lookin' for it, and the cops are gettin' restive. There's been too much gun-play around here. The newspapers are beefin' off, the public are screamin' their heads off. Somebody's gotta be pulled in for something in a minute."

Scansci said: "Yes . . . I sort of heard disa thing before. Well, what do I pay you for? What you going to do about eet?"

Travis said: "Look, boss, maybe the boys think that you're sort of gettin' a little remote these days." He spread his hands, shrugged his shoulders. "I know that's natural," he said. "You just got married so you want a sort of honeymoon, hey? But I got an idea in my head that it's not the sorta time when you have one."

Scansci said: "So what do I do?" He got up, lit a cigar. He looked at Travis through the cloud of tobacco smoke. He said: "You gotta something in your mind. Come on . . . shoot . . . What you theenk? What's in your mind?"

Travis said: "Look, Calsimo's got a coupla gun boys in from New York—Rudy an' Willie Trazzi. O.K. We take 'em just to show him he can't start something around here."

Scansci said: "That's alla right. What's the matter with that?"

Travis said: "But the cops want a pinch. They think they're gonna have an easy one. I've given 'em one."

Scansci said: "Yes? You tella me."

Travis went on: "Shakkey got hold of some mug from the Ozarks—name of Berg—half-starved and lookin' for a job. I've sort of looked after him an' he's grateful, see? He's never met any of the boys an' he's stuck in a small-time hotel. He came to see me yesterday an' he's a gift from Heaven. This is the mug who's gonna knock off the Trazzi boys. You got that?"

Scansci said: "No. Exactly what do you mean?"

Travis said: "Charlie an' Lefty go out with the car an' they take this mug with 'em—this Berg mug. He's got a job, see? He's eaten. He's full of himself. So he gets tight. They go out to Rose Dean. The Trazzi boys will be out there—I've fixed that. The boys get Berg drunk and the Trazzis get fogged. The police find the gun on Berg. They have him. Everybody's happy."

Scansci said: "Well, what's the matter with that?"

Travis said: "That's only the beginning. It's no good beatin' about the bush. We gotta get Calsimo. If he lives, you don't, an' that goes for a lot of us. This is only number one."

Scansci said: "Always you are a very clever one, Travis. You gotta something else in the back of your mind. You tella me what it is."

Travis said: "Look, I'll tell you. The Trazzi boys get bumped, so that's a sort of tip-off for Calsimo, see? Maybe he gets a little scared, maybe he don't. We don't care. O.K. The cops knock off Berg. They're happy. They throw him in the can, but we don't let him stay there." He leaned forward in his chair. "Look, boss," he said, "I've been studyin' this guy, Berg. He's the complete mug—a bonehead—a gift from Heaven. I reckon if that boy felt grateful to us for something in a big way he'd do *anything*. He's that sort of guy. Now this is the big idea."

Scansci said: "You tella me. I listen."

Travis told him.

III

Berg sat on the bed, his arms resting on his knees, his thin face poised on his cupped hands. He looked dully at the wall of the cell opposite him. He was trying to think but found the process both difficult and bitter. His head still ached from the liquor with which the two boys had supplied him so generously. The fact that the final drink had been a Mickey Finn was unknown to Berg. But even if he had known the knowledge would have helped him not at all.

He wondered how long it took to die in the electric chair. They called it the "hot squat." They described the process of being electrocuted as "frying"—not a particularly pleasing word.

He ceased to think about death; turned his mind to other things. So this was the end of the big adventure that Chicago promised to be—a cell and the electric chair. There was no doubt in Berg's mind that he was for the hot squat. They had told him that. There was a weal across one side of his face where one of his interrogators had indulged in a little persuasion with a piece of rubber tubing. For hours, possibly longer, Berg had sweated under the electric light; experienced the joys of third degree. And if he had kept silence it was because there was nothing for him to talk about.

He thought it was unlucky that on his first job he had listened to Charlie and Lefty—the two mechanics with whom he had gone out on his first trip. They'd stopped at several places on the road; had drinks. Berg, who was not keen on liquor, had tried to duck, but they talked him into it. The last drink taken on the road in the cab of the truck out of Lefty's own particular flask, had just about finished him off. After that he was all yours. He didn't know anything about it—nothing until the time when the police car had picked him up; until they had told him he'd shot two men and advised him to come clean and, when he hadn't, had used the usual means of persuasion that were fashionable at that time. He thought it wasn't so good. But his dissatisfaction was not tinged with any great amount of self-pity. Berg, even at the age of twenty-one, had already learned that self-pity got you nowhere. He'd learned that in the Ozarks, the necessary lessons having been inculcated by tough, drunken, vicious, foster-parents. He didn't think there was very much chance. He thought he'd get the hot squat all right. The cops had told him that was a certainty. Well, that was that. It might save a lot of trouble—a lot of inconvenience. But it wasn't the adventure that he had promised himself when he'd got away from the farm in the Ozarks, and hitch-hiked and walked towards the wonderful adventure that Chicago promised. Chicago! The city of dreams! He grinned ruefully.

Upstairs, the Precinct Office clock showed it was seven o'clock. The desk sergeant, drowsy over the blotter, waiting for his relief, looked up as the swing doors opened and Travis Hahn came in. The desk sergeant couldn't see who the person was behind Travis—not for a moment. Then he saw. It was Linney—Scansci's mouthpiece— the cutest lawyer in Chicago. The desk sergeant thought: I know what they're gonna do. They're gonna pull a fast one.

He said pleasantly: "Good-evening, Mr. Hahn."

Travis said: "Good-evening, sergeant. This is Mr. Linney—Mr. Scansci's lawyer. This is just a little matter of *habeas corpus*. You're holding a guy called Rene Berg downstairs. I reckon we wanta see him."

The sergeant said: "Look, Mr. Hahn, you know goddam well this guy held here's on a charge of murder—first degree murder.

He bumped two guys last night and he was caught practically red-handed."

Travis said: "Yeah? That's what *you* think. We don't." He moved to one side.

Linney said: "I don't think we have to argue this thing out here, do we, sergeant? I want to see your prisoner. I have indisputable evidence that he was at least fifteen miles away when this shooting occurred last night. The fact that he was found in a car at the scene of the murder; that he had in his possession the murder gun, means very little against such an alibi. Quite obviously he was taken out there and planted there. He was drunk when he was found. I merely wish to exercise my right to see my client."

The desk sergeant got up. He said: "O.K. . . . O.K. . . . You go and see your client." He bellowed a name; sat down hard on his chair. He looked at Travis and grinned. It was not a particularly nice grin.

Travis was still smiling pleasantly. Now he took out his thin enamelled case and lit a cigarette.

An officer came in.

The desk sergeant said: "Mr. Hahn and Mr. Linney to see the guy Berg." He grinned at the officer.

The officer said: "O.K. This way, please."

He went away. Travis and Linney followed him.

As their footsteps died away the desk sergeant picked up the telephone before him, rang a number. After a moment he said:

"That you, lieutenant? Mr. O'Finnigan . . .? Yeah, this is me. . . . Look, I got an idea that Hahn's pullin' a fast one on you. He's just been here with Linney—Scansci's mouthpiece. Linney's gonna defend Berg. It looks like they got a defence too. They got an alibi—so Linney says, and I reckon if he says so he means it. . . . Yeah. . . . O.K., you'll be around. So long, lieutenant." He hung up.

Downstairs in the cell, Travis sat on the bed opposite Berg. He said: "Well, kid, you got yourself in it pretty bad, hey? You know what this means?"

Berg said slowly: "Yeah . . . they told me . . . the hot squat! They're gonna fry me for this."

Travis said: "Well, that's too bad. I reckon they pushed you around a bit too, didn't they?"

Berg said: "Yeah, they pushed me around a little."

Travis asked: "And what did you tell 'em?"

Berg shrugged his shoulders. He smiled almost wearily. He said: "What the hell could I tell 'em? There was nothing to say. I told 'em I was high and didn't know what I was doin'.'"

Travis said: "Yeah, you couldn't tell 'em much more than that, could you? What did you have to get high for? What the hell's the matter with you, punk? I take you over! I give you a good job, some clothes. I put you in a hotel. I give you dough and fix you up, an' the first time I give you a job to do look what happens. You haveta go about killin' people." He looked at Linney, who smiled acidly.

Travis went on: "Tell me what happened, kid—as much as you can remember."

Berg said: "Goddam little . . . I went down to the garage and met up with those two guys Charlie and Lefty. They got the truck out. I thought they was goin' to give me a drivin' lesson. I thought that was the idea but they said it could wait. They said they reckoned we could go for a ride. So we went. We stopped one or two places and had a drink. Pretty strong sort of liquor it seemed to me, an' I ain't used to drinkin'.'"

Travis said: "Well, what did you want to drink for? Didn't you like it?"

"Yeah, I suppose so," said Berg. "It made me feel good. Besides, they were paying for the liquor, an' they sort of expected me to have a drink with them. They were nice guys."

Travis said: "Yeah . . . they're all right. So what then?"

Berg went on: "We got back into the cab after the last drink. We were goin' along pretty swell too; it seemed fast to me. One of these guys—I think it was Lefty—brings out a hip flask. He told me it was something special—the best liquor in the world. He said to have a long swig. Well, I reckon I don't know very much after that. I got a sort of odd idea about hearin' some shootin' some place, an' the next thing I know I was lyin' in the garden behind that Rose Dean place. I had a gun inside my coat, and the cops arrived."

"Yeah?" said Travis. "An' where the hell did the gun come from? Where'd you get the rod? Hey, kid? How come you was totin' a rod?"

Berg shrugged his shoulders. "I didn't have no rod," he said. "I ain't never fired a pistol. The only thing I fired is a shotgun or a rifle. I'm goddam good with 'em too. But they found the gun on me so I musta got it from somewhere. I reckon I don't know."

Travis asked: "Look, do you reckon you shot those two mugs when you were high? You ever been cut before? Do you get nasty when you get high?"

Berg said: "I've never been properly cut before, but when I've had a snifter I usta get sort of nasty sometimes. Maybe I didn't like these guys. I wouldn't know."

Travis said: "Look, maybe I can fix this for you."

Berg said: "Yeah?" He looked hopefully from Travis to Linney.

Travis said: "This is Mr. Linney. He's an attorney, see? Counsel for Mr. Scansci. Maybe you heard the name Scansci?"

Berg said: "No, I never heard it. Maybe he's what they call a big shot, hey?"

Travis said: "The biggest! Well, he's a friend of mine, see? I been talkin' to him about you. Maybe there'll be room for you in the organisation some place, but you'd have to do what you were told, you know. If you didn't . . . well, you never know what's gonna happen in this city; maybe they'd be able to rake this charge up again. You never know."

Berg said: "Look, Mr. Hahn, you get me out of this an' I'll remember it. I'm not too keen on dyin', you know."

Travis said: "No, nobody is." He turned to Linney. He said: "Go on, Jake . . . he's all yours."

Linney began to speak in his high-pitched, rather pedantic voice: "You've got to understand this, Berg . . . it seems you sort of got yourself mixed up between two rather important liquor concerns in Chicago—one of them Mr. Scansci's, and the other one belonging to a guy called Calsimo."

Berg said: "What . . . me?" His eyes were surprised.

Linney said: "Yes, you . . . just one of those things—an accident, but there it is. I reckon you've been framed." He smiled at Berg.

Berg scratched his head. He said: "Look, Mr. Linney, I don't understand. Maybe you could make this a bit plainer. So I've been framed. All right . . . how?"

Linney said: "We checked up on your movements yesterday evening, Berg. What you've said is perfectly right. You went out with Charles and Lefty in the truck. You had some drinks. Lefty gave you one out of his hip flask, and you passed out. But the truck didn't go anywhere near the Rose Dean Roadhouse. Charlie, who was driving, turned it round and came back into the city."

Berg said: "Wait a minute . . . they told me they were goin' to Rose Dean. They . . ."

Travis said quietly: "Why don't you keep your trap shut? We're tellin' *you* what happened. You don't have to tell *us*. You don't know . . . you were out. You got that?"

Berg said: "Yeah, I got it."

Linney went on: "The truck turned and came back into the city. When they got back to the garage you were right out. They took you out of the cab. They carried you around to Metzler's Skittle Alley. They laid you out on a seat just inside the skittle room."

Berg said: "Hey . . . is this right?"

Linney looked at Travis and grinned. He said: "Yeah . . . that's how it is. There were about seventeen guys playing skittles and drinking, and they're all ready to swear to it. They couldn't make a mistake about a guy like you. You're a distinctive looking mug."

Berg smiled. "Is this good?" he said. "So I never killed nobody?"

Travis rubbed his chin. He said quietly: "Well, kid, I wouldn't go so far as to say that. But we're friends of yours, see? We like you. We're gettin' you out of this. Mr. Linney's got a first-class alibi for you, and there's nobody can break it down. Don't you worry. We'll look after it."

Berg said: "Thanks a lot, Mr. Hahn. You been pretty good to me."

Travis got up. He said: "Well, I'll be on my way. I'll leave Mr. Linney here with you for a bit. He wants to talk to you, Berg. Don't worry. We'll have you out of here sometime to-day or at the latest to-morrow, and you come an' see me. I got a job for you."

Berg said: "You bet I'll be there, Mr. Hahn. You been pretty good to me."

Travis said: "Yeah . . . that's what I thought." He looked at Linney. He said: "Well, so long, Jake. Just get that story right into his head with any frills you wanta put on to it. I'll be seein' you."

He rattled on the cell door to be let out.

Outside on the steel staircase Travis lit a cigarette. He walked slowly up the stairs thinking. He said good-night to the desk sergeant, pushed open the doors of the precinct building. O'Finnigan was just coming up the outside steps. He stopped a couple of steps below Travis.

He said: "You lousy double-crossin' bastard . . . I wonder how you gonna talk yourself out of this one. What's gotten into you, Travis? What's the big idea?"

Travis dropped his voice. He said: "Listen, Pat . . . keep it quiet for a minute, will you? This is serious. I can explain this business all right. I'll tell you something. . . . I'm so goddam steamed up with it myself I don't know what to do. You don't think I'm mug enough to pull a fast one like this on you, do you?"

O'Finnigan looked at him. He said: "You mean somebody else is bein' clever?"

Travis said: "That's what I mean. Come around the corner an' have a drink." They went down the stairs into a nearby speak-easy; over to the corner table.

When the drinks had been brought Travis said: "Listen, Pat, I made a little arrangement with you, and when I make an arrangement I go through with it, you know that. O.K. Well, what happens? Scansci gets word that these goddam Trazzi boys are bein' knocked off. Well, he don't say a word to me about it. What does he do? He sends for Linney. Linney gets crackin', an' they fix up this alibi for Berg."

O'Finnigan said: "All right. But what's the explanation for that one? What the hell does Scansci care about this hick Berg? You tell me that."

Travis said: "I wouldn't know, but I could make a coupla guesses. Look, Scansci gets word that the Trazzi boys have had it. They're fogged see? O.K. Well, that means Calsimo's had lesson number one. His two smart gun-boys from New York have got it. Maybe somebody told Scansci that Berg had pulled this job."

O'Finnigan said: "And he didn't. You're tellin' me he didn't do it?"

Travis said: "Be your age. This mug's never had a rod in his hand in his life. Somebody else did it, see? You know that. But it's pinned on to Berg, and we were gonna give him to you. But Scansci thinks no. So he fixes this with Linney and he gets Berg out. Why?"

The lieutenant of detectives said: "That's what I asked."

Travis said: "It looks to me like there is only one reason. It looks like Scansci thinks he can use this guy Berg. You got that?"

O'Finnigan said: "I got it and I don't like it." He took the cigarette that Travis offered him. He lit it. He said: "You know, sometimes I think that Paul Scansci is askin' for trouble. Maybe he'll get it one day. I reckon this guy Calsimo is gonna be good an' steamed up about this business. Now we're gonna have some gun-play. Now we're gonna have a lot of trouble. We're gonna have another killin' with nobody pulled in for it just because Scansci's got some big idea."

Travis said very quietly: "You know Pat, maybe this mightn't be a bad thing in a way."

The lieutenant of detectives asked: "In what way? It's goddam good for me, ain't it? Who's it gonna be good for?"

Travis said: "These two guys who got bumped weren't local boys. They were New York fellas, see? An' I reckon if somebody could talk turkey to Calsimo and tell him to lay off an' not start anything we might be able to fix something about this."

O'Finnigan looked at him for a long time. He said: "What have you got in the back of your head, Travis?"

Travis said: "Well, I sort of agreed with you that Scansci's slippin'. I reckon this guy Calsimo's got brains. Maybe he's a bigger shot than Scansci. Maybe—"

O'Finnigan whistled. "I got it," he said. "So that's it. You think somebody's gonna sell Scansci out?"

Travis said: "No, I don't think anything like that right now, but I think there's been a lot of talk lately about him; talk about him slippin' and all that sort of stuff. You've heard it yourself."

O'Finnigan grinned. He said: "Yeah, I heard it. . . . Maybe *you* wouldn't know who started it." His grin became broader. He got up. He said: "Well, I'm on my way, Travis. I reckon you've tried to play ball over this. You'd be a mug if you didn't. But I think Scansci's nuts; right now he can't afford to get in bad with anybody"—he smiled sarcastically, "not even with the cops around here. I'll be seein' you. I suppose we shall have to spring Berg to-morrow."

Travis said: "It looks like it. Linney's got a swell case and there's no evidence against Berg except he got that gun on him."

O'Finnigan said: "Yeah . . . but that's evidence all right, you know. A gun's a gun, and it was that gun killed those two Trazzi mugs."

Travis said: "Yeah." Then he played his trump card. "You know what the thing is that knocks me about this, and I didn't know it till this afternoon when Linney told me? You know who that gun belongs to? It belongs to one of Calsimo's mob. Not so good that, hey?"

O'Finnigan said: "Jeez . . . so somebody pinched the gun from one of Calsimo's boys and used it on the Trazzis? For cryin' out loud! Maybe Scansci or somebody else has got more brains than I thought."

Travis said: "Yeah . . . it's a hard world. Well, so long, Pat. You'll hear from me in the morning."

O'Finnigan said: "I better had. I gotta get something out of this. So long." He went away.

Travis finished his drink. He walked slowly up the stairs, meandered two blocks towards the centre of the city. He went into a call-box, called a number.

He said: "Hey, is that you, Mrs. Scansci? . . . Yeah, I'd like to call you Clovis . . . it's a lovely name. . . . Is Paul there? No? Give him a message from me, will you? Tell him it's O.K. about the guy I was talkin to him about. Hell be sprung. You got that?"

She said: "Yes, I've got it, Travis. Is that all?" Her voice was very soft and caressing.

Travis said: "Yeah, Clovis . . . that's all . . . for the moment."

He hung up; went out of the call-box.

IV

It was raining. Berg turned quickly into the entrance to Carlazzi's, threw one of his slow smiles at the girl in the hatcheck room, took off his heavy overcoat, silk scarf and black fedora, laid them on the counter.

The girl, a pert, pretty, thing, wearing the exaggerated uniform fashionable in those days, said: "Good-evening, Mr. Berg. It's nice to see you again."

Berg said: "Yeah . . . me too."

He stood in the centre of the vestibule, looking about him. Now to enter Carlazzi's was no longer an experience. Now he was Rene Berg—a big shot in the Scansci organisation. He was nearly twenty-three years of age. His body, spare, slim-hipped, well-proportioned, made a good peg for the fine cloches that he wore. His double-breasted suit of English cloth was from the best tailor in Chicago. His shirt and collar were silk; his tie had cost five dollars.

He walked through the foyer, through the doors at the end, stood at the back of the restaurant tables, looking at the turn on the dance floor. When the torch singer had finished her number the lights went up. People looked about them. Many turned their heads, saw Berg, whispered to each other. He knew what they were saying. This was Berg—Scansci's ace gunman—the man who had knocked off ten of the Calsimo boys during the last year—a neat quick worker who never put the wrong foot forward and who, since his first unlucky slip-up, had never even been taken in on suspicion. Many of the women took a second look in his direction.

His face was long, oval-shaped, the jaw hard. His thick black well-kept hair flowed back from a forehead that was almost clever. In spite of everything, his eyes still laughed occasionally, and there were humorous lines about them. A good-looking man, Berg.

He sat down at a table. Carlazzi hurried over.

He said: "Good-evening, Meester Berg. It's good to see you. How's every leetle thing with you?"

"Not too bad, Carlazzi," said Berg. He spoke softly and his voice had a good timbre.

Carlazzi, looking down at him, thought how odd it was that a man so good-looking, so young, should be a gunman.

Berg ordered his meal. When it was brought he sat eating it slowly, thinking—thinking about all sorts of things. He sat a little sideways so that he could keep one eye on the door. He had learned that was a good thing to do. Also, sitting that way made the drag of the heavy gun under his left armpit easier.

The floor show started for the second time, but in the darkness that surrounded the tables, Berg's eyes still watched the heavy velvet portieres intently. One of these days, he thought, one of the Calsimo mob were going to have a go for him—one of these days. Sooner or later it must happen. And then . . .? In the darkness he half shrugged his shoulders. When it happened it would happen. It would be the other mug or himself; you just didn't know. Life was like that . . . one of those things!

Berg had learned plenty about life during the past eighteen months. He had also learned quite a little about death. A natural shot, a quick easy mover, a man with the intelligence and intuition of the born hunter, his apprenticeship of four months under Bugsy Trellin—Scansci's ace gorilla—had turned him into the finished product. Even Travis Hahn had been surprised—Travis, who, in these days, boasted that Berg could snap into action, get on his feet, draw his rod, and get the other guy, while the other mug was thinking about it. Berg was a natural. So Travis said. And Travis was usually right.

Berg ate his meal slowly. He was thinking about Travis.

Lauren was leaning up against the mantelpiece; a cigarette hung from one corner of her red mouth. She was watching Travis.

Travis walked up and down the big apartment. His hands were clasped behind his back. He was thinking.

Lauren thought: I know what's on your mind, big boy. You'll get around to it in a minute, *I* know.

At the far end of the room Travis stopped pacing. He stopped at the sideboard, mixed himself a large whisky and soda—his fourth.

She said easily: "You know, honey, you're drinking an awful lot of hooch these days. What's the matter? It can't be so good for you to drink all that whisky even if it *is* good stuff."

Travis put down the glass. He said: "Yeah . . . I know. You're too right. You always are. But what the hell's a guy to do. I'm worried."

She yawned deliberately. She said: "Yeah? So you're worried, Travis, hey? You're worried all the time. You're like a guy with a dog on his shoulder—a big black dog. What's eatin' you?—or maybe I could guess." She yawned again, theatrically delicate in the process. She smiled at him. "Maybe you're worryin' about me, honey." Her smile grew sarcastic. "Maybe you think I'm two-timin' you with some guy—that or somethin' else. I reckon I could make three guesses."

Travis picked up the glass. He drank the remainder of the whisky slowly. He was looking at her.

He said: "What the hell does that mean? Are you tryin' to be smart or something?"

Lauren moved. She stretched luxuriously. She said: "What the hell! I don't haveta be smart. You're the smart guy, ain't you?"

Travis said: "I wonder. But you tell me something. What are those three guesses of yours? I'd like to know what the three things are that are worryin' me."

She said coolly: "I reckon first of all you're worried about Calsimo. That boy's gettin' in your hair, ain't he? He's doing pretty good. The second thing is maybe you're worried a little bit about Scansci."

Travis said: "For Chrissake . . . what the hell do I haveta worry about Scansci for?"

She said: "Nothing very much except that he thinks that Clovis is still stuck on him."

Travis said darkly: "What the hell has Clovis gotta do with me?"

Lauren yawned again. She said: "I wouldn't know, but if you're gonna try and make that baby, you be careful."

He said acidly: "You must be nuts. What the hell!"

She interrupted: "Don't give me that, big boy. You couldn't keep your ringers off any pretty woman, and I reckon Clovis is right up your street. That schoolgirl stuff—those big blue eyes. I gotta hand it to her. She's got a cute line. She's got a cute line all right—the little hoodlum. Every time a guy looks at her an' she looks back with those blue orbs the mug wonders whether it ain't time for him to get around and tell her some of the facts of life. He thinks she wouldn't know. She's that sorta jane."

She took a cigarette from the box on the mantelpiece, lit it with a silver lighter. She went on: "Me—I like her. I think she's got something. She's a friend of mine. Yeah . . . we're buddies. Or are we? But you take a tip from me, Travis, you lay offa her. If you try to lay that baby you're gonna start something you won't finish."

Travis said: "Aw . . . nuts. . . ." He resumed his pacing up and down the room.

Lauren said: "Look, fella, why don't you get it off your chest? You're going to eventually. I know you. You know, a woman doesn't live with a guy for five years without learnin' something about him."

He said: "Well, what the hell's been the matter with the five years? You've had a good time, hey? You got plenty of jack stowed away somewhere an' you got some sweet ice. A lot of dames would like to be you."

She said: "Yeah . . . a lot of dames would like to be me, and a lot of dames would like to look like I do. But I'm like an old book, hey, Travis? You've read me once; you wanta *get* something new out of the library. Only I wouldn't if I was you."

He said over his shoulder: "No, why not? What would you do about it?"

Lauren smiled at him—a slow ominous smile. She said: "What do you think, cutie? You do anything that's sort of public, anything that lets anybody cock an eyebrow at me, and I'll fill your belly so full of lead slugs you'll feel like a buckshot factory, even if I get the hot squat for it. I'd laugh while they was fryin' me."

Travis moved his shoulders uneasily. He said: "Aw . . . what the hell! I believe you would too."

She said: "I *would* an' I'd *like* it."

When he came abreast of her he stopped, stood looking at her. He said: "You're a swell piece, Lauren, except you got a funny sort of mind. You're suspicious. You think all sorts of things that ain't happenin'."

She said: "Nuts! I know men and I know you. Well, what about changin' the subject, sweetie? What's the trouble?"

He said: "What do you think? Calsimo's the trouble. Calsimo's gettin' too big. He's gettin' too big for himself and for us."

Lauren said: "The same old story. But why worry? Chicago's a big place. Calsimo's sittin' pretty an' Scansci's sittin' prettier. Scansci's the big shot around here, especially since you had your little boy friend Rene working for you. That guy's been worth a million dollars to you an' Scansci."

Travis said: "Yeah . . . I know. He's *good*. But that don't help things. There's gonna be trouble."

She said: "Yeah? Why? I thought everybody was behavin' himself. I thought Calsimo was stickin' around on his own territory an' not musclin' in on our take. I thought everything was jake. What's wrong now?"

He said: "I reckon the Feds are gettin' busy around here. They've started passing those goddam new Federal Acts. I don't like it. Nobody likes it. And the cops don't like it. I was talkin' to some goddam copper two days ago. D'you know what he said to me?"

She said: "No, you tell me. Was it good?"

"Was it!" said Travis. "He said they were sick of gettin' cops bumped off in the line of duty. He said they got another big idea. He said that they reckoned if they gave Scansci and Calsimo long enough they'd knock each other's mobs off. The cops could just stick around an' watch it happenin'. And by God he's right. That's what's happenin' now."

Lauren thought for a minute. She said: "Maybe you got something there. What are the figures?"

Travis said: "Well, we started . . . you remember . . . we sort of started this when we bumped those Trazzi boys out at Rose Dean. That was nineteen months ago. O.K. Since then they've had about twenty-three twenty-four of our boys."

She said: "Well, I reckon we've had more of them than that. Why, Rene must have taken about sixteen of that mob himself."

A sarcastic smile spread over Travis's face. He said: "Oh, yeah
. . . you been keepin' a score sheet for him, hey? You like that
guy, don't you?"

She said: "You tell me any dame who gets around with our
mob who don't."

He said: "So it's like that. The guy's lucky!"

She moved to the sideboard languorously. She poured out a
long drink, carried it back to the fireplace. "As if you didn't know,"
she said. "That kid's got something. He's young; he's tough; he
don't drink very much. An' he's brave. I'm tellin' you . . . he's got
all the guts in the world."

Travis said: "Yeah . . . he does what he's told."

Lauren said: "You bet he does. He does what he's told and
what he's told is nobody's business. Every lousy job that everybody else is scared of doin' he gets, but he does it—a great guy!"
She took a sip of the whisky. "That guy mighta been something.
He mighta been something really big if you hadn't framed him
into this goddam racket."

Travis said: "Aw . . . hell! Nobody had to do anything they
didn't wanta do."

"Maybe you're right," said Lauren. "But he hadn't got much
of a chance, had he? It was do what he was told or the hot squat.
He's a good guy. I like him."

Travis said: "All right. So Rene's a good guy an' you like him, and
all the other broads like him. Fine! An' where does that get me?"

She said insolently: "Listen, mug. I could tell you where it
would get you if you'd got any brains."

She moved, and Travis noticed under the frills at her bosom a
new diamond brooch. He said: "Hey . . . hey . . . some rock! Where
did you knock that one off? Maybe you got another boy friend?"

Lauren said: "Nope . . . no soap. I got it from a dame—Clovis
gave it to me."

Travis said: "What the hell! She gave you that brooch? It must
be worth ten fifteen grand."

"I know," said Lauren. "She and I are sort of friendly. So she's
worried too."

Travis stopped again by the sideboard. He turned, leaned against it. He said: "Look, what's goin' on around here? What have you two dames been up to? What's the big idea?"

Lauren said: "Maybe we do a little thinking sometimes, Travis. Maybe we been thinkin' about this Calsimo thing too, and we're sort of interested, see? We don't want the mob to fold up, because if Scansci folds up we fold up with him, hey? So we're two nice little girls standin' four-square behind our men." She blew a polite raspberry.

Travis said: "So what?"

Lauren said: "Listen . . ." Her tone was serious. "I reckon what you been sayin' about the mobs is right. Scansci's got too big. So's Calsimo. The cops reckon that all they gotta do is to stand on one side an' watch the boys iron each other out. So something really serious oughta be done."

Travis said: "Yeah . . . such as?"

Lauren said: "Such as somebody big oughta get fogged. It don't matter who it is—whether it's Calsimo or it's Scansci. If one of the king pins gets fogged the mob folds up and the other guy goes on. Everything would be jake."

Travis said: "Yeah . . . an' how the hell are you goin' to get at Calsimo? How do you do it? That guy's got a bodyguard of three or four boys always sittin' around his front door. It ain't possible. An' what happens to the guy who pulls that one? Supposin' you got somebody to iron out Calsimo. How long would he have to live? They'd have him within twenty-four hours."

Lauren said: "That depends on the guy."

Travis asked: "What are you thinkin' of? What have you got in the back of your head?"

She said: "I got Rene Berg in the back of my head."

Travis said shortly: "Be your age. D'you think he's gonna take a chance on that one? Rene's got guts, but that's big time stuff."

She said: "He'd do it all right if he felt he ought to."

"What the hell do you mean . . . felt he oughta to?" asked Travis.

She said: "Look, sweetheart, that guy is only twenty-two twenty-three years of age, hey? Have you ever known anybody who didn't fall for Clovis? Have you ever known anybody who didn't go weak at the knees when she looks at them with those big blue eyes of hers? Another thing, everybody don't haveta know that she's just a moll like the rest of us feathering her own nest. She's young an' sweet looking. She looks like dairy-milk. Well?"

Travis said: "I got it . . . I got it. . . ." He asked suddenly: "Have you two been talkin' about this?"

Lauren said: "Why not? Somebody's got to do some thinkin' around here. Somebody's got to get some action; otherwise we're all goin' to get the bum's rush. What you've said is right. It's Scansci or Calsimo. All right. You got to get movin'."

He said: "Well, what's the big idea?"

She said: "I'll tell you what the big idea is. You send Rene up to see me some time. Maybe he might fall into Clovis accidentally or somehow else. Maybe she'll have a little story for him. You know, way back in that mug's brain is a rather nice thing. Because he thought he was grateful to you at the beginning he's done all your dirty work. I reckon if he thought he was grateful to Clovis he'd even take Calsimo."

Travis said: "Jeez . . . you got it. . . . I believe you're right."

She said: "You're tellin' me!"

He asked suddenly: "But what about Scansci? What the hell?"

She said: "Look, Scansci is all washed up. He's fat and full of liquor these days. He don't even know he's alive. He sits around an' takes the big dough and you guys keep him where he is. Well, if Calsimo was out of the way, you never know, there might be an accident sometime and if you knew how to play it you'd be sittin' on top of the heap."

Travis moved towards the whisky decanter. He said: "By God, Lauren, you've got something. But it's big. If it went wrong it'd be poison."

She said: "If you don't do something it's gonna be poison anyway."

Travis made up his mind suddenly. He said: "O.K. We might try the first thing. What d'you want me to do?"

She said: "I'll tell you. You tell Rene to ring you up at the apartment here to-morrow night around nine, see? Well, you won't be here, but I'll talk to him. Maybe I'll get him round here. Maybe I'll hand him a nice little spiel. You leave it to me."

Travis said: "O.K. . . . O.K. . . . Ill do that thing." He shot her a glance of ill-concealed admiration. He thought: You've got something, you so-an'-so. If I didn't know you were two-timin' me I could go for you in a big way. If I didn't get so goddamned steamed up about you sometimes I'd hate your guts.

She smiled at him. She said: "What you thinkin', honey?"

"I wasn't thinkin' a thing," said Travis.

"No?" said Lauren. "Like hell you wasn't. I *know* what you were thinkin', honey. Have another drink. You'll feel better about it."

V

Berg came out of Carlazzi's, stood on the edge of the pavement underneath the awning, his hands deep in his overcoat pockets, his chin sunk into the folds of the silk muffler round his throat, his black fedora pulled down over one eye. He presented a dark romantic figure against the whiteness of the snow.

Across on the other side of the street a figure moved in a doorway. Berg grinned. He knew who the figure was. It was Jimmie Rizzi—a small-time gunman employed by the Calsimo organisation—a young man of twenty-seven whose brain and nerves had been fuddled with liquor and drugs. These days he was used as a "tail."

Berg walked slowly across the street. He said: "Hallo, Jimmie. Can't they find you a better job than proppin' up doorways this weather—or maybe you like it?"

Rizzi said: "Aw . . . what the hell! Me—I'm waiting for a dame. I always stick around disa doorway waiting for disa dame."

Berg said: "Yeah . . . so's your old man! You been on my tail since about seven o'clock this evening. You don't want me to smack you down, do you?"

Rizzi's eyes narrowed. He said viciously: "Don' you talk to me like this . . . don' you do it. You know, I'm goddam dangerous."

Berg said: "Yeah!" He began to laugh. "Maybe you usta be one time, Jimmie," he said. "When I first blew into Chi a coupla years ago they told me you was a big shot—a killer. Now you look to me like an exploded air balloon."

Rizzi said: "Looka, Berg . . . you be careful . . ."

Berg said, not unkindly: "Scram, Rizzi, and don't follow me around. If you do I might get sore, and you know what I'd do to you if I got sore, don't you?"

Rizzi looked scared. The belligerent expression passed from his face to be succeeded by a smile. He said: "Aw . . . looka. . . . I was only kidding, see? But it ees the trut'. . . . I am sticking around here waiting for disa dame. I am nota tailing anybody. . . ."

Berg said: "I'm glad to hear it. Good-night, punk."

He walked away. As his back disappeared down the white street Rizzi peered round his doorway—far his lungs were not too good and the wind was very cold—thought how much he would like to put a bullet between the shoulder-blades. He thought bitterly that two-three years ago he would have done that thing. Maybe Berg was right. Maybe he was all washed up. He turned up his coat collar, moved out of the doorway, disappeared into the shadows.

Berg went into the telephone pay-box two blocks past Mulbery at Barrell Street. He rang Travis's number. Whilst he waited he fished a cigarette from his pocket, lit it with his new gold and platinum striped lighter. He drew the smoke into his lungs.

Lauren's voice came on the telephone.

Berg said: "Hallo, Mrs. Hahn. This is Rene Berg. Travis asked me to call him."

She said: "Yeah . . . he told me . . . but he's not here, Rene. He's had to go out. Say, look . . . what are you doin' to-night?"

Berg said: "I'm not doin' anything much. I stuck around. I thought maybe Travis wanted something."

She said: "Well, listen . . . you come over here, kid. I wanta talk to you. Get yourself a cab and come right over."

Berg said: "Yeah? Maybe you got some sort of message for me from Travis?" Always in his heart he had been a little afraid of Lauren. Berg, who could be so ruthless, so merciless, with men, had a peculiar diffidence where women were concerned.

She laughed. When he heard the rich soft notes of her laughter he liked the sound.

She said: "Look, you wouldn't think I was gonna eat you or something, would you? Maybe I *have* got a message from Travis, something I can't shout about on the telephone."

He said: "O.K. I'll come over. Ill come over right away." He hung up the receiver.

Sitting in the corner of the cab, drawing the cigarette smoke down into his lungs, Berg thought about Lauren Harm and women in general. During his period of apprenticeship as a gunman seventeen eighteen months ago, when he had walked around Chicago carrying Charlie and Harry Wells's guns for them in a violin case, he had noticed that every big-time gangster had what seemed an attractive and beautiful woman—one at least. It seemed to Berg a part of the advantages of working in an organisation like Scansci's that beautiful women were available, but somehow he had never got around to them. Time and time again one of the other boys' dames had slung a hot look in his direction, but he had never done anything about it. It seemed to him that women were a lot of trouble. That's how they seemed sometimes. Other times they seemed very necessary; very desirable.

He began to think about Clovis Scansci. There was a hell of a set-up, thought Berg. There was a thing. How the hell does a guy like Scansci—now fifty—get himself a kid like Clovis? Berg thought she must be twenty-two or twenty-three—somewhere about his age. How the hell did Scansci do a thing like that? But you never knew with women. Maybe she went for him. Maybe Scansci had some decent part in his odd nature. Berg's lips twisted into a wry smile at the thought.

But Clovis was no gangster's moll. She had got something. She had style, freshness, and something which none of the other women had. She seemed vaguely unattainable. Berg had only met her twice. But on each occasion he had sensed a peculiar pleasure at being in her company—at being able to look at her. On the second occasion she had looked at him for a long time with her big blue eyes. Just for a moment the idea had occurred to Berg that there was something almost pleading in them.

He knew that idea was ridiculous. Clovis Scansci had everything she wanted. She was sitting right on top of the heap. She had two automobiles, jewels, everything . . . everything that ought to make a woman happy. But still, thought Berg, it was goddam funny how a fat guy like Scansci should make a dame like Clovis.

Berg began to wonder about Scansci. He didn't know him very well, but what he did know he disliked. Most of Berg's instructions came from Travis. He had had little opportunity of studying or analysing Scansci, but there was something repellent in the man—something vague and indefinable which Berg did not like. He threw the cigarette butt out of the window. He dismissed them all from his mind. He leaned back, felt the weight of the automatic under his left arm pressing against him.

He thought that was the thing! If you had a gun and knew how to use it; if you had the right set-up behind you—a mob like the Scansci organisation with attorneys and mouthpieces and crooked lawyers covering up for you, fixing alibis for you, you were a big guy. You could do what you liked. You had powers of life and death. Berg thought that maybe even if the Chicago adventure had not turned out exactly in the way he had planned it when he hitch-hiked down from the Ozarks it had still been exciting anyway. Even if the job was not one which he would have selected it was a big job, he hoped. Still, somewhere in the back of his mind, were those vague ideas which had germinated in the old days, in the hot summers—the ideas of being somebody or something really big. The old heroic figures still passed through his mind and even if there were times when he doubted whether his peculiar profession was particularly heroic, there was always somebody to tell him when the nasty job of the moment was done that he was a big guy.

When he went into the apartment, Lauren, dressed in a blue velvet housecoat, was leaning against the mantelpiece smoking a cigarette. Berg came into the room, stood in the centre of it, his long arms hanging down by his sides.

He said: "Good-evening, Mrs. Hahn. What's new?"

She went over to the sideboard. She poured out two drinks. When she put the ice in, he noticed the whiteness of her fingers, the glitter of the rings on them.

She said: "The first thing is, Berg, we have a drink. And why do you have to call me Mrs. Hahn? My name's Lauren. Lots of people think that's a pretty name."

Berg said: "Yeah . . . I reckon it is." He took the glass from her. "Well, here's to you, Lauren." He drank the drink. He swallowed the liquor in the same prompt and decided way in which he did anything. He walked to the sideboard and put the glass down. He said: "What: was the message that Travis left for me?"

Lauren was back at the fireplace. She looked at him over her shoulder. She said: "Look, Rene, I don't know you very well, but I trust you. Travis didn't leave any message for you. I wanted to talk to you. I'm scared."

Berg raised one eyebrow. He said: "Yeah? Scared . . . what is there to be scared about?"

She said: "I know Travis is worried. He's worried about the mob. Calsimo's gettin' pretty big, you know—too big for his boots."

Berg said casually: "What can he do? We're the only organisation in this city that matters. We pay off plenty. We got everybody in our pockets. If they can't be bought, they can be frightened. What is there to be scared about?"

She shrugged her shoulders. She said: "Look, Rene, maybe I'm talking out of turn. Maybe I ought not to be talking to you like this at all, but I gotta talk to somebody." Lauren, who was a good actress, put on a look of gravest concern. She went on: "Calsimo oughta have been fixed a long time ago; even Travis knows that now. In the old days—a coupla years ago—it would have been easy. Now look at the situation. We're big an' he's big. We're supposed to have our own territories and keep to them, but you know things like that just don't happen. You know that, Rene."

He said: "You're not telling me that Scansci's scared of Calsimo? Is that it?"

She shrugged her shoulders in a little hopeless gesture. She said softly: "Scansci . . . what's happening to him, Rene? Of course you wouldn't know. You don't see much of him. There's something wrong with that guy. He's not worrying about anything any more. He leaves everything to Travis, and Travis has got plenty to take care of. Now the cops have got wise."

Berg raised his eyebrows again. He said: "The cops wise . . . to what? What are they tryin' to do—put the ante up again?"

She said: "It's not graft. The Federal Government's taking an interest in the mobs now. They're passing all sorts of new acts. That's not very good. They get around, these guys, you know—these 'G' men. You can't buy 'em and they're tough. Besides, the cops have got a big idea. They reckon Scansci and Calsimo had got such big organisations around here that somebody is gonna blow something in a minute. They think they'll sort of cancel each other out, see? And they can stick around with their hands in their pockets smoking cigarettes and watching it. Maybe they like it that way."

Berg said: "Yeah . . . maybe they do . . . and maybe they're right." He went on: "You know, Lauren, there's been a lot of killing around here the last year or so."

She said softly: "Yeah . . . there has been. You oughta know."

He smiled. He said: "You bet I know. I've done most of it, haven't I? Maybe these cops have got something; maybe there's gonna be a big war in a minute. I heard the other day that Calsimo was gettin' some machine-guns into town." His eyes brightened a little. "Maybe we're gonna have a pitched battle some day."

Lauren said: "Maybe." She went to the sideboard, refilled the glasses. She brought his drink to him. Under the frills at her throat he could see the plump whiteness of her skin. She went back to the fireplace. Berg still stood in his original position in the centre of the room. Looking at him, she thought he had a peculiar restfulness, a quietness, a relaxation which was uncommon in any of the men who worked for the mobs. She thought he might have been in any other profession—any decent profession. She thought he was a strange man, but rather nice. Lauren thought Berg was a good guy. She thought too he might be very interesting to sleep with.

He drank some of the whisky. He said: "Maybe all this is true, but you never asked me to come here to hear that, did you?"

She said: "No. It's something else."

Berg said: "Yeah? What is it?"

She said: "Look, Rene . . . Clovis Scansci and I are good buddies. She's my pal, see? We women haveta stick together, you know. Well, something's gotten into her; I don't know what it is but she's scared stiff. It's something to do with Scansci or Calsimo, or something. I tried to get it out of her, but she wouldn't tell me. Just before you called through this evening she came around here. She didn't look good to me. I never seen a girl so scared in my life; and, you know, she's nice—Clovis. She ought not to be in this racket. She's a goddam sight too good for it. I'm older than she is and it sort of gets me, see? Another thing, it's a damned shame her being hitched up to that guy Scansci. Oh, I know he's the head of the mob—he's the big shot—but I reckon it's a shame she couldn't have found somebody better than that."

Berg said: "Why did she marry Scansci?"

Lauren shrugged her shoulders. "I wouldn't know," she said. "But Scansci usta have a way of getting what he wanted. If he didn't get it one way he got it another. He can be tough over things that matter."

Berg said: "You mean . . .?"

She said: "I told you I didn't know, but what does that matter? The thing is, the kid's scared stiff. When she came around here to-night I tried to get it out of her, but she wouldn't squeal. Then just as she was goin'—she was over there by the door—she turned round and she said something very funny. She said: 'I met that guy Rene Berg twice. He looks to me like a good guy. Do you think he's the sort to give a girl a hand if she was in a spot?' I asked her what she meant again but she wouldn't let on. I told her I reckoned you were a pretty good proposition."

Lauren moved away from the fireplace. She came close to him. She put her hand on his arm. She said: "Look, Rene, I want you to do something for me, see? I want you to do me a favour. See if you can find out what the hell's going on. Go and see Clovis. I got the idea in my head that this thing she's scared of is something that concerns the lot of us. It's something so big she's afraid to talk about it, but I reckon she's gonna talk to you about it."

Berg said: "Why should she wanta talk to me?"

Lauren said: "That's easy. Look, you been with us a coupla years. You were a kid when you came down here. You've done more in two years than anybody. You're as tough as hell, but you're a nice guy. You're a killer all right, but you got nice eyes. Another thing," said Lauren, dropping her voice almost to a whisper, "you always been goddam nice to the women—sorta polite. I reckon Clovis has heard about you. I reckon she thinks you are the sorta guy could give her a hand." She smiled. "Maybe," she went on, "she's making a little bit of a hero out of you. Well, why shouldn't she? Look, Rene, go and see Clovis. Find out what it is."

Berg said: "I might at that, but if it's me she wants to see I reckon it's got something to do with Calsimo. What else would she want to see me about?"

Lauren shrugged her shoulders. "I wouldn't know," she said. "But why should she wanta see you about Calsimo? What's he gotta do with her? He's just a name to her."

Berg said: "Yeah . . . that's right."

She said: "Look . . . go and see her. Scansci's going out of town to-morrow. He'll be away for two-three days. Go round and have a drink with her to-morrow evening. I'll call her on the telephone and tell her you're going there about eight o'clock. Will you do that, Rene? Will you do it for me?"

Now she was close to him again. She was looking at him. He could smell the perfume she was wearing. He smiled at her. He said: "Why not? I'll try anything once! And if I can be of any use, O.K. Tell her I'll go around there. Ill go round to-morrow night at eight."

She said: "You're a good kid . . . you're a good kid, Rene." She put up her hands and took his face between them. She kissed him on the mouth. She said: "I've always wanted to do that, kid. I think you're terrific."

Berg said: "Yeah . . . why?"

She laughed. She said: "That's the joke. I don't know why. I reckon a woman never does when she falls for a guy."

Berg said: "So it's like that? What about Travis?"

She laughed. She said: "On your way, Rene. One of these evenings when you're not doing anything call through. Come round and have a drink. I'd like to talk to you about my own troubles. But right now you gotta think about this Clovis thing. Another thing," she said, "I don't want Travis to know about this. I don't want him to know about it because she didn't want him to know. She didn't want anybody to know, see? So you'd better scram. Maybe if you like to talk to me about it when you've seen her ... all right."

Berg finished his drink. He gave her the glass. He said: "O.K., Lauren, I'll be seeing you."

He went out of the apartment. After a minute she heard the front door close. She went out into the hallway; waited till she heard the elevator descend. She went back into the sitting-room; moved quickly to the telephone. She called a number.

She said: "Hey, Clovis ... is that you? Honey, it's all right. The sucker's hooked. Now do your stuff, sweetie."

VI

Berg looked at himself in the mirror in the bedroom of his hotel apartment. He was thinking in terms of romance—or as near as his peculiar type of mind could get to that commodity. He thought that perhaps life was throwing something of romance in his way.

At the back of his mind was Clovis. Clovis, who was so beautiful, so wonderful, who had everything, whom he had regarded as being a person set apart from the rest of the world—a person who, in spite of her connection with Scansci, which he imagined was the result of circumstances, possessed every attribute which was good.

Now he was definitely heroic. Clovis was relying on Kim. She was in some sort of trouble. She needed somebody to help her. Surrounded on all sides by big men like Scansci, Travis and the rest of them, it was on Berg she relied—on *him*.

Berg thought that he was not flattering himself. He had no delusions about his position in the Scansci organisation. He was a killer. Just that. But, because he had known no other business in his mature life, he was inclined to take his profession for granted. To him killing was just one of those things.

Had he thought for a moment he would have realised that the only thing that Clovis would want of him was death for somebody. But, because Berg was like most other men, he liked, if possible, to glorify himself, preferred to think that it was not the attribute of being able to deal out death quickly, skilfully, easily, which made him of value to Clovis. He preferred to think it was other things, although had he asked himself the question, what were those other things?

He saw in the glass a fairly tall, slim, well-built, young man with a face that was still clean-cut and attractive, a black fedora over one eye, with humorous lines about the eyes and a mobile, attractive, even just, mouth.

He lit a cigarette, went out of the hotel. He decided not to take a cab, but to walk. He wanted to think. It was cold outside—a cold clear night with a little wind. He liked the feel of the wind on his face.

He began to think about himself being heroic. He remembered what Lauren had said. Berg thought it was fairly easy in Chicago to be a hero. All you had to do was to do what he did. You killed people. You went out—in the old days—in a truck with a sawn-off shot-gun and when it was dark enough and the neighbourhood was lonely enough you waited for the opposition trucks to come along; then you blasted them. Or perhaps the technique was different. Maybe you used a pineapple—a pineapple with a long fuse—and left it in a truck. You waited till the truck got well down the road, and then you heard the explosion. Still later, when you were graduated from the amateur class, you had a car to yourself. You called on people. You saw them in their apartments. You gave it to them there. Then, when you were an expert, as he was now, you made your own plans, your own set-ups. You were told who it was was to "have it"; you saw that they "got it." You used different techniques; thought out different schemes; but the end was always the same—you killed somebody.

And, thought Berg, Lauren had suggested there was something heroic—something romantic—about it, and she was not alone in the thought. All the women—not only the gangsters' women, but some of the nice respectable citizenesses of Chicago—thought that the gunmen were heroic figures. Berg had even heard that that was one of the things that was annoying J. Edgar Hoover—the head of the "G" men. Hoover, Berg had heard, was annoyed because ordinary, respectable, people thought the gangsters were romantic, heroic figures.

He shrugged his shoulders in the darkness. Well, it wasn't hard to be romantic. It wasn't hard to be a hero, especially when you knew you were going to get away with it, especially when you knew that the alibi was laid on; that Scansci's mouthpiece Linney would look after you; that if you shot and killed a man in one part of the town and the cops got on to it—because even the cops had to pull somebody in sometimes—Linney would have five, ten, twenty people quite prepared to go into the box, take the oath, and swear that you were somewhere else at the time. Berg grinned. He thought that people like Linney made life very hard for policemen. The cream of the jest was that the majority of the witnesses that Linney produced on such occasions were good ordinary respectable citizens. Berg wondered how he got them. For a moment he sensed vaguely the tortuous network that Linney must control; had for just a second a glimpse of the terrific organisation for blackmail, bribery and corruption, which must exist in the office of Scansci's attorney.

But on these terms it was easy to be a hero and if it was his fate; if it was ordained that he should be a gangster—a killer; that he should be a hero, a romantic figure, to the women who crossed his path, who was he to quarrel with that decision?

He began to think about Clovis. Thinking about her, his attitude of mind altered. Here was a woman! Something in Berg reached out towards Clovis—something that was possibly decent in him thought that with such a woman he might have made good in some business where life was a little more difficult, where the ordinary everyday life of being a bookkeeper, a clerk, or something like that, did not present the easy angles of a gangster's life.

Let it be said in Berg's favour that he thought nothing of the dangers which he encountered every day of his life. The fact that any day, any night, one of Calsimo's boys might be out looking for him; the fact that he had escaped death a dozen times by a hair-line . . . let it be said in his favour that he thought nothing of these things. He took them for granted. They were part of his profession.

When Berg entered the Scansci apartment block he noticed that the two hefty gorillas who were usually hanging about at the elevator entrance, were gone. He wondered vaguely why. Usually, he understood, there was a man on the main door, two more at the elevator entrance, two more on the third floor where the Scansci apartment was situated. To-night there was none. He dismissed the thought from his mind when he remembered that Scansci was away. Possibly, he thought, with Scansci being away there was no need for protection downstairs. He rang the apartment bell. The door was opened by the girl Truda—a Norwegian.

She smiled at him. She said: "Come in, Mr. Berg. Mrs. Scansci is waiting for you."

She took his hat, his overcoat; indicated the door on the other side of the hall. Berg crossed the hall, went into the large sitting-room of the apartment.

Clovis was standing at the head of the settee. He thought he had never seen anything so beautiful in his life. She was wearing a cornflower blue frock—simple but beautifully cut. Her eyes—blue, lovely—looked at him appealingly. She came to meet him.

She said: "Rene, I'm so glad you have come. You mustn't mind if I call you Rene because that's how I think about you." Her voice was very soft, very melodious. She pronounced her words well; her diction was good.

Berg thought: God, here's a hell of a woman!

She said: "You mustn't stay very long. I don't want you to be here a long time because my husband's away. I couldn't see you when he was here but I don't want anybody to think . . ." She shrugged her shoulders. She went on: "Sit down. Let me give you a drink."

She mixed a drink, brought it to Berg with a box of cigarettes. He took a cigarette and she lit it for him. He sat, cigarette in one hand, drink in the other, looking up at her. She said: "You know, Rene, I'm sorry for you. I'm very sorry for you."

Berg looked surprised. He shrugged his shoulders. He said: "Yeah . . .?" He smiled at her. "I wonder why you should be sorry for me, Mrs. Scansci. What have I done that you've got to be sorry for me?"

She said: "Because, Rene . . . and I wish you wouldn't call me Mrs. Scansci—my name's Clovis. You and I are friends . . . we've got to be friends . . . so we've got to call each other by our first names . . . I am sorry for you because, like me, you've been framed."

Berg said: "Yeah?" He was vaguely amused. "And who's framed me?" he asked.

She smiled. She went and stood in front of the electric fire, one white bare arm resting on the mantelpiece.

She said: "Oh, I don't mean *now,* but when you came to Chicago. I think you'd have done very well in anything you'd gone into; you'd have been a success anyway. But they framed you . . . Travis framed you—you know it . . . he's told you—into working for him . . . for my husband."

Berg said: "Yeah . . . that's as maybe. But I haven't done so badly out of it." He felt a vague sense of discomfort. He felt as if his profession was being patronised.

She said: "Oh, yes, you've done well, Rene. So have I. Look"— she indicated the apartment—"I have lovely clothes and fur coats, and two cars, lots of jewellery. I have everything, except my self-respect."

Berg said: "I wouldn't know what self-respect is. Maybe I never had a chance to find out." He drank a little of the whisky.

She said: "Rene, of course you wouldn't know. You were too young . . . you never had the chance. . . . But I knew. I knew before I was framed into this—" She shrugged her shoulders.

Berg wondered what the hell it was all about. He said: "Listen, Clovis, I was talkin' to Lauren, see? She gave me some line about you being scared about something. She told me you wanted to see me. Well, I reckon Scansci's been pretty good to me one way and another, you know. I know he works through Travis, but I still know who my boss is. The boss is Scansci. That means to me lots of dough, all the things I want, and a cover-up when I want it. So when I hear that you're scared I sort of gotta do something about it. What's the trouble?"

She looked at him for a long time; then she said: "You're a very direct person, aren't you? Very direct and rather nice. Of course what you say about my husband is true. Paul is your boss. He pays you and he pays you well. Why shouldn't he? I wonder what he'd do without people like you."

Berg said: "I wouldn't know." Again he had the vague feeling of discomfort—the feeling that Clovis disliked Scansci; that in some way she was trying to tell him. He wished she'd talk about something else.

He said: "Look, why don't you sit down an' tell me what the trouble is? What's wrong? What's goin' on around here that scares you?"

She said: "Yes, I will. I'll sit down and I'll tell you. But I don't want you to look at me, Rene. Will you come and sit by my side on this settee and I'll try and tell you about it."

Berg thought that women were strange things, but he got up, sat down by her side on the settee. She looked into the fire.

She said: "Listen, I'm about your age. I met Paul Scansci some years ago. I married him because . . . well . . ." She shrugged her shoulders—"I had to marry him. I hadn't any choice. You know, Paul has—or had—a way of getting what he wanted. If he didn't get it one way he got it another. But in the long run he always got it. He used to be a very hard, tough, cruel type."

Berg said: "Yeah? Used to be. . .?"

She threw him a sideways look. She said: "Yes . . . used to be." She looked into the fire again. She went on: "Oh, everybody's noticed the difference in him. For the last four or five months he's done nothing but drink. He's not thinking about his business. It's lucky for the organisation—for people like *you*. . . ." She turned and put her soft white hands suddenly on his . . . "that there are some clever, resourceful people like Linney. He's the person who looks after you—he and Travis. If you were to rely on Paul. . . ." She shrugged her shoulders. She said: "Oh . . . but why am

I talking like this? It doesn't matter. I didn't ask you here to tell you these things."

Berg said: "No? But is that a fact about Scansci? Is it right what you're tellin' me? You mean he's slippin'?"

She nodded her head. "He's slipping badly," she said. "So very badly . . . just how badly, Rene, I'll tell you in a minute."

Berg thought: Maybe she'll get around to it in a minute. He was intrigued. He was wondering what it was all about.

He said: "Look, Clovis, why don't you just sort of tell me what's wrong? What's eatin' you? What are you scared about? I got the rest of the picture. Maybe what you say about Scansci is right. There's been a lot of talk around the town for the last six months about him an' Calsimo. The boys are sayin' that Calsimo is goin' up an' Scansci's goin' down. Well, that may be right even if I haven't noticed it personally, but then I don't see everything." He smiled at her.

She said: "Rene, I won't waste your time. I'll tell you exactly what the trouble is. I've been worried for a long time because I've felt that every time I went out I was being watched. I felt that, even in this place with the boys around, someone was keeping an eye on me—someone who wasn't very nice. During the last three or four weeks I have received four letters. I'm not going into what they say or what they threaten, but I know what they mean."

Berg said: "Yeah . . . well, what do they mean?"

She said: "Calsimo's planning to snatch me. That's how he's going to get back on Scansci."

Berg whistled through his teeth. He said: "For Chrissake . . .! That's a good one." He immediately saw the strength of Calsimo's argument. If Calsimo could succeed in snatching Clovis it would be the end of Scansci. First of all Calsimo would hold her up to ransom, or even if he didn't—even if he returned her unhurt to Scansci—he would make the latter the laughing stock of Chicago.

Berg said: "It's a goddam good idea, I'm tellin' you! Maybe this Calsimo's got brains. From his angle it's a hell of a good idea. From *your* angle not so good."

She looked at him again. She said: "No, I shouldn't think so. Is that all it means to you?"

Berg shook his head. He said: "No . . . not now you've told me. It don't mean a thing to me for a very good reason." He turned towards her and their eyes met. They looked at each other for a long time and into her own eyes Clovis put a message. She willed him to think what she wanted him to think.

She said: "So you're not worrying now." Once again she put her hand over his. She asked: "Why?"

Berg found a little lump in his throat. The background of this scene, the proximity of Clovis, the suggestion of her perfume, the touch of her fingers, were all doing things to him.

He said: "Look, Clovis, now you told me it's O.K. You don't haveta worry."

She said: "No? Are you telling me that? If *you* told me I don't have to worry, Rene, I won't . . . because I think . . ." Her voice broke. "I think to-day of all the friends and people about me, there is only one on whom I can rely . . . you. . . . Now tell me why I don't have to worry."

Berg finished his drink. He got up, put the glass on the mantel-piece. He flicked the cigarette stub into the fire with his forefinger and thumb. He felt a little drunk, although the whisky he had just consumed was the only drink he had had that evening. But it tasted strong; whisky always tasted strong to Berg. His mind was a little uneasy, his tongue free.

He said: "Listen, Clovis, I'm going to tell you something. The guys tell me that in England they've got a proverb 'A Cat May Look At A King.' Maybe I'm just a cat, but I've been lookin' at you. Once or twice when I've seen you I thought you were the greatest thing on earth. I think you're terrific. You've got all the things I think a woman ought to have." He stopped talking, surprised at his own outburst.

Clovis got up. She came slowly towards him. She stood directly in front of him. Once again the perfume she was wearing came to his nostrils.

She said: "Oh, Rene . . . go on . . . go on . . ."

He said: "Well, a cat can look at a king. O.K. I've taken a look at you. You been nice to me to-night. I go for you. I'm not gonna have you scared by Calsimo or anybody else. I'm tellin' you you don't haveta worry."

She said: "Rene, if you say so I believe you. But tell me *why* don't I have to worry?"

She took his glass from the mantelpiece, refilled it. She brought it back. She stood in front of him, holding it up in her two hands, touched the rim of it with her lovely lips. Berg looked at her, hypnotised. She gave the glass to him.

She said: "Drink it, Rene . . . drink it to me."

Berg tossed the drink back. The spirit tasted raw. Again he experienced the sense of discomfort. He wanted to get into the air.

She said: "Now, why don't I have to worry?" She took the glass from him, put it on the mantelpiece behind her.

Berg said: "I'm going to take care of Calsimo. O.K. Maybe Scansci's slipping but *I'm* not. Scansci's been pretty good to me. If you're runnin' a mob you've got to keep on your feet an' look after 'em. If he's not doing that he's no good. If he's not lookin' after you he's no good to you. Goddam it," Berg went on, "if Calsimo were to snatch you we'd be the big laugh around town. Everybody would be bellyachin' about us, even if we got you back. We'd never live it down. It'd be the end of Scansci."

She said: "Yes . . . ?"

"Yes," said Berg. "So I reckon I'll take care of that bastard. Don't you worry. Now I'll be gettin' along."

She put one hand on his shoulder. She said: "Thank you, Rene. I knew I could talk to you. I knew I could rely on you."

Berg moved away from the fireplace. He said: "Well, Clovis, thanks for havin' me around here. Thanks for tellin' me all this. Don't you worry about it. I'll look after that so-an'-so. Maybe we'll be all the better off for it too."

He moved towards the door. He was half-way there when she said: "Rene, aren't you going to say good-night to me?

He put out his hand. He said: "Well, good-night, Clovis. Thanks a lot."

She put her hand in his, but she did not shake it. She drew him towards her. One arm went round his neck. He felt her mouth on his. He thought: What the hell! What the hell!

Somehow the light went out.

VII

Berg stood in the quiet street outside the apartment block. He thought that this was one of those times when something very definite was indicated. He remembered other times in his life when he had been possessed by the same feeling—a desire, an urge, almost uncontrollable, towards harsh action. He stood there, thinking about Clovis Scansci—the whole setup. The thing he had in his mind—the thing he planned to do—seemed to him one of those things which was indicated by a higher fate. The fact that the indication was due to his association with Clovis, with several large whiskies and sodas, was not at all plain to him. In his own rather simple mind the indication was clear-cut.

A yellow cab came by. Berg flagged it; got inside. He told the man where to go. Inside the cab, he relaxed and tried to think logically.

Actually he was unable to think. He was unable to think because a peculiar exultation—due probably to the recent proximity of Clovis; to what had happened—possessed his mind. It was only when the yellow cab stopped outside the three-storey brown stone house that he came back to reality.

He got out, paid the driver. He waited until the cab went away. Then he walked up the short flight of steps, knocked three times—then twice—on the front door. After a moment it opened. Berg went inside. He followed the boy who had opened the door along the dim evil-smelling passageway into the room at the back of the house. The room looked like a small armoury. The workbench on the right of the room was covered with pistols, automatics, every sort of firearm, with sawn-off shotguns predominating.

Berg took off his hat, lit a cigarette. The boy went away. Two or three minutes passed. A man came into the room. He was short, squat, grey-haired, with a peculiar permanently twisted smile.

He said: "Hallo, Rene. You want something?"

Berg said: "Yeah, Charlie. You know you usta have a .38 Police Positive—a nice gun—with a silencer. You still got it?"

Charlie said: "Yeah, I got it."

Berg said: "O.K. You give it to me."

Charlie looked at him for a moment; then he went to a cupboard on the other side of the room; opened it. The cupboard was full of pistols of every sort hanging by the trigger guards on nails. He took a gun down. It was a .38 Police Positive with three inches sawn off the barrel and a silencer fitted over it.

He said: "It's a nice gun. It's done a lot of work. How many shells do you want?"

Berg said: "Just fill it." He waited while Charlie went to a drawer, produced seven .38 cartridges, put them in the gun. He handed it to Berg.

Berg put the gun in his pocket. He said: "O.K., Charlie. Thanks a lot."

Charlie said: "You're workin'?"

Berg said: "Yeah, I'm workin'. I'll be seein' you." He went away.

Outside it was cold. A keen wind was blowing. Berg walked two or three blocks westward. He went into a call-box at Grapevine and Twenty-second. He took a little book from his pocket; looked up a number. He put a nickel in the box; waited.

After a moment he said: "I wanta talk to Mr. Calsimo. This is Rene Berg. Nobody else—just Mr. Calsimo."

He waited. He filled in the time by fishing out a cigarette from his pocket, lighting it. Then someone spoke to him.

Berg said: "Hey . . . that you, Calsimo? This is Rene Berg. Maybe you're surprised at talkin' to me. One of those things, hey? But I wanta talk to you an' it's important."

There was a pause; then Berg said: "Look, you don't haveta worry. I'm comin' round an' I haven't even got a gun. Yeah . . . it's like that. Maybe I'm a wise guy. Maybe I know how things are goin' these days. I like to be on the winnin' side, you know. . . . All right, in half an hour. I'll be seein' you."

He put the receiver back on its hook. He went outside the call-box and stood in the cool night air thinking. He walked two blocks, picked up a taxicab, went back to his hotel.

Up in his bedroom, he took off his hat, coat, underneath coat; washed. He looked at himself in the glass. He thought: This is a star evening with you, Berg. You gotta be good an' I hope it comes off. All the time, at the back of his mind was a picture of Clovis, of her eyes—violet or blue or whatever they were—looking at him beseechingly. He thought to himself: You've got to be a big guy. You must be. Any guy who could make Clovis is good. An' you've made the grade.

He opened a drawer; took out a roll of three-inch adhesive plaster, a pair of scissors. He put the adhesive plaster and the scissors on the dressing-table in front of him. Then he went into the bathroom. He pulled up his trouser leg, took a safety razor, wetted his leg and shaved the hairs from it. He went back into the bedroom. He pulled up his trouser leg; pushed the barrel of the .38 Police Positive into the top of his sock. He stuck a piece of adhesive plaster over the gun, a second piece over the cylinder, a third piece over the butt. He pulled down his trouser leg, shook his leg. The gun was secure, stuck to the inside of his left calf. He put on his coat, overcoat, hat; took a bottle from the cupboard in the corner, put the neck in his mouth, took a long swig. He went out.

He walked until he found a cab; told the man to drive him to a corner a hundred yards east of Riverside Apartments.

When the cab stopped, Berg got out, paid off the man, began to walk. He thought that Calsimo would either believe the story or not, but the way Berg worked it out he would believe it. He thought: If Travis is scared, Scansci's scared. If Scansci's scared, Calsimo's scared. It seemed to Berg that maybe everybody was a little scared.

Five minutes afterwards he turned into the ornate block of apartments on Riverside. He walked down the long luxuriously carpeted passageway. At the end was the elevator. Lounging in front of it, one leaning against the wall, the other extended in a gilt and velvet chair, was Calsimo's bodyguard—two six feet moron-faced gorillas.

Berg said: "Hallo, guys. A nice cold evenin', hey?"

The man in the chair got up. He said: "Yeah . . . you wouldn't be startin' anything, wouldya?"

Berg opened his coat, put his hand in an inside pocket, brought out a cigarette case. He grinned as their hands went towards their hip pockets. He said: "It's all right, fellas. I'm gonna have a cigarette, that's all. You wouldn't be scared of anything, would you?"

The other man said: "Listen, Rene, we heard about you. What's the big idea?"

Berg said: "What the hell's that gotta do with you, bastard? I don't talk to punks like you. I got a date with Mr. Calsimo."

The first man said: "Nice guy, ain'tya? You wouldn't have a rod, would you, Berg?"

Berg said: "I didn't come here and not expect to be frisked. Have a look."

The man did what Berg thought he would do. He ran his hands over both sides of Berg's body, down the hips, down to the thighs. He said: "O.K., Rene, you're all right. Second floor. The big shot's waitin' for you."

Berg said: "Thanks a lot." He stepped into the elevator, closed the gates, pressed the button. The elevator moved swiftly to the second floor. Berg got out. There was another man waiting outside the elevator gate. He grinned sourly. He was a hefty, white-faced Italian.

He said: "Hallo, Boig . . . I never expected to see you kickin' around here."

Berg said: "Well, you never know what's gonna happen. It's a wise guy gets in first."

The Italian said: "So you founda that out. I reckon you're wise enough. Come on."

He took Berg along the passageway, stopped at a door. He knocked. A voice said to come in. The Italian opened the door; said to Berg: "It's all yours. Get in."

Berg went inside. Calsimo was sitting at a table on the right-hand side of the room. He was a thin, black-haired man with a sharp thin face. His eyes were small. He had a little black moustache.

He said: "Good-evening, Rene. This is an unexpected pleasure." He spoke English carefully, almost perfectly. "What's the trouble, boy?"

Berg said: "Look, Calsimo, maybe you heard about me?"

Calsimo nodded. He smiled pleasantly. He said: "I heard about you plenty, Berg . . . quite a lot. Tm terribly interested to know what you want to talk to me about."

Berg said: "It oughta be pretty obvious, Calsimo."

Calsimo shrugged his shoulders. He said: "When a guy out of the Scansci organisation makes a date to see me an' don't bring a gun with him I know it's business. Maybe you'd like a drink?"

Berg said: "Why not?"

Calsimo got the drinks. He poured two big ones; handed one to Berg. He said: "Shoot, kid. So you're coming over to us?"

Berg shrugged his shoulders. He said: "Why not? I'm no mug. I know the way things are goin'."

Calsimo said: "Sure! You'd be a mug if you didn't. I'm taking this town." He laughed. He went on: "I'll tell you something. The only thing that's ever worried me was you. You're tough and you got brains. I like your comin' over here. Maybe we can do some business together."

Berg said: "That's what I thought." He drank some of the whisky.

Calsimo said: "Sit down. Take the weight off your feet an' tell me the story."

Berg pulled up a chair. He sat near the end of the table at an angle from Calsimo. He crossed his legs, bringing the left leg over the right.

He said: "Look, I know what's good for me. I think Scansci's had it. He's been a big boy. He's played it off the cuff the right way. Everything's been fine, but every good thing comes to an end. Maybe he's through."

Calsimo said: "Yeah?" He looked at Berg, his eyebrows raised. He was smiling. His face indicated polite inquiry.

Berg said: "Listen, Calsimo. I'm talkin' straight. I reckon Scansci's out. You know, he's sorta slippin'. . . . I think. Maybe he's drinkin' a little too much. Maybe he's got other interests."

Calsimo said: "Yes, maybe he has. That wife of his—so lovely . . . so beautiful. Maybe he's rather interested in her . . . perhaps too much."

Berg thought: You bastard. I'm wise to you. So what she said was right. That's how you're gonna play it. Like hell you are! But he said: "I reckon you're right, Calsimo. But you an' me don't wanta go into this an' that. If I come over to you how does it break?"

Calsimo said: "What's Scansci giving you?"

Berg said: "Anything I want. I draw up to a thousand a week. I charge the accounts wherever I go where he's got one. He's given me a pretty good deal."

Calsimo said: "I'll give you a better one. You come over to me and I'll give you ten grand as a present." He looked at Berg. His expression changed. His small eyes glittered. "But if you come over, you work, see? There's only goin' to be one boss in this town an' that's goin' to be me. You get ten grand an' one and a half grand a week till we clean the job up. After that we'll talk again."

Berg said: "What about the cops?"

Calsimo laughed. He said: "Look, I know those boys. They never interfere with me. You know that, Berg. You should worry about them."

Berg said: "O.K. That's a bet." He picked up his glass. He said: "Well, here's to it. I'm all yours."

Calsimo said: "I'll tell you something." He finished his own drink. "I'm glad you done this, Berg. With you, we're goin' places. With you, this man's town belongs to me in about three weeks."

Berg said: "Why three weeks? I should think it would take about three days."

Calsimo said: "Yeah? But there's just one little thing. All this is fine, but there's just one little thing."

Berg said: "What's the little thing?"

Calsimo looked at him. He said: "You couldn't guess, could you? Look, I gotta have Scansci. You come over to me an' everything's fine. You get the jake. We look after you. So you sort of got to give us a guarantee, see? We gotta have Scansci. You got me?"

Berg said: "Sure, that's O.K. Why not?"

Calsimo poured some more whisky. He said: "Fella, now you're talkin'. How long is it gonna take you to do that?"

Berg said: "He's away. You know that?"

Calsimo nodded. "You're tellin' me," he said. "You picked a good time to see me. When will he be back?"

"Two three days," said Berg. "I'll have him within a week from the day he comes back." He was thinking to himself: All you big guys are the same. You all think you got something. You all think you can buy anything. He repeated: "I'll have him within a week of the time he comes back. O.K.?"

Calsimo said: "O.K." He picked up his glass. He said: "Here's to it, fella." They drank.

Calsimo opened a drawer. He said: "Here's a sort of little bonus on account. You're a good guy, Rene. I reckon you're the best gorilla around town. There ain't been anybody ever like you in Chi. I'm glad to have you with me." He produced a flat new packet of bills. He put them at the end of the table.

He said: "That's the sort of guy I am. There's ten grand on the side, spare—just to bind the agreement. Buy yourself a coupla drinks, Rene."

Berg said: "Thanks a lot." He picked up the packet of bills, held them in his hand. He said: "Just a little thing I came here straight to-night—you know, no funny business. Just walked in the front entrance. The boys expected me. That was O.K. But you never know. Scansci's been a bit leery lately—sorta funny, see? You never know, he might have told Travis Hahn or some guy to keep an eye on me. When I leave here I'd like to go out the back way."

Calsimo laughed. He said: "You're a wise guy. In the days when I usta carry a gun I was like that myself." He went on: "Look, when you leave here, walk along the passage the opposite way to the way you come in. You'll find a service elevator. They use it to bring the luggage up. Go down in that. There is only one boy on the back entrance an' he knows about you."

Berg said: "Thanks a lot. Well, one for the road, Calsimo. It's been nice meetin' you."

Calsimo said: "Sure, you're a smart guy, you know, the way things are goin'. I like you comin' here." He poured out two more drinks.

Berg split the band round the packet of bills. He split the packet in half, took one-half of the bills, pulled up his right trouser leg, undid the suspender, pushed the packet of bills down inside the top of his sock. He pulled up his sock, reclasped the suspender. Calsimo watched him.

He said: "A wise guy, hey? You carry the dough in your socks?"

Berg said: "Why not? It's an old habit of mine; a silly habit, but that's the way I play it."

He took the second half of the bills in his left hand. He pulled up his left trouser leg, slowly. He put his hand on the butt of the gun and yanked it with the adhesive plaster off his leg. The plaster tore the top skin off. Berg never moved a muscle. He sat quite still in the chair, the gun in his hand.

He said: "Listen, Calsimo, you thought you was gonna get away with something big, hey? You thought you were gonna snatch Clovis Scansci. You made a hell of a mistake, fella. You're all talk. Here's where you get it."

Calsimo looked at him. His hands were flat on the table in front of him. Three or four little beads of sweat stood out on his forehead.

He said: "Listen, Rene . . . you listen to me . . ."

Berg squeezed the trigger four times. The gun made a little noise like the popping of a champagne cork. The four shots took Calsimo in the stomach and upwards. He slumped over the desk. For a moment, his head lying on the desk, he pressed his hands to his stomach. The blood began to drip on to the carpet.

Berg got up. He thought to himself: You were a mug to use four shells. There's a guy on the back door . . . you only got three left. He put the second packet of bills in his left-hand overcoat pocket.

He said: "Well, so long, Calsimo." He went out of the room, closed the door softly behind him.

Downstairs, at the bottom of the service elevator, a redheaded tough was lounging. He pushed himself away from the wall as the elevator came down.

He said: "Hallo, Berg. Nice to see you around here. You had a good time?"

Berg said: "Yeah. I talked turkey an' it's O.K. I'm with you from now on."

The gunman said: "Swell. That's what I like to hear. You're a great guy, Rene. We like you. You got a nice method."

Berg said: "Fine. I'm O.K. for gettin' out? Nobody way down the passage, hey?"

The gunman said: "Well, we're careful, you know. But you're O.K. Stick around here. When the big boy buzzes upstairs you go out. Just a matter of form, you know. That's the system around here. Pretty good, hey? Checked in at the front an' buzzed out at the back."

Berg thought quickly. He said: "You wouldn't have a snifter, would you? It's a cold night an' I'm walkin'. No cab, see?"

The other said: "Wise guy. Those drivers remember too much. Come in here. I got one for you."

They went down the basement stairs into a small room. The drinks were poured out. They drank.

The man said: "You know, when we heard you was comin' here to-night, we thought there was gonna be a lot of trouble until we heard you wasn't carryin' a gun; then we knew how it was. We sort of got the idea you was comin' in with us."

Berg said: "Sure . . . have a cigarette." He put his hand into the pocket of his overcoat. He brought out the gun. He said: "You guys indulge in daydreams, don't you? Why don't you grow up?"

He fired once. The glass made an odd sound as it smashed on the cement floor. Berg looked at the man as he lay on the floor. There was a surprised expression on his face.

Berg tipped his hat. He said: "Well, that's how it is, fella! That's how it is!"

He walked out of the room, up the stairs, along the passage-way, into the street.

Berg lay on his bed smoking a cigarette, looking at the ceiling. He grinned. He thought next day there would be a fine how-d'you-do about the Calsimo thing. They'd have something to think about all right. He wondered what Margolez—Calsimo's lieutenant—now the big shot of the Calsimo organisation—would do about it. Maybe now that the big boy was dead they'd take things easy. They might even let it ride. They might. Or else . . .

Well, if they weren't going to let it ride he'd have to look out for himself. He looked at his watch. It was just after three. Berg thought to himself: Fella, you've had a busy evening what with one thing and another. He remembered Clovis. The very thought of the two hours he had spent with her affected him to such a degree that he wondered at it. He remembered another biblical expression from his Sunday School—something about a man's knees turning to water. That was how Clovis made you feel.

He swung his legs off the bed, went over to the sideboard, took a flask out of the drawer, took a long pull. The whisky tasted good. Berg went back and sat on the bed, the flask in one hand, a cigarette in the other. He was thinking: Fella, now you've gotta be careful. Positively you got to be careful.

The telephone jangled. Berg put the flask down on the bed, took up the receiver. It was Travis.

Travis said: "For Chrissake . . . you've pulled a fast one, hey? The whole town's talkin'. Wait till the news-sheets hit the street to-morrow morning. They tell me they're printin' special editions now. For God's sake . . . what's the matter with you? What did you haveta pull that one for?"

Berg said: "Listen, Travis. Do I have to go in for long spiels on the telephone? What the hell! An' what's the matter anyway? I thought you'd be plenty pleased. What's eatin' you?"

Travis said: "Look, fella, I'm pleased enough. That's O.K. by me, but I'd like to know what Paul Scansci's gonna say about this one."

Berg said: "You mean to say he's not gonna like it? He's got to like it. He's sittin' on top of the heap now."

Travis said: "Well, maybe he is. For how long? What d'you think the Calsimo mob are gonna do about this? D'you think Margolez is just gonna sit down an' smoke cigarettes? That boy is gonna get crackin'. I reckon Scansci'll haveta live inside a bullet-proof car now permanently."

Berg put his hand out, picked up the flask. He took another swig. He said: "You mean Margolez is liable to get tough?"

Travis said: "Why not?"

Berg said: "O.K. If he gets funny we'll have him too."

Travis sighed. "Look, fella, we don't wanta start a Battle of Waterloo around here. Our job is sellin' hooch."

Berg said: "Yeah . . . I know all about that. Maybe I know one or two things that you don't know. Maybe when you get wise you'll say I was right in doin' what I did—right every time." He went on: "As a matter of fact I like it. I never liked that guy Calsimo."

Travis said: "I'll say one thing for you, Rene, you've got your nerve all right. You'll haveta watch out for yourself now. They'll be after you."

Berg said: "Yeah? So what?"

There was a pause; then Travis said: "Say, listen, Rene, what's the big idea? What did you do it for? You said just now you knew something I didn't know. I reckon this is the first time you've gone off sky-rocketin' on your own creasin' some guy before I told you to. Maybe you'll wise me up to this. Maybe you'll tell me what it is that you know an' I don't."

Berg said: "You ask Lauren. Lauren gave me a tip-off. She asked me to do something. Well, I did it. I'm not gonna say what I did or who I was with or what we talked about. Maybe I'll tell you next time I see you. I'll think it over. But take it from me, Travis, that what I did is right. If I hadn't, I reckon Calsimo woulda put paid to us. He'd have finished us."

Travis said: "Yeah . . ." His tone was doubtful. He went on: "Well, what's done is done. We'll haveta see what happens, but I'm not feelin' so good. Any time I go out from now on I'll wish I was wearin' a suit of armour plate."

Berg said: "Aw . . . hell! What's the use of bein' scared? It's the guy who's afraid of gettin' bumped off who always gets bumped off. Personally, if somebody can pull a gun quicker than I can then I'm gonna *get* it and that's that."

Travis said cynically: "Maybe you like the idea of dyin', Rene?"

Berg said: "No . . . definitely not—not *now*."

The inflection in Travis's voice went up. "What's this . . . not now? What's happened that you're so keen on goin' on livin, fella, *after* you bumped this mug Calsimo?"

Berg said: "It don't matter, Travis—just one of those things." He took another swig at the flask.

Travis said: "O.K. If I was you I'd stick around in your hotel for a day or two. There's gonna be hell poppin' over this. You stay where you are until I see you. You got that? Maybe we can straighten this out. I've got an idea Margolez will be callin' through some time in the mornin'."

Berg said: "Yeah? What for?"

Travis said: "It's natural, ain't it? He'll have made up his mind what he's gonna do. I reckon he's liable to tell me too."

Berg said: "O.K. To-morrow oughta be good. But I'll do what you say, Travis. Ill stick around here until I see you; then maybe I'll know where I am. So long, fella." He hung up. It seemed to him now that Travis was not a very big personality after all. Berg began to see himself as a big—important—person. Margolez and the Calsimo mob scared him not at all. He was above himself and the whisky had made him feel very good. He went over to the bedroom door, locked it. He undressed, took a shower in the adjoining bathroom, got into bed. He put one of the .45 automatics under the pillow, butt downwards where his hand could quickly find it . . . in case.

Lauren, who was wearing a padded silk dressing-gown, her small feet encased in velvet mules, brought the whisky bottle and the glass over to Travis where he sat by the fire.

She said: "Well, he's done it. I knew he would."

Travis said: "Yeah, it's come off. The next thing is how's Scansci gonna take it."

Lauren said: "Paul's not gonna take it so well. He's gonna be all steamed up about this—more than you think."

Travis said: "Is he? Why should he be? Maybe this thing'll sort of blow over. Look . . ." He leaned forward, poured out the whisky, took a gulp. He repeated: "Look . . . maybe the cops are gonna be pleased about this, see? They got rid of Calsimo. O.K. This guy Margolez, who'll be runnin' the mob now, he's a brainy guy. So I reckon he's gonna be for a quiet life. I reckon we can do a deal with that guy. Maybe it's gonna be better than it was before. Anyhow, I reckon it's gonna be easier for us."

Lauren said: "Scansci's goin' to be burned up to hell over this."

Travis looked at her. He said: "Look, gorgeous, what is it that you know that I don't? You're holdin' out again, hey?"

She came over, stood on the opposite side of. the fireplace, looking down at him. A little smile played about the corners of her mouth.

She said: "Look, Unconscious, where's Scansci now? He was goin' away for three days, wasn't he? O.K. Where was he goin' to? He usually lets you know, doesn't he? But he didn't this time. Nobody knew where he was goin'."

Travis said: "Yeah, that's right. He just took one of the boys, said he'd be back in three days an' scrammed. Anyhow, that's what Clovis said."

Lauren nodded. "You know what the other thing is?" she went on. "Maybe you didn't know, but Calsimo was goin' away. He was takin' a trip too. He was goin' to-morrow morning. Not that he'll haveta worry about it now. You got that?"

Travis said: "Why the hell don't you say what you mean? I've got nothing. I don't know what you're talkin' about."

Lauren said: "Listen . . . Calsimo an' Scansci had fixed up to have a meetin'. Calsimo was goin' to join in with Scansci. They were goin' to run the town together. What d'you know about that one?"

Travis said: "Jeez . . . what d'you know? And Scansci told nobody. Maybe he was right." Travis, his eyes excited, got up. He put the bottle and the glass on the mantelpiece. He said: "Look, where'd you get this from?"

Lauren said: "Clovis. Scansci never talked to anybody much over this, but there's one time he does talk. He talks in his sleep."

Travis said: "For cryin' out loud! Is he gonna be steamed up?"

Lauren laughed. "Steamed up," she said. "He's gonna blow his top. Wait till he hears about this. I reckon he's sittin' in some dump on Long Island or somewhere or other waitin' for Calsimo to turn up, thinkin' that everything is hunky dory, thinkin' that nobody need be scared any more because they're gonna run the job together. Wait till somebody tells him!" She laughed again. "Is he goin' to be pleased when he hears that Rene's bumped off Calsimo at the wrong moment? Is it funny or is it?"

Travis said: "It might not be so funny for Berg."

Lauren raised her eyebrows. She said: "No? D'you think Rene'll be scared?"

Travis shook his head. "Nothin' scares that guy," he said.

Lauren said: "Listen, Travis, when Paul comes back he's not goin' to be so pleased with Berg, is he? Supposing . . . supposin' just for the sake of argument . . ." She stopped.

Travis said: "Go on . . . cough it up. What's the next move?"

Lauren said softly: "Scansci ain't gonna be so pleased with Berg. Supposin' somebody was to tell Scansci that Rene was around there in the apartment with Clovis for nearly three hours to-night, after which he goes an' knocks off Calsimo . . ."

Travis said: "Yeah? An' who's gonna have the guts to tell Scansci that . . . me?"

Lauren shook her head. She said: "No . . . but Truda, the maid around there, might, mightn't she?"

Travis whistled through his teeth. He said: "Jeez! She might at that."

"All right," said Lauren. "So Scansci is gonna have a showdown with Rene, hey? He's goin' to be goddam rude to Rene. He's goin' to say things about Clovis. Maybe he's goin' to have the Berg boy knocked off. You see what happens?"

Travis said: "You tell me."

Lauren said: "You know, Rene don't like Scansci. He's certainly not gonna like him after . . ." She smiled slowly . . . "the three hours with Clovis. He's a bad-tempered fella, that Rene. I know what he'll do."

Travis said: "You mean he'll take Paul?"

She nodded. "If he don't fog Scansci I'm an Indian princess with a cork leg," she said. "Anyway, it's worth tryin'. No harm can come of it if no good does."

Travis said: "You think! So if somebody gets this maid to spill the beans to Scansci it's not gonna be so good for Clovis."

Lauren said: "Don't worry about her. She can look after herself. Besides, it's her idea."

Travis said: "My God, you frails! You're worse than any goddam gunsel in Chicago."

Lauren put a curl back into place. She said: "Yeah, somebody's got to look after you mugs. Listen, honey, supposin' this thing comes off . . . supposin' Rene creases Paul. O.K. You make a deal with Margolez. Let's have a little quiet around here, with you an' Margolez runnin' this dump."

Travis said: "Yeah . . . and what about Rene?"

She shrugged her shoulders. She said: "Well, the cops'll want somebody, won't they?"

Travis looked at her. His eyes narrowed. He said: "You beat everything. I reckon inside you're as black as hell. I reckon you'd send me out without a thought if you wanted to."

She poured some whisky into the glass, handed it to him. She said: "An' why not? You'd do the same for me any time. Don't let you an' me kid each other, Travis."

They both drank from the same glass.

VIII

Eight nights after the Calsimo shooting, Berg knocked on the back door of the Barrell Street garage. The door was a small wooden one, set in the steel shutter which moved up and down by electricity. Berg tapped impatiently on the door for the third time; stood, his back against the shutter, his hand in his right-hand pocket, looking up and down the street.

It was very late. There was a cold wind and a little rain. A sudden gust of wind blew the large drops against Berg's face. He found the process refreshing. The door opened.

Shakkey, a gun in one hand, a torch in the other, put his head out. He said: "Hallo, kid. What's new? Somebody on your tail?"

Berg said: "I wouldn't know, Shakkey. I need a drink."

Shakkey said, grinning: "Come on in. We got lots of liquor."

Berg stepped through the frame door. Shakkey shut it, locked it, pulled down the additional steel shutter behind it. The garage was practically a fortress. He switched on his torch. Berg followed him across the wide stone floor between the rows of carefully parked trucks into the little office in the corner. He sat down.

Shakkey got a bottle and two glasses. He poured out the drinks. He said: "You know, Rene, it's goddam funny. Seein' you sittin' in this office makes me remember the day when you first come to town—that night I found you lyin' outside. I sorta suggested to Travis we might give you a job down here in the office, sort of keepin' an eye on the truck drivers an' guards. Maybe it was a pity you didn't take the job, although there wouldn't have been quite so much dough in it."

Berg said: "Maybe you're right, Shakkey." He finished the whisky. Shakkey poured out another slug.

He said: "You started something when you did this Calsimo thing. I reckon it ain't gonna be so healthy for you for a bit, not until it sort of settles down."

Berg said: "I reckon it ain't gonna settle down—not now. Not for a long time."

Shakkey lit a cigarette. He said: "I wouldn't go so far as to say that. I reckon Margolez is gonna play this the easy way. Maybe he'll want to patch it up with Scansci. Everybody's pretty fed up with the killin's around this city. They're gettin' sort of tired of it."

Berg said: "Margolez won't patch anything up with Scansci."

Shakkey reached for the bottle. He said: "No? Why not?"

Berg said: "I fogged Scansci half an hour ago up in his apartment."

Shakkey put the bottle on the table. He said: "Jeez . . . are you ribbin' or do you mean this?"

Berg said: "I'm not ribbin'. I went up there to-night. He wanted to talk to me about this Calsimo thing. He was steamed up." He laughed. "You know why he was steamed up."

Shakkey said: "Maybe I could make a guess."

Berg said: "He went out of town to meet Calsimo. They were gonna patch this thing up and go in together, see? One organisation to supply the whole city. Calsimo was due to leave to meet Scansci the mornin' after I shot him. So you can bet Scansci wasn't so pleased when he heard the news."

Shakkey said: "No, he wouldn't be. Did you haveta kill him for that?"

Berg said: "Not for that. Look, Shakkey, I shot Calsimo because I heard he was gonna try an' snatch Clovis Scansci. That's why I shot him."

Shakkey began to laugh. "Ain't you the nut?" he said. "So Calsimo was gonna snatch Clovis Scansci just at the time he's meetin' up with Paul Scansci to go into partnership with him. It don't make sense. Who told you that one?"

Berg said: "Clovis Scansci told me. Why should she tell a lie? A good dame, that one. She's had a tough time. She was scared."

Shakkey said: "Scared my fanny!" He poured out two more drinks. He picked up his own glass and sat looking at the amber fluid. He thought for a long time. He said: "You know, Rene, when you came round to this burg I offered you a job-—not much of a job—but I wish you'd taken it. You ain't a bad kid, see? So Travis hadta frame you into that Rose Dean job an' you went in on the gun side. It looks to me like somebody's been takin' you for a ride again."

Berg said: "How come?"

Shakkey said: "Listen, here's the story. Scansci an' Calsimo are gonna meet, straighten things out, go in together. Well, somebody don't like that. I reckon that somebody was Clovis Scansci. So she tells you a hard-luck story . . . Calsimo's gonna snatch her. So you fix Calsimo. I don't know what there was on between you an' Clovis Scansci but she's a tough egg, that one. I know her. Maybe she let Paul hear about it somehow when he came back. Maybe that's why he got funny with you to-night. Maybe he told you he was gonna have you took for a ride, hey?"

Berg said: "Yeah . . . something like that."

Shakkey nodded. "So you give it to him first," he said. "It's a pretty good position for somebody."

Berg said: "Yeah? Who?"

Shakkey said: "I could make a coupla guesses. It's a pretty good position for Clovis an' the guy she's stuck on."

Berg said: "Yeah? Who's the guy?"

Shakkey looked at him. He grinned. "Who d'you think, mug?" he said. "Travis Hahn. Now it's in the bag for Travis. He an' Margolez settle this job up an' they're the big shots."

Berg said: "Yeah . . . an' what about me? Where do I come in?" For once there was a little bitterness in his voice.

Shakkey said: "You don't. Everybody around here is tired of this gunplay. Chicago's sick of it. The Feds are comin' in. This place is gonna be cleaned up. This killin' has just about put the edge on it. Somebody'll haveta go up for this. You know who that somebody's gonna be, don't you?"

Berg gave a little sigh. "It looks like me."

Shakkey said: "You're right. An' this time you'll find Mr. Linney won't be around tryin' to pull a *habeas corpus* act to get you out again. This time they'll let 'em fry you, kid."

Berg said softly: "Yeah? So what? Maybe I'll have a talk with Travis."

Shakkey shook his head. He said: "Look, mug, why don't you get some sense? You go an' have a talk with Travis. There's only one thing you can talk with an' that's a rod. An' you've been doin' a little too much talkin' with rods lately." He smiled—not an unfriendly smile. It illuminated his thin comedian's face. He said: "Look, fella, you take a tip from me. You get outa here. You get outa here before this thing gets around. Nobody's heard about it yet."

Berg said: "No, they wouldn't, but they will in a minute."

Shakkey went to a desk in the corner. He unlocked it. He came back to the table, threw a thick wad of bills tied with string in front of Berg.

He said: "Look, this is the first time I double-crossed the organisation. That's to-day's take on the East Side for liquor. There's a car in the garage with new number-plates on it—a fast one. You get outa here an' keep goin'. What the hell d'you wanta stay an' be fried for? They tell me it's goddam uncomfortable in the hot seat."

Berg looked at the bills on the table. He said: "It's swell of you, Shakkey. But what the hell's the use of me scrammin' out of here? Maybe they'll get me some place else."

Shakkey said: "An' maybe not. Look, maybe the cops aren't gonna be so unpleased about this. Of course they'll have to beef off about it, but with the two big bad wolves in this town bein' ironed out inside two weeks of each other, I bet the cops are chortlin'. No more Calsimo and no more Scansci. I reckon they can get in now an' fix things so there'll be a little peace. An' Travis is the sort of guy to want peace, an' so is Margolez. Nobody could accuse either of those two as bein' too nervy—too brave. They like livin'. Maybe if you got outa here good an' quick they wouldn't worry about you so much. Maybe you'd get away with it. It's worth tryin'."

Berg said: "Yeah? Why?"

Shakkey said: "What have you got to lose, kid? Look, you been taken for a ride. You been taken for a ride by Travis an' by Clovis Scansci. Every goddam person in the organisation has had somethin' from you one way or another. You're just the world's biggest mug, hey? You're not twenty-five; you've got a lot of years in front of you. Why don't you get the hell out of here an give yourself a break?"

He poured out two more drinks. "Go on, kid," he said. "Do something for me for once. For Chrissake get outa here."

Berg picked up the glass. He drained it slowly; then he got up, picked up the bills, put them in his pocket. He said: "Thanks a lot, Shakkey. I reckon you're a good guy. I wish I'd taken the little job you offered me a long time ago."

Shakkey said: "Me too. Come on. You've got to get goin'."

They went into the garage. The car, newly sprayed, just serviced, showed resplendently under the electric light.

Shakkey said: "The place for a guy like you is South America. If you wanta get scrappin' you can get it down there. There's always a civil war goin' on, an' nobody gives a hell how many people you kill. I reckon you'd do well there."

Berg got into the car.

Shakkey said: "There's fifteen gallons in the tank; another twenty in the big reserve tank at the back. Don't stop before you're a long way out. Ill give you the route an' garages to fill up at—places where they won't talk."

He tore off a sheet from the invoice book from his hip pocket, took a stub of pencil from behind one large ear. He began to write. When he had finished he handed the piece of paper to Berg.

He said: "There you are, kid. You got a car, dough an' juice. Now get out here. Try an' go on livin'."

He went to the wall; threw over the lever. Slowly the wall shutter of the garage began to rise. He stopped it at eight feet.

He said: "So long, kid."

Berg said: "So long, Shakkey. Thanks a lot."

The car moved slowly out into the street. Shakkey threw over the lever. The shutter came down. He turned out the lights; walked back into the little office in the corner. He poured out a drink.

He said to himself: "The goddam silly young bastard! The goddam nut!" He shrugged his shoulders.

CHAPTER THREE
HILDE
Norway—September, 1940

THE girl Ingrid walked with slow almost hesitant steps to the spot where the country road leading away from Skaalund divided. She took the left fork. A hundred yards down the road she could see a crack of light from one of the side windows of the *kroj*.

Now she hastened her steps a little. When she arrived at the door of the one-storied beer-house she looked quickly up and down the road; pushed the door open enough for her to edge sideways through. She shut the door behind her; stood, her back to the door, the palms of her hands pressed flat against it, looking about her. The bar parlour was long, low-ceilinged. The walls were of logs. An open fire burned at one end. There were rough tables here and there, and at the right end a bar. Two or three men leant against the counter and two sat at opposite tables. The silence was heavy in the room.

The girl Ingrid went up to the counter. The host, portly, red-faced, looked at her for a moment. His eyes were a little pitiful. He filled a mug with dark beer, pushed it towards her. They stood looking at each other. Then she picked up the mug; moved to a table by the side of the fire. She put the mug on the table, sat down in the chair. She was looking at the froth on the top of the mug. At the same time she was biting her lips to stop the tears from welling into her eyes. She thought that she had never felt so bitterly before.

She sat there, her eyes on the beer mug, her hands in her lap. After a while she looked down, saw that her fingers were trembling. She concentrated on keeping them still, but she could not do this. She found that the only way to master the trembling in her hands was by locking the ringers together in her lap.

One of the men at the counter began to speak to the landlord in a low voice. He was not a local man. He was from Bardu. He said: "What's the matter? Is it those swine again? Is it those swine?"

The landlord said: "Keep quiet, Sven. It isn't good to talk. It is much better to keep quiet."

The man called Sven said: "I never thought I should have to keep my tongue silent in Norway."

The landlord shrugged. He said: "What is there to talk about, Sven?" He poured out another mug of beer. Drinking it, he looked over the edge of the mug towards the girl Ingrid, who sat looking into the fire, her fingers locked together.

Berg came out of the house, which had been taken as a local police barracks, with Nielenberg. They stood at the top of the steps. Berg turned up his overcoat collar.

Nielenberg stretched, banged his great hands on his chest. He was a big fine specimen of manhood, over six feet; his uniform, that of a Feldwebel in the German Field Gendarmerie, sat well on his compact body. The tunic was a little tight, the collar a little too high, but Neilenberg liked that. He knew he was a fine figure of a man. He hoped the women would eventually know it. The fact that he had not been very successful since he had been in the Skaalund district annoyed him very little. He thought there was lots of time. All sorts of things would be happening in Norway, and the women must, finally, learn sense.

Nielenberg spent a great deal of time thinking about Norwegian women. He was a product of the Army and the S.S. Police Training School—big, strong, intelligent, if anything over-trained.

He said to Berg in careful, good English: "My friend, you can take it from me that what I tell you is right. We have got too big a start. The British, who are very good at makeshift measures, cannot possibly compete with or catch up with our German military production. Realise the poorness of their equipment used here—a few territorial regiments, practically no artillery, certainly no air support."

They began to walk down the street. "Make no mistake," the Feldwebel continued, "these British are brave men. They can fight, but to fight you have to have weapons and leaders. By the time they begin to develop the resources of their Empire for war; by the time they get into their stride . . ." He shrugged his shoulders, "The war will be over. This Norway is just a little thing. The Fuehrer has everything tied down to a timetable. You will see."

Berg said: "Yeah?" He thought maybe the German was right.

"Also there is another thing," the Feldwebel continued. "An important thing. Your own country. People say that the Americans are helping the British." He shrugged his shoulders again. "That's all right. People also say," he went on, "that America may even come into the war on the side of the British." He smiled. "I think there will be a great deal of trouble in America before that happens. I do not believe that your countrymen realise the strength of the German Secret Service movements in America—of our secret *Bunds* out there. But supposing that eventually America were to come in, it would still be too late."

Berg said: "You might be right at that." He looked at the Feldwebel sideways. "And the thing for me to do is to join the German Army, hey?"

Nielenberg said: "Why not?" He laughed. "I know all about you, my friend," he said, "just as we know all about every foreigner who is in this country. It is our business to know. Besides, you have told me some things. You are an experienced fighter. You have killed men. You are young, intelligent, strong. Now you have your chance. Become a German; adopt our nationality; go to one of our training schools. The army will look after you. Before you know where you are you will be wearing a shoulder strap—a red and silver shoulder strap like mine."

Berg grinned. He said: "Yeah . . . it would be funny to see me walkin' around with that make-up on. But maybe I wouldn't look so bad in a uniform."

The Feldwebel said: "You'd look very good."

Berg said: "O.K. Well, now what: about gettin' out of here? I often wonder why in heck I came to this goddam country. Anyhow, I came at the wrong time."

Nielenberg said: "You mean you wish you'd stayed in South America?"

Berg said: "Yeah. Maybe I do. I liked it there, you know. It was good. But I made a little jack an' I thought I'd like to get around a bit an' see the world. Nobody told me there was gonna be a war. If they had," he continued, "I wouldn't have thought it woulda come over here to Norway. Maybe I would have been better off to have stayed back in South America."

The Feldwebel shook his head. They were walking in step and the sound of the German's heavy boots echoed down the quiet street.

"No, my friend," he said. "It would have been just the same. This year Norway, next year South America. I tell you most of the republics there will go National Socialist or Fascist within the next year. They have got to. First of all our influence is great. Secondly, they will realise who is winning the war. They will realise that wise people go with Germany."

Berg said: "Yeah . . . maybe you're right. What about this liquor you was tellin' me about?"

The Feldwebel looked at his wrist-watch. The gesture of putting up his arm and turning over the wrist was theatrical and extravagant. Everything that Nielenberg did was theatrical. Berg had noticed that.

The German said: "We have time, but not too much time, because to-night I have some work to do—some very interesting work."

Berg said: "Yeah? Something really good, hey?"

The Feldwebel said: "An opportunity. It is a thing which does not normally come my way, but the Oberleutnant is away at Narvik. I am in charge here." He turned to Berg with a smile. He said: "If you like to come to the Gendarmerie Command Headquarters, of which I am at the moment in charge, in about an hour's time, I will show you something very amusing, I think."

Berg said: "O.K. Maybe I will, but I think I'll take a walk around first."

Nielenberg said, rather patronisingly: "That will be all right, because you have the pass I have given you. You can walk about even at this time of night. You see, you are a neutral at the moment, my friend."

Berg said: "Yeah . . . when do you think those papers are comin' through? When d'you think I'll be able to get outa here?"

The Feldwebel spread his hands. "Any moment," he said. "The despatch rider might bring them to-morrow. Directly I have them you can go down to the port, but your journey home will be a long one, and"—he looked at Berg sideways and smiled—"I hope you get there. You see, our submarines are not being so particular in this war as they were in the last one. It would be unfortunate if your ship were torpedoed, my friend. If you are a wise man you will consider staying here; applying to join the German Army; to be a German. We shall allow all good people who wish to, to do that. With me behind you—and I can recommend you—and your own experience, you will be much happier." He looked at Berg sideways again. He said: "Supposing you got back to America, my friend. Maybe the police have got a record against you. Maybe they might want to talk to you about one or two things that happened a long time ago. You see, I know what I am talking about."

Berg said: "Yeah, I can see you know what you're talkin' about, but maybe I'll chance it. I reckon I'd like to see the United States again." He grinned. "Maybe they've forgotten about me by now."

They stopped outside the Feldwebel's billet. Nielenberg said: "Well, we'll talk about this again. I have only ten minutes for drinking, but we can drink quite a lot in ten minutes. Then you have your walk and if you like to come to my headquarters as I told you in an hour or so, perhaps after I have done my duty, we might have time for another drink."

Berg said: "Yeah . . . maybe . . ."

They went into the house.

When the boy slipped round the edge of the door and came into the bar-room the girl Ingrid was still sitting looking into the fire with her fingers interlocked. The mug of beer on the table in front of her was untouched. The boy was about fourteen years of age, thin, straight, wiry. He threw a quick look round the room. His eyes rested for a moment on the man Sven who came from Bardu. Sven had his back to the boy.

The boy pointed with a grubby forefinger towards Sven's back. His eyes were inquiring. The landlord, who was moving a barrel behind the counter, looked at the boy over his shoulder.

He nodded. He said: "It's all right. We know him."

The boy moved from the door; went over to the table where the girl Ingrid sat. He said: "Well, Ingrid?" He stood, relaxed, looking down at her. His face was sad.

She said: "It is not good, Gunnar." The tears welled up into her eyes.

The boy said: "You must be brave, Ingrid. These things happen. We must do our duty. Perhaps there is something to be done. Perhaps I could tell—"

She said: "No, there isn't anything to be done now. All we can do is to wait."

The boy asked: "For what . . . what do we wait for?"

Ingrid said: "Listen . . . they were taken to-night about two hours ago. They were dropped in the little wood—the pine-wood. They were taken by accident. Nobody had talked. Nobody knew they were coming to-night. Some wandering patrol found them before they had time to do anything."

The boy said: "Well . . . where are they?"

She went on: "They put them in a cell at the old police station. They have been there since. To-night they are going to question them."

The boy said: "I see." He looked at her white, tight-gripped fingers. He said: "I am very sorry, Ingrid."

She went on: "You know what they do to people when they want to question them. They will not do very much to the man. They prefer to deal with women. They think it is easier to make them talk."

The boy said: "You are afraid for Hilde? You are afraid what they will do."

She said: "I am afraid of that, Gunnar. And I am afraid that if Hilde breaks down . . . if she talks . . . what will happen to the rest of us?"

The boy smiled. He said: "Do not fear, Ingrid. Hilde will never talk. If things get too bad I know what she will do."

Ingrid nodded. She said: "Yes . . . so do I. She will kill herself—if she can. But sometimes that is not easy." She sighed. "You must be thirsty, Gunnar. You've come a long way. Would you like the beer?" She indicated the mug on the table.

The boy said: "Thank you." He picked up the mug, drank a little of the beer. He said: "Here's to Hilde. And to Norway!"

He handed her the mug. She smiled at him. She put the mug to her lips, drank some of the beer.

She said: "Did you come in by the town? Did you see anything?"

He shook his head. "I came in the town," he said, "by the back alleyways. You know, inside the town limits no one is allowed to be out at night. I saw Nielenberg—the Police Feldwebel—with the other man. They were going into his billet. I waited because I had to pass the house to get into the alleyway on the other side. After a little while the other man came out. He began to walk down the road. He was walking slowly, with his hands in his pockets. I did not know he was a friend of Nielenberg's."

She said: "I don't think he is. I don't think he has any friends. He is waiting for a permit to get out of Norway. He is an American."

The boy said: "He can move about at night. They let him. If we knew something about him . . . one never knows, he might help."

She looked up at him. "One dare not chance a thing like that. One dare not chance a thing like that."

The boy said: "You ought to know, Ingrid. You have talked to him. You have been about with him. People have talked . . ."

She said: "I like him very much, Gunnar. He is a strange man, but I like him." She looked into the fire. She was thinking.

The boy said: "I must go. I will see you again in the morning if I can get back into the town. If not, I will wait till night at the usual place. Good-bye, Ingrid."

He went quietly out of the bar, slipped into the shadows by the side of the road, moving noiselessly away into the night.

She sat looking into the fire. She was wondering what was happening to her sister Hilde. She thought it was a pitiful thing that had happened; that more pitiful things would happen. But what was one to do? One could only try. She remembered the happy years that had gone, when she and Hilde were little girls playing in the woods on the edge of the town. A lump came into her throat.

She looked up as the door opened. Berg stood in the doorway. He did not come in as the Norwegians came in. He opened the door wide, stood framed against the darkness outside for a moment; closed the door behind him. He had the *bravura* of a man who had a police pass, entitled to move about. He came over to the table. He grinned at Ingrid.

He said: "Well, babe, how's it goin?"

She said: "Not very well, Rene Berg. Not at all well."

Berg raised one eyebrow. He said: "Nope? It's funny to hear that anything goes or don't go in this dead an' alive hole."

She said: "Would you like some beer?"

Berg nodded. He drew up a chair, sat down by the fire. She walked over to the counter. She asked the landlord for the beer. Sven and the other two men were in the far corner, talking in whispers.

The landlord whispered: "What are you going to do, Ingrid?"

She said softly: "There is just a chance." She looked at Bergs back. "He knows Nielenberg. You never know . . ."

The landlord said: "Be careful. They say he is a friend of Nielenberg's."

She smiled. "No," she said. "I know him. He is not the type. He has contempt for Nielenberg—for all these Germans."

The landlord said: "You should know, Ingrid."

She picked up the beer, returned to the table. She put the mug down, sat on her chair. Berg turned his own chair round so that he faced her.

He said: "You're not drinkin'?"

She said in her soft, slightly guttural, English: "No, I am not drinking. Rene . . . do you think I have been kind to you?"

He cocked one eyebrow. He said: "Yeah . . . I suppose you have. You're a nice girl, Ingrid."

She asked: "Have you ever asked yourself why I have been kind to you? Do you think that I sleep with any man?"

Berg said: "Why not? I sort of never thought about it like that."

She said in a flat voice: "I have been good to you because somebody has got to find out about strangers in the town."

Berg said: "Yeah . . . why?"

She gave him a little whimsical smile. She asked: "Cannot you guess? Do you think we shall always have these swine here?"

Berg said: "Well, it looks as if you got 'em here now, don't it? An' it looks as if they're gonna stay."

She said: "Not always. The British will come back. I tell you that I believe that. We must believe it."

Berg said: "Yeah? Well, if you feel like that it's better to go on believin' it."

She said: "There is something else. Some of us who love our country believe that we should help the British to come back."

Berg drank some more beer. He said: "That's O.K. by me. But I don't reckon you've got much chance of doin' it, kid."

She asked suddenly: "What sort of man are you, Rene? Are you a good man?"

He grinned at her. He said: "No. I reckon by your standards I'm a lousy type. You know . . . I've never been very good at anything much except maybe one or two odd things that wouldn't interest you."

She said: "No? I have heard things about you in the town. They say you were a big man in America at one time; that you used to work for one of the bootleg organisations; that you were clever."

Berg said: "I would know about being clever. I usta work for a guy called Scansci. I reckon he was a pretty big liquor guy one time."

She said: "You must have had all sorts of difficult things to do in your work."

"You're tellin' me," said Berg. "But I don't know that they were so difficult. It was getting away with it that was difficult."

She said: "Rene, I would like to tell you a story. I am putting my life and the lives of my friends in your hands. I must do it, because there is no other chance."

Berg said: "Say . . . what is all this? Everything's sort of goddam dramatic around here to-night. I reckon you could cut the atmosphere with a knife." He turned and looked at the other men in the bar. They were standing looking towards him now, their hands hanging straight down by their sides. Berg thought they looked very grim—very unpleasant.

She said: "There is a great deal of strain for us all to-night. I will tell you why. Early this evening a British Secret Service Agent, whom we know, and a Norwegian woman, were dropped out beyond the town from an aeroplane. They were unfortunate. The man came down badly. He hit his head; was unconscious. Before the woman had time to do anything about it they were discovered by an infantry patrol. They have been handed over to the Field Gendarmerie."

Berg said: "So that's it. Nielenberg was tellin' me something was breakin' around here." He lit a cigarette. He went on: "Look, kid, what the hell's all this to you? Supposin' they have knocked off these guys, what's it to you?"

She said: "It means a very great deal to me, Rene. The woman is my sister Hilde."

Berg whistled through his teeth. "That's not so good, is it?" he said.

She said: "It is not very good. It may be terrible. You know, or probably you do not know, the German police—especially the Field Gendarmerie—have some very unpleasant methods of making people talk."

Berg drew on his cigarette. "I get it," he said. "You reckon that Nielenberg an' the boys are sort of gonna get to work on this guy an' your sister?"

She nodded.

He said: "Not so good." He looked at her quickly. "An' you got another idea," he went on. "You reckon if they get busy on her an' she cracks up she's got to give some other guys away maybe."

She nodded again. "That is correct," she said.

Berg said: "Look, are there a lot of you bozos in this? What is this . . . sort of underground stuff, hey?"

She said: "Yes, underground stuff. And we are all in it, Rene. Every Norwegian, except just a little scum, is in it."

Berg said: "Well . . . well . . . well. . . . I reckon I'm sorry about this." He smiled at her. "You're not a bad kid," he said. "I hope for all your sakes nobody talks." He finished the beer, threw his cigarette stub into the fire. He lit a fresh cigarette.

She picked up the mug, took it to the counter, handed it to the landlord, who refilled it. She brought it back, put it beside Berg's elbow. He threw her a quick sideways smile.

She put out her hand. He noticed that the fingers were thin and white. Then he looked into the fire. He was drawing the smoke down into his lungs, exhaling it slowly through pursed lips.

After a bit he said: "So you didn't sorta fall for my manly beauty or anything like that. You weren't sort of stuck on me. You just thought that whatever it cost you you had to get around to knowin' who an' what I was."

She said: "That is perhaps half the truth. The other half is that you are rather a strange and attractive man. I have liked you, Rene. I should have liked you in any event, but I do not suppose—if I tell the truth—that I would have been so good to you unless it was necessary that I should find out about you. We do not like strangers here. Too often they come from the Gestapo."

Berg grinned. He said: "Well, not me. I'm an American citizen." For some unknown reason he felt proud of the fact.

She said: "Yes? That is the only free country at peace at the moment. It must be nice to be American." She picked up the beer mug. She looked at him. She said: "Here's to you, Rene." She drank some of the beer.

Berg threw his cigarette into the fire. He looked at his wrist-watch. He said: "Well, maybe I'll go an' take a look at this sister of yours. The Feldwebel asked me to go along there."

She said: "You might not like it. It is not amusing for a man to see a woman beaten."

Berg said: "No? I've seen worse than that. So long, kid. I'll be seein' you."

He went out. The door banged behind him.

The landlord said: "If he talks . . . it is going to be very unpleasant. You have taken a very great risk, Ingrid."

She said sadly: "Maybe . . . I don't know. In these days one guesses at things."

She went back to the chair by the fire; sat looking into the embers.

Berg walked briskly down the road towards Skaalund. He was stopped at the crossroads where the woods ended by the German Gendarmerie patrol. They examined his pass; allowed him to proceed.

Berg thought to himself: These guys are goddam funny—these Norwegians. Are they funny guys? He turned the thought over and over in his mind.

He felt vaguely uncomfortable. A peculiar mental irk possessed him. He wondered what it was. It was rather as if he had drunk a glass of really bad hooch—as if his stomach was turning over. Actually, because inside Berg there was some peculiar feeling of pride, he was infuriated with himself because of Ingrid, although he did not care to admit the implication.

He said to himself: "Are they goddam funny—these dames! A babe like Ingrid—good-looking—a young kid—so she lays a guy because she wants to find out about him, not because she likes him." Berg, who had been in his own way fond of Ingrid, did not like this thought.

The mental process continued. He said to himself: But you got to have something sticking around here, being kicked around by these heinies—and they're not so hot either—they're very tough—guys like Nielenberg. A babe like Ingrid is just sticking around ready to lay a guy so that they can find out about him!

He dismissed the thought from his mind because it was not pleasant. He began to think about what she had said to him. So they were all in the underground—this poor puny hidden thing that was trying to fight the might of the German Army. He remembered what she had said. They were all in it except perhaps for a little scum. Berg began to think about all the people he had met in Skaalund. He wondered which of them were in the movement, and which few constituted the little scum. He shrugged his shoulders. You just didn't know! Anyway, these Norwegians had had it. They had lost and if you lost there was nothing to be done about it. They were living on day-dreams; believing that the British would come back. Berg, who knew very little about the British, thought such a process was not very possible. He had heard about the British invasion of Norway—a handful of not very well-trained troops, inadequately supported by artillery, with no aircraft, who had put up some sort of show and been kicked out again by the organised might of the German Army. He began to think about the British. They were odd too. They weren't unlike the Norwegians. They might even come back. Berg remembered somebody telling him that the English always lost every battle except the last. But it seemed to him that the last battle had been fought.

The Germans were on the up-and-up. His own country—America—was wise enough to keep out of it. He had heard the stories about Roosevelt sending over stores, food and ships. Well, maybe that was a gesture from one country to another. It didn't mean a thing.

He turned out of the main street down to the left. At the bottom on the right side at an angle he could see the windows of the Gendarmerie headquarters. A despatch rider was outside, sitting across his motor-cycle, lighting a cigarette. At the top of the stone steps Berg could see the figure of the Gendarmerie sentry, his rifle with the bayonet fixed held lightly in his hand, the two stick grenades tied, on the left side of his belt. He was laughing and saying something to the despatch rider.

Berg thought: They're easy, these guys. They've got everything all set. They know what they're doing. They've got organisation. He thought of Scansci in the old days. He'd had a good organisation too. The thought occurred to Berg suddenly that the Scansci organisation had slipped a little. He shrugged his shoulders. Maybe one day the organisation of these Jerries would slip. Maybe! But he did not think so.

He approached the entrance. The sentry stiffened. His rifle came up. Berg heard the safety catch go off. Simultaneously, from a window which was half-opened, with a dark blind behind it, there came the sound of a whimper—a moan. It was a woman's voice.

Berg thought casually: I reckon that's Hilde—Ingrid's sister. I reckon Nielenberg is getting to work on her. He stopped and lit a cigarette. Then he took his pass out of his pocket, went towards the stone steps. The despatch rider looked at him inquiringly as he passed the front of his motorcycle with its subdued headlight.

Berg held out his pass towards the sentry. He said: "Herr Feldwebel Nielenberg?"

The sentry looked at him; then he motioned him to go inside.

Berg walked towards the door at the far end of the stone passage. He knocked, pushed it open, put his head round the corner. The room was the office of the Oberleutnant, which Nielenberg was using in his superior's absence. There were three people in the room. Nielenberg, the collar and top buttons of his tunic undone, sat on the desk facing the other two.

The man and the woman were seated in high straight-backed chairs with their arms pulled backwards over the tops of the chairs and tied to the cross-bar at the back. Each ankle was tied to a leg of the chair.

Berg looked at the two. Furthest from him was the man.

He looked dazed and there was a bruise on his head. His head was sunk forward. Berg thought he was a good type. He had a thin face with a good jaw. His eyes were half-closed, but Berg could not tell whether this was through tiredness or whether the man was shamming semi-consciousness.

In the other chair was the woman Hilde. She was fair, and her hair, which Berg thought might be beautiful when it was dressed, hung down to her shoulders. Her face was oval and very white. A thin stream of blood was running from one corner of her mouth down her chin, dripping down to the rough frieze coat she wore. Across her face was a red weal.

Nielenberg looked at Berg's head as it protruded through the opening of the door. He said: "Come in, my friend. This might be very interesting. And close the door behind you. You will find some beer in the cupboard in the corner."

Berg entered the room. He noticed that Nielenberg carried in his right hand a thin rubber quirt. Quite obviously, he had slashed the girl across the face with this. Berg looked at her again. Her eyes were filled with tears; she was biting her lips in an endeavour to keep them back.

Nielenberg said: "All these damned Norwegians are the same. They all think they are very strong and very brave. They all think that none of them is going to talk. Eventually, we find some way of making them talk. The devil of it is it sometimes takes a long time and I do not want it to take a long time—not on this occasion." He grinned at Berg. He said: "And you might give me a mug of beer too."

Berg opened the cupboard; took out two mugs and the large stone jar of beer. He filled the two mugs, brought one to Nielenberg.

Nielenberg went over to the man. He stood over him, the rubber quirt in his right hand, the beer mug in his left.

He said: "You do not look very well, my English friend. You do not look very well because you made a very bad landing. You look to me as if you came down head first. This may help to revive you." He threw the mug of beer into the man's face, passed the rubber quirt into his left hand, drew back his right fist and struck the man between the eyes. The force of the blow was so great that the chair heeled over sideways and crashed to the ground.

No sound came from the man. He lay there on his side, his arms still fastened over the back of the chair, in a most grotesque position. Nielenberg leaned over, seized the chair, yanked it upright. He came back to the desk.

Berg picked up the mug. He said: "I thought you wanted some beer. You'd better have some more." He poured out another mug. He sat down on the side of the desk opposite Nielenberg. He drank his beer; lit a cigarette.

Nielenberg said: "These two are going to talk before the Oberleutnant comes back. I would like very much to have my report all ready for him when he arrives."

Berg said: "So the boss is comin' back, hey? Maybe he'll have some news about my papers when he comes."

Nielenberg said: "Perhaps . . . and perhaps not. In any event he will have more important things to think about if I can make these swine talk."

He finished his beer; passed the mug back to Berg. Berg refilled both mugs.

He asked: "What's goin' on around here? What's all this about?"

Nielenberg laughed. He said: "These people think they have a chance of making some sort of what you call a comeback. This one"—he motioned to the man—"is an Englishman. We've heard about him. He's been dropped a dozen times before. They are dropped by plane. They organise what they call resistance and underground movements—stupid little organisations which never achieve anything. The woman is Norwegian. Also she thinks she is very tough. We shall see in a minute."

Berg said: "When does the boss come back?"

The Feldwebel thought for a moment; then he said: "If the despatch rider is right he should be here by a quarter to ten." He looked at his wrist-watch. "That gives me twenty-five minutes." He grinned. "Now let us analyse the twenty-five minutes. Five minutes to make this woman talk, three minutes to dictate the report, ten minutes for it to be typed, and I will meet the Ober-leutnant at the landing strip and present it to him."

Berg drank some beer. He said: "Yeah . . . that's *if* she talks."

Neilenberg walked over to the girl. He stood in front of her. From where he stood Berg could see that she had well-cut ankles, slim legs. He thought she was like her sister Ingrid. He thought it damned funny that a sweet piece like Ingrid should lay a man just to find out what he was doing; just to find out where he came from. Immediately afterwards, he thought was it so goddam funny? Maybe it wasn't. Maybe they *had* to play it that way.

Nielenberg said to the girl: "Who were you going to meet? Where were you going to meet them and why?"

She answered in German. She said one word: "Scum . . .!"

Berg knew what the word meant. It reminded him again of Ingrid. She had used that word. She had said that everybody was in the underground movement except for a little scum. All the people who were not in the resistance movements were scum, and the Germans were scum. Berg thought: These Norwegians have their nerve all right.

Nielenberg slapped the girl across the face with the back of his hand—hard. The slap made a peculiar staccato sound. When he stepped back, Berg could see that her lips were cut and bleeding.

He said casually: "You got a lot to learn, Feldwebel. In the old days in the States when we wanted to make some guy talk we never batted him across the face like that."

Nielenberg said: "No?" He turned his head towards Berg. "And what used you to do, my friend?" he asked.

Berg said: "I always found a cigarette lighter held between the fingers was a good thing to start off with."

Nielenberg said: "It's not bad. I've tried it. Also a needle under the finger-nails. Perhaps we shall have to use such methods in a moment."

Berg grinned. He said: "You'll have to hurry up if you're goin' to make her talk before the Oberleutnant comes back."

The Feldwebel said to the girl: "How would you like to have some needles run under your finger-nails? After you had had two or three nails done you would *have* to talk. Why not talk now?"

She said: "I shall never talk whatever you do. Scum . . .!"

Nielenberg hit her again. Now the top of her rough jacket was covered with the blood which was streaming from her mouth and teeth. Berg thought that Nielenberg was not at all artistic.

He drew on his cigarette. He said: "Look . . . I could save you a lot of trouble."

Nielenberg raised his eyebrows. He said: "Yes? What do you mean?"

Berg said: "You come over here. I want to talk to you."

Nielenberg, a puzzled look on his face, came over.

Berg said: "I'll tell you something funny. When I went for my walk to-night I overheard something." He dropped his voice. "I got talking to some people. Well, when I got back here and saw these two here I was able to put two and two together. I know who they were going to meet, and I know where they were goin' to meet 'em."

Nielenberg said: "My God, you don't mean that?"

Berg said: "Yeah, I do. It's just one of those things. So I thought we might make a little deal."

Nielenberg asked suspiciously: "What sort of deal?"

Berg said: "Look, I want to get out of here—you know that. You get me my papers through so I can get down to Narvik and get away and I'll give you the works. But I'm not talkin' till the Oberleutnant tells me he's goin' to give me my papers. He can do it."

Nielenberg said: "Yes, I daresay if he wanted to hurry it up he could get them in a day."

Berg said: "O.K. How long is it before he arrives?"

Nielenberg looked at his wrist-watch. He said: "He will be here in about fifteen minutes."

Berg said: "Look, Feldwebel, why don't you chuck these two in the can. Lock 'em up, see? All right. You an' I go down to the air-strip. We meet the Oberleutnant. Have you got a car?"

Nielenberg said: "Yes, I shall take a car with me."

"O.K.," said Berg. "When we have met him we drop him back here; then you and I go down an' get the other guys. I'll show you where they are. We bring 'em back an' we hand 'em over. Then your boss has got the lot of 'em and to-morrow he gets my papers for exit. Is that O.K.?"

Nielenberg said: "I have no doubt it will be all right. The Oberleutnant will be pleased at a neutral assisting the Germans. Perhaps he'll think it's good propaganda." He looked at his watch again. "We must be going," he said. "We will lock up these two here. They are quite safe . . . like trussed chickens. We will meet the Oberleutnant. In any event he should be pleased with what has been done in his absence. Come, my friend."

He led the way out of the room. Berg waited only long enough to finish his mug of beer; then he went after the Feldwebel. As he passed the woman he looked at her. She raised her eyes to his and he could see the hatred shining in them.

The long straight road that led to the air-strip was bounded on each side by tall fir-trees. The trees were thick and the moon shining on the white surface of the road gave it the appearance of a river between two high banks.

Berg, sitting in the passenger seat of the open gendarmerie car beside the Feldwebel, who was driving, thought about the girl Ingrid.

For some reason which he could not quite explain, her image persisted. Actually it was because his pride was hurt. Berg thought he had made a conquest in Skaalund; that Ingrid had fallen for him; that she was really fond of him. Now he knew that this was not so. She had not been thinking of him; she had been thinking of her sister Hilde, of the man who was with her—the Englishman; of the resistance movement; of anything but Berg. He did not like the thought.

In five minutes' time they were at the entrance to the airfield. The sentry recognised the car; stood on one side. They drove through the wooden gates. Nielenberg stopped the car twenty yards down the landing strip. High above them came the sound of an airplane.

The Feldwebel looked at his watch. He said: "Good timing! This is the Oberleutnant. He will be pleased." Then as an afterthought he said: "Why did you not tell me immediately you came to Gendarmerie headquarters of what you knew? Why did you allow me to try to get it out of that girl?"

Berg grinned at him sideways. He said: "I was sort of keen to see what your technique was goin' to be. I heard you guys are pretty tough, but it didn't look tough to me. I don't reckon you'd ever have made that girl talk. Or the guy either. I know those types. They keep their traps shut no matter what happens."

Nielenberg shrugged his shoulders. "Perhaps you are right," he said. "In any event we shall make somebody talk somehow."

The plane—of a small passenger-carrying type—came down. The pilot made a perfect landing. After a moment three people got out of the plane. The pilot walked towards the control tower, followed by another man. The other man—an officer—walked straight towards the gendarmerie car.

Nielenberg said: "This is the Oberleutnant."

He moved away from Berg; advanced to meet his superior officer. The click of his heels could be heard distinctly as he saluted. He began to talk. Slowly they walked back towards Berg. When they arrived, the officer—a young man of about twenty-seven with blond hair and moustaches—nodded to Berg.

Nielenberg said: "The Oberleutnant is very pleased. He knew that there was some sort of resistance movement going on in these parts. Now he says we shall be able to kill it. I have told him all about you. I have also told him that you and I have been friendly; that I know your background; that you are well disposed towards Germany. I have told him that you wish to leave as quickly as possible, and he says that in consideration of your services he will arrange for your exit permit to come through quickly. But he also says—and if you take my advice you will accept his offer— that if you care to stay here, do your training and take the oath of allegiance to the Fuehrer, there is no reason why you should not adopt German nationality. There would be a place for you in the Gendarmerie." Nielenberg looked at Berg and grinned cynically. "I told him that you had been a killer in your time," he said.

Berg said: "That's as maybe and I'd like you to thank the officer. But I'm still keen on gettin' out. So I'll have the exit permit if it's all the same to him. Now, what's the big idea? How're we gonna play this?"

The Feldwebel began to speak to the Oberleutnant. They talked for a long time softly. Then Nielenberg said: "The Oberleutnant says we will take two police trucks down to this place wherever it is, and arrest everybody; then we can sort them out afterwards."

Berg said: "Just a minute. Do you think that's a good idea? I reckon they got some sort of scouts out posted about that place. I saw one or two guys hangin' about along the road by the forest. I'd like to make a suggestion. I got an idea."

The Feldwebel translated. After the officer had finished speaking, he said to Berg: "The Oberleutnant says he would like to hear your ideas. He thinks you are intelligent."

Berg said: "Thanks a lot. Look, the obvious thing to do is to go down an' get the girl who told me about this business; not let her know what's goin' on."

Nielenberg said: "So there's a girl? You haven't been wasting your time in Skaalund, my friend."

Berg said: "No, I never do. Anyway, she trusts me. If I go down there an' ask her to come for a walk she'll come. I'll bring her along the road. Then we stick her in the car an' we tell her all about it; then nobody has a chance to get warned. We get from her the names of the people in the resistance movement or whatever they call it. If you want to send a couple police trucks down and knock them off in that beer house you can do it. But the thing is to get hold of the girl first."

Nielenberg translated. After a moment he said to Berg: "The Oberleutnant agrees. He thinks it's a good idea. We will take him back to headquarters; then we will go and *get* this girl. After we have got her back for questioning we can either arrest them singly if we get the names from her; if not, we can arrest everybody at the inn. Let us go."

The car moved swiftly towards the Gendarmerie headquarters.

Nielenberg said quietly: "This is all very good. Things are working out well, my friend Berg. The only thing is that I am sorry you are leaving us. We could have used a man like you."

Berg said: "Yeah." But he had not heard what the Feldwebel had said. He was looking straight ahead at the shiny surface of the road which stretched before him.

Something had suddenly occurred to Berg. He had realised suddenly that everything he had done and planned during the last hour had been the result of a sudden feeling which he could not quite analyse, but which he thought was one of hatred for the girl Ingrid. Ingrid had made a fool of him. Under the pretence of being attracted to him she had used him. She had used him to find out anything she could, to be in a position to know what was happening; what the German police were doing. That was all. A surge of the old anger which had come to him on the night when Shakkey had told him how Clovis and Lauren had fooled him, came to Berg. He was all right with men. He could handle men; kill them if necessary. But he wasn't so good with women. They laid for him; they made a sucker out of him.

Berg's mind was obsessed by the thought. Yet at the same time, beneath it all, there was another, almost a strong, feeling of compassion or sorrow for the girl Ingrid and the fools who thought they could match themselves against the German military organisation.

The car stopped outside the headquarters. Nielenberg sprang out; opened the door for the Oberleutnant. They spoke for a moment and the officer entered the headquarters.

Nielenberg got back into the car. He was about to drive off when Berg said: "Listen, buddy, I'll move my seat. I'll get down in the back of the car. If one of those guys was to spot us driving through the town together—and they might have somebody keepin' an eye open—it wouldn't be so good."

Nielenberg smiled. He said: "You think of everything, my friend Berg."

Berg got out of the car: re-entered by the back door. He sat down on the floor. The car started. Nielenberg began to talk quietly but distinctly so that Berg could hear.

He said: "Exactly what is the plan?"

"Here's the way we play it," Berg answered. "There is a little bit of woodland about a quarter of a mile before you get to that beer-house. It's a dark deserted place and the police patrol turn off about half a mile away. They never get down there, see? O.K. You stop the car in the forest just off the road. I get out. I go back there. I talk to this baby that I was talkin' to earlier to-night. I say I've met up with a guy in the town—one of their boys—somebody who might be of use to them. I tell her I've got him waiting down on the edge of the wood. So she comes, see?"

Nielenberg said: "Yes, of course she comes. Excellent, my friend."

"All right," said Berg. "So we get *her*. She's the important one. Well, they won't expect her back for a bit, will they? So we take her back to headquarters. We get busy on her. It don't matter if she doesn't talk because in the meantime you send some of your cops down to the *kroj* an' take the rest of 'em. Then we get the lot. Then we can tell them one at a time that she's talked; that she's blown the works. Once they get the idea in their head that the game's up they'll all start talkin', hey?"

The Feldwebel said: "I think you are right, my friend. In any event, it is worth trying."

There was silence. Ten minutes passed; then Nielenberg drove the car off the road on to a little pathway that led into the thick fir forest. He stopped the car twenty-five yards in, put in the clutch; sat relaxed, his shoulders easy, in the driving seat.

Berg got up and sat on the seat. He said: "I'm surprised at you, Nielenberg."

The Feldwebel turned his head. "Surprised? Why?" he asked.

Berg said: "Have you seen the back of your helmet. That's the first time I've ever seen you with mud on the back of your helmet. Here . . . give it to me."

Berg put his hand on the back of the German's steel helmet and tipped it off his head. He said: "Look at this . . ."

As the Feldwebel turned, Berg brought the heavy steel helmet crashing down on the top of his head. Nielenberg slumped forward over the wheel.

Berg got out of the car. He threw the helmet into the back of the car; then he pushed the unconscious Feldwebel back into the driving seat. Berg put his right hand round the man's throat. He began to squeeze. He kept it there for three-four minutes. Then he undid the top buttons of the policeman's tunic, slipped his hand inside. Nielenberg was dead.

Berg grunted. He undid the remaining buttons of the tunic, pulled it off the recumbent figure, threw it into the back of the car with the helmet. He took Nielenberg's pistol and two ammunition clips from his holster; put them in his pocket. He opened the door, pulled Nielenberg's body across his shoulders, took it another fifteen or twenty yards into the wood. He threw it in the middle of a thick coppice.

He said: "Well, fella . . . now you've had yours! Now you'll be happy all right . . ."

He went back to the car. Looking at it, he thought it was unlikely that it would be observed by anybody. He turned off the parking lights; lit a cigarette. He went along the pathway, back on to the road; began to walk towards the beer-house.

He was there in ten minutes. Outside the door he felt a peculiar sense of excitement. He was wondering whether she would be there; whether she had already left. He found himself hoping that she would still be sitting by the fire. He opened the door: went in.

The girl was still sitting in the wooden chair, looking at the fire. Her hands were clasped together. At the other end of the room the landlord was deep in conversation with the three men who had been there before and another two who had arrived since. They all looked up as Berg came in.

He crossed the room, sat down in the chair opposite the girl. He said: "Hallo, babe!"

She looked up. She said: "Well, Rene? What is your news?"

Berg said: "Things have been movin' a little, sister. When I went back, Nielenberg had got this guy and Hilde, your sister, up at the Gendarmerie headquarters. I reckon he'd been puttin' them through it—but not too bad. Maybe he'd have gone on, but a message arrived from the air-strip that the Oberleutnant was coming back."

She said: "Yes? Had they hurt Hilde much?"

"Nothin to speak of," said Berg. "Just a bit of pushin' around. Anyway, I got an idea."

She raised her eyebrows. Looking at her white face and her big eyes, Berg realised that in the right atmosphere, and properly fed, Ingrid would be very beautiful.

She said: "So you have an idea? What is the idea?" She looked at him doubtfully.

From the other end of the room Berg could feel six pairs of eyes boring into his back.

He said: "Well, I told Nielenberg that it might be a good thing to lay off them an' come along an' make a pinch down here." He went on: "I had to play it that way. I had to make them certain they could trust me, see?"

She said: "I see."

"O.K.," Berg went on. "He fell for it. So we went an' met the Oberleutnant. He's back at headquarters. Nielenberg an' I came down here. He's back in the forest with a car. His idea was that I got you out of here. We took you back an' we made you talk. While this was bein' done they were knockin' off the rest of the guys here."

She said: "Yes . . . and then?"

Berg grinned at her. He said: "Well, then I croaked Nielen-berg. I killed him. His body's away back there in the wood. I got an idea there's a slim chance of gettin' outa here for all of us. We might as well try it."

She said: "How do I know that I can believe you? How do I know that what you say is true?"

A wave of anger swept through Berg. He said: "Ain't you the little pip? You make a pass at me. You lay for me because you want to find out what Fm doin'—if I come from the Gestapo. When they knock your sister off, you get fed up an' you ask me to help you. When I take a chance—because you can imagine what these heinies'll do to me if they get wise to what I'm doin'—you ask me if you can trust me. I reckon you make me sick."

She said: "I may make you sick, but people's lives are in my hands. I want to know that I can trust you."

"O.K.," said Berg. "But we haven't got a lot of time to lose. You'd better come along an' look at the stiff."

She asked: "How did you kill him?"

Berg said: "I crowned him with his own steel helmet. When he went out I strangled him."

She said: "I would like to see him."

Berg said: "O.K. This way, sweetie."

They got up. They were moving towards the door when Berg stopped suddenly. He looked at her and grinned.

He said: "I might still be havin' you on. This might be just a fairy story to get you outside. Have you thought of that one?"

She said: "Yes, Rene. I thought of it. Sometimes one has to take a chance."

They went through the doorway. Berg led the way silently up the road, keeping in the heavy shadows thrown by the fir-trees. He took her down the little path, past the car, to the coppice. He showed her the Feldwebel's body lying there, the head resting at an odd angle on one arm. She looked at it.

After a minute she turned to Berg. She put her hand on his arm. She said: "Thank you very much. I think you are a very brave man. I am not sorry that I have given you what I have given you."

Berg grinned at her. He said: "Thanks a lot. But the thing is how we get out of here. I got an idea. Maybe it would work."

She said: "Yes? What is it?"

Berg said: "You listen to this one. I put you in the back of the car down on the floor, an' I drive the car back to Gendarmerie Headquarters. The sentry knows me. I've got a pass. He won't think it funny my drivin' the car because he's seen me with Nielenberg the whole evening. He knows we went out on some sort of job. Now you tell me something . . . this English guy who's with Hilde—does he speak German?"

She said: "But of course. He is called Ransome—a naval officer. He's one of their most clever Secret Service Agents. He speaks several languages."

"That's. O.K.," said Berg. "All right. When we get to Gendarmerie headquarters I go in. I got to take a chance on what the situation is there, but I reckon the Oberleutnant hasn't moved anything much. I reckon Hilde an' this guy Ransome are still tied up to chairs like they were when I left there. I reckon the Oberleutnant has been talkin' to them; tellin' them how goddam clever he is. You got that?"

She said: "Yes, go on . . ."

"That's how I think it might be," said Berg. "O.K. When I open his office door an' walk in, he's not gonna be surprised to see me, is he? You bet he's not. He knows I went down with Nielenberg. He knows Nielenberg might be turnin' out some coppers to round up these guys. So I take a chance. I walk straight up to him an' I crown him. I've got Nielenberg's gun. He goes out."

She nodded. She said: "It might happen. And then?"

"Then," said Berg, "we got to get movin'. Ransome will have to take a hand. Anyway, it's gonna be a lot of fun." He smiled at her in the darkness. "When I was in that office before," he said, "I opened a cupboard to get some beer out. The Oberleutnant keeps his beer on the top shelf in an arms cupboard. There were three machine-pistols underneath with two extra ammunition clips for each one. Even if they get us," said Berg, "we can make ourselves damned unpleasant first."

She said softly in the darkness: "You sound almost as if you *like* this."

Berg said: "Well, I been kickin' around here not doin' very much. I like a little excitement." He went on: "Maybe I won't take you right up to Gendarmerie headquarters. Maybe I'll leave you in a dark side street somewhere near. The patrols won't be goin' out again for another hour or an hour an' a half. Everything's quiet now. The guard room is about a hundred yards from the headquarters. There's only one sentry on—he's not changed till three o'clock in the mornin'. If we can fix him we've got the car. If we can get on that air-strip an' the plane's still there that the Oberleutnant came in. . . . Maybe they've refuelled it. He got right out of it an' didn't give any orders, so maybe they're keepin' it there for him in case he wants to go some place. Maybe our pal Ransome can fly a plane?"

She nodded. "He can do that too," she said.

"O.K.," said Berg. "You listen to me. You keep your eye on the door of the headquarters. After I've dropped you, I'll drive around an' come back on the main road from a different direction. But you watch the sentry; watch him if he goes inside an' don't come back again. If that happens an' if you see me come out an' get inta the car you scram across an' get in too. You got that?"

She said: "Yes, I understand."

"If anything goes wrong," said Berg, "well, you'll know. You'll hear the shootin'. In that case you just scram. Nobody knows about you. Nielenberg was the only one who knew an' he can't talk. Well, let's get goin'."

He started to move back to the car.

She said: "A moment please, Rene. I want to talk to you."

Berg said: "Yeah?" He turned back to her.

A gleam of moonlight came through the trees. He could see her face, thin and white, turned up to him.

She said: "I would like you to kiss me, Rene. I would like to tell you that I'm very glad that I love you."

Berg said: "Aw . . . what the hell!"

He turned away; began to walk towards the car.

*

Fifteen minutes later Berg brought the car to a standstill outside Gendarmerie headquarters. The sentry stood nonchalantly at the top of the steps. He yawned as Berg got out of the car. Berg grinned at him; walked slowly up the steps through the doorway, along the passage. His heart was beating a little quickly. He wondered what the situation would be inside the room. His right hand was in his coat pocket. He clasped Nielenberg's heavy Mauser pistol by the barrel.

Berg opened the door; stepped into the room. Almost he could hear himself breathing a sigh of relief. Ransome and Hilde were still seated, bound to the chairs, where he had left them. The girl's face was tired and drawn. Ransome was leaning his head on one side on his shoulder. As Berg stepped into the room he saw his eyes brighten. Ransome was conscious.

Berg, standing in the doorway, paused for a moment and looked over his shoulder smilingly. He gave the impression that behind him down the passageway was Nielenberg. The Oberleutnant, seated at his desk writing, looked up and saw the movement. He nodded to Berg.

Berg stepped quickly into the room. He covered the four paces between himself and the officer in split seconds. Then the butt of the Mauser automatic crashed down on the Oberleutnant's skull. He slumped forward across the desk.

Berg darted to the door; shut it. He put the pistol back in his pocket; took a knife from his trouser pocket; began to cut the cords which bound Ransome.

He said: "Don't talk. Listen, there's no time to lose. What you got to do is this. Have you heard that guy talk?" He pointed to the recumbent figure of the officer slumped across the desk.

Ransome said: "Yes."

"All right," said Berg. "You go to the doorway. Open the door a little bit an' call the sentry in German. Give as near an imitation as you can of the officer's voice. I'll be waitin' for him."

Ransome said: "Right." He got out of the chair, stretched himself. He moved stiffly to the door. He opened it a little and, standing so that he could not be seen, called some words in German.

Berg watched. His heart jumped as he heard the heavy clatter of the sentry's boots walking down the corridor. Berg pushed the door open, turned and gave a half salute towards the slumped figure at the desk. Then he walked out of the room. The sentry stood on one side to allow him to pass. Berg walked two more steps; then, as the sentry reached the threshold of the room, turned, sprang forward, tipped the man's helmet off the nape of his neck with his left hand and smashed the butt of the automatic into the base of the sentry's skull.

The man pitched forward into the room. Berg shut the door. Ransome, with Berg's knife in his hand, had already cut Hilde's bonds.

Berg said: "All right. Listen: This is how we play it. The Gendarmerie car is outside. Ingrid is just across the road, on the corner. Get outside—both of you—into the car. But have this before you go." He went to the cupboard behind the desk. He opened it. At the bottom of the cupboard in the rack provided for them were half a dozen machine-pistols with extra ammunition clips by their side. Berg gave one to Ransome; two more, with three extra clips, he put under his coat. He said: "Now get out, you two. The street outside's empty. Get in the back of the car an' duck."

They went out quickly. Berg stood in the middle of the office looking at the sentry, who lay on his face, and then at the recumbent figure of the Oberleutnant. He thought to himself: For Chrissake . . .! It looks as if it's comin' off . . .!

Outside, the streets would be deserted. No one was allowed out after eight o'clock and the rule was so well-kept that the German patrols went round now only two-hourly. Berg wondered about the two unconscious men; then he shrugged his shoulders. By the time they were sufficiently interested to do anything about it, the job would have either come off or not. He took the key from the door, passed through, locked it on the outside, walked quickly down the passageway, down the front steps, into the car. Ransome and the girl were in the back.

Berg started the engine. He swung the car round, drove over to the corner of the dark street diagonally opposite to the headquarters. He stopped in the shadow.

He said: "Come on, Ingrid."

He waited. Then he got out of the car. He looked into the doorway where he had left her. She had gone.

Berg went back to the car. He said: "This is not so good. Ingrid's gone. I reckoned we oughta try an' take her with us. There's a plane down on the airfield—the Oberleutnant's plane."

Ransome said: "She wouldn't go back with us. She's got a job to do here. Is there anybody could give her away?"

Berg said: "Nope. The only guy who could do anything about it was Nielenberg. I've croaked him. Nobody knows about her."

Ransome said: "That's why she's gone. She's a good girl."

Berg said: "O.K. If that's how she wants it, that's how it is." He felt angry with the girl.

He got into the car, began to drive towards the long road towards the air-strip. He said over his shoulder: "Hey, you, Ransome . . . in the bottom of the car there's a German Gendarmerie tunic and helmet. Put 'em on. Get over inta the front seat an' sit by me. The sentry at the air-strip will think you're Nielenberg. He's seen me with him before.

"Now, look . . . the Oberleutnant arrived here about an hour ago. He came right out of the plane, an' they left it there. If he didn't leave any orders about it, maybe they'll have refuelled it. If it's still there, you an' the girl get outa the car an' get it. Try an' get her goin'."

Ransome said: "Yes, that sounds all right. And what about you?" His voice was natural, cool.

Berg said: "Look, I'm hangin' about with these little machine-guns. I like machine-guns. I go for 'em in a big way, an' I'm used to shootin'. I reckon if anybody comes outa the control tower I can keep things goin' nice an' easy until you've got that plane started. When she starts to rev up I'll make a run for it an' get in. How's that?"

Ransome said: "That's all right." He had already struggled into Nielenberg's tunic. It was too big for him, but the buttons could be seen, and the shape of the helmet was obvious. He stepped over the back seat of the open car, sat down by Berg's side. Away in the distance they could see the gate to the air-strip.

Ransome said: "You're a pretty cool sort of customer. Who are you?"

Berg said: "The name's Berg—Rene Berg. I'm an American. I've been kickin' around here tryin' to get out of this place. I had trouble about gettin' my exit permit. Well, one thing led to another an' I thought maybe I'd get out this way."

Ransome grinned. He said: "And you've done this job to-night just to get out this way?" He looked at Berg quizzically.

Berg said: "Aw . . . well, maybe . . . what the hell!"

The gate was fifty yards ahead. The sentry—one of the ground staff of the Luftwaffe unit—stood easily by the side of the gate. He looked at the car. He saw the helmet and tunic on Ransome. As Berg slowed down he grinned. He recognised Berg's face. Berg waved his hand. The car moved through the gates. Over his shoulder Berg could see the sentry leaning up against the gate-post. So that was that.

He swung the car diagonally to the right. The airplane was where it had landed. Berg accelerated. He drove the car almost to the tail of the plane, stopped it. He jumped over the side.

He said: "Now . . . for Chrissake . . . get crackin' . . .!"

He knelt on the running board behind the car. He could just see over the top of the tonneau. One machine-pistol he laid at his right hand. The other, loaded, with the reserve magazine close at hand, was in his hands ready for action.

Berg felt good. It was like the old days when you went out with a machine-gun and blasted places. He felt a surge of the old excitement. A minute passed; then with a roar the propeller of the plane began to revolve.

Berg grinned. So that was that! He knelt there, looking over his shoulder as the plane revved up. Then, from somewhere across the strip from behind the control tower, came the sound of a shot and a whistle blast. Berg thought: Some mug's discovered those guys at the Gendarmerie headquarters. He's phoned through here. This is where the fun starts.

Berg saw the light as the door of the control tower opened. A figure came out: He stood up. He squeezed the trigger of the machine-pistol and began to spray the control tower. It was with a feeling of pleasure that he heard the glass of the windows smashing; then the lights went out. Presently, from round the side of the tower came two or three figures running. The guard had turned out. Berg began to spray the left side of the control tower. He fired in short staccato jerks, saving his ammunition. He thought: I'll keep the second gun till they get here. I'd better keep that.

He looked over his shoulder. The girl Hilde was leaning out of the cabin of the plane waving to him. Berg threw down the empty pistol, picked up the second one and ran for the plane. As he stood on the wings she put her hand out under his collar. She pulled him through the now open doorway.

Ransome said: "Nice work, Berg." The plane began to move. From somewhere on the air-strip came the sound of a machine-gun.

Hilde said: "I hope we get off."

Ransome said: "I think we're going to make it."

Berg looked down. The plane had already left the ground. From below came the sound of shots and whistles. Somewhere a gun was firing. The staccato rattle of a machine-gun came to his ears from time to time.

He sat back in the seat. He looked at the girl Hilde. He grinned. He said: "Well, what d'you know about that? So it came off!"

She said: "Are you all right?"

Berg said: "Yeah. I think so. I got a slug in one arm—just one of those accidental things—-but it don't matter a damn. What happens now?"

Ransome looked over his shoulder. He said: "That depends. I hope we've got enough juice to get across. If we get across we've got to find a place to come down. That is, unless we're shot down by one of our own planes or our own anti-aircraft guns. We're not out of the wood yet."

Berg said: "Maybe not. But we're out of the worst part of the wood. I wonder what those guys woulda done to us if they'd caught up with us."

Ransome said: "Yes, I don't think it would have been so good."

Berg was smiling. He brought out his cigarette case. He gave one to the girl; lit one for himself. Ransome refused to smoke. Berg sat there listening to the hum of the engine. He felt unhappy.

He felt unhappy because the girl Ingrid was not there.

There was a long silence. Berg lay back, resting his injured arm against the side of the seat. He smoked silently.

Hilde said something in Norwegian to Ransome. He answered. They smiled at each other.

Berg asked: "What was that you said? Let me in on the joke."

She said: "It isn't a joke. You know, we have many fairy stories in Norway. There is one about the man called The Dark Hero. When things get very bad and very difficult, the fairy tale says that The Dark Hero comes and puts everything right. I have just said that I thought *you* were The Dark Hero."

Berg grinned at her. He said: "Aw . . . what the hell!"

He began to think about Ingrid.

CHAPTER FOUR
SHAKKEY
December, 1944

BERG came out of the bathroom, went into the bedroom, began to dress. He was whistling. Outside it was cold. He moved to the window, pulled aside the blackout curtain, looked out. It was very dark.

When he had finished dressing, he took a bottle of whisky from a cupboard in the corner, poured out a good measure into the tooth-glass, mixed some water, drank it. He looked at himself in the glass. He thought to himself: You're not a bad-looking guy. You got a funny sorta mug, but you're not *too* bad. He felt vaguely happy.

Actually, although he did not know it, Berg was subconsciously pleased with having created for himself a background. His work with Ransome for nearly four years had produced in him a certain sense of discipline. He had made himself invaluable to Ransome. He was trusted. He liked that. Although Berg preferred to think of himself as a cynic, especially where women were concerned, he was beginning to find that self-esteem paid dividends. Life had begun to interest him.

He finished the whisky, went down the stairs. Out in Knights-
bridge, the wind met him. He liked the feel of it on his face. He
began to walk towards Piccadilly. He turned up Bond Street, turned
right, began to walk down Sackville Street. Along the roadway he
could see the dimly lit sign of the Club. He went in.

Berg liked looking at the girl with the hennaed hair behind
the bar. He thought she was a scream. She had mascaraed eyes,
a fully-blown figure and alarmingly high heels. Sometimes he
wondered how she managed to keep her balance. He ordered a
drink. When it was served, he picked it up, took it to a table in
the corner.

He sat down, lit a cigarette. The door opened and a man came
in. He was in the uniform of a Chief Machinist's Mate in the U.S.
Navy. He went to the bar, sat on a high stool, ordered a drink.
He turned his face towards Berg.

It was Shakkey. They recognised each other at the same instant.
Shakkey slid off the stool. He came over to the corner.

He said: "Jeez . . . Rene . . .! For cryin' out loud . . . what d'you
know about this one! Is life strange or is it strange? An' you look
pretty good to me."

Berg said: "You don't look so bad yourself, Shakkey. A sailor,
hey?"

Shakkey said: "Yeah . . . you know, in the old days when we
was in that liquor business with Scansci, when things got a bit hot,
I usta sit back in my little office an' think how peaceful it would
be at sea. So when this man's war started I got me a job in the
Navy." He grinned. "An' it ain't been so peaceful!"

Berg said: "Go get your drink, Shakkey."

Shakkey went to the bar, came back with his drink. He sat
down on the other side of the table.

Berg said: "I oughta say thank you to you. I reckon it was pretty
decent of you to get me outa Chicago in the old days. I reckon if
I'd stuck around there they'd have fried me, hey?"

Shakkey said: "Yeah, they'd have fried you all right, but you
wasn't there an' I reckon the cops was pretty pleased with Scansci an' Calsimo bein' shot up. I reckon it suited 'em so they just
let it ride."

Berg asked: "What happened to Travis an' Lauren?"

Shakkey shrugged his shoulders. "They got out some place after a bit," he said. "The Feds came in an' started cleanin' up Chicago in a big way. An' how! Things got pretty hot around there. I don't know what Travis an' Lauren were doin' or where they got to." He drank some of the whisky. He went on: "What happened to you, Rene?"

Berg said: "Well, I went down to South America. It wasn't so bad around there. The liquor was good. I made a little jack too. Then I got out an' started wanderin' around. I was over in Norway when the war started over there. I was there some time."

Shakkey asked: "What you doin' now, Rene?"

"Aw . . . just kickin' around," said Berg.

Shakkey said: "Like hell . . .! You know, the world's a goddam funny place. You go for years an' years an' you never see guys. An' then all of a sudden you see 'em all in a bunch."

Berg said: "Yeah . . . who else have you seen?"

Shakkey said: "That's what I was comin' to. I reckon I saw you the other day. I was on top of a bus goin' down Piccadilly. I saw a guy an' I thought to myself: For cryin' out loud . . . that's Rene Berg. I looked again an' he was gone. Maybe it was you."

Berg said: "Yeah, it could have been me."

Shakkey picked up the two empty glasses. He took them back to the bar. He brought them back refilled.

"That afternoon," he said, "I was walkin' down on Sloane Street an' who d'you think I ran into, looking like all the flowers in May an' in some sorta uniform? Who else but Clovis."

Berg said: "No? You're not telling me that she's over here?"

Shakkey said: "I'm tellin' you that thing. What a dame!"

He rolled his eyes in ecstasy. "Boy, if that dame was good in the old days, you oughta see her now. What a figure!" He shrugged his shoulders. "Me—I never had a chance with Clovis," he said. "But how I would like to make that dame. Brother, how I would like to make that dame! She's got every thing—"

Berg said: "Yeah, you're tellin' me! What had she gotta say?"

Shakkey said: "We was talkin' about the old days, an' your name came up. I told her that I reckoned I'd seen you that mornin' in Piccadilly, or somebody who looked goddam like you. Well, she said a helluva lot of nice things about you. She said she'd always been sorta stuck on you; that you was a good guy."

Berg said: "Yeah . . . like hell she was stuck on me! An' Lauren was stuck on me. So they sell me out in the old days in Chicago. If she does that to a guy she's stuck on, I'd like to see what she'd do to a fella she don't like."

Shakkey said: "Well, there it is. Dames are funny things. An' anyhow she's too goddam beautiful to criticise. I think she's tops. It looks as if she's doin' a good job too."

Berg said: "Yeah, what's she doin'?"

Shakkey said: "I wouldn't know. There's so many goddam uniforms kickin' around here I don't even know what they are. But she got an idea about you."

Berg said: "An idea about me . . . what idea?"

Shakkey said airily: "She heard somethin' about you; that you was workin' with a Norwegian resistance movement or somethin' like that, doin' some under-cover job. Somebody had said somethin' like that to her some place. She asked me if I knew about you. I thought she seemed keen to meet up with you again."

Berg said: "She's got me all wrong. An' what do I wanta see Clovis for?"

Shakkey said: "Well, the years go on, an' people change. Maybe she ain't like she usta be. Let's have another drink."

Berg said: "Yeah, why not?" He began to think about Clovis—about the old days. He went to the bar; ordered more drinks. When he came back, Shakkey said: "D'you know what I think, Rene? D'you know what I think? You an' me are two very lucky guys. I reckon we both oughta been stuck in Alcatraz in the old days. I reckon they *woulda* stuck us there too if they'd been able to find us when they wanted to. An' now here are you a big shot in somethin' or other an' lookin' good, an' me a Chief Machinist's Mate in a destroyer in the U.S. Navy. Is life funny or is it? I reckon we oughta make a night of it."

Berg said: "Yeah . . . why not?"

Meeting Shakkey had brought a strange nostalgic feeling to him. Memories of the better parts of the old days crowded into his mind. He said: "O.K. But I gotta date to keep first, Shakkey." He looked at his wrist-watch. "Look," he went on, "it's eight o'clock. I'll meet you here at half-past nine. We'll have some drinks an' talk about the old days."

"Okey doke," said Shakkey. "I reckon we'll stick around here an' drink till they chuck us out. Then we'll go along to my place. I got a little apartment back in a mews off Sloane Street. We'll finish up there."

Berg said: "That's O.K. by me. I'll see you here at nine-thirty, Shakkey. So long."

He got up, walked out of the bar, down the stairs. At the bottom of Sackville Street, Berg was lucky enough to get a taxicab. He told the man where to go.

He got out at a house near Birdcage Walk. There was an iron gate and a little pathway leading up to the door. Berg rang the bell. A man in the uniform of the Royal Marines opened the door.

He said: "Good-evening, Mr. Berg."

Berg said: "Good-evening. The commander in?"

The marine said: "Yes, he's waiting for you. He's on the phone at the moment, but go in. I don't think he'll be very long."

Berg walked down the passage; went into the room at the end. It was a large room, comfortably furnished as a study. A desk with a shaded light stood in the corner. On a table nearby there was a bottle of whisky, a syphon, some glasses and a box of cigarettes. Berg opened the box, took a cigarette, lit it. He began to walk about the room, looking at the pictures. He paused at the desk and looked down. There was a folder on it—a red folder—and on a label on the front was "*U.S. Military Intelligence Liaison. Report Rene Berg. Chicago* 1932."

Berg made a little whistling noise. He switched the folder round, opened it. Inside were a dozen typewritten foolscap sheets. Berg began to read. He stood there, smoking quietly, reading the long official report on the activities of Scansci, Travis, himself and all the other boys and girls of the old mob. After a while he closed the folder. He turned towards the door as Ransome came in.

Ransome was in uniform. Berg thought he was a swell looking type. He said: "Well, Commander, how's it going?"

Ransome said: "Not too bad, Rene." He pointed to the folder on the table. "Have you seen that?" he asked.

Berg said: "Yeah, I was just lookin' at it. You boys get around to finding things out, don't you?"

Ransome said: "Yes, we have to sometimes too. Things aren't always what they seem. I never imagined that you were an angel with wings—in the old days I mean, in Chicago. I've always had some ideas about you, but I'm rather inclined to judge people on what they are, not on what they have been." He smiled. "You've done a pretty good job with me, you know—four years' service—and you've taken a hell of a lot of chances."

He helped himself to a cigarette, poured out two whiskies and sodas. He said: "Things aren't always what they seem. That folder is not there because I particularly wanted to delve into your past, but because I had to have the information because of some activities that might be coming along. But that can wait. When we've done the job that I'm planning now, we'll get around to this other thing." He pointed to the folder with a long forefinger. "You can do a lot to help me too. It's a job that I think will suit you."

Berg said: "O.K. What you say."

Ransome handed him the drink. He said: "Sit down, Rene. Let's deal with this big job first. The time has come when we have got to get three or four people out of Norway—from the Skaalund district. The Germans know too much about them, and I think the war's not going to last for more than another year. So the time has come to get them out. I think we can do it. I think you'll be interested."

Berg drew on his cigarette. He said: "Yeah? Why?"

Ransome said: "Because one of the people I want to get out is Ingrid. You remember Ingrid?"

Berg said softly: "Yeah, I remember her."

He had. Most days her white face had been before him. Most days he had thought about her, wondered about her.

Ransome said: "How many times have you been dropped over in Norway since we all got out on that night?"

Berg said: "I should think seven or eight. But never around there—always other places where they wanted somebody tough who could use a gun."

Ransome said: "I know, but this isn't going to be so easy. The Germans know that we've got a strong resistance headquarters in that district. They'll be keeping an eye on it. We'll have to play it carefully."

Berg said: "I've never known you not play it carefully. You always seem to me to take a lot of trouble about anything you do." He grinned at Ransome.

Ransome said: "We've got a contact over there. The contact is already in touch with Ingrid and the two other resistance leaders we propose to bring over. But we cannot take any chances. They dare not move out of the district and we've got to know that they can come out of hiding and have a chance of being picked up by the plane. We can't have any slip-ups. They're much too valuable."

Berg said: "Yeah, I can understand that. What's the idea?"

"The idea is this," said Ransome. "An air-raid will have to be put on—the usual thing—a box barrage of bombers dropping bombs, making a lot of noise, keeping the attention of the Germans concentrated. We'll drop you in the middle of the box. That will be on the edge of the forest, just outside Skaalund. It's good ground there for dropping." He grinned. "It's not too far from that air-strip," he said. "You remember? The place where we took the plane and got away from?"

Berg said: "I remember."

"We drop you there," said Ransome. "I'll give you directions as to where you go to pick up Ingrid and the other three. If everything's well, you can give us a signal that's arranged. A plane will land and pick the lot of you up. It's got to be done quickly. There mustn't be any mistakes."

Ransome got up; helped himself to another cigarette. He said: "You've taken a lot of chances with me, Berg. You've done good work. I could send somebody else to do this, but I had an idea"—he smiled at Berg—"you'd like to go."

Berg said: "Yeah? Why?"

Ransome said: "I don't know . . . both Hilde and I always had an idea in our heads that you were a little stuck on Ingrid, if you know what I mean."

Berg shifted his feet uncomfortably. He said: "Well, maybe I am, and maybe I'm not. But I'd like to go."

Ransome said: "All right. Come and see me on Thursday. We do the job at the end of next week. By then I'll have everything cut and dried."

"All right," Berg said. "That's O.K. with me."

Ransome said: "Have one for the road."

Berg said: "Thanks, I will." He drank the whisky. He said: "Well, so long, Commander. Thanks for the job."

Ransome said: "I thought you'd like it. Are you all right for money?"

Berg said: "Yeah, I'm doin' fine. You've always been swell about that anyway."

Ransome said: "Why not? Good-night, Rene."

Berg went out. He began to walk across the park in the direction of Piccadilly. He felt strangely elated—almost excited. Before him in the darkness he could see Ingrid's white face.

It was one o'clock in the morning when Berg pushed open the door of Shakkey's rooms in the Mews; walked unsteadily down the stairs towards the street. He was drunk. He thought to himself: Why the hell should I be high like this? What's happening to me? He found it difficult to understand. He stood in the middle of the staircase swaying a little; then he went back, pushed open the door of the flat, passed through the sitting-room into the bedroom.

Shakkey was lying across the bed. He had passed right out. Berg thought: Well, maybe it's knocked him too. Maybe I'm taking it better than he is. He closed the door; walked down the stairs. At the bottom, when he opened the street door, the cold night air made him a little more unsteady. He walked out into the dark Mews, moved across to the other side, leant for a moment against the wall. His head was going round and round. He had a pain at the base of his skull. When he put his hand to his forehead he found it was wet with sweat.

He stood, leaning against the wall, thinking. He thought: This is goddam funny. He felt almost as if somebody had given him a Mickey Finn. But people didn't do that in England. And why should Shakkey do it—Shakkey, who was in a worse condition himself? Berg fumbled in his pocket for his cigarette case. Now his head was beginning to clear a little. He lit a cigarette, stood leaning against the edge of a doorway, smoking quietly. He was trying to collect his thoughts; to think about the evening with Shakkey. Berg discovered that he remembered very little about it. They had talked a hell of a lot, but his mind was not as clear as usual. He could not pinpoint it down to any particular point of conversation. The cigarette tasted acrid and bitter. He threw it into the gutter.

The sound of high heels came towards him. A woman was walking with short staccato steps down the Mews. She stopped opposite him, put a key in the lock, opened the outer door of Shakkey's flat. There was a light inside. From where he was Berg could see her distinctly. It was Clovis.

He ran his tongue over his dry lips. He said: "Hey . . . Clovis. . . ."

The woman, who was about to close the door behind her, stopped. She looked out into the darkness. Berg walked across the Mews. He leaned against the side of the door, looking at her.

He said: "Well, Shakkey said you'd improved with the years. He said he reckoned you was plenty beautiful. I reckon you are too. An' you look good in that uniform."

She looked at him for a moment; then she put her hand on his arm. She said: "You don't know how good it is to see you. I was talking to Shakkey about you the other day. He said he thought that he'd seen you some place. I hoped we might have an opportunity to meet."

Berg said: "Yeah? Well, now we have met. I reckon you oughta be happy."

She made a little moue. He noticed that her lips were still full and red, her teeth still perfect and white. She looked at him with her large blue eyes.

She said: "Rene, why do you sound so bitter?"

Berg began to laugh. He said: "Ain't you the little pip? Maybe your memory's not as good as mine is. Maybe you've forgotten the old days back in Chi. Maybe you and Lauren and Travis have all of you forgotten the little ride you took me; how you framed me into the mob; how you framed me inta killin' Calsimo an' then Scansci. You were a little sweetie-pie, weren't you? An' you'd got your nerve. If the cops had got their hooks on me in the old days after what I'd done, they'd have fried me so hard that I'd have just been a cinder. An' what would you have done about it? You was gonna let 'em do it. An' you have the goddam nerve to stand there an' tell me that I'm bein a little bitter. You know what I'd like to do? I'd like to smack you down, baby. I think you're poison."

There was a silence; then she said: "Rene, I'm afraid you don't understand. We all make mistakes. We all do things that we regret. Maybe in those days I was rather like a squirrel running round in a cage trying to escape."

"Yeah?" said Berg. "Some squirrel! A squirrel with a coupla Chinchilla coats an' all the ice you wanted. You weren't no squirrel. You were more like a goddam rattlesnake."

Clovis sighed. She looked away from him. Berg could see the full beauty of her profile; the line of her neck and bosom.

She said: "Rene, I can understand you saying hard things to me. You don't know how I regret everything that happened in the old days. One day you'll know it wasn't all my fault. One day you'll know that. And I'd like to tell you something else. I gave you something once, Rene, back in those old days, because I loved you. Supposing I told you now that I still love you. What would you say?"

Berg said: "I'd say you was a goddam liar like you've always been." An idea struck him. "Look, Toots," he said, "what're you doin' around here? Maybe you're stuck on Shakkey now. You used not to think very much of Shakkey in the old days, did you? You bet you didn't. Then he was just the guy who looked after the trucks down at the garage. What're you stuck on him now for? He's not much more—a Chief Machinist's Mate in the U.S. Navy. An' here's little Clovis payin' him visits at nearly two o'clock in the mornin'. Maybe you've fallen for Shakkey as well as bein' in love with me—you little so-and-so!"

Her eyes blazed. She said: "There are moments when I could be very angry with you, Rene, but I'm not going to lose my temper with you whatever you say."

Berg said: "How could you lose your temper with me? You can't afford to lose your temper with anybody. You know what you are, Clovis? You're just a tramp! I'm wise to you."

She drew her hand back. She hit him across the face. Berg never moved.

He said: "Well, that got you. sweetiepie, didn't it? I hope you liked it, because I meant it. When you get upstairs give Shakkey my regards; that is if he's come to yet. But maybe that wouldn't bother you."

He stepped back. She slammed the front door. Berg stood for a moment in the Mews looking at the door. He was trying to piece together some odd bits in a jigsaw. Clovis . . . Shakkey . . . himself. . . . He could not do it. His mind was muzzy. None of the pieces would fit. Vaguely, for some reason unknown to himself, he remembered the folder on Ransome's desk—the dossier about himself—the report of the American Intelligence on him—the job that Ransome had talked about.

Berg shrugged his shoulders. One day he had no doubt everything would be plain. In the meantime there was little use in worrying. He looked up at the window of Shakkey's flat. The blackout curtain had moved a little. There was a chink of light.

Berg walked slowly away. He thought Clovis had descended in the social scale. Scansci, Travis, himself . . . now Shakkey . . . and who else? He wondered what she wanted from Shakkey. He wondered what Shakkey had to give a woman like Clovis.

Clovis pushed open the bedroom door and stood, looking at the recumbent figure of Shakkey. He presented a disgusting picture. He lay across the bed, his shirt collar undone, his mouth open. He was breathing stertorously, muttering, twisting about.

She went into the kitchen, opened the cupboard, found a bottle of concentrated coffee, prepared to boil water. After a while she went back into the bedroom. She carried in one hand a cup of black coffee, in the other a towel.

She put down the coffee; dipped the towel in the cold water jug on the wash-stand. She poured some of the cold water over Shakkey's face and head; began gently to flick him across the face with the wet towel. After some five minutes Shakkey opened his eyes. He looked up at her stupidly.

Clovis said: "Drink this, Cyram. It will put you right." She raised his head on one arm; sat on the bed beside him, began to feed the coffee to him spoonful by spoonful. After a while Shakkey got to his feet. He stood looking at her; then, with a grunt, staggered out of the room. She heard him stagger to the bathroom. When he returned she had more hot coffee ready for him.

Shakkey sat on the bed. He began to drink the coffee. He said: "Well . . . so you got around here. Goddam it, I didn't think you woulda come. I didn't think you meant it."

Clovis said: "I always do what I promise . . . well . . . most of the time." She smiled at him. It was an odd smile.

Shakkey walked over to the wash-stand; began to bathe his face in cold water. When he was through he said: "That was *some* hooch you sent around. For Chrissake . . .! I ain't never drunk stuff like that. It was like somebody had made it in the bath-tub. I'm tellin' you that a Mickey Finn was a clover-leaf cocktail compared with that stuff."

She said: "It wasn't very tough. I knew he'd never talk unless he was half-cut. And that guy could always drink liquor and remember to keep his mouth shut."

Shakkey said: "You don't like the guy. You don't like Rene . . . hey?"

She said: "No . . . I don't like him. I don't *have* to like him." There was a pause. Then: "Well . . . what did he say? What's he going to do? Where's he going next?"

Shakkey looked at her. He ran his tongue over his lips. He drank some more of the coffee. After a while he asked:

"What's the big idea? Whaddya wanta know about him for? Do you care where he goes an' what he does? What's it to you, Clovis?"

She shrugged her shoulders. She said: "I always like to know what he's doing. I can't sort of get away from him. Sometimes I think I'm still stuck on him, and sometimes I hate his guts. That's the way I feel right now. But I'm curious about that guy. I'm like a child that's got to keep on pokin' its finger in the fire just to see if it's still going to hurt. Can you understand that?"

Shakkey nodded. He thought he could. He said: "Yeah . . . I reckon dames are like that. Didn't some mug say that Hell ain't got any fury like a baby that's been given the air." He grinned at her. He went on: "It was pretty swell of you to come around here. I didn't think you'd come. I reckon you're the tops, Clovis. Jeez . . . are you a baby or are you?" He looked at her ankles.

She said in a flat voice: "When you called through to me that you'd met him; that you were going to meet again tonight, I sent that hooch round because I wanted him to talk. It was doctored all right . . . you bet it was. I couldn't tell you about that, because if I had you'd have laid off it yourself and he'd have suspected something. He's very smart . . . that one." There was another silence; then she said: "Well . . . what did he say? I reckon he'd talk to you. You're the only one he trusts. I reckon he thinks you're his one pal."

Shakkey wetted his lips again. He said, in a voice that was a little hoarse: "You remember what you said . . . you remember what you promised?"

Clovis said: "I remember. Tell me what he said, and I'll keep my promise . . . maybe . . ."

She got off the bed; began to walk about the room. Shakkey watched her. She moved gracefully. She knew his eyes were on her.

Shakkey said: "Well . . . when he'd had three or four, he started to go funny. I'd only had one . . . like you told me. I was listenin'. He was nearly right out. Then he started mutterin' an' moanin'. He was sittin' in that chair over there. He said somethin' about some dump called Skaalund or somethin' like that. He was talkin' about some dame Ingrid an' Norway an' somethin' about takin' a jump. Afterwards . . . when we'd laid off, an' he was gettin' straighter an' I talked about seein' him again next week, he said he couldn't do it. He said he was goin' away."

Clovis said: "I see . . . I see. . . ." Her eyes were gleaming. She said: "I'm going out now. I'll be back."

Shakkey got up. He moved in front of the door. He said: "Jeez . . . are you gonna stand me up now! Are you gonna take a powder on me after I done what I said?"

She came over to him. She stood in front of him. She made a little grimace.

"I'm coming back," she said. "I'll keep my word. But I've got to do something. I'll be back in a few minutes. Get out of my way."

Shakkey moved away from the door. She went out. When she had gone he went back and sat on the bed. He muttered to himself: "For Chrissake . . . for Chrissake . . .!" He sat there muttering and waiting.

Clovis walked down the Mews into the main street. There was a telephone booth on the corner. She went in, dialled a number. She waited; then someone answered.

She said: "This is Clovis. All right. Am I talking to Mr. Maston? Well, listen. . . . It's what I thought. Skaalund . . . in Norway. Some tie-up with some girl Ingrid . . . and it's probably going to be next week. . . ."

The voice said: "Excellent. Thank you very much. Goodnight!"

She came out of the call box. She stood for a moment looking up the dark street. Then she shrugged her shoulders.

She began to walk back to Shakkey's flat.

Berg sat in the seat behind the pilot. The pilot was a young man of twenty-three—a crack flyer in a Mosquito squadron. He had a permanent smile and the large handlebar moustaches at one time fashionable in the R.A.F. From time to time he looked over his shoulder at Berg and grinned.

Berg sat stiffly in his seat. He had a .45 automatic in a shoulder holster on each side of his parachute jacket, one of the German machine-pistols which he had taken from the Gendarmerie head-quarters some four years ago, and of which he was fond, three clips of ammunition, and a spring parachute knife.

The pilot throttled back, began to glide. He said to Berg through the ear-phones: "Well, the boys ought to be starting in a minute. I must say you've got a nice night for it." His grin broadened. "And I hope you don't come down in a ditch."

Berg said: "Me too." He grinned back at the pilot.

There was silence for a moment; then the pilot said: "There she goes. The boys are in."

He opened the taps. The sound of bombing came to Berg's ears. They were flying low and the crashes as the bombs exploded reverberated. Two miles away, on the right, an ammunition dump or something of the sort went up in flames. Now the German anti-aircraft went into action. The noise was terrific.

Berg looked down at the buckle of his safety belt. They were banking now. The pilot called:

"Where do you want to go from—eight hundred or lower? It's what you say. I always try to please the customers!"

Berg said: "You have it your way. Last time it was about eight hundred and it was good."

The pilot said: "I don't think so . . . not to-night and with this bus. You get out at five hundred feet. It'll be better for you."

Berg said: "All right." He undid the buckle of his safety belt.

The pilot started his approach to the D.Z. Berg could feel the sharp turn of the bank as he came into the wind. The pilot put down his flaps and landing wheels to make a greater resistance against the wind.

He said to Berg over the intercom.: "Flaps and landing wheels down. Get over the hatch."

Berg knelt down over the escape hatch. He knelt behind it, slightly to one side.

The pilot said: "Here you go, fella. . . . Good hunting!"

The escape hatch opened in front of Berg. He said: "So long! Thanks for the trip."

He went out though the hatch head first. When he was clear he pulled the cord. He dropped nearly seventy feet; then checked. He began to descend slowly. Away on the left and right of him he could see the gun-flashes of the German anti-aircraft batteries. The British bombers were still at work. Berg thought, as the keen wind hit his face, that it was a nicely organised job. He hoped that he was clear of the forest.

He hit the ground, crumpled, fell backwards, gathered in the parachute cords, took his spring knife, cut them. Now he began to haul on the cords, pulling in the parachute. When he had got it he sat on one end and began to fold it. Nearby was a shell hole. He pushed the parachute into the shell hole; threw some earth on it. They'd find it some time, but there was lots of parachutes lying about. One more or less meant little.

Berg got up. He began to walk forward. After a minute he recognised where he was. He was about a hundred and fifty yards off the edge of the forest that bounded the airstrip from which Ransome, he and Hilde, had escaped four years ago. On the other side of the air-strip was the road that led into Skaalund. The contact was to meet him in the northeast corner of the fir-wood at three o'clock. If all went well, the plane which Ransome was sending for them should pick them up in another locality not too far away, where there was a good landing place, at ten minutes to five.

Now the noise of bombing was dying away. The anti-aircraft guns began to check down. Berg walked slowly forward towards the edge of the wood. Now there was a little moon and he could see the tops of the fir-trees silhouetted, against the sky. In the right-hand pocket of his parachute jacket was a flask of whisky. He took it out, took a long swig. The spirit warmed him. He felt better.

He had walked another twenty yards when he stopped; dropped on one knee. Somewhere near him he had heard a voice. He listened. More voices came to him. Ten yards from Berg, on the right, was a patch of gorse. He crawled over to it on his hands and knees. Covered by it, he stood up.

He stood there, the palms of his hands suddenly wet, his mouth dry. Advancing in extended order from the edge of the wood, some hundred yards away, was a body of German infantry; away on the left another section.

Berg thought: Well, here it is! Somehow they were wise to what had happened. They were sweeping the ground in extended order. They were going to get him some time. High above him he could hear the noise of an engine. It was the fighter pilot who had brought him circling, waiting for the signal that everything was O.K.

Berg thought quickly. If the pilot did not get the signal he might hang about for a bit thinking that Berg had made a bad landing; was pulling himself together. He'd probably wait some little while; then he might be late getting back, or if he stayed too long—if that happened, the plane that was to pick up Berg, Ingrid and the rest of them, might leave. Whatever happened that had got to be stopped, because even if Berg was not there to give the signal to the plane to land, if Ransome were in it he'd come down. He'd want to know what had happened to Berg. He'd want to have a look.

Berg thought this mustn't happen. Quite obviously the Germans knew something. Quite obviously, they had been waiting. He looked again. The line of men, extended, about three or four paces between each man, their bayonets snowing plainly in the moonlight, advanced slowly across the flat field. They were beating every bush, every bit of scrub.

Berg thought of Ingrid. Maybe the contact who was to meet him on the north-east corner of the fir-wood was already on his way there. He must be warned somehow. The Germans arrested anybody out after curfew, and with all these men about somebody was certain to spot him. There was only one thing to be done.

Berg unstrapped the machine-pistol and the two clips of ammunition. The two .45 automatics, strapped to each side of his jacket, were heavy. He took off the jacket, took the guns out of their holsters. He looked at them for a minute. They were old friends of his. He hated parting with them but they were too heavy for quick movement. He wrapped the guns in the parachute jacket, pushed it into the coppice. Maybe some other parachutist, dropping on the same sort of job, would find it; would guess what had happened to Berg.

He loaded the clip into the machine-pistol. He moved to the edge of the coppice. Now the line of men was only fifteen to twenty yards away. Berg snapped the safety catch off the pistol. He cuddled it into his shoulder. The gun made a staccato noise as he squeezed the trigger and sprayed the advancing line. Five of the German soldiers immediately in front of Berg went down. He fired another burst to his left; then, bent double, started to run for the fir-wood. Half-way there he stopped, fired another burst.

Now the shooting started. Bullets whistled past him. Berg grinned. That's what he wanted. Ingrid's contact, on his way to the appointment, would hear. He would guess what had happened. He would go back.

Berg ran swiftly. He was almost on the edge of the wood. He was thinking to himself: There is still a chance if I can get into the wood; if they don't find me before morning I might get out and hide up somewhere. One of the resistance guys might find me and hide me up. The thought was hopeful, but useless. At this moment Berg was hit. The bullet struck him in the chest, knocked him flat. He lay there. He could not get up. A blackness descended on him.

When Berg came to, he was propped against a tree just inside the wood. People stood about him. Nearby, somebody switched on the headlights of an ambulance. The lights illuminated the faces of the men who stood regarding him curiously. Berg thought: This is it!

Two men stood together, a little apart from the rest, looking down at him. One was the Oberleutnant of Gendarmerie whom he had knocked unconscious and left at headquarters years before. He spoke to the other man in German.

The other man turned to Berg. He said: "The Oberleutnant says that you were here four years ago; that you got away. He says he knows about you. So, my friend, you decided to come back again. Do you not think it was rather stupid?" He laughed. "But I admire your nerve," he said.

Berg said nothing. The German went on: "Let me present myself. I am Major Kramen of the Gestapo. We have been waiting for you, my friend. We are very glad to see you. I expect you have a lot to tell us."

Berg said: "Yeah? Well, I was unlucky. It can happen."

The German nodded. "It can happen," he said. "I agree with you. Also you have very little chance. It might have come off, but we knew."

Berg said: "You knew? How the hell did you know?" He coughed a little. "I don't believe you."

The German said: "We're not such fools. We have people in London. They are not fools either. We knew you were coming."

Berg sat, looking into the dark avenue on the other side of the lights between the fir trees. Now he understood. Now he understood Clovis's visit to Shakkey—the hooch that he had thought was doctored. He must have talked to Shakkey. All this time she had been waiting to get even with him. He shrugged his shoulders.

The German said: "We're going to send you to hospital. We shall look after you. You're much too valuable to be allowed to die, and you will not die. But when you are better we shall make you talk, my friend. You'll save yourself a lot of trouble now if you tell me who your contact was here. Somebody was due to meet you to-night. Who was it?"

He came forward. He knelt down opposite Berg. He said: "What is the name of the man or woman who was going to meet you to-night?"

Berg said: "I'll tell you." He pushed himself up on his left hand. He struck upwards with his right elbow. The blow struck the German on the mouth and nose.

Kramen fell sideways. One of the German soldiers pulled back the bolt of his rifle. Kramen, rising to his feet, his mouth, lips and nose bleeding, rapped out an order in German. He brushed the leaves and twigs from his breeches. He stood,

looking down at Berg; then he drew back his right foot. He kicked Berg in the face.

He said: "My friend, we have heard about you. Always when a certain parachutist has been dropped in Norway, there has been trouble and killing and shooting. Perhaps you are the one. Perhaps *you* are the one they call 'The Dark Hero.'"

Berg put his hand to his mouth. Two of his teeth were gone. When he took his hand away it was red with blood. He looked up at Kramen.

He said: "Fella . . . all my life I been tryin' to be a hero. Well, by God, it looks as if I *gotta* be one now."

Kramen said: "My friend, I agree with you. In Germany we have a very nice Concentration Camp for people like you. It is going to take you a long time to die. The interesting part is," he went on, "I am leaving this accursed country. I shall be in charge of that camp. I shall make you my own especial pleasure—my hobby. I shall make you surfer very much, my friend."

Berg said nothing. He was thinking of the words "*Dark Hero.*" So that's what they called him. He remembered the night when Hilde, flying back with Ransome and himself, had first used the words.

Strangely enough, he was not unhappy.

EPILOGUE
INGRID
August, 1945

WHEN Berg saw the little car in the shadow of the hedge by the white gate, he stopped. He turned and looked back to the spot where Clovis's body was lying at the foot of the tree.

He felt very little—certainly not regret. But somewhere there was a vague feeling of disappointment. He shrugged his shoulders. He could not work out exactly what this feeling meant; but then, he thought, he had never been awfully good at working out things to do with the mind. Sometimes you felt something. Sometimes an odd thing made you feel a little happy or sad. But most of the time you went on, because it wasn't too good to feel too happy or too sad. If you felt anything very much you were disappointed.

He got into the car and started the engine. He began to drive slowly back to Dartmouth. He drove slowly because he was thinking, and because he knew that the last act of the drama which had been his life was now being played. He grinned. Anyway, it was going to be a sensational act. He wondered what Ransome would think about it.

Berg knew exactly what would happen. He'd been long enough in England to know the strictly impartial processes of the English law. The English did not play around with situations. If you murdered somebody you swung for it. They hanged you by the neck until you were dead. You had a trial and even if you wanted to plead guilty they wouldn't let you. If you hadn't got lawyers or counsel they gave you the best for nothing. They gave you a chance all right, but if you'd killed somebody, especially if you were prepared to admit it, as he was, well, you were hanged. They sentenced you to be hanged by the neck until you were dead, and the judge put a black triangular thing on his head and hoped that the Lord God would have mercy on your soul. Berg had heard all about that. And then they weren't content with that. Even if you'd been sentenced, they'd appeal just to see that you got even another chance. And the appeal would be dismissed and within three weeks of the sentence they took you out and they hanged you nicely, quietly and in an orderly manner.

And that was what was going to happen to him.

But there was just one thing had to be done. There was one person whom Berg wanted to know a little more of the story than he would produce. He was not concerned with defending himself. Maybe he was bored with the whole setup. But he'd like Ransome to know.

It was a quarter past one when he stopped the car on the quay at Dartmouth. The moon was brighter now. Lying out in the broad part of the river he could see the destroyer *Whelp*. He thought that she looked a fine ship in the moonlight.

He lit a cigarette; walked along to the landing steps opposite the Raleigh Hotel. The river was quiet. Nothing moved. Berg walked towards the next landing steps—thirty to forty yards down the road. At the bottom of them two or three dinghies were tied up. Berg got into one. He began to pull out towards the destroyer. It was hard work. The tide was bad for him. He was glad when he arrived.

The watch officer, seeing the dinghy, stood at the top of the accommodation ladder. He said: "Well, what is it?"

Berg said: "I wanta see Commander Ransome. Tell him the name's Rene Berg. I reckon he'll see me all right."

The sub-lieutenant said: "I bet he will. He's been trying to get in touch with you all day."

Berg tied up the dinghy. He went up the ladder; stood, drawing on his cigarette.

The watch officer said: "Just stay here a minute. I'll be back." He returned in two or three minutes' time. He said to Berg: "Come with me. The commander will see you now."

When Berg went into the cabin, Ransome was seated at his desk, writing. His back was to Berg. He turned round on the revolving office chair. He was smiling.

He said: "Well, Berg, I'm glad to see you. But you've been a little elusive, I. must say. When I heard that you'd picked up the cheque book and the money I left for you at the old place; when I heard that you'd been to the American Club for the guns, I thought it was time that you and I had a talk."

Berg said: "Yeah. Well, we're having one, aren't we, Commander?"

Ransome said: "Yes. You look pretty good to me. I bet they gave you a lousy time in that concentration camp."

Berg said: "It wasn't so good. They pushed me around a bit. I've been back over three months, but I didn't feel I wanted to talk to you. So I kept away as long as I could. I went and picked up the money and the cheque book when I had to. I picked up the guns because I wanted 'em. I thought Shakkey had left 'em there."

Ransome said: "Why should you think that?"

Berg said: "I'll tell you why. The night the heinies took me I wrapped up those two guns in my parachute jacket. I left them in a coppice. I thought maybe that one of your people would find 'em an' bring 'em back. I reckoned if they did. that you'd give 'em to Shakkey, because I told you if anythin' happened to me I wanted anythin' that was comin' to me to go to him. So when I found 'em I thought he'd left 'em."

Ransome said: "Well, he didn't. I did." He smiled again. He went on: "But what did it matter, Rene?"

Berg said: "It mattered a lot to me. I wanted to get hold of this guy Shakkey, an' I was lucky. I found him." Berg grinned. "I found him down here to-night," he said. "He's a Chief Machinist's Mate on one of the U.S. destroyers here. But he was away—absent without leave. Then I went over to the Raleigh, and I got a tip-off from some dame. So I found him. I found him over at some dump called the Chateau de la Tours. You know it?"

Ransome said: "I know it. Why were you so keen on meeting Shakkey?"

Berg said: "I reckoned if I found Shakkey I'd be able to find a woman I was lookin' for—a dame called Clovis Scansci. Well, I was lucky. She was over there stayin' at this chateau place. After I'd had a talk with Shakkey he scrammed. So then I had a talk with her. And I fogged her. I shot her three times. She is lyin' at the foot of a tree in a little wood that's at the back of the big lawn behind the Chateau."

Ransome said: "Ah!" He took a box of cigarettes from his desk, handed one to Berg, took one himself. He snapped on his lighter, lit the cigarettes. He said: "Tell me, Berg, what did you have to do that for?"

Berg said: "I reckon it's a long story, Commander-—a goddam sight too long. But you'll only be interested in a bit of it. I met this Clovis Scansci a long time ago in Chicago. I got myself framed into a mob. I was a killer for Scansci. I killed a lotta guys out there. I reckon it was the only thing I knew. Then I got stuck on this Clovis dame a bit, an' she framed me inta shootin' a couple of other guys. Then I got out.

"O.K. The night I met you when I came to your place near Bird-cage Walk, an' you told me I was gonna be dropped at Skaalund to get Ingrid an' the others out, after I left you I had a date with Shakkey. I drank some hooch that had been doctored. I musta talked a little. When I was leavin' the place I met Clovis comin' in. I mighta guessed what the game was. Shakkey was crazy about her. He's nuts about women. I reckon she had schemed to get outa him what I was doin'. She just wanted to know because she was waitin' for a chance to get even with me. She wanted to get even with me because I'd been goddam rude to her; because I'd told her where she got off, an' she was the sorta baby who didn't like that. I reckon it was a case of love turned to hate—you know the stuff."

He grinned at Ransome. "So somehow she slips this informa-tion to some fella called Maston, who was workin' over here for the Jerries. His real name was Schlengel. An' when I dropped that night they were waitin' for me—about three infantry companies all of them probin' about the place. I hadn't got a dog's chance."

Ransome said: "What about a drink?"

Berg said: "I reckon I could use one."

Ransome went to a cupboard. He produced a bottle, a syphon and two glasses. He poured out the drinks, handed a glass to Berg. He said: "Go on."

Berg said: "All the time I was in that goddam concentration camp there was only two things I wanted to do before I died. One of 'em was to get the guy Kramen—the sub-commandant there who had pushed me around good an' plenty. An' the other thing—it was a sorta day dream—was if ever I got back here—or wherever I went—I'd find Clovis Scansci an' I'd kill her."

He shrugged his shoulders. "Well, I've done both those things," he said. "An' I'm not sufferin' from any delusions about what's gonna happen to me. If you kill somebody over here they hang you. I know that.

"That's O.K. All I wanted to do was to have a word with you. I reckon you've been the only pal I've ever had in my life. I wanted you to know. After that, all I haveta do is go ashore, see the local cops an' tell 'em." He finished the whisky.

Ransome said: "No, it isn't like that at all. Of course you're quite right about the woman Scansci." He held up his glass, looked at the amber liquid in it. He drank a little. He said: "Rene, do you remember that on the night you came to see me, when I first talked to you about this Skaalund jump, you found a folder on my desk? You had a look at it and you saw I'd got your record from the U.S. Military Intelligence. You remember that?"

Berg said: "Yeah."

Ransome said: "Do you remember I told you that when you got back from the Norway thing there was another job I was going to ask you to do—a job you were particularly suited to do?"

Berg said: "Yeah, I remember."

Ransome finished his whisky. He said: "It's rather extraordinary, but if you turned over two or three more pages of the folder you'd have seen I wasn't only concerned with you, but very much more concerned with Mrs. Clovis Scansci, whom we knew had been working for the Germans since a year before the war. We knew she was in England. I intended to put you on to finding her. That's rather funny, isn't it?" Ransome grinned. "It looks to me as if she found you first," he said.

Berg said: "Well, that beats everything. So you was out lookin' for her an' she gets me first. An' I come back an' I get her."

Ransome said: "Yes. But so far as I am concerned it's not murder. You're still working for me, Berg. You're still working for the Allied Intelligence Liaison. If you shot Clovis Scansci to-night you merely executed her a little before her time. We were going to pick her up. We could have done it any time we wanted to, but she's led us on to other people. We got Schlengel and a half a dozen others through her. If ever a woman deserved to be executed it was that one. She'd have had it anyway."

Berg looked at Ransome. He said: "What the hell . . .! D'you mean I get away with this?"

Ransome said: "Yes." He went on: "You've worked for me for a long time. You're a brave man. I know all about you, Berg. I've had your whole story. I know it. I don't think you ever had much of a chance in the old days, but during the time you were with me you produced the qualities that I think go to make a man—courage and loyalty. You had a damned bad time in that concentration camp, but I don't believe you ever squealed, and as I've said, if ever a killing was justified, it was the woman Scansci."

Berg said: "Well, what do you know? What are you gonna do, Commander?"

Ransome said: "I'll look after this thing. I'll have the body moved to-night. You can take it from me that nobody's going to miss Mrs. Scansci very much. You can also take it from ma that our own M.I. Department are going to be very pleased to know that she is no longer with us. The story is of course that you went there to-night on my instructions to identify her—to bring her back. Well, she tried to escape. She did what would be a natural thing for her to do. She pulled a gun on you. So you did"—Ransome smiled—"what would be a natural thing for you. You killed her. I'll take care of that."

Berg said: "Thanks a lot. So what happens?"

Ransome got up. He said: "You'd better pull ashore. I'll give you a chit to the American Club. You can sleep there to-night. Come and see me in the morning. Maybe I'll find another job for you. And there's something you can do for me when you get ashore to-night. Go over to the Ferris Hotel and knock up the night porter. He's an old man and he'll take some knocking up, but he'll turn out eventually. When he lets you in, tell him that you're delivering a message for me to the occupant of Room 29 on the first floor. Deliver the message personally. You understand?"

Berg said: "I got it. Room 29 at the Ferris Hotel. An' I see you to-morrow mornin' at eleven o'clock. That O.K.?"

Ransome said: "That's all right. Now I'll give you the note." He sat down at his desk, wrote a note. He put it in an envelope, sealed it. He gave it to Berg. He said: "Well, Berg, you've been an unlucky person for quite a part of your life, but perhaps your luck's changed. You've certainly been lucky to-night."

Berg grinned. He said: "You're tellin' me!"

Ransome held but his hand. They shook hands. Berg went away.

Berg knocked at the door of the Ferris Hotel for a good ten minutes before the night porter—grey-haired and rheumaticky— turned out. He stood in the doorway regarding Berg with suspicion.

Berg said: "I've got a letter to deliver to Room 29 and I've got to do it myself. I've come from Commander Ransome."

The night porter said: "That's all right. I know the Commander. Up the stairs—it's the third door on the left. And shut the door after you when you go out and see it's locked."

Berg said: "O.K."

The old man shuffled away.

Berg went slowly up the stairs. He was feeling a little dazed. He thought life was goddam funny. Just when you thought it had got you right down on the floor; just when you thought you'd had it; that you were out, it turned around and lifted you up again. He shrugged his shoulders.

At the top of the stairs a dim light burned. Berg found No. 29, knocked on the door. There was a pause. Then he heard someone moving inside the room. He heard the light switched on; then the door opened.

Berg held out the letter. He said: "This is from Commander Ransome." He looked up.

Standing in the doorway, smiling at him, was Ingrid.

Berg looked at her, his eyes wide with amazement. He said: "For Chrissake . . . Ingrid . . .!"

She said: "Yes, Rene . . . it's me." She held out her hand for the letter.

Berg gave it to her. He stood staring at her stupidly. He thought: So this is what being in love with some dame really is. All this time I've been crazy about this kid, and I've never known it. Is that funny or is it?

She said: "Rene, do you know what's in this note?"

Berg said: "Nope."

She said: "I'd like you to read it." She held the piece of quarto paper out towards Berg.

He took it; stood sideways to the door so that the light fell on the paper. He read:

"Dear Ingrid,

"I am sending you The Dark Hero once again. You always said that he would come back and that you would wait for him. Well, here he is.

"Good luck to you both. You deserve it.

"Yours ever,

"C. T. R. Ransome."

Berg stood there, looking at the piece of paper. For some reason which he could not understand he saw that the fingers holding it were trembling.

Ingrid said: "Come in, Rene. You and I have a great deal to talk about."

THE END

Printed in Great Britain
by Amazon

24994035R00111

C000006043

Remember This?

People, Things and Events
FROM **1954** TO THE **PRESENT DAY**

UK EDITION

Copyright © 2021 Say So Media Ltd.
All rights reserved.

No part of this book may be reproduced in any form or by any electronic or mechanical means including information storage and retrieval systems, without permission in writing from the publisher.

All product names and brands are property of their respective owners. No endorsement is given or implied.

With thanks for additional research by Dale Barham, Nicola Gardiner and Janice Morton.

Baby names: Office of National Statistics.

Cover images: Mary Evans - Grenville Collins Postcard Collection, Keystone Pictures USA/zumapress.com, Roger Mayne Archive, Marx Memorial Library. Cover icons from rawpixel/Freepik.

Cover Design: Fanni Williams / thehappycolourstudio.com

The Milestone Memories series including this *Remember This?* title is produced by Milestones Memories Press, a division of Say So Media Ltd.

First edition: October 2021

We've tried our best to check our facts, but mistakes can still slip through. Spotted one? We'd love to know about it: info@saysomedia.net

Rewind, Replay, Remember

What can you remember before you turned six? If you're like most of us, not much: the comforting smell of a blanket or the rough texture of a sweater, perhaps. A mental snapshot of a parent arriving home late at night. A tingle of delight or the shadow of sorrow.

But as we grow out of childhood, our autobiographical and episodic memories – they're the ones hitched to significant events such as birthdays or leaving school – are created and filed more effectively, enabling us to piece them together at a later date. And the more we revisit those memories, the less likely we are to lose the key that unlocks them.

These fragments are assembled into a more-or-less coherent account of our lives – the one we tell ourselves, our friends, our relatives. And while this one-of-a-kind biopic loses a little definition over the years, some episodes remain in glorious technicolour – although it's often the most embarrassing incidents!

But this is one movie that's never quite complete. Have you ever had a memory spring back unbidden, triggered by something seemingly unrelated? This book is an attempt to discover those forgotten scenes using the events, sounds, and faces linked to the milestones in your life.

It's time to blow off the cobwebs and see how much you can remember!

It Happened in 1954

The biggest event in the year is one that didn't make the front pages: you were born! Here are some of the national stories that people were talking about.

+ Runner Roger Bannister breaks four-minute mile (right)
+ Britons witness first total solar eclipse since 1927
+ First book in JRR Tolkien's Lord of the Rings trilogy published
+ William Golding's classic Lord of the Flies published
+ Fourteen years of food rationing ends
+ IRA seizes weapons cache in Armagh barracks raid
+ Queen Elizabeth first reigning monarch to visit Australia
+ First episode of radio sitcom Hancock's Half Hour airs
+ Sir Winston Churchill celebrates 80th birthday
+ First Wimpy Bar opens in central London
+ Dockers across the country go on strike
+ Saucy seaside postcards ruled 'obscene'
+ Treaty ends 70 years of British occupation of Suez Canal Zone
+ Government announces link between smoking and cancer
+ Diane Leather first woman to run mile in under five minutes
+ Ethiopian emperor Haile Selassie visits UK
+ Prestwick air crash kills 28
+ First broadcast of Dylan Thomas' radio play Under Milk Wood
+ 100th University Boat Race won by Oxford
+ English Electric's supersonic jet fighter Lightning takes off
+ Operation Anvil cracks down on Kenyan Mau Mau rebels

Born this year:
&⁓ Eurythmics singer Annie Lennox born in Aberdeen
&⁓ Scottish sci-fi author Iain Banks born in Dunfermline
&⁓ Pet Shop Boys' Neil Tennant born in North Shields, Tyneside

In less than auspicious weather on 7 May 1954, medical student Roger Bannister achieved the unachievable in Oxford: the first sub-four-minute mile. The timekeeper was Norris McWhirter, co-founder of the Guinness Book of Records. After one more epic race later that year, Bannister decided that his future career in neurology would take precedence over his athletic abilities; he viewed his achievements in science as more significant than his world record. He died in 2018.

On the Bookshelf
When You Were Small

The books of our childhood linger long in the memory. These are the children's classics, all published in your first ten years. Do you remember the stories? What about the covers?

1954	The Eagle of the Ninth by Rosemary Sutcliff
1954	Horton Hears a Who! by Dr Seuss
1956	Kenny's Window by Maurice Sendak
1956	**Hundred and One Dalmatians by Dodie Smith** Dodie Smith wrote the book after one of her friends commented that her dalmatians would make a lovely coat. She had nine – including a Pongo.
1956	The Silver Sword by Ian Serraillier
1956	Little Old Mrs Pepperpot by Alf Prøysen
1957	Moominland Midwinter by Tove Jansson
1957	The Cat in the Hat by Dr Seuss
1958	Five Get into a Fix by Enid Blyton
1958	A Bear Called Paddington by Michael Bond
1958	Tom's Midnight Garden by Philippa Pearce
1959	Silly Verse for Kids by Spike Milligan
1959	The Rescuers by Margery Sharp
1960	**Green Eggs and Ham by Dr Seuss** A $50 bet, laid and won: could Dr Seuss write a book with 50 unique words or fewer? Oh yes, he can!
1960	Tintin in Tibet by Hergé
1960	Weirdstone of Brisingamen by Alan Garner
1961	**James and the Giant Peach by Roald Dahl** The giant peach was originally a giant cherry, inspired by a tree in Dahl's garden.
1961	The Phantom Tollbooth by Norton Juster
1961	Gumble's Yard by John Rowe Townsend
1962	Wolves of Willoughby Chase by Joan Aiken
1963	The Secret Passage by Nina Bawden
1963	Stig of the Dump by Clive King
1963	Where the Wild Things Are by Maurice Sendak
1964	On the Run by Nina Bawden

Around the World in Your Birth Year

Here are the events from abroad that were big enough to make news at home in the year you were born. And you won't remember any of them!

- ✦ European football association UEFA formed in Basel, Switzerland
- ✦ Marilyn Monroe weds baseball star Joe DiMaggio in San Francisco
- ✦ World's first nuclear-powered submarine USS Nautilus launched
- ✦ World's first Burger King opens in Miami, Florida
- ✦ Alabama woman hit by 9lb meteorite survives
- ✦ First portable transistor radio Regency TR-1 goes on sale in USA
- ✦ Earthquake in northern Algeria kills over 1,000; 5,000 injured
- ✦ Sun Myung Moon founds Moonies' Unification Church in South Korea
- ✦ McCarthy hearings investigate US army 'communists'
- ✦ Gateway to the US, Ellis Island's immigration station closes
- ✦ US firm Swanson & Sons create first frozen TV dinners
- ✦ First mass vaccination of children against polio begins in USA
- ✦ Italian climbers reach summit of world's second highest peak K2
- ✦ World's first atomic power station opens at Obninsk, near Moscow
- ✦ Gamal Abdel Nasser becomes first prime minister of Egypt
- ✦ Elvis Presley releases his first single That's All Right
- ✦ First successful kidney transplant carried out in Boston, USA
- ✦ US Supreme Court rules racial segregation of schools 'unlawful'
- ✦ First Indochina war ends – communists take over North Vietnam

Born this year:
- ✐ German Chancellor Angela Merkel born in Hamburg
- ✐ Actor/martial artist Jackie Chan born Chan Kong-Sang in Hong Kong
- ✐ TV host and actress Oprah Winfrey born in Kosciusko, Mississippi
- ✐ US actor Denzel Washington born in Mount Vernon, New York

Boys' Names When You Were Born

Stuck for a name in the early 20th century? The answer was simple: use your own. Will nobody think of the genealogists? Here are the most popular names in England and Wales in 1954.

David
David has wrestled control of the top spot from John, and he'll keep it for twenty years.

John
Stephen
Michael
Peter
Robert
Paul
Alan
Christopher
Richard
Anthony
Andrew
Ian
James
William
Philip
Brian
Keith
Graham

Rising and falling stars:
Farewell Bernard, Frank, Norman, Leonard, Lawrence and Clifford. Give a big Top 100 welcome to Jeremy, Julian and all the G's: Gerard, Garry, Gareth and Gregory and Glenn.

A note about other parts of the UK:
Baby name data isn't available until 1974 for Scotland and the turn of the century for Northern Ireland. How different are they? In the mid-seventies around a third of Scotland's Top 100 boys' names weren't in the English and Welsh equivalent – but the highest ranked of these was Gordon at number 30. By 2019, Scotland-only names ranked 4th (Harris), 7th (Lewis), 18th (Brodie), 22nd (Finlay) and more.

Girls' Names When You Were Born

Some parents pick names that are already popular. Others try to pick something more unusual – only to find out a few years later that thousands had the same idea.

Susan
After thirty years, Susan takes the top spot from Margaret.

Linda
Christine
Margaret
Janet
Patricia
Carol
Elizabeth
Mary
Anne
Ann
Jane
Jacqueline
Barbara
Sandra
Gillian
Pauline
Elaine
Lesley
Angela
Pamela
Helen
Jennifer
Valerie

Jean
Slides from the Top 100 are usually gentle. But not for Jean: by the sixties, she was gone.

Rising and falling stars:
A quarter of names in this Top 100 haven't been seen since, including Rita, Geraldine and Doreen. Taking their place are names such as Gail, Dawn, Anna, Fiona and Beverley.

Things People Did When You Were Growing Up...

...that hardly anyone does now. Some of these we remember fondly; others are best left in the past!

+ Use a mangle
+ Do your National Service (it ended in 1960)
+ **Use an outside toilet**
  Slum clearances and grants saw the end of most outside toilets, although in 2010 around 40,000 properties still had one.

+ Take the trolley bus to school
+ Fetch coal from the cellar
+ Wear a hat to work
+ **Use a coal tar vaporizer**
  A coal tar inhaler or vaporizer – probably made by Wright's, with the matching liquid – seemed like a good idea for treating whooping cough. It wasn't. A 1930s example held by the National Trust has a simple caption: 'This is poisonous.'

+ Travel without a seatbelt
+ **Rent a TV**
  When tellies cost a fortune (and frequently broke), renting a TV made sense. Where to go? Radio Rentals, who promised, 'You'll be glued to our sets, not stuck with them!'

+ **Wear a housecoat**
  Who can think of a housecoat and curlers without remembering Coronation Street's Hilda Ogden?

+ Scrub your doorstep
+ Creosote the fence (banned for DIY in 2003)
+ **Smoke a pipe**
  Stephen Fry was the last Pipe Smoker of the Year, in 2003.

+ **Spank (or be spanked)**
  Corporal punishment ended in most schools in 1986. It is illegal in Scottish and Welsh homes, but not in England or N. Ireland.

+ Pay the Pools collector
+ Build a soapcart
+ **Write a letter**
  Royal Mail still handles 10 billion letters each year but very few are handwritten. More than a fifth of UK children have never received a letter.

Old-fashioned Games

In a pre-digital age, boardgames ruled. Many of these predate you buy decades, centuries or more but still played; others gather dust in attics and charity shops.

1928	Escalado
1934	Sorry!
1935	**Monopoly**

The origins of this stalwart lie with The Landlord's Game, an education tool patented in 1904 by Elizabeth Magie. (The anti-monopoly version – Prosperity – didn't catch on.) It was the first game to feature a never-ending path rather than a fixed start and finish.

1938	Buccaneer
1938	Scrabble
1935	Whot!
1947	Subbuteo
1949	**Cluedo**

Cluedo, or Clue as it is known in the USA, introduced us to a host of shady country house characters and a selection of murder weapons. For years those included a piece of genuine lead pipe – thankfully replaced on health grounds.

1925	Dover Patrol
1851	**Happy Families**

The original and much-copied Happy Families card game was launched for the Great Exhibition in 1851. For 20th Century children, Happy Families also means the million-selling book series by Allan Ahlberg, based loosely on the card game, which in turn inspired a BBC series.

1889	**Tiddlywinks**

Trademarked as Tiddledy-Winks by Joseph Fincher, this much-maligned game has nevertheless found fans at elite universities, spawned countless spin-offs and rule variations (known in Tiddlywink parlance as 'perversions').

1896	Ludo
1892	Chinese Chequers
1938	Totopoly
Ancient Egypt	Mancala

Things People Do Now...

...that were virtually unknown when you were young.
How many of these habits are part of your routine or even
second nature these days? Do you remember the first time?

- Shop on Sunday (made possible in England and Wales in 1994)
- Microwave a curry
- **Leave a voicemail**
  At least you'll never have to change the cassette again!
- **Watch last night's TV**
  Nowadays, you don't have to remember to set the VCR (and get a
  small child to help you do it). BBC iPlayer was the UK's first
  on-demand, streaming service, launched in 2007.

- Strim grass
- Change a fitted sheet
- Recharge your toothbrush
- Order a takeaway meal... to be delivered
- Delete a photo
- **Fit a disposable nappy**
  The first disposable 'napkins' went on sale in 1949 as two-part
  Paddis, invented by Valerie Hunter Gordon.

- Eat an avocado
- Use Google
- Take a shower
- **Make a video call (right)**
- Buy a cheap flight
- **Floss your teeth**
  Not a flosser? Take heart from a 2016 US research review:
  evidence for its benefit is very weak, and official advice to floss
  was dropped. Poking around with those pesky interdental
  brushes is how you should be spending your time (and money).

- Pressure wash your patio
- **Stick a self-adhesive stamp**
  You can probably still remember the taste of stamp glue, even
  though the sticky versions were introduced in 1993.

- Answer an email (or send it to spam)
- **Use a duvet**
  Sir Terence Conran is credited with finally persuading Brits to
  ditch the blankets when he introduced duvets in his Habitat
  stores in the sixties.

Zoom, Skype, FaceTime and more: if you weren't making face-to-face calls before the lockdowns of 2020, that's probably when you made your first. But it has taken 50 years to catch on and for technology to catch up: shown above is AT&T's PicturePhone, demonstrated in 1964 at New York's World's Fair. (The cost didn't help: renting a pair of devices for three minutes cost

Popular Food in the 1950s

Few would wish the return of fifties food, even the dishes introduced after rationing finally ended in 1954. Tinned food, stacked high. For flavour, take your pick: ketchup, brown sauce, or salad cream. Keep your olive oil in the bathroom cabinet. But a few favourites live on: who can resist a coronation chicken sandwich?

Milkshakes
Thick, creamy and an ideal hiding place for a lethal dose of poison. That's what the CIA thought when they plotted to slip a pill into Castro's beloved chocolate milkshake. Fortunately for the Cuban leader, the pill stuck to the freezer door.

Chop Suey

Real cream cakes

Bananas
In the 1950s, Gros Michel bananas – the dominant banana sold – were wiped out by the Panama disease, nearly destroying the banana industry.

Peaches

Frosties
Introduced in 1954 as Sugar Frosted Flakes, this new cereal was an instant hit – as was Tony the Tiger.

Frozen chicken

Tinned pineapple
Think pineapple, think Hawaii. Pineapples are still cultivated there, although the state's last cannery closed in 2006.

Spam fritters
Dubbed the 'Miracle Meat' when it was introduced in the late thirties, Spam is no longer made in the UK but it's still popular. Worldwide, around 7 billion cans have been sold; 44,000 cans are still produced every hour.

Baked Alaska

Devilled eggs

Coronation chicken

Hamburgers
In the US during WWII, hamburgers were briefly rebranded 'liberty steaks' in a renewed bout of food-as-propaganda. In World War I, sauerkraut was 'liberty cabbage' while French fries became 'freedom fries' during the Iraq war.

Pre-war Chocolate

Many of the chocolate bars we enjoy today were dreamed up long before WWII – though recipes, sizes and names have mostly been given a tweak or two over the decades to keep them as our newsagent favourites.

1800s	**Fry's Chocolate Cream** The first chocolate bars to be mass-produced.
1905	Cadbury Dairy Milk
1908	Bourneville
1914	Fry's Turkish Delight
1920	Flake
1926	Cadbury's Fruit & Nut
1927	**Jaffa Cake** Her Majesty's Customs and Excise tried to argue that a Jaffa Cake is a biscuit and subject to VAT. McVitie's won the day, in part because Jaffa cakes go hard when stale, unlike biscuits which go soft.
1929	Crunchie
1932	**Mars Bar** Want to buy a Mars bar in the US? Ask for a Milky Way.
1932	Penguin
1935	Aero
1935	**Milky Way** The Milky Way is not named after our galaxy, but instead after a type of malted milk, or milkshake as it's now known.
1936	Milky Bar
1937	**Kit Kat** Before Joseph Rowntree trademarked the term 'Kit Kat' in 1911 and the snack's eventual launch in the thirties, the name was most commonly associated with a mutton pie made by pastry chef Christopher Catt. He served it in his London Kit-Cat Club during the late 17th Century.
1937	Rolo
1939	**Marathon** In 1990, Marathon became Snickers: the US name since its 1930 launch (named after Frank Mars's horse). In the seventies, Mars sold a chocolate bar in the US called the Marathon – and it's still on sale here as the Curly Wurly.

Cars of the 1950s

Do you remember your first road trip? Bare legs welded to the hot plastic seats, buffeted by gusts of warm air through the open windows and not a seatbelt to be seen. There's a fair chance you'll have been cooped up in one of these fifties favourites.

Austin Westminster
Ford Prefect
In The Hitchhiker's Guide to the Galaxy, an arriving alien picks the name Ford Prefect thinking it would be inconspicuous.

Vauxhall Velox
Sunbeam Talbot
Rover 60
Ford Anglia
Features on the cover of Harry Potter and the Chamber of Secrets.

Ford Consul
Hillman Minx
Morris Minor
Originally named Mosquito, the name was changed at the last minute as it was feared that the name would deter conservative buyers. It went on to become the first million-selling British car.

MG Magnette
Morris Oxford
Singer Gazelle
Standard Vanguard
Named after a Navy battleship to appeal to ex-servicemen.

Austin Cambridge
Wolseley / Riley One Point Five
The Riley One Point Five and the Wolseley shared features including the engine, suspension and dimensions. The Riley was originally intended as a replacement for the Morris Minor.

Ford Popular
Land Rover
The first Land Rover was inspired by World War II jeeps, with the steering wheel in the middle. A Land Rover with tank tracks for agricultural work and a monster truck version followed.

Austin A30
Dubbed the steel teddy bear due to its rounded, cute appearance.

1958 brought a rather less welcome motoring innovation: the parking meter. The first meters installed in Mayfair, London (sixpence for an hour, a shilling for two), triggered the predictable result from day one: parked cars crammed onto neighbouring streets without restrictions, below.

The Biggest Hits When You Were 10

Whistled by your father, hummed by your sister or overheard on the radio, these are the hit records as you reached double digits.

Glad All Over 🎵 The Dave Clark Five
Needles and Pins 🎵 The Searchers
Anyone Who Had a Heart 🎵 Cilla Black
Can't Buy Me Love 🎵 The Beatles
It's Over 🎵 Roy Orbison
House of the Rising Sun 🎵 The Animals
A folk song, recorded by an electric rock band:
this was the song which convinced Bob Dylan to abandon his roots and go electric.

It's All Over Now 🎵 The Rolling Stones
A Hard Day's Night 🎵 The Beatles
A Hard Day's Night was the feature song from The Beatles' movie of the same name – their first motion picture.
It was a commercial success despite low expectations and a correspondingly low budget.

Do Wah Diddy Diddy 🎵 Manfred Mann
You Really Got Me 🎵 The Kinks
I'm Into Something Good 🎵 Herman's Hermits
Oh, Pretty Woman 🎵 Roy Orbison
The track found a new lease of life when it was used as the theme for Julia Robert's iconic movie, Pretty Woman nearly 30 years later.

Baby Love 🎵 The Supremes
Little Red Rooster 🎵 The Rolling Stones
Little Red Rooster was the first big hit for The Stones, but was actually a cover of a song by one of their blues heroes, Howlin' Wolf.

Tech Breakthroughs Before You Turned 21

Much of the technology we use today stands on the shoulders of the inventions made while you were small. Here are some of the most notable advances.

1953	Heart-lung machine
1955	Pocket transistor radio
1956	Hard Disk Drive
1956	Operating system (OS)
1957	**Laser** The strength of the first laser was measured in 'Gillettes', as scientists tested the laser by assessing how many Gillette razor blades it could slice.
1958	Microchip
1959	Xerox copier
1959	**Three-point seatbelt** The patented three-point safety belt was first installed by Volvo in 1959. Volvo waived the patent rights so other manufacturers could use the design for free.
1959	Weather satellite
1962	**Red LEDs** It took a further ten years to develop yellow LEDs; blue and white LEDs weren't commercially viable for a further two decades.
1964	Plasma display
1965	Hypertext (http)
1966	Computer RAM
1967	Hand-held calculator
1967	**Computer mouse** Doug Engelbart patented an early version of his 'X-Y indicator' in 1967. By the time a (very large) mouse became available with a Xerox computer in 1981, the patent had expired.
1969	Laser printer
1971	Email
1973	Mobile phone

On the Silver Screen When You Were 11

From family favourites to the films you weren't allowed to watch, these are the movies that drew the praise and crowds when you turned 11.

The Collector 🎬 Terence Stamp, Samantha Eggar
The dark ending of The Collector would have been deemed illegal, but the censor fell asleep and missed the final scene.

Darling 🎬 Julie Christie, Dirk Bogarde
The Ipcress File 🎬 Michael Caine, Sue Lloyd
For a Few Dollars More 🎬 Clint Eastwood and Lee Van Cleef
Van Cleef only takes one eighth of a second to draw, cock and fire his pistol – just three frames of film.

The Sound of Music 🎬 Julie Andrews, Christopher Plummer
The Sound of Music proved to be the last ever Rodgers and Hammerstein musical.

Thunderball 🎬 Sean Connery, Claudine Auger
The Knack... and How to Get It 🎬 Rita Tushingham, Ray Brooks
Doctor Zhivago 🎬 Omar Sharif, Julie Christie
Von Ryan's Express 🎬 Frank Sinatra, Trevor Howard
A Patch of Blue 🎬 Sidney Poitier, Elizabeth Hartman
Cat Ballou 🎬 Jane Fonda, Lee Marvin
On winning the Oscar for Best Actor, Marvin dedicated half of the award to his horse co-star, Smoky.

Bunny Lake Is Missing 🎬 Carol Lynley, Laurence Olivier
The Intelligence Men 🎬 Eric Morecambe, Ernie Wise
Operation Crossbow 🎬 Sophia Loren, George Peppard
Help! 🎬 John Lennon, Paul McCartney
The Hill 🎬 Sean Connery, Harry Andrews
Dr Who and the Daleks 🎬 Peter Cushing, Roy Castle
The Heroes of Telemark 🎬 Kirk Douglas, Richard Harris
What's New Pussycat? 🎬 Woody Allen, Peter Sellers
She 🎬 Ursula Andress, Peter Cushing
Lord Jim 🎬 Peter O'Toole, Daliah Lavi
King Rat 🎬 George Segal, James Fox
Battle of the Bulge 🎬 Henry Fonda, Robert Shaw

Comics When You Were Small

Did you spend your childhood hopping from one foot to the other, longing for the next edition of your favourite comic to appear on the shelves? If so, these may be the titles you were waiting for.

Boys Own ✳ (1879-1967)
The Eagle ✳ (1950-1969)
Robin ✳ (1953-1969)

Some of the most popular Robin comic strips included BBC children's characters Andy Pandy and the Flower Pot Men.

The Hornet ✳ (1963-1976)
Look And Learn ✳ (1962-1982)

The first issue of Look and Learn featured a photograph of a very young Prince Charles on the front cover.

TV Comic ✳ (1951-1984)
Jack and Jill ✳ (1954-1985)
Tiger ✳ (1954-1985)

The Tiger comic strip character Roy Race was so popular, he eventually became the star of his own eponymous publication in the late 70s – Roy of the Rovers.

The Topper ✳ (1953-1990)
Jackie ✳ (1964-1993)
The Beezer ✳ (1956-1993)

For the first 25 years of its run, Beezer – companion to Topper – was printed in large-format A3.

Buster ✳ (1960-2000)
Bunty ✳ (1958-2001)
The Dandy ✳ (1937-2012)
Beano ✳ (1938-present)

The most valuable copies of the first issue of Beano fetch over £17,000 at auction. There are only 20 left in the world today.

Around the UK

Double digits at last: you're old enough to eavesdrop on adults and scan the headlines. These may be some of the earliest national news stories you remember.

- Peter Allen and Gwynne Evans last men to be hanged in UK
- BBC2 begins broadcasting with episode of Play School
- ITV's motel soap opera Crossroads takes to the screens
- Pirate radio station Caroline begins broadcasting offshore
- First edition of The Sun rolls off the press
- Great Train robbers jailed for total of 307 years
- Roald Dahl's Charlie and the Chocolate Factory published
- Milton Keynes, Havant and Basingstoke 'new towns' proposed
- Mods and Rockers battle it out on Brighton beach
- TV chart show Top of The Pops first airs on BBC
- Innovative design firm Habitat opens its first store in London
- The Queen opens Forth Road bridge to traffic
- Malta gains its independence from Britain
- Labour's Harold Wilson becomes prime minister
- Elizabeth Taylor and Richard Burton wed in Montreal
- Girls' teen magazine Jackie first published
- The Beatles first film A Hard Day's Night released
- Government votes to abolish death penalty for murder
- Construction of London's Post Office Tower completed
- UK and French governments agree to build Channel Tunnel
- British Northern Rhodesia becomes Republic of Zambia

Born this year:
- Prince Edward, Earl of Essex, born in Buckingham Palace
- Actress and comedian Kathy Burke born in Camden, London
- UKIP leader and MEP Nigel Farage born in Farnborough, Kent

UK Buildings

Some were loathed then, loved now; others, the reverse. Some broke new architectural ground, others helped to power a nation or entertain. All of them were built before you were 40.

1961	**Dungeness Lighthouse** When you build a nuclear power station that blocks out the view of a lighthouse, what do you do? Build another one.
1961	**Guildford Cathedral** Scenes from 1976 film The Omen were shot here; cathedral staff had to encourage the locals to attend after filming.
1961	Park Hill, Sheffield
1962	Coventry Cathedral
1963	Bankside Power Station
1964	**Post Office Tower** The tower was previously a designated secret under the Official Secrets Act and didn't appear on any OS maps. It was a pretty prominent secret, though, and was used as a filming location for TV and film during this time.
1966	Birmingham GPO Tower
1966	Centre Point
1966	**Severn Bridge** Grade I listed, and since 2018, free to cross (both ways!).
1967	Queen Elizabeth Hall
1974	**Birmingham Library** Looked like 'a place where books are incinerated, not kept' said Prince Charles. It was demolished in 2013.
1976	National Exhibition Centre (NEC)
1976	**Brent Cross Centre** The UK's first American-style indoor shopping centre. The car park was used for the James Bond film Tomorrow Never Dies.
1980	NatWest Tower
1982	Barbican Centre
1986	Lloyd's Building
1991	**One Canada Square, London** This Canary Wharf icon spent 20 years as the UK's tallest building before The Shard stole its thunder.

Early Radio 1 DJs

Do you remember the first time you heard 'the exciting new sound of Radio 1'? Replacing the BBC Light Programme in 1967, it soon won over the UK's youth to become the world's most popular station, and the DJs – all men until Annie Nightingale joined in 1970 – became household names.

Tony Blackburn
The man who started it all with those immortal words and span the first disc (Flowers in the Rain, by The Move). And don't forget his canine co-presenter, Arnold.

John Peel
Peel's life-long service to music is well known. But before this took off, his aspiration to be a journalist while selling insurance in Texas led him to bluff his way into the midnight news conference where Lee Harvey Oswald was paraded before the press.

Keith Skues

Ed Stewart
For children of the seventies, Ed Stewart means Crackerjack; but for those of us born earlier, it was Junior Choice on Saturday mornings where we'd get to know 'Stewpot'.

Mike Raven

Jimmy Young

Dave Cash

Kenny Everett
Everett was a Radio 1 DJ for less than three years before being sacked. He also appeared in 1980 on Just a Minute and was given the subject of marbles. Nicholas Parsons let him talk (while hesitating, repeating *and* deviating) for 90 seconds as a joke – assisted by the other panellists. He wasn't on the show again.

Terry Wogan

Duncan Johnson

Tommy Vance

Emperor Rosko
'Your groovy host from the West coast, here to clear up your skin and mess up your mind. It'll make you feel good all over!' – Rosko, aka Mike Pasternak, introducing his Midday Spin show.

Pete Murray

Bob Holness

Female Wimbledon Winners

Aged 15 in 1887, Lottie Dod was the youngest to win Wimbledon. Aged 37 in 1908, Charlotte Cooper Sterry was the oldest. These are the winners when you too were still in with a (slim) chance! Men, PTO!

1969	Ann Jones
1970	Margaret Court
1971	Evonne Goolagong
1972-73	**Billie Jean King**

King's 1973 Wimbledon marks the last time any player won all three tournaments (singles, doubles, mixed doubles). She didn't win them all in the same day (as Doris Hart did in 1951), but she did manage it twice – she'd scooped the 'triple crown' back in 1967, too.

1974	Chris Evert
1975	Billie Jean King
1976	Chris Evert
1977	**Virginia Wade**

Wade competed at Wimbledon 15 times before winning. It was to be Britain's last female grand slam victory until Emma Raducanu's epic US Open win in 2021.

1978-79	Martina Navratilova
1980	Evonne Goolagong Cawley
1981	**Chris Evert Lloyd**

Nicknamed the Ice Maiden, Evert was the first tennis player to win 1,000 matches and the first female tennis player to reach $1 million in career prize money.

1982-87	Martina Navratilova
1988-89	Steffi Graf
1990	Martina Navratilova
1991-93	Steffi Graf

Wimbledon: The Men

In the men's tournament, Becker won at the tender age of 17. At the top end, Federer won in 2017 at the age of 35. But in 1909, in the amateur era, Arthur Gore was a nimble 41 years young – giving us our 'winning window' of 17 to 41.

1970-71	John Newcombe
1972	**Stan Smith** Outside tennis, Stan Smith is best known for his best-selling line of Adidas sports shoes.
1973	Jan Kodeš
1974	Jimmy Connors
1975	**Arthur Ashe** Ashe contracted HIV from a blood transfusion following a heart operation, and worked to raise the awareness of HIV and AIDS before his death at the age of 49. The Arthur Ashe Stadium in New York was named in his memory.
1976-80	Björn Borg
1981	John McEnroe
1982	Jimmy Connors
1983-84	John McEnroe
1985-86	**Boris Becker** As a child, Becker would sometimes practice with Steffi Graf. He dropped out of school to join the West German Tennis Federation.
1987	Pat Cash
1988	Stefan Edberg
1989	Boris Becker
1990	Stefan Edberg
1991	Michael Stich
1992	**Andre Agassi** Agassi started losing his hair at 19 and wore hairpieces to hide it. The night before the 1990 French Open final, his wig was damaged. He wore it during the match but was so worried about it falling off that he lost.
1993-95	Pete Sampras

Books of the Decade

Ten years that took you from kids'
adventure books to dense works of
profundity – or maybe just grown-up
adventures! How many did you read
when they were first published?

1964	Herzog by Saul Bellow
1964	Last Exit to Brooklyn by Hubert Selby
1965	Dune by Frank Herbert
1966	Wide Sargasso Sea by Jean Rhys
1966	The Jewel In The Crown by Paul Scott
1967	One Hundred Years of Solitude by Gabriel Garcia Marquez
1967	The Outsiders by SE Hinton
1967	Poor Cow by Nell Dunn
1968	2001: A Space Odyssey by Arthur C Clarke
1969	Slaughterhouse-Five by Kurt Vonnegut
1969	Portnoy's Complaint by Philip Roth
1969	The Godfather by Mario Puzo
1969	The French Lieutenant's Woman by John Fowles
1969	Them by Joyce Carol Oates
1970	Deliverance by James Dickey
1971	An Accidental Man by Iris Murdoch
1971	The Day of the Jackal by Frederick Forsyth
1972	**Watership Down by Richard Adams** Watership Down was the first story Adams ever wrote, at the age of 52, based on tales he told his daughters in the car.
1973	Gravity's Rainbow by Thomas Pynchon
1973	Crash: A Novel by J G Ballard

Around the UK

Here's a round-up of the most newsworthy events from across the country in the year you turned (sweet) 16.

- ✦ Tory leader Ted Heath becomes prime minister
- ✦ State of Emergency declared as national dock strike disrupts ports
- ✦ Half-crown coin withdrawn from circulation
- ✦ Teenage prank sets Menai Strait railway bridge alight
- ✦ British Petroleum discovers vast Forties oilfield off Aberdeen
- ✦ Ban on importing pets issued after Suffolk rabies outbreak
- ✦ Anarchic comedy trio The Goodies debuts on BBC TV
- ✦ Tonga and Fiji gain independence from Britain
- ✦ Royal Navy serves last daily rum ration
- ✦ British mountaineers first to climb Annapurna's south ascent
- ✦ Government lowers voting age from 21 to 18
- ✦ Irish nationalist hurls CS gas into House of Commons
- ✦ T-Rex tops bill at first Glastonbury festival
- ✦ First topless Page 3 girl appears in The Sun newspaper
- ✦ Paul McCartney announces Beatles' split
- ✦ The British Army impose a 36-hour curfew in Belfast (right)
- ✦ Rolling Stone Mick Jagger fined £200 for cannabis possession
- ✦ England captain Bobby Moore cleared of bracelet theft in Colombia
- ✦ Wakefield gran Miriam Hargrave passes driving test on 40th try
- ✦ Manchester-Barcelona holiday flight crashes, killing 112
- ✦ Sir Clive Sinclair invents first handheld TV

Born this year:
- ☙ Supermodel Naomi Campbell born in Streatham, London
- ☙ Welsh singer and TV presenter Aled Jones born in Bangor
- ☙ Premier League top scorer Alan Shearer born in Gosforth

Following the Belfast riots of late June, the British Army conducted a search for weapons in the Falls district of the city. A riot erupted and a curfew was imposed, covering around 3,000 households.

An extensive house-to-house search uncovered explosives and guns, although soldiers were also accused of looting. The Official IRA attacked troops with hand grenades and rifles. Four people were killed by the British Army. The curfew was only ended when thousands of women and children marched to the area, demanding to be admitted.

TV Newsreaders: The Early Days

Trusted, familiar, and mostly with received pronunciation: these are the faces that brought you and your family the news, and the dates they shuffled their papers.

Richard Baker 📺 (1954-82)
In 1954, Baker introduced the BBC's first TV news broadcast. Seventies children know his voice as the narrator of Mary, Mungo and Midge.

Robert Dougall 📺 (1955-73)
Kenneth Kendall 📺 (1955-69)
Angela Rippon 📺 (1975-2002)
The UK's first regular female newsreader and known nationwide for her 1976 Morecambe and Wise appearance.

Jill Dando 📺 (1988-99)
The shocking murder of Dando on her doorstep in 1999 remains unsolved.

Moira Stuart 📺 (1981-2007)
Peter Woods 📺 (1964-81)
Woods is the biological father of BBC journalist and presenter Justin Webb.

Nan Winton 📺 (1960-61)
Winton was the BBC's first on-screen female newsreader in a shortlived 1960 trial deemed unacceptable by viewers.

Reginald Bosanquet 📺 (1967-79)
Michael Aspel 📺 (1960-68)
Corbet Woodall 📺 (1963-67)
Anna Ford 📺 (1976-2006)
Jan Leeming 📺 (1980-87)
Lynette Lithgow 📺 (1988-96)
Selina Scott 📺 (1980-86)
Sue Lawley 📺 (1981-88)
Alongside her news duties, Lawley is best known for her 18-year stint presenting BBC Four's Desert Island Discs. She left the role in 2006.

Julia Somerville 📺 (1983-99)

Fifties TV Gameshows

Gameshows got off to a rocky start in the UK, but the advent of commercial TV in 1955 – and ad-funded prizes – boosted the format into primetime, where it has remained ever since. Many of these early shows have since been remade, but how many of the originals do you remember?

Tell the Truth

Twenty Questions

Host Gilbert Harding, dubbed by the BBC as Britain's 'best-loved and best-hated man', was particularly drunk during one recording. He insulted two of the panellists, caused chaos by failing to recognise an answer, and ended the show early. Read more about Harding on page 36.

What's My Line?

Arguably the nation's first TV gameshow, first on screens in 1951.

Round Britain Quiz

Top of the Form

Twenty-One

Beat the Clock

Concentration

Crackerjack

Do You Trust Your Wife?

Double Your Money

In 1959, Sir Bobby Charlton appeared as a contestant on the show and won the top prize of £1,000, answering questions on pop music. Dame Maggie Smith also appeared as a hostess for a short time before her acting career took off.

Name That Tune

Opportunity Knocks

Spot the Tune

Take Your Pick!

Take Your Pick! was the first gameshow to be broadcast on commercial TV, debuting on the newly launched ITV in 1955. The income generated by adverts made it the first UK gameshow to give away cash prizes.

Two for the Money

Keep it in the Family

Make Up Your Mind

Stamps When You Were Young

Stamp collecting was the first serious hobby for many 20th century children. Commemorative issues weren't issued until the twenties, but soon became highly collectible – and the perfect gift for uncles in need of inspiration. These stamps may well have started your collection.

1924-5	**British Empire Exhibition** Designed to showcase Britain's strengths in an era of declining global influence, the exhibition left a legacy: the Empire Stadium (later renamed Wembley Stadium). The stamps were the UK's first commemorative issue, sixty years after the USA did the same.
1929	**9th Universal Postal Union Congress, London** Arguably of little interest to few outside philatelic circles, this was the first of several self-referential issues over successive decades. See also the Inter-Parliamentary stamps first issued in 1957.
1935	George V Silver Jubilee
1937	George VI Coronation
1940	**Centenary of the first adhesive postage stamp** Everyone has heard of the first adhesive stamp, issued in 1840: the Penny Black. (Perforations didn't come along until the 1854 Penny Red.) The glue on commemorative stamps contained around 14 calories!
1946	Victory
1948	Royal Silver Wedding
1948	Olympic Games
1949	The 75th Anniversary of the Universal Postal Union
1951	Festival of Britain
1951	George VI (high value 'definitives')
1953	The coronation of Queen Elizabeth II
1955	Castles (high value 'definitives')
1957	**World Scout Jamboree** Held in Sutton Coldfield; 50,000 Scouts attended. After heavy rain, the US Air Force was called in to help.
1957	46th Inter-Parliamentary Union Conference
1958	6th British Empire and Commonwealth Games

The Biggest Hits When You Were 16

The songs that topped the charts when you turned 16 might not be in your top 10 these days, but you'll probably remember them!

Love Grows ♪ Edison Lighthouse
Wand'rin' Star ♪ Lee Marvin

Bridge over Troubled Water ♪ Simon & Garfunkel
The album from which this song was taken stayed at the top of the charts for a whopping 35 weeks, cementing Simon & Garfunkel as one of the biggest acts in the world at the time.

All Kinds of Everything ♪ Dana

Spirit in the Sky ♪ Norman Greenbaum
According to Greenbaum, he only needed 15 minutes to write the lyrics to this fuzz-rock anthem.

Back Home ♪ England World Cup Squad 70

In the Summertime ♪ Mungo Jerry
Originally called Good Earth, the band chose the name Mungo Jerry after considering alternatives including 'Duran Duran'. They didn't have a drummer when they recorded this track; instead, they made the percussion sounds by wearing big boots and stamping their feet.

The Wonder of You ♪ Elvis Presley
The Tears of a Clown ♪ Smokey Robinson
Band of Gold ♪ Freda Payne
Woodstock ♪ Matthews Southern Comfort

Voodoo Child ♪ Jimi Hendrix Experience
Voodoo Child was the last song Jimi Hendrix ever performed live before his barbiturates-related death in 1970. The track was often written by Hendrix as Voodoo Chile.

I Hear You Knocking ♪ Dave Edmunds

Gameshow Hosts of the Fifties and Sixties

Many of these men were semi-permanent fixtures, their voices and catchphrases almost as familiar as our family's. Some were full-time entertainers, born to the stage; others seemed rather less suited to the spotlight!

Ted Ray... ➤ (Joker's Wild)
and his son, Robin Ray ➤ (Face the Music)
Peter Wheeler ➤ (Crossword on Two, Call My Bluff)
Robert Robinson ➤ (Brain of Britain, Ask the Family)
McDonald Hobley ➤ (Come Dancing, It's a Knockout)
David Jacobs ➤ (Juke Box Jury)
Shaw Taylor ➤ (Password, Pencil and Paper)
Eamonn Andrews ➤ (Crackerjack!)
Roy Plomley ➤ (Many a Slip)

Gilbert Harding ➤ (Twenty Questions, What's My Line?)
Harding was a teacher and policeman before working in radio and television. Resentful of his fame, Harding was once left mortified on the London Underground when he was recognised by fellow passengers who failed to notice that TS Eliot was also in the same carriage.

Bamber Gascoigne ➤ (University Challenge)
Tommy Trinder ➤ (Sunday Night at the Palladium)
Bruce Forsyth ➤ (Beat the Clock)
Bruce Forsyth first appeared on television in 1939. He had many talents including playing the ukulele and accordion, singing, dancing and acting. In his later years, Forsyth stated that he regretted presenting so many gameshows.

Leslie Crowther ➤ (Billy Cotton Band Show, Crackerjack)
Bob Monkhouse ➤ (The Golden Shot)
While serving in the RAF, Bob Monkhouse drafted a letter to the BBC from his group captain, stating that 18-year-old Monkhouse was a war hero and deserved an audition. His group captain signed the letter without reading it; Monkhouse got his audition.

Hughie Green ➤ (Opportunity Knocks)
Derek Batey ➤ (Mr and Mrs)
Wilfred Pickles ➤ (radio show Have a Go)

Kitchen Inventions

The 20th-century kitchen was a playground for food scientists and engineers with new labour-saving devices and culinary shortcuts launched every year. Here are some your parents – and now you – wouldn't be without.

1929	**Dishwasher** The first hand-operated dishwasher was created in 1885 by inventor and socialite, Josephine Cochrane, who was tired of her servants chipping her fine china. In 1929, Miele brought out an electric, top-loading model. Front-loading and drying functions followed in 1940; automation in 1960.
1937	Blender
1939	Pressure cooker
1940	Chest freezer
1945	**Fridge** If you think today's American-style fridges are big, consider the Large Hadron Collider in Geneva. With a circumference of 17 miles and 9,300 magnets, it's chilled to -270C before use. That would definitely keep your milk cold.
1948	Kenwood mixer
1955	Automatic kettle
1956	**Non-stick pan** You can thank a French angler's wife for your non-stick pans: it was she who noticed her husband's habit of coating his gear in non-stick Teflon, and suggested he did the same to her pans. Scrambled egg fans owe her a life-long debt.
1960	**Tupperware** In 1960, Tupperware parties arrived in the UK. Earl Tupper's 1948 invention took off when a US single mother called Brownie Wise started home sales and the social selling concept proved equally successful here. This icon of female entrepreneurship was dismissed in 1958 for being too outspoken.
1974	Microwave
1974	Food processor
1976	**Deep fat fryer** The Egyptians, Romans and Greeks were all known to have been keen on deep frying their food – often items that look uncommonly like today's doughnuts (minus the jam).

Around the World When You Turned 18

These are the headlines from around the globe as you were catapulted into adulthood.

- Palestinian terrorists kill 11 Israelis at Munich Olympics
- Spanish jet crashes into Ibizan peak, killing all 104 aboard
- Japanese soldier in Guam jungle learns WWII ended 28 years ago
- US swimmer Mark Spitz wins record 7th gold at Munich Olympics
- President Amin gives Ugandan Asians 90 days to leave country
- Stranded rugby team in Andes air crash survives by cannibilism
- President Nixon covers up break-in at Democrats' Watergate HQ
- Photo of burned 'Napalm Girl' captures horror of Vietnam War
- Hutu-Tutsi ethnic violence in Burundi – over 300,000 feared dead
- Avalanche on Japan's Mount Fuji kills 19 climbers
- Ceylon becomes Republic of Sri Lanka
- Fischer is first US World Chess champ after beating USSR's Spassky
- British parliament votes to join European Economic Community
- Mafia drama The Godfather premieres in New York cinema
- UK declares state of emergency over 47-day miners' strike
- Nicaraguan quake devastates Managua, up to 10,000 dead
- Countries sign treaty to ban use of biological weapons

Born this year:
- US basketball player Shaquille O'Neal born in Newark, New Jersey
- Quirky singer Björk Guðmundsdóttir born in Reykjavik, Iceland
- US tennis player Michael Chang born in Hoboken, New Jersey
- Award-winning actress Toni Collette born near Sydney, Australia

Toys of Your Childhood

In the sixties, the toy industry got serious: no more lead paint. New licensing models (Thunderbirds! Batman! Doctor Who!). And a Toy of the Year award – the James Bond Aston Martin car was the first winner. Hop into the seventies and you'd soon be needing some batteries to go with some of those Christmas surprises...

Sindy
Katie Kopykat
Betta Bilda
Plasticraft

Peter Powell Stunter
Not to be confused with the popular Radio 1 DJ, Powell was a kite designer who hit the big time after one of his models was featured on the BBC show Nationwide. His revolutionary idea was to use two lines for added control. 'It tugs at the heart strings,' he told the BBC in 2014.

Playmobil
Action Man
Duplo

Spacehopper
Just sneaking into this decade (if Spacehoppers can sneak): these went on sale in 1969. Sold as Hoppity Hops in the USA. In 2018, Steven Payne crossed the Alps on one. Madness.

Ping Pong
Nerf ball
Skateboards

Lego
The world's biggest manufacturer of tyres is not Goodyear, or Michelin – it's Lego. They produce around 300 million tiny tyres every year.

Evel Knievel Stunt Cycle
Etch-a-Sketch
Magna Doodle
Simon

Speak and Spell
The Speak and Spell was the first mass-produced item to include a digital signal processor, a precursor to the computers we have in our homes today.

Around the UK

Voting. Placing a bet. Buying a legal drink. Turning 18 is serious stuff. Here's what everyone was reading about in the year you reached this milestone.

- BBC quiz show Mastermind screened for first time
- IRA car bomb kills seven at Aldershot barracks
- Duke of Windsor, formerly King Edward VIII, dies in Paris
- Bloody Sunday – UK troops kill 14 on Derry civil-rights march (right)
- Second Cod War begins as Iceland declares 50-mile exclusion zone
- UK far-left group The Angry Brigade go on trial for bombings
- British direct rule imposed; Northern Irish parliament suspended
- SAS parachutes into Atlantic to deal with QE2 bomb threat
- Thousands join CND four-day march to Aldermaston
- Long-running ITV soap Emmerdale broadcast for first time
- Luxury electric train Brighton Belle makes last trip from London
- UK unemployment tops one million
- School leaving age raised from 15 to 16
- Staines air crash kills all 118 onboard
- UK's last UK trolleybus makes final journey in Bradford
- Coal miners accept pay offer after seven-week strike
- First official UK Gay Pride rally held in London
- Deported Ugandan Asians start to arrive in UK
- Rock opera Jesus Christ Superstar opens in London's West End
- First official England-Scotland women's football match played
- Rose Heilbron first female judge to sit at Old Bailey

Born this year:
- Ginger Spice Geri Halliwell born in Watford
- Olympic gold-medallist rower James Cracknell born in Sutton, Surrey
- Actor and DJ Idris Elba born in Hackney, London

Two days after 14 unarmed civilians were killed on Bloody Sunday, thousands marched on the British Embassy on Dublin's Merrion Square. Protesters pelted the building with petrol bombs and it burned to the ground.

Medical Advances Before You Were 21

A girl born in the UK in 1921 had a life expectancy of 59.6 years (boys: 55.6). By 2011 that was up to 82.8 (79 for boys), thanks to medical advances including many of these.

1956	Paracetamol
1957	EEG topography (toposcope)
1958	Pacemaker
1959	Bone marrow transplant, in-vitro fertilisation
1960	Kidney transplant, CPR and coronary artery bypass surgery
1961	The pill
1962	Hip replacement, beta blockers
1963	**Valium** Valium was famously dubbed 'mother's little helper' by The Rolling Stones. Valium was hailed as a wonder drug as it worked was a far less risky alternative to barbiturates.
1963	Lung transplant, artificial heart
1964	Measles vaccine
1965	**Portable defibrillator** CPR on TV is successful one time in two, a 2009 study found: roughly the same as reality. However, the lack of follow-up or age-related differences on TV means people's expectation for a life-saving result is unrealistically high.
1966	Pancreas transplant
1967	Heart transplant
1968	Liver transplant, Controlled drug delivery
1969	**Cochlear implant** Cochlear implants aren't always a success. Some can't get on with them; others believe they undermine deaf culture.
1969	Balloon catheter
1971	CAT scan
1972	Insulin pump
1973	MRI scanning, Laser eye surgery (LASIK)
1974	Depo-Provera contraceptive injection
1974	**Liposuction** Liposuction did not take off until 1985 when techniques had improved to decrease the chance of serious bleeding.

Popular Girls' Names

If you started a family at a young age, these are the names you're most likely to have chosen. And even if you didn't pick them, a lot of British parents did!

Sarah
Claire
Nicola
Emma
Lisa
Joanne
Michelle
Helen
Samantha
At number 9, Samantha's first appearance is among the highest of the century. She'll stay around until 2003.

Karen
Amanda
Rachel
Louise
Julie
Clare
Rebecca
Sharon
Victoria
Caroline
Susan
Alison
Catherine
Elizabeth
Deborah
Donna
Tracey
Tracy

Rising and falling stars:
Just like the boys, several names are all-too-briefly on the lips of many new parents: Vanessa, Nichola, Tara, Clair and Sonia.

Animals Extinct in Your Lifetime

Billions of passenger pigeons once flew the US skies. By 1914, they had been trapped to extinction. Not every species dies at our hands, but it's a sobering roll-call. (Date is year last known alive or declared extinct).

1960	Candango mouse, Brasilia
1962	Red-bellied opossum, Argentina
1963	Kākāwahie honeycreeper, Hawaii
1964	South Island snipe, New Zealand
1966	Arabian ostrich
1967	Saint Helena earwig
1967	**Yellow blossom pearly mussel, USA** Habitat loss and pollution proved terminal for this resident of Tennessee.
1968	Mariana fruit bat (Guam)
1971	Lake Pedder earthworm, Tasmania
1972	Bushwren, New Zealand
1977	Siamese flat-barbelled catfish, Thailand
1979	Yunnan Lake newt, China
1981	Southern gastric-brooding frog, Australia
1986	Las Vegas dace
1989	Golden toad (see right)
1990	Atitlán grebe, Guatemala
1990	Dusky seaside sparrow, East Coast USA
1990s	Rotund rocksnail, USA
2000	**Pyrenean ibex, Iberia** For a few minutes in 2003 this species was brought back to life through cloning, but sadly the newborn female ibex died.
2001	Caspian tiger, Central Asia
2008	Saudi gazelle
2012	**Pinta giant tortoise** The rarest creature in the world for the latter half of his 100-year life, Lonesome George lived out his days in the Galapagos as the last remaining Pinta tortoise.
2016	Bramble Cay melomys (a Great Barrier Reef rodent)

The observed history of the golden toad is brief and tragic. It wasn't discovered until 1964, abundant in a pristine area of Costa Rica. By 1989 it had gone, a victim of rising temperatures.

Popular Boys' Names

Here are the top boys' names for this year. In many instances it's merely a reshuffle of the popular names from the previous decade; but in the lower reaches, change is afoot…

Paul
After John, then David, came Paul: the nation's favourite name, but he'd keep the spot for less than a decade.

Mark
David
Andrew
Richard
Christopher
James
Simon
Michael
Matthew
Stephen
Lee
John
Robert
Darren
Daniel
Steven
Jason
Nicholas
Jonathan
Ian
Neil
Peter
Stuart
Anthony
Martin
Kevin

Rising and falling stars:
It's rare that names become popular enough to make the Top 100 only to fall out of favour as quickly as they came. Rarer still to have three flashes-in-the-pan: Glen, Brett and Damian.

Popular Movies When You Were 21

The biggest stars in the biggest movies: these are the films the nation was enjoying as you entered adulthood.

Jaws  Roy Scheider, Richard Dreyfuss
Steven Spielberg invited his good friend, George Lucas, to check out the mechanical shark used in production. When inspecting the inside of the fish's mouth, Lucas became trapped and had to be pulled out.

Night Moves  Gene Hackman, Jennifer Warren
The Stepford Wives  Katharine Ross, Paula Prentiss
Mary Stuart Masterson makes her film debut playing the daughter of actress Katharine Ross and her real-life father, Peter Masterson.

The Man Who Would Be King  Sean Connery, Michael Caine
Rooster Cogburn  John Wayne, Katharine Hepburn
Royal Flash  Malcolm McDowell, Oliver Reed
Love and Death  Woody Allen, Diane Keaton
Shampoo  Warren Beatty, Julie Christie
Brannigan  John Wayne, Richard Attenborough
The Ghoul  Peter Cushing, John Hurt
Funny Lady  Barbra Streisand, James Caan
Barry Lyndon  Ryan O'Neal, Marisa Berenson
Galileo  Chaim Topol, Edward Fox
The Sunshine Boys  Walter Matthau, George Burns
Rollerball  James Caan, John Houseman
The fictional game of Rollerball was so popular, the actors and crew would play the game in their spare time between takes.

Dog Day Afternoon  Al Pacino, John Cazale
The famous scene where Pacino screams 'Attica!' at the crowd was completely improvised on the spot.

The Hindenburg  George C Scott, Anne Bancroft
Tommy  Roger Daltrey, Ann-Margret
Nashville  Ronee Blakley, Keith Carradine
The Land That Time Forgot  Doug McClure, Susan Penhaligon
Picnic at Hanging Rock  Rachel Roberts, Dominic Guard
The Eiger Sanction  Clint Eastwood, George Kennedy

Around the UK

A selection of national headlines from the year you turned 21. But how many can you remember?

✦ IRA bombs London Hilton Hotel, killing two, injuring 63
✦ Icelandic gunboat fires on UK trawler provoking third Cod War
✦ IRA bomb explodes outside London's Green Park tube station
✦ Dozens killed in Moorgate tube crash
✦ Motor-racing champion Graham Hill dies in helicopter crash
✦ Nine held hostage in Spaghetti House siege (right)
✦ Tories choose Margaret Thatcher as first female party leader
✦ Flaming June replaced by snow and wintry weather
✦ Silent-film legend Charlie Chaplin knighted by Queen
✦ Author Ross McWhirter shot by IRA for offering bomber bounty
✦ Dougal Haston and Doug Scott first Brits to climb Everest
✦ 33 OAPs die in Yorkshire bus crash
✦ Sex Pistols play first gig at London art school
✦ Birmingham Six jailed for city pub bombings
✦ First episode of comedy classic Fawlty Towers airs on BBC2
✦ British public votes resoundingly to remain in EEC
✦ IRA gunmen free hostages after six-day Balcombe Street siege
✦ Sex Discrimination and Equal Pay Acts tackle equality of sexes
✦ UK coal miners accept not-so-minor 35% government pay rise
✦ Elizabeth Taylor and Richard Burton remarry
✦ UK radio broadcasts parliamentary proceedings for first time

Born this year:
🎗 Oscar-winning actress Kate Winslet born in Reading
🎗 TV chef and cookbook author Jamie Oliver born in Clavering, Essex
🎗 Football star David Beckham born in Leytonstone, east London

September 1975: three gunmen take eight Italian staff at the Spaghetti House restaurant hostage, after an attempted robbery is foiled by an escaping staff member. But are they criminals? Or political activists, fighting the oppression of black people? Claiming membership of the Black Panther movement, the gunmen ask for prisoners to be released, a car to Heathrow and a plane to Jamaica. But police believe this to be a cover story and elect to sit out the siege, spying using fibre optic cables. After six days and psychological mindgames using the media, the siege ends. The remaining hostages are released unharmed; the gang leader shoots himself in the stomach but survives. Their motives remain unclear to this day.

The Biggest Hits When You Were 21

The artists you love at 21 are with you for life. How many of these hits from this milestone year can you still hum or sing in the bath?

Down Down ♪ Status Quo
Quo had some difficulty recording the track because their amps would be interrupted by a morse code signal from the Chinese embassy up the road.

Make Me Smile ♪ Steve Harley
If ♪ Telly Savalas
Bye Bye Baby ♪ Bay City Rollers
Oh Boy ♪ Mud
Stand by Your Man ♪ Tammy Wynette

I'm Not in Love ♪ 10cc
10cc were ready to scrap their iconic ballad when they heard the secretary and window-cleaner singing the song. This was enough to convince them to keep the track.

Tears on My Pillow ♪ Johnny Nash
Give a Little Love ♪ Bay City Rollers
Sailing ♪ Rod Stewart
Hold Me Close ♪ David Essex

Space Oddity ♪ David Bowie
Space Oddity received its television debut when it was played during a broadcast of the Apollo 11 mission after Neil Armstrong and his crew had made it to the moon safely.

Bohemian Rhapsody ♪ Queen
Lyrics to Bohemian Rhapsody were taken from one of Freddie Mercury's scrapped song ideas called The Cowboy Song.

Popular Food in the 1960s

Convenient ready meals, 'fancy foreign food'… the sixties menu had it all. The chemists joined the dinner party, too, with additives and processes that made our new favourites easy and cheap to produce. We'd take a while to work out if this was always such a good idea!

Vesta curry or Chow Mein

Lager
'Lager' comes from the German word 'lagern', meaning 'to store', as lager takes longer to produce than other ales.

Coco Pops

Fish fingers
The largest fish finger ever made was 6ft long and weighed 136 kg. No word on whether the chef dipped it in ketchup.

Spaghetti Bolognese
You shouldn't include oregano, basil or garlic in the 'ragu' (not bolognese). And for goodness' sake, use tagliatelle, not spaghetti. Or… accept that it is as inauthentic as the Vesta curry and enjoy, like millions of Brits learned to do in the sixties.

Chicken Tikka Masala

Cheese and onion crisps
The first flavoured crisps were created by Joe 'Spud' Murphy (founder of Irish brand Taytos) in the late 1950s.

Crêpe Suzette

Chicken liver pâté

Angel Delight
Angel Delight doubled the dessert market when it was invented in 1967. Wallace and Gromit gave it another push in 1999.

Fray Bentos pies

Instant coffee

Frozen vegetables
Clarence Birdseye was the first person to freeze food for mass production, having got the idea from an Inuit in 1912.

Swedish meatballs

White bread
A new Chorleywood process introduced enzymes and additives and high-speed mixing. The result? Soft, cheap bread that sticks to the roof of your mouth. A nation couldn't get enough of it.

Fashion in the Sixties

As a child, you (generally) wear what you're given. It's only in hindsight, on fading slides, that you recognize that your outfits carried the fashion imprint of the day. Whether you were old or bold enough to carry off a pair of bell bottoms, though, is a secret that between you and your photo albums!

Shift dresses
Mini skirt
Popularised by Mary Quant who named the skirt after her favourite car – although not everyone was a fan. Coco Chanel described the skirt as 'just awful', and it was banned in some European countries.

Five-point cut
Vidal Sassoon
Sassoon had a temper. He would give clients a slap of a comb if they touched their hair while he was cutting it.

John Bates
Biba
Biba started as a mail order business, advertising a pink gingham dress in the Daily Mirror. 17,000 orders were placed and a shop was opened. On its opening day, the store sold out of its only product line.

St Michael American Tan tights
Dr Scholl
Orlon, Crimplene, Terylene, Spandex, PVC and Vinyl
Paper dresses
Twiggy
Jackie Kennedy
In 1962, Jackie Kennedy wore a leopard print coat which caused a spike in demand for leopard skin, leading to the death of up to 250,000 leopards. The coat's designer, Oleg Cassini, felt guilty about it for the rest of his life.

Little black dress
First introduced by Coco Chanel in the 1920s, the little black dress received a fifties update from Christian Dior. Audrey Hepburn's LBD sold for £467,200 in 2006.

Jean Shrimpton
Jane Birkin

Around the World When You Turned 25

By your mid-twenties, TV coverage of news in far-flung places brought global stories into our homes almost as fast as they happened. How many do you remember?

- ✦ Pol Pot's brutal regime ends as Vietnam takes Cambodian capital
- ✦ Iranian radicals storm US Embassy in Tehran, taking 90 hostages
- ✦ Dutch firm Philips unveils first compact disc and player
- ✦ Shah of Iran flees country as Muslim fundamentalists take power
- ✦ First black-led government of Zimbabwe-Rhodesia takes power
- ✦ China institutes one child per family rule
- ✦ Ixtoc well blowout off Mexican coast causes massive oil spill
- ✦ Last British soldier leaves Malta after 166 years of UK rule
- ✦ US space station Skylab falls to Earth in Australia and Pacific
- ✦ Ugandan dictator Idi Amin overthrown
- ✦ Nuclear melt-down at Three Mile Island plant in Pennsylvania, USA
- ✦ US and USSR sign SALT II nuclear arms reduction treaty
- ✦ Two families escape East Berlin in homemade hot-air balloon
- ✦ Snow falls in world's hottest desert the Sahara
- ✦ War breaks out as Chinese troops invade northern Vietnam
- ✦ Freak storm lashes 300 yachts in UK's Fastnet race – 19 drown
- ✦ Pink Floyd's concept album The Wall released
- ✦ Personal stereo tape-deck Sony Walkman goes on sale in Japan

Born this year:
- ⚙ Ireland rugby captain Brian O'Driscoll born in Dublin
- ⚙ Oscar-winning actor Heath Ledger born Perth, Australia
- ⚙ Homeland actress Claire Danes born in New York, USA
- ⚙ US comedian/actor Kevin Hart born in Philadelphia, Pennsylvania

Cars of the 1960s

For every much-loved Hillman Imp or trusted Vauxhall Victor, the sixties boasts a glamorous Aston Martin DB5 or a covetable Jaguar E-type. Has any decade delivered for the motoring public like the sixties?

Mini
Famously featured in the 1969 film The Italian Job, Mini manufacturer BMC didn't want the car used in the film and refused to donate any. However, the director insisted that British cars should be used in a British film and over a dozen were used.

Triumph Herald

Vauxhall Victor
The design of the Vauxhall Victor was based on the style of American cars, which didn't appeal to everyone's taste in 1960s Britain. The car also gained a negative reputation for rusting.

Austin 1100

Sunbeam Tiger

Aston Martin DB5
The Aston Martin DB5 has been described as the most famous car in the world, following its 1964 debut in Goldfinger. In 1968, the car used by James Bond in the film was stripped of the weapons and gadgets and resold as a used car. It was stolen in 1997 and is rumoured to be in the Middle East.

Hillman Hunter

Lotus Elan
The Lotus Elan was designed by Ron Hickman, who subsequently left Lotus and went on to design the Black & Decker Workmate. Early versions of the Elan were also available as a kit that could be assembled by the buyer.

Ford Cortina
The Ford Cortina was launched in 1962 and later proved to be the best-selling car of the 1970s in its Mk3 guise. Designed as a new version of the Ford Consul, the name was changed to Cortina after the Italian ski resort Cortina d'Ampezzo, host to the 1956 Winter Olympics.

Rover 3500

MGB

Vauxhall HA Viva

Books of the Decade

Were you a voracious bookworm in your twenties? Or a more reluctant reader, only drawn by the biggest titles of the day? Here are the new titles that fought for your attention.

1974	**Tinker, Tailor, Soldier, Spy by John le Carré** David Cornwell, the man behind the pseudonym John le Carré, drew on his personal experience working for MI5 and MI6. He appeared as an extra in the film of the book.
1974	**Carrie by Stephen King** Carrie was King's first novel, published when he was 26. He disliked the first draft and threw it in the bin; his wife found it and encouraged him to continue with the story.
1974	The Bottle Factory Outing by Beryl Bainbridge
1975	Shogun by James Clavell
1975	The Periodic Table by Primo Levi
1976	Interview with the Vampire by Anne Rice
1977	Song of Solomon by Toni Morrison
1977	The Shining by Stephen King
1978	The World According to Garp by John Irving
1978	The Sea, The Sea by Iris Murdoch
1978	Tales of the City by Armistead Maupin
1979	**The Hitchhiker's Guide to the Galaxy by Douglas Adams** If 42 is the meaning of life, what's the meaning of 42? Nothing. Adams said it was simply a random number he chose. There's a message in there somewhere…
1979	A Bend in the River by V S Naipaul
1979	Sophie's Choice by William Styron
1980	A Confederacy of Dunces by John Kennedy Toole
1980	The Name of the Rose by Umberto Eco
1981	Midnight's Children by Salman Rushdie
1982	The Color Purple by Alice Walker
1982	**Schindler's Ark by Thomas Keneally** Keneally wrote Schindler's Ark – later retitled Schindler's List – after he met Holocaust survivor Leopold Page. Schindler is credited with saving over 1,000 lives.
1983	The Colour of Magic by Terry Pratchett

Stamps in the Sixties

The UK hit its stride with commemorative stamps in the sixties. There were dry centenary and congress issues, but in 1965 the Postmaster General, Tony Benn, removed the need to include a large monarch portrait. The result? The kind of stamps every young collector would want.

1963	Freedom From Hunger
1963	Lifeboat Conference
1963	Red Cross Centenary Congress
1964	Opening of the Forth Road Bridge
1965	Winston Churchill Commemoration
1965	700th anniversary of Parliament
1965	Centenary of the Salvation Army
1965	**Antiseptic Surgery Centenary** Celebrates the introduction of surgical sterilisation by Joseph Lister.
1965	Commonwealth Arts Festival
1965	25th Anniversary of the Battle of Britain
1965	Opening of the Post Office Tower
1966	Westminster Abbey
1966	Landscapes
1966	**1966 World Cup** Stamps to mark England's role as hosts were hastily reissued in August 1966 with ENGLAND WINNERS added.
1966	British birds
1966	British technology
1966	900th anniversary of the Battle of Hastings
1966	**Christmas** The first UK Christmas stamps. The idea was championed by Tony Benn and the stamps designed by two 6-year-olds – winners of a Blue Peter competition.
1967	British wild flowers
1967	British paintings
1967	British discoveries and inventions
1967	Sir Francis Chichester's solo circumnavigation
1968	British bridges
1969	Concorde's first flight

Sixties TV Gameshows

Gameshows in the sixties were dominated by a few stalwarts, though a few short-lived experimental formats and US adaptions were tried. Without any serious competition, audiences were enormous. How many do you remember watching with your family?

Call My Bluff
Almost every episode from the first eight series of Call My Bluff has been wiped from the BBC archives. There were 263 episodes in series one to eight, and only seven episodes still survive.

Face the Music

Just a Minute

Ask the Family

University Challenge
Several celebrities appeared on University Challenge before they became famous. These include Stephen Fry, David Starkey, Sebastian Faulks, Julian Fellowes, and Miriam Margolyes (who swore when she answered a question incorrectly). University Challenge has a claim to be the longest running TV quiz show, alongside A Question of Sport.

For Love or Money

Mr and Mrs
After watching the Canadian version of Mr and Mrs, Derek Batey was inspired to develop a UK version of the show for Border Television. Batey hosted over 500 episodes, as well as 5,000 on stage after developing a theatrical version.

Play Your Hunch

Take Your Pick

Brain of Britain

Double Your Money
A November 1966 episode drew the nation's highest gameshow audience of nearly 20 million viewers.

Exit! It's the Way-Out Show

Many a Slip

Three Little Words

Crossword on 2

Around the UK

Another decade passes and you're well into adulthood. Were you reading the news, or making it? Here are the national stories that dominated the front pages.

- ✦ British Telecom privatised – 50% shares sold to investors
- ✦ Miners walk out in long battle over pit closure threat
- ✦ Financial Times Stock Exchange FTSE 100 Index set up
- ✦ First Virgin Atlantic plane takes off
- ✦ Half pence coin withdrawn from circulation
- ✦ Church of England supports ordaining women as priests
- ✦ Skaters Torvill and Dean win Olympic gold with Boléro routine
- ✦ Police and miners clash at Orgreave colliery – 64 injured (right)
- ✦ Band Aid charity single Do They Know It's Christmas? released
- ✦ Brunei becomes independent of UK
- ✦ York Minster roof set ablaze by lightning bolt
- ✦ Magnitude 5.4 earthquake shakes north Wales
- ✦ South African runner Zola Budd granted British citizenship
- ✦ IRA Brighton hotel bomb targets Tory cabinet, killing five
- ✦ Sinn Fein president Gerry Adams wounded in loyalist shooting
- ✦ One dead, 11 injured in 294-day London Libyan Embassy siege
- ✦ Princess Diana gives birth to second son Harry, Duke of Sussex
- ✦ UK geneticist Alec Jeffreys discovers DNA fingerprinting
- ✦ Police drama The Bill airs on ITV
- ✦ Government bans union membership at Cheltenham GCHQ
- ✦ Civil servant Sarah Tisdall jailed for cruise missile leak

Born this year:
- ಱ TV personality and daughter of Ozzy, Kelly Osbourne born in London
- ಱ Singer and TV presenter Olly Murs born in Witham, Essex
- ಱ The Crown actress Claire Foy born in Stockport

For years after the events of 18 June 1984, the establishment narrative largely held: thousands of violent picketers at Orgreave Colliery had confronted the police in their attempt to stop deliveries of coal. Truncheon and horse charges and the use of snatch squads were made in self-defence as the rioters ran amok.

As the decades passed, the truth emerged. Trials collapsed and compensation was paid as police evidence proved unreliable and malpractice uncovered; evidence was prefabricated and links at a senior level between the manner of policing at both Orgreave and Hillsborough were revealed.

The Biggest Hits When You Were 30

How many of these big tunes from the year you turned thirty will still strike a chord decades later?

Pipes of Peace ♪ Paul McCartney

Relax ♪ Frankie Goes to Hollywood

99 Red Balloons ♪ Nena

Hello ♪ Lionel Richie
Lionel Richie was instructed to write this song after Ritchie jokily crooned the eponymous line at his producer.

The Reflex ♪ Duran Duran

Wake Me Up Before You Go-Go ♪ Wham!
Andrew Ridgeley accidentally came up with title for this song when he accidentally left his mother a note saying 'wake me up up...' Ridgeley took the idea to complete the song's title.

Two Tribes ♪ Frankie Goes to Hollywood

Careless Whisper ♪ George Michael

Freedom ♪ Wham!

I Feel for You ♪ Chaka Khan
In order to meet Chaka Khan, I Feel for You songwriter Prince rang her on the phone and pretended to be her good friend Sylvester Stallone.

I Should Have Known Better ♪ Jim Diamond

The Power of Love ♪ Frankie Goes to Hollywood
The Power of Love marked a stellar year for Frankie Goes to Hollywood when it became their third number one of 1984.

Do They Know It's Christmas ♪ Band Aid

...and the Movies You Saw That Year, Too

From award winners to crowd pleasers, here are the movies that played as your third decade drew to a close.

Gremlins 🎬 Zach Galligan, Phoebe Cates
Beverly Hills Cop 🎬 Eddie Murphy, Judge Reinhold
Romancing the Stone 🎬 Kathleen Turner, Michael Douglas
Footloose 🎬 Kevin Bacon, Lori Singer
Another Country 🎬 Rupert Everett, Colin Firth
Ghostbusters 🎬 Bill Murray, Dan Aykroyd
Nearly every word from Murray is an ad-lib. In fact, most of the actors were given the nod to improvise as much as possible.

Amadeus 🎬 Tom Hulce, F Murray Abraham
The Company of Wolves 🎬 Sarah Patterson, Angela Lansbury
Purple Rain 🎬 Prince, Apollonia
Prince made co-star Apollonia promise to break up with David Lee Roth and not date anybody famous during the promotion of Purple Rain. He also dictated what she wore and when she could eat.

A Passage to India 🎬 Judy Davis, Victor Bannerjee
Splash 🎬 Tom Hanks, Darryl Hannah
Paris, Texas 🎬 Harry Dean Stanton, Dean Stockwell
Police Academy 🎬 Steve Guttenberg, GW Bailey
Against All Odds 🎬 Rachel Ward, Jeff Bridges
The Killing Fields 🎬 Haing S Ngor, John Malkovich
The Karate Kid 🎬 Ralph Macchio, William Zabka
Macchio was given the famous 'wax on, wax off' car as a present and brought it out of retirement for the Cobra Kai TV series.

The Bounty 🎬 Anthony Hopkins, Mel Gibson
A Private Function 🎬 Maggie Smith, Michael Palin
The Natural 🎬 Robert Redford, Glenn Close
This Is Spinal Tap 🎬 Michael McKean, Christopher Guest
The Terminator 🎬 Arnold Schwarzenegger, Linda Hamilton
Linda Hamilton broke her ankle before shooting The Terminator. She spent most of the shoot in pain and had to film all her action scenes at the end of the production schedule.

The Never Ending Story 🎬 Noah Hathaway, Barret Oliver

Around the House

Sometimes with a fanfare but often by stealth, inventions and innovations transformed the 20th-century household. Here's what arrived between the ages of 10 and 30.

1964	Flat screen and Portable TVs
1965	**AstroTurf** AstroTurf was originally called ChemGrass, and invented by chemicals giant Monsanto. It was rebranded in 1966.
1965	Cordless phones
1965	Plastic chairs
1967	Ariel detergent
1968	Plastic wheelie bins
1969	Bean bags
1969	Comfort fabric softener
1970	**Blu-Tack** The largest Blu-Tack sculpture is a 2007 creation called Spider Biggus. it uses 4,000 packs of the blue stuff.
1971	Garden strimmers
1973	BIC lighter
1974	Sticky notes
1975	Betamax movies
1976	**VHS movies** The last film ever released on VHS was David Cronenberg's 2006 thriller, A History of Violence.
1977	Sony Walkman
1977	Auto focus cameras
1978	Electronic (computer-controlled) sewing machines
1978	Slide Away (sofa) beds
1979	**Black + Decker DustBuster** Black + Decker came up with the idea of a cordless vacuum while working on a cordless drill for NASA.
1979	Shake n' Vac
1982	CD Players
1983	Dyson bagless vacuum cleaner
1983	**Nintendo Entertainment System (NES)** Super Mario Bros is the best-selling NES game of all time.

British Prime Ministers in Your Lifetime

These are the occupants of 10 Downing Street, London, during your lifetime, not including Larry the resident cat. Don't be deceived by that unassuming, black, blast-proof door: Number 10 features a warren of more than 100 rooms.

1951–55	**Sir Winston Churchill** Churchill was made an honorary citizen of the United States in 1963, one of only eight to receive this honour.
1955–57	Sir Anthony Eden
1957–63	**Harold Macmillan** Macmillan was the scion of a wealthy publishing family, but the biggest secret of his life was kept under wraps: his wife Dorothy's 30-year affair with fellow Conservative (and Krays associate) Robert Boothby. Macmillan died aged 92; his last words were, 'I think I will go to sleep now.'
1963–64	Sir Alec Douglas-Home
1964–70	Harold Wilson
1970–74	Edward Heath
1974–76	Harold Wilson
1976–79	James Callaghan
1979–90	**Margaret Thatcher** 'Today we were unlucky,' said the chilling statement from the IRA, 'but remember we only have to be lucky once.' The 1994 bombing of the Grand hotel in Brighton may not have killed the prime minister, but five others died and others were left with lifelong injuries.
1990–97	John Major
1997–2007	Tony Blair
2007–10	Gordon Brown
2010–16	David Cameron
2016–19	**Theresa May** Asked in a pre-election interview about the naughtiest thing she'd ever done, May said that she'd once run through a field of wheat with her friends, and that the farmers 'weren't too happy'.
2019–	Boris Johnson

Household Goods in 1962

In 1947, the government calculated inflation for the first time using a basket of frequently purchased goods. This list has been reviewed ever since; the changes mirror our ever-changing tastes and habits. Here's what housewives were buying when you were small.

Sliced white bread
Chocolate coated biscuits
Dry cleaning
Potato crisps
Crisps entered the basket of goods in 1962, the same year Golden Wonder (bought by Imperial Tobacco) launched cheese and onion flavoured crisps. Golden Wonder, Smith's and soon Walkers fought for the market, and consumption rocketed.

Oven ready chicken
Cuts of halibut
Second-hand car
Welfare milk scheme
Ground coffee
Frozen croquettes
As more homes had freezers and the desire for ready meals increased, frozen food was all the rage. Frozen croquettes were released in the early 1960s and were a resounding success.

Canned fruit salad
Canned fruit salad was designed to use the fruit scraps that couldn't be used in canning. Fruit salad arrived in the 1940s and became one of the most popular canned fruits available. You could even use it to make a fruit salad cake.

TV set rental
Gloss paint
Ceiling paper
Jeans
Latex backed carpet
Refrigerator
Ready-made suit
Terylene slacks
Created in Manchester in 1941, Terylene revolutionised clothing in the 1950s. It was used by Mary Quant to make the original miniskirts, and Ray Davies of The Kinks advertised it.

Around the World When You Turned 35

It's a big news day every day, somewhere in the world. Here are the stories that the media thought you'd want to read in the year of your 35th birthday.

✦ George HW Bush sworn in as 41st US president
✦ South Africa's President Botha meets prisoner Nelson Mandela
✦ Nintendo releases handheld video game console Game Boy
✦ Icelanders celebrate legalisation of beer after 74 years
✦ 'Tank Man' stands up to army in Beijing's Tiananmen Square
✦ East Germans flock to border as Berlin Wall comes down
✦ NASA launches Galileo spacecraft to study Jupiter
✦ FW de Klerk succeeds Botha as South African president
✦ Overthrown Romanian dictator Ceauşescu executed by firing squad
✦ UK inventor Tim Berners-Lee creates World Wide Web
✦ Oil tanker Exxon Valdez spills millions of gallons off Alaska
✦ Bush and Gorbachev declare end of Cold War at Malta summit
✦ 14th Dalai Lama Tenzin Gyatso wins Nobel Peace Prize
✦ France celebrates 200th anniversary of storming of Bastille
✦ Revolutions in Eastern Bloc countries end communist regimes
✦ Iran's ayatollah urges Muslims to kill UK author Salman Rushdie
✦ Hoffman-Cruise film Rain Man wins four Oscars
✦ Infamous US serial killer Ted Bundy executed in electric chair

Born this year:

🐾 US politician Alexandria Ocasio-Cortez born in New York
🐾 US pop singer Taylor Swift born in West Reading, Pennsylvania
🐾 Grammy-winning DJ Avicii born Tim Bergling in Stockholm, Sweden

Beer of the Seventies

You could haul a seven-pint tin of Watneys Party Seven to a celebration. Someone would be drinking bland Watneys Red, or Courage Tavern ('It's what your right arm's for'). But how about a drop of that cold, refreshing lager you tried on holiday? 'Mine's a pint!' said millions of Brits.

Watneys Party Seven
Whitbread Tankard
Watneys Red
Double Diamond

Carlsberg
The inventor of Carlsberg, JC Jacobsen, gave a Ted Talk on his life philosophy in 2017 – 130 years after he died. He was brought back to life via hologram and even fielded questions from the audience.

Heineken
The Heineken International company owns more than 250 other brands, many of which you'll probably recognise such as Amstel, Desperados and Strongbow.

Tennant's Gold Label

Guinness
When Arthur Guinness started his now-famous business he rented an unused brewery on a 9,000-year lease – though the contract was eventually voided when the company bought the land and surrounding areas to expand the business.

Worthington E
Carling Black Label
Harp
Stella Artois
Ind Coope Super
Younger's Scotch Ale
Bass Charrington

Strongbow
HP Bulmer named his drink after one of the greatest knights in English history, Richard de Clare, who was given the nickname Strongbow.

Long Life

Seventies TV Gameshows

With light entertainment increasingly becoming the bedrock of TV channel success, the seventies saw an explosion of formats from gimmicks to US imports. Which ones got you shouting at the telly?

It's a Knockout
Although this show began in 1966 and it limped on into the new century, the seventies was It's a Knockout's golden age, thanks in no small part to presenter Stuart Hall. The winning teams proceeded to represent the UK at the European final, Jeux Sans Frontières.

I'm Sorry I Haven't a Clue

Jokers Wild

My Music

A Question of Sport
A Question of Sport is the world's longest running TV sports quiz. The first episode was recorded in 1970 in a converted chapel in Rusholme, Manchester, and the show is still recorded in the city as it surpasses 1,300 episodes.

Quote... Unquote

Whodunnit?

Mastermind

Screen Test

Celebrity Squares
Inspired by the game noughts and crosses, Celebrity Squares was based on the US gameshow Hollywood Squares. The original run was presented by Bob Monkhouse, who also returned to host the revival of the show in the 1990s.

Gambit

The Generation Game

The Golden Shot

The Indoor League

Password

Runaround

Sale of the Century

The Sky's the Limit

Winner Takes All

Popular Boys' Names

40

Just as middle age crept up unnoticed, so the most popular names also evolved. The traditional choices – possibly including yours – were fast losing their appeal to new parents.

Thomas
Paul, Christopher and now Thomas takes the top spot: but Jack is coming up fast in the nation's affections…

James
Jack
Daniel
Matthew
Ryan
Joshua
Luke
Samuel
Jordan
Adam
Michael
Alexander
Christopher
Benjamin
Joseph
Liam
Jake
William
Andrew
George
Lewis
Oliver
David
Robert
Jamie
Nathan

Rising and falling stars:
Jake makes an unusually high debut at 18, and Connor does the same at 28. Shortened names are in vogue: Joe, Billy, Josh, Max; Darren, Mathew, Gareth and Stuart leave us.

Popular Girls' Names

40

It's a similar story for girls' names. Increasing numbers took their infant inspiration from popular culture. The worlds of music, film and now the internet are all fertile hunting grounds for those in need of inspiration.

Rebecca

It's a few short years for Rebecca as the nation's favourite girl's name. Sarah may be vanquished but Chloe waits in the wings.

Lauren
Jessica
Charlotte
Hannah
Sophie
Amy
Emily
Laura
Emma
Chloe
Sarah
Lucy
Katie
Bethany
Jade
Megan
Alice
Rachel
Samantha
Danielle
Holly
Abigail
Olivia
Stephanie
Elizabeth

Rising and falling stars:

This is the last year when we see lots of change in the Top 100. Bethany is in at number 15 and Megan at 20; 28 other names are new. Among those making for the exit are Toni, Jemma, Lisa and Helen.

F1 Champions

If you fancy your chances in Formula One, start young. Sebastian Vettel won at 23. *El Maestro*, Juan Manuel Fangio, is the oldest winner to date, at 46. The field is wide open for an older champ, right?

Niki Lauda 🏁 (1975,77,84)
Niki Lauda was also an aviation entrepreneur, founding three airlines in Austria. He also held a commercial pilot's licence.

Mario Andretti 🏁 (1978)
Jody Scheckter 🏁 (1979)
Alan Jones 🏁 (1980)
Nelson Piquet 🏁 (1981,83,87)
Nelson Piquet lost his civilian driving licence in 2007 due to numerous speeding and parking offences. He was ordered to attend a week of lessons and pass an exam.

Keke Rosberg 🏁 (1982)
Alain Prost 🏁 (1985-6,89,93)
Ayrton Senna 🏁 (1988,90-1)
Two days before Senna's fatal crash at Imola, he was early to the scene of a near-fatal crash for Rubens Barrichello. One day before, he inspected the car of Roland Ratzenberger as the mortally-injured Austrian was taken to hospital – the same facility that would attempt to save Senna's life the following day after his crash on the same corner. An Austrian flag was later found in Senna's cockpit, intended to be unfurled as a tribute to Ratzenberger.

Nigel Mansell 🏁 (1992)
Michael Schumacher 🏁 (1994-5,2000-04)
Michael Schumacher was one of a handful of drivers to appear as themselves in the Pixar film Cars, voicing a Ferrari F430.

Damon Hill 🏁 (1996)
Jacques Villeneuve 🏁 (1997)
Mika Häkkinen 🏁 (1998-99)

Fashion in the Seventies

The decade that taste forgot? Or a kickback against the sixties and an explosion of individuality? Skirts got shorter (and longer). Block colours and peasant chic vied with sequins and disco glamour. How many of your seventies outfits would you still wear today?

Flares
Platform shoes
Laura Ashley
While working as a secretary, Laura Ashley was inspired to produce printed fabric after seeing a display at the Victoria and Albert Museum. Struggling to make a profit, Laura Ashley and her husband and children once lived in tents in Wales for six months.

Gucci
Diane Von Furstenberg
Tie Dye
Kaftans
Brought to western culture via the hippie trail, the kaftan's popularity was boosted further when Elizabeth Taylor wore a kaftan-inspired dress for her second wedding to Richard Burton in 1975.

Liza Minnelli
Lurex and suede
David Bowie
Afro, braids or a perm
Jumpsuit
Sequin hot pants
Moon boots
Double denim
Double denim garnered the nickname the 'Canadian tuxedo' after Bing Crosby was refused entry to a hotel in Vancouver because he wore a denim ensemble. Levi subsequently designed Crosby a denim tuxedo.

Vivienne Westwood
Previously a primary school teacher, Vivienne Westwood lived in an ex-council flat in Clapham until 2000. Her son from her relationship with Malcolm McLaren founded lingerie brand Agent Provocateur.

Household Goods in 1970

Frozen foods and eating out swallow up an increasingly larger share of the family budget in the seventies. Or how about a day trip (don't forget your AA membership and your mac), then home for a sweet sherry?

Frozen chicken
Mushrooms
Frozen beans
Sherry
Sherry consumption peaked in the UK in the 1970s following the development of sweet versions – often using added syrups or sugars – known as creams and developed for British palates.

Night storage heater
Plastic Mackintosh
MOT test
Introduced in 1960, the MOT was designed to test the brakes, lights, and steering of all vehicles over 10 years old. This was progressively reduced to every three years by 1967, and the test changed to include tyres.

State school meal
Canteen meal
Cup of tea
The 1970s saw a significant increase in eating out, so a cup of tea was added to the basket. Despite Britain's reputation as tea lovers, coffee sales overtook tea sales for the first time in 1986.

Cafe sandwich
Local authority rent
Local authority rent was added to the basket of goods in the 1970s; by 1979, 42% of Britons lived in council homes.

Paper handkerchiefs
Auto association subs
Keg of ale
Fresh cream
Gammon
While gammon gained popularity during the 1970s due to its unlikely pairing with pineapple rings, the word 'gammon' is now also used as an insult towards the political right, coined in response to 'snowflake'.

Post-war Chocolate

You'll find nearly all of these on the supermarket shelves, even though the most recently invented chocolate bar here was brought to market thirty years ago. Gulp.

1948	Fudge
1951	**Bounty**

If you wanted to sell a chocolate bar with curved ends and swirls on the top, in theory there's nothing that maker Mars could do to stop you: the shape was decreed not distinctive enough to trademark in 2009. Do check with a lawyer first, though.

1957	Munchies
1958	Picnic
1962	**After Eight Mint Chocolate Thins**

A billion of these are churned out every year (although we've never heard anyone call them chocolate thins).

1962	Topic
1963	Toffee Crisp
1967	Twix
1970	Chomp
1970	Curly Wurly
1973	Freddo
1976	**Double Decker**

Double Deckers contain raisins, don't they? Not any more: they were removed from the recipe during the eighties.

1976	Starbar
1976	**Yorkie**

'It's not for girls,' said the adverts. The sexist marketing of Yorkie reached its peak – or trough – in 2005 with special pink editions. By 2011 the complaints outweighed the commercial advantage. The 'men only' angle was dropped.

1978	Lion Bar
1980	Drifter
1983	**Wispa**

For twenty years, Wispa was the go-to Aero alternative. But then in 2003 it was gone. A predictable outcry followed and in 2007 it was back on the shelves. Phew.

1992	Time Out

Books of the Decade

Family, friends, TV, and more: there are as many midlife distractions as there are books on the shelf. Did you get drawn in by these bestsellers, all published in your thirties?

1984	Money by Martin Amis
1984	Neuromancer by William Gibson
1984	The Wasp Factory by Iain Banks
1985	**The Handmaid's Tale by Margaret Atwood**

The Communist reign of Nicolae Ceaușescu in Romania partially inspired Atwood to write The Handmaid's Tale. While he was in power, women had to have four babies; abortions were illegal, contraception was banned, and women were examined for signs of pregnancy at work.

1985	Blood Meridian by Cormac McCarthy
1985	Perfume by Patrick Suskind
1986	The Old Devils by Kingsley Amis
1986	It by Stephen King
1987	Beloved by Toni Morrison
1987	Bonfire of the Vanities by Tom Wolfe
1988	Satanic Verses by Salman Rushdie
1988	The Alchemist by Paulo Coelho
1988	Oscar and Lucinda by Peter Carey
1988	The Swimming-Pool Library by Alan Hollinghurst
1989	A Prayer for Owen Meany by John Irving
1989	The Remains of the Day by Kazuo Ishiguro
1989	London Fields by Martin Amis
1990	Possession by AS Byatt
1990	The Buddha of Suburbia by Hanif Kureishi
1991	Regeneration by Pat Barker
1991	**American Psycho by Bret Easton Ellis**

Ellis received death threats on account of the violent and misogynistic content. He had to indemnify his publisher from being sued by his family if he were murdered.

1992	The Secret History by Donna Tartt
1992	All the Pretty Horses by Cormac McCarthy
1992	The English Patient by Michael Ondaatje
1993	The Shipping News by E Annie Proulx

Around the World When You Turned 40

Which of these international news events were on your radar as you clocked up four decades on the planet?

- ✦ Elvis' daughter Lisa Marie weds popstar Michael Jackson
- ✦ US grunge rock singer Kurt Kobain leaves rehab and takes own life
- ✦ Work on China's mega hydro project Three Gorges Dam begins
- ✦ Car ferry MS Estonia sinks in Baltic Sea, killing 852
- ✦ World's first smart phone IBM Simon launched in US
- ✦ Doomsday cult releases deadly Sarin gas in Japan
- ✦ Hutu extremists slaughter 800,000 Tutsis in 100 days in Rwanda
- ✦ Jeff Bezos founds e-commerce giant Amazon from his Seattle garage
- ✦ TV tycoon Silvio Berlusconi's Forza Italia wins Italian election
- ✦ First episode of sitcom Friends airs on US TV
- ✦ Channel Tunnel linking UK and France officially opened
- ✦ Nelson Mandela becomes South Africa's first black president
- ✦ Crowbar attack wounds top US skater Nancy Kerrigan
- ✦ Art thieves snatch Munch's The Scream from Oslo gallery
- ✦ Sony releases PlayStation video console in Japan
- ✦ Berlin bids farewell to Allied troops after 49-year presence
- ✦ Exiled Soviet writer Solzhenitsyn returns after 20 years in US
- ✦ Brazilian F1 champion Ayrton Senna killed in grand prix crash
- ✦ Hungarian chess player Péter Lékó youngest grandmaster at 14
- ✦ Spielberg's Holocaust epic Schindler's List wins seven Oscars

Born this year:
- ☛ American actress Dakota Fanning born in Conyers, Georgia
- ☛ Canadian singer and teen idol Justin Bieber born in London, Ontario
- ☛ Irish-American actress Saoirse Ronan born in New York

The Biggest Hits When You Were 40

Big tunes for a big birthday: how many of them enticed your middle-aged party guests onto the dance floor?

Twist and Shout 🎵 Chaka Demus and Pliers
Without You 🎵 Mariah Carey
Without You was originally written by British band, Badfinger. It has also been covered by Harry Nilsson and dozens of others.

Doop 🎵 Doop
Everything Changes 🎵 Take That
Gary Barlow wrote Everything Changes when he realised their latest album didn't have any song for Robbie Williams to sing lead vocal.

The Real Thing 🎵 Tony Di Bart
Inside 🎵 Stiltskin
Come On You Reds 🎵 Manchester United FC
Love Is All Around 🎵 Wet Wet Wet
Love Is All Around was woven into the plot of the movie Love Actually, recorded as a seasonal money-spinner for the character Billie Mac (Bill Nighy), crooning Christmas is All Around.

Saturday Night 🎵 Whigfield
Sure 🎵 Take That
Baby Come Back 🎵 Pato Banton
Let Me Be Your Fantasy 🎵 Baby D
Stay Another Day 🎵 East 17
Stay Another Day was written about Tony Mortimer's late brother. It went on to become Christmas number one after a producer suggested adding sleigh bells into the mix.

Popular Food in the 1970s

Roll out the hostess trolley, seventies food is ready to be served. If it's not highly processed, artificially coloured, moulded and served in a novelty dish, is it even food? Still, most of it went down very well with the kids – and still does today, given half a chance.

Lemon meringue pie

Cheese and pineapple

Black Forest Gâteau

The Black Forest Gâteau is named after the kirsch alcohol made from Black Forest sour cherries, rather than the Black Forest region in Germany.

Dream Topping

Mateus Rose, Liebfraumilch and Chianti

Cornetto

Cornetto cones were created by Spica, an Italian ice-cream company, in 1976. The company was bought by Unilever not long after, who then marketed the dessert in Europe.

Quavers

Quiche

Unlike the gâteau above, quiche Lorraine *was* named after the area in which it was created. It is considered a French dish, even though Lorraine was under German rule at the time.

Pot Noodle

The original Pot Noodle made in 1979 did not contain a sauce sachet – these were only added in 1992.

Fondue

Smash

Scampi in a basket

Banoffee pie

Chili con carne

Chili is the state dish of Texas, where many people think the recipe originated. Before WWII, hundreds of individual parlours all insisted they had their own secret recipe.

Prawn cocktails

Profiteroles

The Full English Breakfast

Cars of the 1970s

How did you get around in the seventies? Was it in one of the decade's fancy new Range Rovers, or perhaps something more modest like a Morris Marina? Here are the decade's most famous (and infamous) cars.

Ford Capri

Vauxhall HC Viva

Ford Escort

Introduced in 1968, the Ford Escort went on to be the best-selling car in Britain in the 1980s and 1990s. The car was brought back into the spotlight in 2013, when it was featured in Fast & Furious 6.

Jaguar XJ

Triumph TR7

Austin Allegro

Austin Maxi

The Austin Maxi was the first British five-door hatchback, and one of the first cars to be featured on the BBC's Wheelbase show.

Ford Cortina

Ford Granada

Designed as a European executive car, the Granada was popular for taxi and police car use. It was also modified for use as a hearse and limousine, and was often seen in The Sweeney.

Leyland Princess

Triumph Dolomite

Vauxhall Cavalier

Range Rover

Morris Marina

The popular Morris Marina is ranked amongst the worst cars ever built. The car was released with poor suspension, chronic understeer, and windscreen wipers fitted the wrong way round.

Hillman Avenger

Saab 99

Datsun Sunny

BMW 316

Volkswagen Beetle

Affectionately known as the bug in English-speaking countries, it is called turtle in Bolivia, frog in Indonesia, and hunchback in Poland.

Household Goods in 1980

Mortgage interest rates were around 15% as we went into the eighties, not much lower as we left, and added to our basket in 1980. If you had any money left over perhaps you were spending it on home perms, cement and lamb's liver!

Lamb's liver

Tea bags

Tea is one of the few items included in the basket since the start. Tea bags were added in 1980; loose tea was removed in 2002.

Smash

Smash sales soared following the 1974 TV adverts featuring the Smash Martians. It was replaced in 1987 by oven chips.

Cider

Wine

Mortgage Interest

White spirit

Cement

Toilet seat

Electric plug

Colour TV

Colour TV sets outnumbered black and white sets in 1976.

Record player

Cassette recorder

Cassette recorders were first introduced by Philips in the 1960s and were originally intended for dictation and journalists.

Electric hairdryer

Carpet sweeper

Continental quilt

Drycell batteries

Colour photo film

Briefcase

Home perm

National Trust fees

Membership to the National Trust significantly increased throughout the 1980s (around 5.6 million people are members today). The Giant's Causeway is the most visited national attraction.

Olympic Medallists in Your Life

With seven gold medals, Jason Kenny is without equal while the unique achievements of Laura Trott – now Mrs Kenny – brings the household tally to twelve. Meanwhile, over at the Paralympics, swimmer-cyclist Sarah Storey has an incredible 17 gold medals. And medals of all colours? Here are the heroes of Team GB at the Summer Olympics.

Jason Kenny (9) ⚷ Cycling

Bradley Wiggins (8) ⚷ Cycling
Britain's most decorated Olympian until Kenny took the crown in Tokyo, Wiggo acquired various nicknames throughout his career. In France he was referred to as 'Le Gentleman', while the Dutch apparently called him 'The Banana with the Sideburns'.

Chris Hoy (7) ⚷ Cycling

Laura Kenny (6) ⚷ Cycling
Our most successful female Olympian with five gold medals, Trott (now Kenny) began life with a collapsed lung and asthma.

Steve Redgrave (6) ⚷ Rowing

Max Whitlock (6) ⚷ Gymnastics

Charlotte Dujardin (6) ⚷ Equestrianism

Ben Ainslie (5) ⚷ Sailing
Known for his hot temper, Ben Ainslie has accused competitors of teaming up against him. He was disqualified from the world championships in Australia for confronting a photographer who Ainslie felt had impeded his progress.

Adam Peaty (5) ⚷ Swimming

Katherine Grainger (5) ⚷ Rowing
Grainger is the first British woman to win medals at five successive Olympic games, from Sydney to Rio.

Mo Farah (4) ⚷ Athletics

Matthew Pinsent (4) ⚷ Rowing

Ed Clancy (4) ⚷ Cycling

Ian Stark (4) ⚷ Equestrianism

Louis Smith (4) ⚷ Gymnastics

Becky Adlington (4) ⚷ Swimming

Seb Coe (4) ⚷ Athletics

Ginny Leng (4) ⚷ Equestrianism

It's striking that our most decorated Olympians did so in recent decades. Of the 18 athletes earning four medals or more since you were born, Seb Coe came off the starting blocks first: he won his first medal at the 1980 Moscow Olympics at the age of 23 (shortly after breaking the 1,000 metre record in Oslo, above).

Run the slide rule over every modern Olympics, starting in 1896, and only six more GB athletes have achieved the same phenomenal success.

Winter Olympics Venues Since You Were Born

Unless you're an athlete or winter sports fan, the Winter Olympics can slip past almost unnoticed. These are the venues; can you remember the host countries and years?

Lillehammer
Cortina d'Ampezzo
Salt Lake City
Sapporo
Albertville
The last Games to be held in the same year as the Summer Olympics, with the next Winter Olympics held two years later.

Turin
Grenoble
Sarajevo
Lake Placid
Sochi
Innsbruck (twice)
This usually snowy city experienced its mildest winter in 60 years; the army was called in to transport snow and ice from the mountains. Nevertheless, twelve years later, the Winter Olympics were back.

Squaw Valley
Nagano
Calgary
Vancouver
PyeongChang

Answers: Lillehammer: Norway, 1994; Cortina d'Ampezzo: Italy, 1956; Salt Lake City: USA, 2002; Sapporo: Japan, 1972; Albertville: France, 1992; Turin: Italy, 2006; Grenoble: France, 1968; Sarajevo: Yugoslavia, 1984; Lake Placid: USA, 1980; Sochi: Russia, 2014; Innsbruck: Austria, 1964; Squaw Valley: USA, 1960; Nagano: Japan, 1998; Calgary: Canada, 1988; Innsbruck: Austria, 1976; Vancouver: Canada, 2010; PyeongChang: South Korea, 2018

Fashion in the Eighties

Eighties fashion was many things, but subtle wasn't one of them. Brash influences were everywhere from aerobics to Wall Street, from pop princesses to preppy polo shirts. The result was chaotic, but fun. How many eighties throwbacks still lurk in your closet?

Shoulder pads or puffed sleeves

Scrunchies
Patented in 1987 by nightclub singer Rommy Revson, the first scrunchie was designed using the waistband of her pyjama bottoms. The softer alternative to hair bands was named after Revson's dog Scunchie (no, that's not a typo).

Conical bras
Inspired by 1950s bullet bras, Jean Paul Gaultier introduced the cone bra in 1984. As a child he fashioned the bra for his teddy bear; years later he reworked the look for Madonna's Blonde Ambition tour in 1990.

Acid wash jeans

Slogan t-shirts
Designer Katharine Hamnett introduced slogan t-shirts, famously revealing one displaying an anti-nuclear statement when meeting Margaret Thatcher in 1984. Wham opted for 'Choose Life'; for Frankie Goes to Hollywood it was 'Frankie Says Relax'.

Leotards and leg-warmers
Leg-warmers reached the masses following the release of Fame and Flashdance, as well as Jane Fonda exercise videos. Nowadays, leg-warmers are even worn by babies while they have their nappies changed.

Deely boppers, bangle earrings or a polka dot hair bow

Pedal pushers or leggings

Guyliner

Levi 501s

Pixie boots

Ra-ra skirt and PVC belts

Dr Martens
Dr Martens were designed by a German soldier to aid the recovery of his broken foot. Pete Townshend of The Who was the first rock star to wear the boots on stage, and the shoe was adopted by numerous subcultures.

World Buildings

Buildings that are known the world over for all the right (and the wrong) reasons and were opened before you turned 40.

1955	**Hiroshima Peace Museum, Hiroshima** Built following the atomic bombing of Hiroshima as an enduring symbol of peace and to educate, the museum receives over a million visitors each year.
1958	Tokyo Tower, Tokyo
1958	Expo '58 World's Fair, Brussels
1958	Seagram Building, New York
1959	**The Guggenheim, New York** Architect Frank Lloyd Wright produced over 700 sketches of the museum. Upon opening, Woody Allen commented that it looked like a giant lavatory basin.
1961	**Space Needle, Seattle** Built for the 1962 World's Fair. Early shape designs included a tethered balloon and a cocktail shaker before the iconic final design was chosen.
1968	Madison Square Garden, New York City, New York
1969	John Hancock Center, Chicago
1973	Sears Tower, Chicago, Illinois
1973	World Trade Center, New York
1973	**Sydney Opera House, Sydney** The estimated cost for the construction was AU$7m (£4m). It ended up costing AU$102m (£59m), and took 14 years to build rather than the four years planned.
1976	CN Tower, Toronto
1977	Pompidou Centre, Paris
1981	Sydney Tower, Sydney
1990	Washington National Cathedral, Washington DC
1983	**Trump Tower, New York** How many floors there are in Trump Tower? An easy question, right? It was built with 58 floors. But Trump wasn't happy... the ceilings are high on some floors, so the numbers jump from the 6th to the 13th floor. Now it has 68!
1988	Parliament House, Canberra

Grand Designs

Governments around the world spent much of the 20th century nation building (and rebuilding). Here is a selection of striking civil engineering achievements between the ages of 0 and 30.

1955	Disneyland Castle, Anaheim, California
1955	Battersea Power Station, London
1959	**M1 Motorway, London & Leeds**

The M1 was the second motorway built in the UK, and it was the first motorway to join two cities. The first section opened in 1959, and the most recent section was added in 1999.

1959	Kariba Dam, Kariba
1962	Butlins, Minehead
1965	Mont Blanc Tunnel, France & Italy
1965	Zeeland Bridge, Netherlands
1966	**Almondsbury Interchange, Bristol & Gloucester**

The Almondsbury Interchange was the first example of a four-level stack in the UK, and remains one of only three of its kind in the country.

1967	**Second Blackwall Tunnel, London**

The second Blackwall tunnel is relatively straight, unlike the first which is curved. That was to avoid a sewer, but also reportedly so that horses (the main means of transport when built) didn't see daylight at the other end and bolt.

1969	Humber Refinery, Northern Lincolnshire
1970	Aswan Dam, Aswan
1970	Hyde Park Barracks, London
1971	**Spaghetti Junction, Birmingham**

Officially the Gravelly Hill Interchange, Spaghetti Junction was named by the Guinness Book of World Records as 'the most complex interchange on the British road system'.

1973	Bosphorus Bridge, Istanbul
1976	**Sonnenberg Tunnel, Lucerne**

A 5,000 ft road tunnel that was built to double up as a nuclear shelter for up to 20,000 people. Blast doors at the entrance weigh 350 tons...but take 24 hours to close.

1981	Humber Bridge, Kingston upon Hull

Household Goods in 1987

The shelves, fridges and freezers are piled high with convenience foods. What did we do with all that extra time we'd saved? First, dig out the indigestion tablets. Then tackle a spot of DIY and finally move house, it seems!

Squash racket
The classic eighties sport. Prince Philip played squash to relax while Queen Elizabeth II was in labour with Prince Charles.

Muesli

Spaghetti

Jam doughnuts

Swiss roll

Beefburgers

Mince

Garlic sausage

Frozen prawns

Brie

Red Leicester
Originally called Leicestershire Cheese, the cheese was renamed Red Leicester after World War II to differentiate it from 'White Leicester' made during rationing when the use of colouring agents was banned.

Conifer

Frozen curry and rice

Fish and chips
Synonymous with British cuisine and described by Winston Churchill as 'the good companions', fish and chips were exempt from rationing during World War II, as the government feared any limitations would damage the morale of the nation.

VHS recorder

Ready mixed filler

Home telephone
The popularity of mobile phones has led to a decrease of landlines. Only 73% of British households had a landline used to make calls in 2020.

Fabric conditioner

Estate agent fees

Indigestion tablets

Books of the Decade

By our forties, most of us have decided what we like to read. But occasionally a book can break the spell, revealing the delights of other genres. Did any of these newly published books do that for you?

1994	A Suitable Boy by Vikram Seth
1994	Snow Falling on Cedars by David Guterson
1995	A Fine Balance by Rohinton Mistry
1996	Infinite Jest by David Foster Wallace
1996	A Game of Thrones by George RR Martin
1996	Bridget Jones's Diary by Helen Fielding
1997	**Harry Potter And The Philosopher's Stone by J K Rowling** **In the film of the book, Rik Mayall played the part of** **Peeves the Poltergeist. The scene was cut before release.**
1997	American Pastoral by Philip Roth
1997	The God of Small Things by Arundhati Roy
1997	Underworld by Don DeLillo
1997	Memoirs of a Geisha by Arthur Golden
1997	Blindness by José Saramago
1998	The Poisonwood Bible by Barbara Kingsolver
1999	Disgrace by J M Coetzee
1999	Being Dead by Jim Crace
1999	Ghostwritten by David Mitchell
2000	White Teeth by Zadie Smith
2000	The Blind Assassin by Margaret Atwood
2001	The Corrections by Jonathan Franzen
2001	Austerlitz by W G Sebald
2001	Life of Pi by Yann Martel
2002	Everything Is Illuminated by Jonathan Safran Foer
2002	**The Lovely Bones by Alice Sebold** **At university, Sebold was beaten and sexually assaulted in** **a location where a girl had previously been murdered. Her** **experience and her subsequent reactions to it informed** **a novel called Monsters about the rape and murder of a** **teenager, later retitled as The Lovely Bones.**
2003	The Kite Runner by Khaled Hosseini
2003	Vernon God Little by DBC Pierre

US Vice Presidents in Your Lifetime

The linchpin of a successful presidency, a springboard to become POTUS, or both? Here are the men – and the woman – who have shadowed the most powerful person in the world in your lifetime. (President in brackets.)

1953–61	Richard Nixon (Dwight Eisenhower)
1961–63	Lyndon B Johnson (John F Kennedy)
1965–69	**Hubert Humphrey** (Lyndon Johnson) Christmas 1977: with just weeks to live, the former VP made goodbye calls. One was to Richard Nixon, the man who had beaten Humphrey to become president in 1968. Sensing Nixon's unhappiness at his status as Washington outcast, Humphrey invited him to take a place of honour at the funeral he knew was fast approaching.
1969–73	**Spiro Agnew (right)**
1973–74	Gerald Ford
1974–77	Nelson Rockefeller
1977–81	Walter Mondale
1981–89	**George HW Bush** He is only the second vice president to win the presidency while holding the office of vice president.
1989–93	**Dan Quayle** You say potato, Quayle said potatoe: he famously told a student to add an 'e' during a 1992 school visit.
1993–2001	**Al Gore** Gore won the Nobel Peace Prize in 2007. Two others have won: Teddy Roosevelt (1906) and Charles Dawes (1925).
2001–09	Dick Cheney
2009–17	Joe Biden
2017–20	**Mike Pence** In the 90s, Pence took a break from politics to become a conservative radio talk show and television host.
2020–	**Kamala Harris** Harris is the highest-ranked woman in US history and the first woman of colour to hold the office of Vice President. 'While I may be the first woman in this office, I will not be the last,' she said.

Spiro Agnew resigned in 1973, the second VP to quit in America's history (the first was John Calhoun in 1932). He stepped down after being charged with tax evasion and taking bribes. He covered his legal debts with a loan from friend Frank Sinatra. In 1983, Agnew was compelled to repay $268,000: the money he had taken in bribes, plus interest.

Stamps in the Seventies

By the seventies, any hobbyist intent on keeping a complete ongoing collection needed deep pockets (or a rich uncle). New stamps were churned out several times a year and the subjects became ever more esoteric: not just flowers and trees but racket sports, or paintings of horse races. Was your album gathering dust by then?

1970	Commonwealth Games
1971	British rural architecture
1972	Polar explorers
1972	Village churches
1972	Royal Silver Wedding celebration
1973	Plant a Tree Year
1973	County Cricket
1973	**400th anniversary of the birth of Inigo Jones** Not a household name by today's standards, Jones was an early and influential architect. He designed Covent Garden Square and parts of St Paul's Cathedral.
1973	Royal Wedding (Princess Anne and Mark Phillips)
1973	Britain's entry into the EC
1974	Medieval Warriors
1975	Sailing
1975	100 years since the birth of Jane Austen
1976	100 years of the telephone
1976	**British cultural traditions** The four chosen were a Morris dancer, a Scots piper, a Welsh harpist and an Archdruid.
1977	Racket sports
1977	Silver Jubilee
1977	Wildlife
1978	**Energy resources** In an era before renewable energy the choices made were oil, coal, natural gas and electricity.
1978	Horses
1979	Dogs
1979	Spring wild flowers
1979	Paintings of horse races
1979	150 years of the Metropolitan Police

More Things People Do Now…

… that nobody ever did when you were small – because they couldn't, wouldn't, or definitely shouldn't!

+ **Place a bet *during* a sporting event**
  This became popular in the 1990s; first on the phone, now online.
+ Turn on underfloor heating
+ **Buy soft toilet rolls**
  In 1942, a wonder was created in Walthamstow's St Andrews Road, one for which the bottoms of the world owe a huge debt: two-ply, soft toilet roll ('It's splinter-free'!). It was christened Andrex.

+ Talk to a smart speaker
+ Clean up dog poo (not doing it has been an offence since 1996)
+ Listen to a podcast
+ **Do a Sudoku puzzle**
  How many Japanese words do you know? Tsunami? Karaoke? Sake? In 2005, you likely added another: Sudoku (meaning 'single number'). The puzzle originated in the USA – but was popularised by Wayne Gould, a Hong Kong judge from New Zealand who found a translated version in a Tokyo bookshop.
+ **Cheat in a pub quiz**
  Which two capital cities mean the same in different languages? Who knows? Google knows, and a quick trip to the loo (phone in hand) is a modern phenomenon. (The answer is Sierra Leone's Freetown and Gabon's Libreville – but of course you knew that.)

+ Order something for same day delivery
+ Use chopsticks
+ Fly a drone
+ **Never watch live TV**
  Owning a TV but not watching any live programmes (just streamed content) might sound odd. But that is the reality for many – and around 1.5m have ditched the TV completely.

+ Eat in the street
+ Buy water
+ **Use SatNav**
  In the 1980s, Ronald Reagan permitted civilian use of satellites for navigation and opened up a world in which we never need to get lost again – unless we want to. Or the USA pulls the plug.

+ Argue for hours with strangers you'll never meet

A Lifetime of Progress

It's easy to lose sight of the breadth and pace of life-enhancing inventions made as you grew up – although some of these didn't stand the test of time! These are the biggies before you turned 50.

1976	Apple Computer
1979	Barcodes
1979	Compact disc
1982	**Emoticons** The inventor of the smiley emoticon hands out 'Smiley' cookies every Sept 19th – the anniversary of its first use.
1983	Internet
1983	Microsoft Word
1984	LCD projector
1984	Apple Macintosh
1985	Atomic force microscope
1985	**Sinclair C5** Despite a body and a chassis designed by Lotus and assembled by Hoover, the ahead-of-its-time Sinclair C5 was plagued with problems including poor battery life, the inability to climb gentle hills and safety concerns.
1986	Mir Space Station
1988	**Internet virus** The first Internet worm (ie self-replicating) was designed to go after passwords. Its inventor was the son of the man who invented… computer passwords.
1989	World Wide Web
1990	Hubble space telescope
1991	Websites
1994	Bluetooth
1995	Mouse with scroll wheel
1996	DVD player
1998	Google
1999	Wi-Fi
2000	Camera phone
2001	**Wikipedia** Around 5 million articles in English now await the curious, with many more in languages from Swedish to Tagalog.

FA Cup Winners Since You Were Born

Many fans have waited decades to see their team lift the cup; many more are still waiting. Here are the teams that have hoisted the trophy in your lifetime (last win in brackets).

Newcastle United ⚽ (1954-55)
Aston Villa ⚽ (1956-57)
After Aston Villa won the final in 1895, the FA Cup was stolen from a shop window display in Birmingham. The thief confessed 63 years later, stating he had melted the trophy down to make coins.

Bolton Wanderers ⚽ (1957-58)
Nottingham Forest ⚽ (1958-59)
Wolverhampton Wanderers ⚽ (1959-60)
West Bromwich Albion ⚽ (1967-68)
Leeds United ⚽ (1971-72)
Sunderland ⚽ (1972-73)
Southampton ⚽ (1975-76)
Ipswich Town ⚽ (1977-78)
West Ham United ⚽ (1979-80)
Coventry City ⚽ (1986-87)
Wimbledon ⚽ (1987-88)
Wimbledon shocked the country in 1988 when they beat First Division champions Liverpool in the FA Cup final, overcoming 17-1 odds.

Tottenham Hotspur ⚽ (1990-91)
Everton ⚽ (1994-95)
Liverpool ⚽ (2005-06)
Portsmouth ⚽ (2007-08)
Wigan Athletic ⚽ (2012-13)
Manchester United ⚽ (2015-16)
Chelsea ⚽ (2017-18)
Former Chelsea and Ivory Coast striker Didier Drogba is the only player to score in four separate FA Cup Finals.

Manchester City ⚽ (2018-19)
Arsenal ⚽ (2019-20)
Leicester City ⚽ (2020-21)

Gameshow Hosts of the Seventies and Eighties

What do points make? I've started so I'll finish. Shut that door! You can't beat a bit of Bully! The catchphrases echo down the ages from these much-loved TV favourites.

David Vine ⋈ (A Question of Sport)
Stuart Hall ⋈ (It's a Knockout)
Anneka Rice ⋈ (Treasure Hunt)
Kenneth Kendall ⋈ (Treasure Hunt)
Cilla Black ⋈ (Blind Date)
Born Priscilla White, the stage name of Cilla Black came about by mistake. Featured in the first issue of Mersey Beat newspaper, the journalist accidentally called her Cilla Black. Cilla liked the name and opted to keep it.

Barry Cryer ⋈ (Jokers Wild)
Nicholas Parsons ⋈ (Just a Minute, Sale of the Century)
Jim Bowen ⋈ (Bullseye)
After completing his national service in the bomb disposal unit, Jim Bowen worked as a teacher and was promoted to deputy head, but gave up teaching once he appeared on The Comedians alongside Mike Reid.

Mike Read ⋈ (Pop Quiz)
David Coleman ⋈ (A Question of Sport)
Prof. Heinz Wolff ⋈ (The Great Egg Race)
Bob Holness ⋈ (Blockbusters)
Magnus Magnusson ⋈ (Mastermind)
Angela Rippon ⋈ (Masterteam)
Noel Edmonds ⋈ (Telly Addicts)
Noel Edmonds has made headlines for plotting to buy the BBC, starting a pet counselling service, and driving a mannequin called Candice around in his black cab to dissuade the public from trying to flag him down.

Ted Rogers ⋈ (3-2-1)
Terry Wogan ⋈ (Blankety Blank)
Les Dawson ⋈ (Blankety Blank)
Larry Grayson ⋈ (The Generation Game)

Popular Food in the 1980s

Our last trolley dash takes us down the aisle at lunchtime, piled high with eat-on-the-go snacks and sandwiches. Stop on the way home for a deep pan pizza and a Diet Coke; end the day with a slice of Battenberg cake. Congratulations, you've just eaten the eighties!

Crunchy Nut Cornflakes
The cereal was invented in Manchester in 1980. Pity the poor Americans: it took 30 years for Crunchy Nut to cross the Atlantic.

Kellogg's Fruit and Fibre
Prepacked sandwiches
The prepacked sandwich was first sold by M&S in spring 1980. The range was small, conservative, made in-store and used whatever ingredients were plentiful (even if that was pilchards).

Viennetta
Trifle
In 1596, Thomas Dawson recorded the first recipe for trifle in his books, *The Good Huswifes Jewell*. It was essentially thick cream, rosewater, sugar and ginger. Jelly didn't appear until the 1700s.

Chicken Kiev

Vol au vent

Battenberg cake
Pizza
Pizza Hut claim to be the first company to sell food online – one of their signature pizzas via their Pizanet website, back in 1994.

Garlic bread

Kiwi

Sun-dried tomatoes

Potato waffles

Happy Meals
Diet Coke
Within two years of its unveiling in 1982, Diet Coke became the most popular diet soft drink in the world, and the third most popular soft drink overall behind Coca Cola and Pepsi.

Rowntree's Drifters

Hedgehog-flavoured crisps

Burton's fish 'n' chips

Chicken satay

Eighties Symbols of Success

In the flamboyant era of Dallas and Dynasty there were many ways to show that you, too, had really made it. Forty years on, it's fascinating to see how some of these throwbacks are outdated or available to nearly everyone, while others are still reserved for today's wealthy peacocks.

Car phone
Dishwasher
Children at private school
Waterbed
The modern-day waterbed was designed by a US student for his master's thesis project. Original fillings included corn syrup, and then jelly, before he settled on water. They were popular but problematic due to their weight and susceptibility to puncture, as Edward Scissorhands found out.

Second cars
Holidays abroad
Conservatory
Pony
Colour TV
Diamonds
Cordless phone
Birkin bag
A chance encounter between Hermès Executive Chairman Jean-Louis Dumas and Jane Birkin on a plane inspired the Birkin bag. The contents of Birkin's bag spilled out, and Dumas suggested she needed a bag with pockets, so Birkin sketched her idea on a sick bag.

Double glazing
Rolex watch
Leather Filofax
Mont Blanc pen
Newton's Cradle desk toy
Named after Isaac Newton and the cat's cradle, an early version was wooden, expensive and sold at Harrods. Chrome imitations followed. TV programme Myth Busters built a supersized cradle with concrete-filled chrome wrecking balls… it didn't work.

Stone cladding

The first UK car phone call was made in 1959 from outside the Lymm Hotel in Cheshire; human operators were used to connect calls until the 1980s. John Lennon wrote the lyrics for I'm Only Sleeping on the back of a car phone demand letter.

Cars of the 1980s

Many cars you might associate with the eighties were on the road long before then, from the Ford Granada and Escort to the Porsche 911. But this is the decade they arguably hit their stride alongside other automotive icons.

Toyota Corolla
Introduced in 1966, the Toyota Corolla became the best-selling car worldwide by 1974. The car was named after a ring of petals.

Volvo 240

BMW 3 Series

Volkswagen Golf
Sold as the Rabbit in the US and the Caribe in Mexico.

Volkswagen Passat

Vauxhall Astra

Triumph Acclaim

Porsche 911
Originally the Porsche 901 on its 1964 debut, the name was changed after Peugeot claimed they had exclusive rights to naming cars with three digits and a zero in the middle.

Jaguar XJS

Nissan Micra

Peugeot 205

Austin Maestro

Vauxhall Nova
The Vauxhall Nova inspired a series of comical bumper stickers, including 'You've been Novataken', and 'Vauxhall Casanova'. It was called the Corsa everywhere but Britain where it sounded too much like the word 'coarser'. It was renamed anyway in 1993.

Ford Sierra
Neil Kinnock had one of the first Sierras. He wrecked it in a crash.

Austin Montego

Volkswagen Polo

Austin Metro
Promoted with comical adverts, the car became one of the best-selling cars in UK history, and even Princess Diana owned one.

Ford Fiesta
The Fiesta is the UK's best-selling car of all time.

Vauxhall Cavalier

Eighties TV Gameshows

By the eighties, new formats aimed at youngsters – your youngsters? – were introduced. Some shows went digital or took to the skies; others kept it (very) simple, and a few remain family favourites to this day.

The Adventure Game

Treasure Hunt

Blind Date

The pilot episode of Blind Date was hosted by Duncan Norvelle, but he was quickly replaced by Cilla Black. Black presented the entire original run of the series for eighteen years, before unexpectedly announcing her departure on the show's first ever live episode.

Surprise Surprise

Countdown

Catchphrase

Blockbusters

Telly Addicts

3-2-1

The show's mascot and booby prize, Dusty Bin, cost around £10,000 to build. He was built by visual effects engineer Ian Rowley, who also operated Dusty Bin in the studio.

Blankety Blank

Bob's Full House

The instantly recognisable scoreboard was dubbed Mr Babbage by original host Bob Monkhouse. This was a nod to Charles Babbage, the inventor of the first programmable computer. In the reboot, Mr Babbage was replaced with a colour scoreboard, but the original board soon returned.

Bullseye

Cheggers Plays Pop

Family Fortunes

The Great Egg Race

Give Us a Clue

The Krypton Factor

Play Your Cards Right

The Price is Right

The Pyramid Game

Popular Girls' Names

60

Of the fifty names that made the Top 10 from 1900-74, only four have appeared since: Claire, Emma, Samantha and Sarah. (Oddly, names beginning with 'D' are now a rarity with no Top 10 entries in the last fifty years!)

Amelia
Olivia
Along with other names ending in 'a', Olivia rose to popularity in the late nineties and has remained a favourite ever since. She's been number one or two from 2008 to the present day.

Isla
Emily
Poppy
Ava
Isabella
Jessica
Lily
Sophie
Grace
Sophia
Mia
Evie
Ruby
Ella
Scarlett
Isabelle
Chloe
Sienna
Freya
Phoebe
Charlotte
Daisy
Alice

Rising and falling stars:
Thea, Darcie, Lottie and Harper: welcome to the Top 100!
Amy, Mollie, Faith and Isabel: we're afraid your time is up.

Books of the Decade

Our final decade of books are the bookstore favourites from your fifties. How many did you read…and can you remember the plot, or the cover?

2004	The Line of Beauty by Alan Hollinghurst
2004	Cloud Atlas by David Mitchell
2004	Gilead by Marilynne Robinson
2004	Small Island by Andrea Levy
2005	Never Let Me Go by Kazuo Ishiguro
2005	The Book Thief by Markus Zusak
2005	The Sea by John Banville
2005	**The Girl with the Dragon Tattoo by Stieg Larsson**

Larsson died before the first three books in the Millennium series were published. Larsson's partner has a partially completed fourth book – but not the publishing rights.

2005	No Country for Old Men by Cormac McCarthy
2005	Saturday by Ian McEwan
2006	The Road by Cormac McCarthy
2007	A Thousand Splendid Suns by Khaled Hosseini
2007	The Ghost by Robert Harris
2008	The White Tiger by Aravind Adiga
2008	**The Hunger Games by Suzanne Collins**

The myth of Theseus and the Minotaurs inspired Collins to write The Hunger Games. She didn't intend to write a trilogy but felt compelled to continue the story.

2009	Wolf Hall by Hilary Mantel
2009	The Help by Kathryn Stockett
2010	The Hand That First Held Mine by Maggie O'Farrell
2010	The Finkler Question by Howard Jacobson
2011	**Fifty Shades of Grey by EL James**

The story originated as a piece of Twilight fan-fiction.

2011	A Dance with Dragons by George RR Martin
2012	Gone Girl by Gillian Flynn
2013	Doctor Sleep by Stephen King

April 17 1970: Jim Lovell is brought aboard a helicopter, the last of the three astronauts from the Apollo 13 mission to be lifted from the floating

Apollo Astronauts

Not all of those who have been to the moon are equally well known. Twelve landed; twelve remained in orbit. Gus Grissom, Ed White, and Roger B Chaffee died in training. BBC and ITV broadcast the Apollo 11 landing live, in the first all-night transmission. The landing was at 9.17pm, but Armstrong didn't take one monumental step until 3.56am.

Landed on the moon:

Alan Bean

Alan Shepard
Shepard was the oldest person to walk on the moon at the age of 47.

Buzz Aldrin

Charles Duke

David Scott

Edgar Mitchell

Eugene Cernan

Harrison Schmitt

James Irwin

John Young

Neil Armstrong

Pete Conrad

Remained in low orbit:

Al Worden

Bill Anders
Anders took the iconic Earthrise photo.

Dick Gordon

Frank Borman

Fred Haise

Jack Swigert

Jim Lovell

Ken Mattingly

Michael Collins

Ron Evans
Made the final spacewalk of the program to retrieve film cassettes.

Stuart Roosa
On the Apollo 14 mission he carried seeds from 5 species of trees. They were planted across the US and are known as Moon Trees.

Tom Stafford

Popular Boys' Names

The most favoured names are now a curious blend of the evergreen (Thomas), the rediscovered (Harry), and those enjoying their first proper outing (Joshua).

Oliver
With the exception of 2011-12 when Harry was briefly the nation's favourite, Oliver has been the first choice ever since 2009.

Jack
Harry
Jacob
Charlie
Thomas
George
Oscar
James
William
Noah
Alfie
Joshua
Muhammad
Henry
Leo
Archie
Ethan
Joseph
Freddie
Samuel
Alexander
Logan
Daniel
Isaac
Max

Rising and falling stars:
While lots of names fell in and out of fashion in the eighties and nineties, the pace has slowed. Just one new name in 2014: Joey (not seen since). Out: Owen, Robert and Finlay.

Things People Did When You Were Growing Up (Part 2)

Finally, here are more of the things we saw, we did and errands we ran as kids that nobody needs, wants, or even understands how to do in the modern age!

+ Drink syrup of figs
+ Preserve vegetables
+ Save the silver chocolate papers from Roses
+ **Eat offal**
  Tripe was never on ration but long out of favour by the time the tripe dresser's fate was sealed in 1992, when BSE broke out.

+ **Make a carbon copy**
  Carbon paper was first patented by Ralph Wedgwood, son of Thomas Wedgwood, in 1806, for his Noctograph – designed to help blind people write without ink. The smell and texture are just a memory, but emails sent in 'cc' (carbon copy) might remind you!

+ **Wash handkerchiefs**
  You'd have to keep (and wash) a hanky for nine years to outweigh the CO2 emissions of its tissue cousins.

+ Use talcum powder
+ Make a penfriend
+ **Wire a plug**
  Strip and route wires to the terminal; fit the right fuse. Not any more. In 1994, it became illegal to sell appliances without fitted plugs.

+ Darn a hole in your sock
+ Refill your pen from an inkwell
+ Wind on your camera for another shot
+ See the bones in your foot at the shoe shop through a Pedoscope
+ Pluck a chicken
+ **Smoke on a bus**
  'When will this fanaticism going to stop?' asked one MP in 1962, about a proposed ban on lower-deck smoking.

+ Scrape ice patterns off the inside of your bedroom window
+ Service your own car
+ Buy starch or blue bags for your washing
+ **Play Spot the Ball**
  Spot the Ball was launched in 1973. More than 10 years passed without a jackpot winner as its popularity declined.

Printed in Great Britain
by Amazon

70997907R00061